THE OLD AND THE YOUNG

▸◂[I VECCHI E I GIOVANI]▸◂

BY

LUIGI PIRANDELLO

AUTHOR OF "THE OUTCAST," "SHOOT!" "SIX CHARACTERS
IN SEARCH OF AN AUTHOR," ETC.

Authorized Translation from the Italian by
C. K. SCOTT-MONCRIEFF

VOLUME
I

E. P. DUTTON & COMPANY
681 FIFTH AVENUE   NEW YORK

PUBLISHER'S NOTE.—"The Old and The Young," a novel by
Luigi Pirandello, translated by C. K. Scott-Moncrieff, is one
of a series of novels and plays by Pirandello which will be
published by E. P. Dutton & Company under the general
supervision of Arthur Livingston.

AI MIEI FIGLI
GIOVANI OGGI,
VECCHI DOMANI.
    LUIGI PIRANDELLO

A N. D.

COI VECCHI E COI GIOVANI
UGUALE,
E PER ME, SEMPRE,
AMICO.

Londra, 1926   C. K. S.-M.

CONTENTS OF VOLUME I

PART I

Contents

CONTENTS OF VOLUME II

PART II

Contents

PART I

The Old and the Young

THE OLD AND THE YOUNG

PART I

CHAPTER I

Monsignore is quite right. . . .

THE rain, which had fallen in torrents during the night, had churned into a quagmire the long highroad that wound, in a succession of twists and turns, as though in search of some less laborious ascent, some less abrupt slope, over the broken surface of the vast, deserted plain.

The damage done by the storm appeared all the more depressing, inasmuch as there were already signs, here and there, of the disregard, not to say the contempt, shewn for the labours of those who had planned and constructed the road in order to give their fellow-men an easier passage over the natural obstacles of the country by means of those bends and coils, erecting now a retaining wall, now a dyke. The retaining walls had fallen, the dykes had been trampled down, where short cuts had come into being.

3

guard, notwithstanding the cold and rain that chilled and drenched him, would sit erect in his saddle, assuming an air of martial disdain; martially, were he passing one of the shrines, would he raise his hand in salute; then lowering his eyes to study the trained and trimmed points of the scanty black moustaches (most inadequate!) beneath his bold aquiline nose, would alter his friendly encouragement of the animal to an imperious "Up, there!" followed by a tug of the rein and an inward thrust of his spurs, to which as often as not Titina—the besom—finding herself treated with such violence in her torpid senility— would respond with scant courtesy.

But these encounters, so gratifying to the Captain, had become extremely rare. Everybody knew now about that bodyguard at Colimbètra, and either laughed at it or waxed indignant.

"The Pope, in the Vatican with his Switzers; Don Ippolito Laurentano, on his estate with Sciaralla and Co.!"

And Sciaralla, who, within the marches of Colimbètra, felt himself to be in his proper place, every inch a Captain, once he was outside the gates did not know what air to assume to escape from jeers and insults.

Already everybody was beginning to degrade him from his true rank, addressing him as *caporale*. Idiots! The impertinence! When he was in command of fully five and twenty men (yes, five and twenty!) and you ought to see how he drilled them in all the military exercises and kept them on the trot. Besides. . . . But surely, do not all the great gentlemen keep an escort of *campieri* in livery on their estates? Quite so, but to admit that he was merely a *campiere* was something of a wrench to poor Sciaralla, who was a "man of family" and held an elementary teacher's and gymnastic instructor's certificate. He had, nevertheless, reluctantly compelled himself at times to describe his position in these terms, lest he should hear himself called by a yet more opprobrious name. A *campiere,* yes . . . the chief *campiere,* the *capo.*

"*Caporale?*"

"*Capo,* chief! Where d'you get the corporal from? You do admit, then, that we are a military force?"

"Whose? How? And why are they dressed like that?" Sciaralla would shrug his shoulders, screw up his eyes and heave a sigh.

"One uniform is as good as another. . . . One of His Excellency's whimsies, what is a man to do?"

But with others of greater credulity he allowed himself to indulge in mysterious confidences: to the effect that the Prince, whose views made him be looked at askance by the Italian Government, which—imagine such a thing—would be only too glad to hear that he had been ruthlessly murdered

or pillaged, did really stand in need, in this lonely
part of the country, of the escort of which he,
Sciaralla, was the unworthy chief. This, however,
did not explain why the escort were obliged to go
about dressed in that hated uniform.

"Hangmen, that's what you are!" was the retort that had more than once been made to poor
Sciaralla, who would then think a trifle bitterly
how easy it was for the Prince to maintain with
such dignity and constancy that proud attitude of
protestation, remaining always shut up within
the walls of Colimbètra, whereas he and his subordinates were obliged to face the perils of the
outer world and to answer there for him.

In vain, in private conversation, did he swear
and forswear himself that never on any account
would he, in the days of the Bourbons, have put
on that uniform, a symbol, at that time, of
tyranny, a symbol of the oppressors of the country; and he would add, throwing up his hands:

"But nowadays, gentlemen, why not? Now that
it is you who are the masters. . . . You let me be!
It's my daily bread, gentlemen! You don't really
mean it."

In vain. They tried to turn his blood to gall,
by pretending not to understand that he, after all,
in his real self, was not simply a part of the dress
he wore; that inside the uniform was a man, a
poor man like all the rest, obliged to earn his living in some vile manner. By his smiles, by his

glances, composing his features with an air of keen interest in other people's affairs, he sought in every possible way to distract their attention from his coat; after which, he would feel a fierce inward resentment of all these tricks and grimaces, because, when he looked at the coat without thinking of what it meant, why, good Lord, it seemed to him a very fine coat indeed, and one that suited him down to the ground; and he almost felt remorseful at having to pretend that it distressed him to wear it.

He had heard it said that up in town, at Girgenti, a certain official from the mainland, a bearded, bilious creature, had publicly declared with furious gesticulations that such an indecency, such insolence, so open an insult to the glory of the Revolution, the Government, the Country, Civilisation itself, would not be tolerated in any other part of Italy, nor perhaps in any other province of Sicily itself except this province of Girgenti, so . . . so . . . he had preferred not to express in words what he thought of it; with his hands he had sketched a certain gesture. . . .

Lord, could it really be meant for him, for that Bourbon uniform of the five and twenty men of the bodyguard, all that contempt and ill-feeling? Why, oh why, did not these indignant folk turn their attention rather to His Worship the Mayor, to the Aldermen, the Municipal and Provincial Councillors, who came tumbling over one another, strutting along in their best clothes, to pay their respects to H. E. the Prince of Laurentano, who received them in his villa like a king in his royal palace? Not to mention the higher ranks of the clergy, with the Lord Bishop at their head, who, of course, might regard a Legitimist like his Excellency as his natural ally.

Sciaralla swelled with pride and joy at the sight of all these visitors; and nothing gave him greater pleasure than to stand to attention whenever they called, and present arms to them. If Monsignore came, or the Mayor, the sentry at the gate would turn out the little picket from the adjoining guard-room, and give a first salute then and there, in the best military style, with a fine clatter of arms presented and brought down to the order in quick time; another salute followed beneath the pillars of the porch outside the villa, at a shout from the second sentry by the carriage door. As for earning their pay, they had so little to do that he and his men deliberately made work for themselves, seeking whatever pretext they might find; and one of their most serious occupations was just this military salute, which was wonderfully effective in ridding them of the degrading sense that—for all their fine uniforms—they served no purpose whatsoever.

When all was said, with all these powerful protectors, Sciaralla might have laughed at the mockery he received from the lower orders, had he not,

like all vain men, felt a longing to be received and
greeted by everyone with courtesy and goodwill.
And so he was unable to laugh at it, indeed for
some time past he had been more than a little
alarmed by it, for another reason.

There was a rumour going about, which acquired
greater strength every day, that all the workmen
of the larger towns on the island, and the peas-
antry, and, nearer at hand, the workers in the sulphur pits were seeking to combine in unions, or,
as they called them, *fasci,* to rebel not so much
against the gentry as against all law and order,
they said, and to overturn everything.

Over and again, when he was on duty in the
ante-room, he had heard the matter discussed in
the drawing-room. The Prince—of course—threw
the blame on the usurping Government, which had
first of all caged up and had then proceeded to
starve the populace of the island by unjust and
infamous taxes and appropriations; the rest of
the party agreed in chorus; but the Lord Bishop
seemed to Sciaralla to know better than any of
them where the evil lay.

The evil, the true evil, the greatest of all the
evils committed by the new Government consisted
not so much in their usurpation, which still, and
rightly, made the heart of H. E. the Prince of
Laurentano bleed. Monarchies, civil and social
institutions: these were temporary affairs; they
pass away; it would be a mistake to alter or abol-

ish them if they are just and holy; a mistake however which it might be possible to remedy. But if
you abolish or obscure in the sight of men what
ought to shine eternally in their spirit: their
Faith, their Religion? Well, this was what the
new Government had done! And how could the
people remain quiet amid all the tribulations of
life, if they no longer had their faith to make them
accept these with resignation, or rather with jubilation as a proof and promise of reward in another
life? Is there one life only? This life on earth?
Will not your tribulations have their recompense
in the world beyond, if they are endured with
resignation? If not, what reason have we left for
accepting and enduring them? Let numbers triumph then, and the bestial instinct break loose for
satisfying here below all the base appetites of the
body!

He was quite right, was Monsignore. The true
reason of all the evil was this. No less than Monsignore, who, to tell the truth, with all the money
he had could scarcely feel the tribulations of life,
Sciaralla would have liked to see all the poor folk
realize this reason. But he could not succeed in
putting out of his thoughts a holy man, an aged
mendicant, who had appeared one day at the gate
of the villa, rosary in hand, and, as he stood waiting for alms and heard a long rumbling sound in
his own stomach, had drawn Sciaralla's attention
to it, with a sorrowful smile:

"Did you hear? It wasn't I that spoke; it's the voice of hunger speaking. . . ."

Sciaralla's consternation at this grave peril which overhung all the gentry arose more than from anything else from the calm confidence with which the Prince, there in his drawing-room, appeared to defy it. It was based, certainly, upon Sciaralla, and upon the valour and devotion of his men, this confidence on the Prince's part, and. it might be good enough for him to say that he himself was not afraid, leaving all other considerations to other people.

Fortunately, up to the present at Girgenti nobody stirred a finger nor shewed any sign of proposing to stir a finger! A city of the dead. So much so—said evil tongues—that the crows reigned there, in other words the priests. An inertia, whether for good or for evil, had taken root in the most profound distrust of destiny, in the conviction that nothing could possibly happen, that every effort must prove futile to shake off the utter desolation in which were engulfed not only the souls of men but everything else as well. And Sciaralla felt that he had a convincing proof of this in the dreary spectacle presented to him, that morning, by the surrounding country and by that endless road.

Courage, Titina!

He had by this time covered the section of road hewn out of the vertical face of the long brow, from which rise majestic against the sky the remains of the old Akragantine temples, and where at one time opened the Golden Gate of the ancient vanished city. Now he came stumbling down the slope that declines to the valley of Sant'Anna, through which there trickles, with an occasional obstruction, a rivulet of undrinkable water, the ancient Hypsas, now Drago, dry in summer and a source of malaria throughout the surrounding country, owing to the stagnant pools that form beneath the tangled vegetation of its banks. Swollen to a torrent by the heavy rain of the night, it surged, this morning, against the low arch of the bridge, accustomed in summer to bestride an empty bed of stones and gravel.

Indeed from that dreary tract of country, abominated by such peasants as were compelled by necessity to inhabit it, wasted, yellow, fever-ridden, there seemed to be exhaled in the murk of the frigid dawn an agonizing oppression, by which even the trees were penetrated; those centenarian, writhing olives, those almonds stripped bare by the first winds of autumn.

"Wet morning, eh?" Captain Sciaralla would hasten to say, whenever, on this part of the road, he encountered any of the peasants or carters who

knew him, to forestall jeers and insults, and would
put spurs to poor Titina.

It was not without reason, though, that he
chose, this morning, as a topic of conversation the
rain of the past night. As he trotted along, and
looked up at the black and ragged mass of drift-
ing clouds, his thoughts turned to the rain in
search of an excuse that would set his conscience
at rest, he having disobeyed an express order received the evening before from the Prince's secretary: the order to set off at once with a letter
to Don Cosmo Laurentano, Don Ippolito's brother,
who lived in similar isolation on the other estate
of Valsanìa, about four miles from Colimbètra.

Sciaralla had not felt inclined to venture forth
at that hour of the night, and ride down the valley
in such vile weather; it had occurred to him that
Lisi Préola, the old secretary, having a scapegrace
son who aspired to become captain of the bodyguard, would like nothing better than to dispatch
Sciaralla himself into the next world; that, after
all, the letter was probably not so urgent as to require him to risk his neck on a villainous road, in
pitch darkness, under pelting rain, amid thunder
and lightning; and that in short he might as well
wait for the dawn and slip off quietly, without
having to forego his evening game of *briscola* in
the barrack-room on the crest of the Sperone, to
which he retired for the night with his three chief

subordinates, each of them taking his turn of three hours on guard.

Captain Sciaralla always disliked having to leave Colimbètra, but he felt that he was taking his life in his hands when he had to go to Valsanìa. There he was always required to endure in patience the fury of an old fiend, the terror of all the country round, named Mauro Mortara, who, taking advantage of the easy-going nature of Don Cosmo, whose great tomes of philosophy had undoubtedly addled his brains, played the master there, refusing to take orders from anyone else.

"Courage, courage, Titina!" Sciaralla kept sighing, whenever the figure of this old man appeared to his mind's eye: of low stature, slightly bent, jacketless, wearing a thick, rough shirt of violet flannel checked with red, unbuttoned to expose his hairy chest, a huge shaggy cap on his head which he had made for himself from a lambskin, the tan of which, melted by his sweat, had stained to a deep yellow his flowing locks and the untrimmed white whiskers on either side of his face: comic and savage, with a brace of big pistols always in his belt, even at night time, since he lay down to sleep fully clad on a straw mattress for a few hours only: still more alert and stronger, at seventy-seven, than a lad of twenty.

"And he won't ever die!" groaned Sciaralla. "I should think not! He has everything he wants!

After all these years he is looked upon as one of the family by Don Ippolito himself, which is saying a good deal. As for Don Cosmo, the wonder is they don't call each other *tu*."

And he turned over in his mind as he rode the extraordinary adventures of this man who, in Forty-Eight, had followed into exile in Malta the old Prince, Don Gerlando Laurentano, who had shown a fondness for him ever since the time when, deprived of his place as Gentleman in Waiting, *Gold Key*, owing to some scandal at the Court of Naples, he had retired to Valsanìa, where Mortara had been born and bred, the son of poor peasants, and was a peasant boy himself, tending the sheep, in fact, at the time.

One in particular among the man's countless adventures arrested Placido Sciaralla's attention: the adventure that had won for Mortara the nickname *Monk;* an adventure of his earliest days, before Forty-Eight, when at Valsanìa, round the old Prince of Laurentano, there used to assemble in secret, from Girgenti, the section leaders of the revolutionary committee. Mauro Mortara kept guard for the conspirators at the gate of the Villa. Well, on one occasion a Franciscan friar was so ill-advised as to make his way there in search of alms. Mortara at once took him for a spy: seized him, bound him, kept him tied to a tree all day long: at nightfall he untied him and sent him pack-

ing; but the friar was unable to get over his
fright, and shortly afterwards died.

This adventure remained more vivid than any
of the rest in Sciaralla's imagination, not only because in it Mortara showed himself, as he liked to
believe himself, a fierce man, but also because the
tree to which the Franciscan had been tied was
still standing there by the villa, and Mauro never
failed to point it out to him, accompanying the
gesture with a mute, sardonic smile and a slight
nod, his face contorted with rage at the sight of
that Bourbon uniform.

"Courage, Titina, courage!"

It was best to suffer in peace the insults and
taunts of this old man. A man who had, indeed,
met and faced dangers and mishaps of every sort
in the course of his life, beyond counting; but how
fortunate he was now to be serving Don Cosmo,
who never took any notice of anything except those
great books which kept him wandering all day in
a sort of waking dream about the avenues of Valsanìa!

What a difference between the Prince, his own
master, and this Don Cosmo! What a difference,
too, between either of the brothers and their sister
Donna Caterina Auriti, who lived—a penniless
widow—at Girgenti!

For years past all three had been at daggers
drawn with one another.

Donna Caterina Laurentano, alone of the three, had been influenced by their father's new ideas; in addition to which it was said that, as a girl, she had brought shame on the family by running away with Stefano Auriti, killed later on in Sixty, as a Garibaldino, at the battle of Milazzo, while fighting side by side with Mortara and with his own son Don Roberto, who now lived in Rome and had then been a boy of twelve, the youngest soldier in the Thousand.

It may be imagined, therefore, whether the Prince could have any dealings with such a sister! Don Cosmo was another matter—why not he? He, to all appearances at least, had never taken sides with anyone. And yet perhaps he did not approve of his elder brother's protest against the new Government. Which of the two was right, though? Their father, before turning Liberal, had been a Bourbonist, a Gentleman of the Chamber and *Gold Key:* what wonder, then, if the son, deeming his father disloyal, had remained faithful to the late Government? Indeed, he was entitled to respect for showing such constancy: respect and veneration; and was in no way to be blamed if he chose that everybody should know what his views were, even by the way in which he dressed his dependents. "Yes, gentlemen, I am a Bourbonist! I have the courage of my convictions!"

"Courage, Titina!"

Ohè!

At this stage a clod of earth struck Captain
Sciaralla on the back, followed by a burst of mock-
ing laughter.

The Captain started up in his saddle and
turned round, furious. There was no one to be
seen. From a hedge beyond the ditch, however,
came the following lines of verse, declaimed in a
tone of derision, very slowly:

> Sciarallino, Sciarallino,
> sei scappato dalla storia?
> dove vai con tanta boria
> sul ventoso tuo ronzino? [1]

Captain Sciaralla recognized the voice as that
of Marco Préola, the scapegrace son of the
Prince's secretary, and felt his blood boil. But a
moment later Préola made his appearance in such
a state that the Captain's frowning brows rose to
the brim of his cap, and his lips, tight pressed in
anger, parted with stupefaction.

He bore no resemblance to a human being, this
creature: saving the grace of Baptism, it was a
hog that he suggested, fresh from his wallow,
muddy and dishevelled. Standing with his legs
apart, his body reeling backwards from the waist
in a drunkard's balance, Préola continued to

[1] (Sciarallino, Sciarallino, have you just stepped out of the
history-book? Where are you off to, so proud and stiff, on your
broken-winded nag)

declaim from above with loose and feeble gesticulations

> Dimmi, corri, Sciarallino,
> all'assalto d'un molino?
> od a caccia di lumache
> vai così di buon mattino,
> con codeste rosse brache
> e il giubbon chiaro turchino,
> Sciarallino, Sciarallino? [2]

"You dear fellow!" said Sciaralla, as he felt with one hand behind his back, where the clod had plastered his coat with mud.

Marco Préola slid down, on the seat of his breeches, from the slimy bank of the ditch, and came up to him.

"Dear, am I?" he said. "No: I sell myself cheap! Do you like my poetry? It's fine! And there's more of it, you know? I am going to print it in next Sunday's *Empedocle.*"

Captain Sciaralla continued to gaze at him, his face now contracted in a grimace in which pity was mingled with disgust. He knew that the other was liable to epileptic fits, that often he would wander about by night like a stray dog, and disappear for two or three days on end, until he was found lying like a dead animal with his face to

[2] (Tell me, are you hastening, Sciarallino, to the assault of a windmill? Or is it hunting snails that you come out like this at cockcrow with those red breeches and that sky-blue coat, Sciarallino, Sciarallino?)

the ground and froth on his lips, up at the Culmo delle Forche or on the Serra Ferlucchia or in the fields. He saw the man's puffy face, disfigured by a long, livid scar on the right cheek, with a thin, irregular growth of colourless hair on lip and chin; he stared at the old cap, faded and filthy, which did not come far enough down to hide the deformity of a precocious baldness; he noticed that the hair of his eyebrows had fallen out also; but he could not face the glare of those pale, green-ish, impudent eyes, in which all the vices imagin-able seemed to swarm. Expelled from the Mili-tary School at Modena, Préola had been in Rome for about a year on the staff of a blackmailing little paper; after serving a term of eight months' im-prisonment, he had tried to commit suicide by jumping off one of the bridges into the Tiber; his life saved by a miracle, he had been sent back to his home by order of the court, and was now liv-ing at his father's expense in Girgenti.

"What have you been doing?" Sciaralla asked him.

Préola looked at his clothes and with a frigid grin replied:

"Nothing. I've made myself a bit . . . mucky."

He waved his hands in such a way as to indicate that he had been rolling on the ground, and added:

"A slight attack. . . ."

All of a sudden, with a change of tone and man-ner, gripping Sciaralla by the arm:

"Give me the letter," he shouted. "I know you have it!"

"Are you mad?" exclaimed Sciaralla, recoiling from him with a jerk.

Préola uttered a nervous laugh, then said to him:

"Out with it; I'm only going to take a sniff at it. I want to see if it smells of wedding-cake. Creature, don't you know that your master is getting married?"

Sciaralla stared at him in amazement.

"The Prince?"

"His Excellency, yes indeed! Don't you believe me? I bet that's what the letter is about. The Prince is announcing his marriage to his brother. Haven't you seen Monsignor Montoro? He's the match maker!"

Certainly Monsignor Montoro had, during the last few days, shewn his face far more often than usual at Colimbètra. Could it be true? Sciaralla made an effort to prevent these incredible tidings, of such an astounding event, from revealing to him in a flash a vision of sumptuous entertainments, of a gay animation quite novel in that austere, vast, silent retreat; the hope of reward for the brave show that he would make with his men and the faultless service that he would render. ... But the Prince, was it possible? So serious a man ... and at his age? Besides, how was anyone to believe what Préola might say?

Endeavouring to hide his amazement and curiosity with an incredulous smile, he asked:

"And who is the lady?"

"If you give me the letter, I'll tell you," the other replied.

"To-morrow! Get along with you! I see your game."

Whereupon Sciaralla leant forward in his saddle as a signal to the mare to move.

"Wait!" exclaimed Préola, grasping Titina by the tail. "A lot I care about the wedding, or whether you believe me or not! Perhaps . . . now this is what I really should like to know . . . perhaps the Prince is writing to his brother about the election, and their nephew's candidature. Haven't you heard about that either? Don't you know that Roberto Auriti, the 'twelve-year-old hero,' is standing for Parliament?"

"I know all I want to know, you can't take me in," said Sciaralla. "Haven't we got a Member already, Fazello?"

"Why, you're all a hundred years behind the times, at Colimbètra!" sneered Préola. "We're to have a General Election, and Fazello's not standing again, donkey, because of his son's death!"

"His son? But he's not married!"

Again Préola uttered his nervous laugh.

"And can't a bachelor, a clergyman too, have children? Idiot! We're to have Auriti, sup-

ported by the Government, against the lawyer
Capolino. A fierce fight, tense excitement. . . .
Give me the letter!"

Sciaralla thrust his spurs into Titina and jerked
himself free from Préola. Whereupon the latter
flung a stone after him, then a second; he was preparing to fling a third, when from round the corner came a furious voice:

"Ohè, what the . . . Who's that throwing
stones?"

And a second voice, addressed evidently to the
escaping Sciaralla:

"For shame! For shame! You dressed-up
doll! Idiot! Clown!"

And from round the corner there appeared, beneath a huge, tattered umbrella, tired and travel-
stained, the two inseparables, Luca Lizio and
Nocio Pigna, or, as everyone had now begun to
call them, *Propaganda and Co.*: the former, a pale,
shockheaded lamp-post of a man, with a pair of
spectacles that kept slipping to one side of his
nose, hunching his shoulders with cold, and with
the collar of his light summer jacket turned up;
the other squat, deformed, with a crooked back, one
arm dangling down almost to the ground and the
other hand resting on his knee, in an attempt to
establish some sort of equilibrium.

The Naked Truth!

They were the two revolutionaries of the place.

Captain Sciaralla was wrong in thinking that there was no one stirring at Girgenti.

They were stirring, Lizio and Pigna.

It must be admitted that the appearance of the pair, that morning, so drenched and numbed, under their tattered umbrella, did not suggest that there could be anything very terrible in their revolutionary enterprises.

No one could be better aware of this than Marco Préola, who, having long since abandoned to the will of destiny his own life, which he himself was the first to belittle and despise, a life in which there was no affection, no faith in anything left, unbound not only by any rule but by any force of habit, and flung to the mercy of every sudden, violent caprice, regarded everything as absurd and fatuous, and laughed at everything, finding an outlet in that laughter for the exceptional, if disordered, energies of his embittered spirit.

He knew that, three days earlier, the pair had gone down to the harbour of Porto Empedocle to catechize the porters employed in loading sulphur, the wharfingers, stevedores, lightermen, carters, checkweighmen, with a view to combining them in a *fascio*. Seeing them return at such an hour and in such a state, he wrinkled his nose, stopped in the middle of the road to wait for them and ac-

company them as far as Girgenti; as they drew
near, he flung out his arms as though to gather
up a full-sized *fiasco* of wine, and said to them:
"Come along; don't worry: I can carry it."

Pigna stopped and, drawing himself up as far
as he could with the support of his arm, stared contemptuously at Préola. His body was all twisted
and knotted; but he had the face of a great doll,
without a hair on it, cheeks burnished by the salt
sweat that exuded from his skin, and a pair of
black eyes, glinting and darting, the eyes of a
madman, beneath a big blue bonnet, battered out
of shape, which gave him the appearance of a
jack in the box.

Marco Préola hailed him by a contemptuously
friendly nickname, and said with a smile:

"*Nociarè,* don't take on about it! It's a vile
world we live in, full of ungrateful wretches.
Sailors, flat-feet. . . . Oh, yes, and put away your
umbrella, Luca! God sends us down water, and
you refuse His gift? Let us give our faces a
wash, like this. . . ."

He raised his muddy face to the sky. There
still spattered down from the clouds, which were
reddening now at their ragged edges as they
moved towards the almost risen sun, an icy, stab-
bing drizzle.

"What are a few pins and needles?" he cried,
throwing off a shower of water like a horse, shaking his head and deliberately charging into Pigna.

Filthy as he was, from head to foot, and soaked to the skin by the rain, he felt that he need no longer bother to keep himself dry and clean, and had the satisfaction, as he wallowed whole-heartedly in the mire, of being able to splash the others with impunity.

"Get away with you!" Pigna shouted at him. "Who asked you to come here? Who wants your company? Who ever told you you could take such liberties?"

Without turning a hair, Préola replied:

"I do love to see you in a rage! Mother earth, my dear fellow, mother earth! I was trying to stick some of it on you. . . . Nature's seal? You would run away from me, would you? And then you complain that other people are ungrateful."

"Did you ever hear such impudence . . ." Pigna growled, as he turned to Lizio.

But the latter was absorbed in his own thoughts, and walked on in frowning indifference. He shrugged his shoulders as who should say that he did not wish to be disturbed from his train of thought, and on he went.

Préola followed them in silence for some way, keeping his distance, gazing at each of them in turn.

He felt himself torn by a gnawing desire to be doing something, that morning; what, he did not know. In another moment he would have begun to howl like a wolf. To keep himself from howling, he opened his mouth, gripped his lower jaw in his hand and pulled it down until he had almost dislocated it. His only relief was to vent himself on the pair of travellers; but what amusement was there in teasing Lizio? A desperate fellow like that, and one moreover whose head was always in the clouds. A twofold calamity, the suicide of his father, an excellent lawyer but of unbalanced brain, followed by that of his brother, had won him a certain sympathy in the place, in which horror blended with pity, and a certain respect to boot. He studied hard and spoke little, indeed he scarcely spoke at all. There was good reason for this: he was able to pronounce barely half the alphabet. One thing only brought him into derision, that he had found his barrel-organ in Pigna, and organ and grinder invariably appeared together on platforms. If Pigna went out of tune, he brought him back to the right pitch, with the utmost gravity, plucking him by the sleeve. Social Revolution . . . Brotherhood of Man . . . Stand Up for the Rights of the Downtrodden . . . big ideas, indeed! And perhaps that was why, in his distraction, he had fastened meanwhile upon a crust of bread that others had earned for him. He was doing well, oh rather! Only, with this touch of cold in the air . . .

"A nice little pot of coffee, by God!" Préola burst out suddenly, waving his arms in the air.

"Three lumps of sugar, a jug of cream, four slices of toast. Oh, Holy Souls in Purgatory!"

Luca Lizio turned sharply round to gaze at him. A cup of coffee was just what was in his mind at that moment, behind those knitted brows; he saw it and was almost intoxicated by it in imagination, as he inhaled its steaming fragrance; and in the force of his desire clenched the numbed fist in his pocket. Having started before dawn, and in the bitterness of defeat, from Porto Empedocle, he was starved with cold; he was longing to reach his destination. Abashed by this base need, he felt himself to be wretched, deserving of comfort, of a comfort which no one (he well knew) could provide.

A moment earlier, what with that dressed-up doll bolting off on his white mare, and Préola standing there waiting for them, his lips curved in a sneer, he had received a sudden strange impression of himself, which had penetrated to the depths of his being and stirred up a feeling that was entirely new to him, a feeling almost of stupefaction at all his red rags, all his blazing furies, which in a flash had revealed themselves to him, as though seen from outside, as foolish and vain, there in the midst of that scene of utter squalor and desolation. In the wretched emaciation of his body shivering with cold and sticky with a viscid sweat, he felt that he resembled one of those trees that rose from behind the crumb-

ling walls, dead and dripping. He too was dripping, with cold, from the tip of his nose, and
trickling from the peering, watery eyes behind
his spectacles. He had huddled himself together;
and, as though that impression, after plumbing the
depths of his consciousness and vanishing in stupefaction, had now closed round him with a crushing grip, he felt himself a mass of aches; his narrow brows ached, and the sharp protuberance of
his back, over which the stuff of his summer jacket
had worn shiny, and the wrists exposed by the
shortness of his sleeves, and the soaked feet in
his broken shoes. And everything seemed to him
now unbearable, an excess of cruelty: every fresh
turn in that road, become a torrent of mud; the
crude light of dawn which, notwithstanding the
blackness of the clouds, struck a reflexion from
the mire which dazzled his eyes; but most of all
the company of that miserable scarecrow, spattered with mud from head to foot, mud without
and mud within, who kept goading Pigna to speak.
He, being accustomed for so many years now to
remaining silent, felt a bewilderment that grew
more and more confused at his own silence, which,
though no one knew this, fed and waxed strong
within him upon certain fantastic impressions,
such as that which he had just received, which he
could not have expressed in words to himself even,
save at the cost of forfeiting all faith in and
support of his work.

Marco Préola, meanwhile, went on speaking, as though to himself:

"As for me, that's another matter; what am I? A vagabond; I deserve all this and more. But look at the weather the Lord God sees fit to send us, when two poor humanitarians are taking the road on a sacred mission, after an irreverent crowd has driven them out, at night, with a whipping!"

Pigna made as though to stop, quivering with rage; but Luca Lizio drew him on with a clutch at his sleeve and an angry growl.

"Whipping . . . just you wait!" he muttered through his teeth. "I'll give them a whipping, I will . . ."

"And I would take one from you, Nociarè," Préola hastened to assure him with a bow, "as sure as God's in Heaven! Why, do you know, you're a hero! Stinking filth! Or is it I that am always smelling stinks. . . . The nose; something in the nose. . . . I ought not to smell them, accustomed as I am to filth. . . . A true hero, Nociarè! The common people can't understand you. They can't understand you, because an idea, unfortunately, has no eyes or legs or mouth. What has an idea to say for itself? It speaks by the mouths of men. And the ignorant masses are incapable of distinguishing between the idea and the person who expresses it, do you follow me? You may sing like a nightingale, and yet, my

Nòcio, you can have no effect. Suppose you say:
'Men and women, humanity is on the march! I
will teach you to march!' they are quite capable
of looking at the way you throw your shanks
about, and jeering: 'Just look at the fellow who
wants to teach us to march!' "

"Ass!" roared Propaganda, who could contain
himself no longer. "Reasoning with the feet is
what you call that."

"I? The people!" retorted Préola.

"The People, let me tell you," replied Pigna,
rolling his eyes like a madman; then suddenly he
broke off. "Don't you dare to utter the word
People; you are not fit even to name the People!
The People have learned too much, my good man,
let me tell you; and, first and foremost, that your
patriots have deceived them. . . ."

"Mine?" came with a laugh from Préola.

"Yours, the men who drove them into the Revolution of 1860, with promises of a Golden Age!
Not we! Not we, as you fellows go about preaching! The patriots and the priests deceived them
and are deceiving them now! We, my good man,
let me tell you, prove to them, in so many words,
with the proof in our hands, that (you follow me?)
by virtue of their own force (you follow me?)—
by virtue, I repeat, of their own force, not by any
concessions from outside, they can, if they choose,
improve their condition."

"By force of their own virtue would be bet-

ter," Préola observed placidly, without thinking
of what he was saying.

Pigna stared at him in astonishment. But the
other at once made haste to calm him:

"It's nothing, don't worry about it. It was
only a joke!"

"By virtue . . . by virtue of their own force,"
Pigna went on in a low tone, none too certain of
himself, turning to Lizio to read in the latter's
eyes whether he had used the right words; and
went on, somewhat disconcerted: "To improve,
yes, Sir, this unjust economic system, under which
men are living . . . that is to say, no . . . I
mean, yes . . . some men are living without working, and others, who do all the work, cannot live!
Do you follow me? We say to the People: 'You
are everything! You can do anything! Unite,
and dictate your own law and your own justice!' "

"Splendid!" exclaimed Préola. "Will you allow me to speak now?"

"Your own law and your own justice!" Pigna
repeated, furious at the interruption. "Speak,
speak."

"You won't take offence?"

"I shall not take offence: speak."

"Were you or were you not, until recently, a
sacristan?"

Propaganda turned round again to gaze at him
in astonishment.

"What has that got to do with it?"

To which Préola, calmly:

"You're not to take offence! Answer me."

"A sacristan, yes, Sir," Pigna courageously admitted. "Well? What do you mean by that? That I've changed the colour of my coat?"

"Colour of your coat, indeed! That's nothing . . ."

"I have learned to know the priests, that is all!"

"And how to breed children," retorted Préola: "seven daughters, one after another; can you deny that?"

Nocio Pigna stopped for the third time to gaze at him. He had promised that he would not take offence. But what was the fellow driving at with this string of questions? He had lost his post in the church because one of his daughters, the eldest, and a certain Canon Landolina . . .

"On condition that you keep off certain topics," he warned the other, darkening and lowering his gaze.

"No, no, no," Préola broke out, placing his hand on his heart. "Listen, Nocio, I am, 'by the universal judgment of the wise,' what is commonly called a scoundrel. Is that clear? I have been eight months *in quod* . . . think of that! And do you see this?" he added, pointing to the scar on his cheek. "When I jumped *in river*, as they say in Rome. . . . Yes, indeed! . . . You can imagine, then, whether certain things can make any impression on me! Do you know, though, what has made an impression on me? The fact that you, with that poor girl . . ."

"I told you, we were to keep off certain topics."

"My dear sir," sighed Préola, shutting his eyes. "Let me go on. . . . You must know that the people I fight against are the only ones for whom I feel any respect. But these same people, naturally enough, since my . . . let us say misfortunes, refuse to feel any for me, and would prevent me, if they could, from living. I must live! In order to live I fight against them and stand by the priests. Men do not forgive; God, on the other hand, so the priests say, has forgiven me long ago; and on that pretext they make use of me. . . . Look at this vast expanse, Nocio!" he went on, pushing back his hat so as to expose his brow. "And there's plenty of stuff behind it, you know! If things had gone the right way with me. . . . But enough of that. I, you, . . . everything . . . just look! Mud, mud, mud . . . Here we are, all three of us, up to our ankles in the mud of this road. Let us speak plainly, openly, Holy God, for once in a way! Let us state things nakedly and crudely, as they are, without dressing them up in fine language. The naked truth, come; let us give ourselves that pleasure! I am a swine, yes, but what are you, Nociarè? What do you do? What is your work, can you tell me that? Put your hand on your heart, now, and tell the truth: you don't work at all!"

"I?" exclaimed Pigna, astonished, stupefied, rather than offended by the injustice of the remark, extending his arm and folding it over his bosom with outstretched forefinger.

"You are working for the cause? Words!" Préola was ready with his retort. "I asked you to tell me the naked truth! Instead of which you clothe it, you cover it up, as you please, to quiet your conscience. You did work . . . they turned you out of the church; then, from a lottery office. . . . Slander, yes, I know! Still, supposing you really did pocket the half-pence of the idiots who came to bet in your shop, do you imagine that I would call that wrong? You would have been perfectly right! But now, what are you doing? Your daughters do the work, and you eat and preach. And this other fellow here, this Saint Luke the Evangelist. . . . What is it you call it? Free love. Very good: words! The fact of the matter is that he has been going with another of your daughters and . . ."

At this point Luca Lizio, livid, speechless, quivering with rage, sprang forward with outstretched arms at Préola's throat. But the other drew back with a laugh, caught hold of his arms and thrust him away without undue violence.

"What are you doing?" he shouted at him, his

eyes and teeth gleaming with malicious joy.
"What is the joke? I am telling you the truth."

"Let him rip!" Pigna here interposed, holding
Luca Lizio back and preparing to move on his
way. "Don't you see that he makes it his business to play the gadfly?"

"A gadfly, yes. . ." said Préola. "What part
of you did I sting? Your nakedness? Ah, we are
naked and ashamed, my friends. . . . And in this
cold weather, too. . . . Let us cover it up quickly
with the cloak of charity! I was only trying to
explain to you, dear Nocio, without offending you,
why you are unable to create any effect . . ."

"Because the people here are carrion!" cried
Pigna, turing upon him with a savage glare in
his eyes.

"I quite agree!" Préola made haste to assure
him. "And I myself . . . carrion too, don't you
mean? I agree! But you don't work; your daughters do the work, and Luca eats and reads, and
you eat and preach. Now the people who do work,
my dear fellow, and who hear you preaching to
them, 'Just look,' they say, 'who it is that wants
to save us! Nocio Pigna! *Propaganda!* That's
the man!' And they burst out laughing. You
preach and you don't see yourself: you see the
idea! The people, however, don't see the idea;
they see the man who is preaching. You see them
laugh, and you say: 'But why?'—puzzled, pained,
because at that moment you identify yourself en-

tirely with your idea, and can think of nothing
else. But the audience facing you, my dear fellow, see in you the quondam sacristan, the quondam lottery clerk; they see a hunchback, a twisted
cripple (it's God own truth); they remember that
you are living upon your daughters, and—let us
be quite frank—how could you have any effect,
my dear Nocio?"

Pigna made no reply; he shook his head several
times and once again muttered to himself:

"A lot of carrion! They ought to listen to me,
if I am a hunchback or a cripple. . . . And when
have I ever said: 'I am saving you'? 'Your salvation rests with yourselves,' is what I say. But
go to Aragona, a stone's throw from Girgenti; go
to Favara, Grotte, Casteltermini, Campobello,
. . . Who are they? Peasants and sulphur workers, poor illiterates. Four thousand of them, at
Casteltermini alone! I was there last week; I
was present at the formation of the Fascio . . ."

"With a lamp burning before the Madonna,"
inquired Préola. "Wasn't there?"

"God is one thing, a priest is another, idiot!"
Pigna replied haughtily.

"And the bugles sounding the royal salute?"

"Discipline! Discipline!" exclaimed Pigna.
"They're doing splendidly! You ought to have
seen them. . . . All ready and in earnest . . .
four thousand . . . a solid mass . . . they were
like the earth itself, the earth come to life, you

know, moving and thinking . . . eight thousand eyes conscious and looking up to you . . . eight thousand arms. . . . And my heart turned in my bosom at the thought that only among ourselves, here at Girgenti, the capital, at Porto Empedocle, a sea port, open to trade: nothing! Nothing! One can do nothing! What dumb brutes they are! Worse than brutes! But do you know how they live down at Porto Empedocle? How the shipping of the sulphur is still being done? Do you know?"

Marco Préola was tired: his head drooped, as he murmured:

"Porto Empedocle . . ."

And each of the three formed a mental image of that straggling village by the sea which had grown in a few years at the expense of the old town of Girgenti and had now become an independent *comune*. A score of huts, originally, down there on the beach, with a short loading stage of flimsy beams, known now as the Old Harbour, and a sea fortress, foursquare and frowning, in which the convicts were kept at hard labour, who subsequently, as the sulphur trade increased, had thrown out the two broad reefs of the new harbour, one on either side of the little wharf, which, by virtue of its landing stage, had retained the honour of carrying the harbour master's office and the white tower of the principal beacon. Prevented from spreading inland by the

cliff of marl that overhung it, the village had extended laterally along the narrow beach, and right
up to the foot of the cliff the houses were packed
and squeezed together, almost on the top of one
another. The loads of sulphur were piled up
along the beach; and from morning to night there
was a continuous rumbling of carts which came
loaded with sulphur from the railway station or
even direct from the nearest pits; an endless coming and going of barefooted men and animals,
and a din of quarrels and curses and cries blended
with the rumbling and whistling of a train which
crossed the beach, making alternately for each of
the two breakwaters, constantly under repair. Beyond the eastward arm the beach was fringed by
the lighters, with their sails furled at half mast;
at the foot of the sulphur heaps were the scales,
upon which the sulphur was weighed before being
loaded on the backs of the carriers, known as *men
of the sea,* who, barefoot, in canvas trousers, each
with a sack on his shoulders, pulled down over his
head in front and twisted round the back of his
neck, plunging waist-deep into the water, carried
out their loads to the lighters, which then, hoisting
their sails, went out to unload the sulphur into
the holds of the trading steamers anchored in the
harbour or outside it.

"Slave labour," said Pigna; "it makes one's
heart bleed, on cold days in winter. . . . Bowed
down under their loads, with the water up to their

bellies. . . . Men, do you call them? Beasts is what they are. . . . And if you tell them that they could become men if they chose, they open their mouths in a fatuous laugh and insult you. Do you know why they are not putting landing stages on the breakwaters of the new harbour, where the loading could be done more quickly and easily from carts or trucks? Because the big pots of the place are the people who own the lighters! And all the time, in spite of the fortunes they are making out of the trade, the drains are still uncovered on the beach, and the people die of fever; with the whole sea at their feet, there is no supply of drinking water, and the people die of thirst! No one takes any trouble; no one complains of the state of things. They are like a lot of lunatics, all those men, bestialized in the war for profits, a vile and savage war."

"But do you know, you really do speak well?" Préola expressed his approval. "Do you know, you really have profited by all the sermons you had to listen to as a sacristan?"

"*Bye bye,* as the English say!" Nocio Pigna went on, stretching out his long arm with a menacing gesture. "There are three hundred thousand of us, my boy, at this very moment. And you shall hear of us again before long."

In the realm of Orcus.

Having climbed to the summit of the road, from
which the ground fell away down the slope of the
valley beyond, Placido Sciaralla was now trotting
along on Titina in the direction of Valsanìa,
plunged in fresh and even more complicated considerations after what he had heard from Préola.
After a while he shrugged his shoulders and began to look about him.

There stretched out now, on his left, the smiling seaboard country, covered with almond trees
and olives. He was already in sight of Seta, a
hamlet of some fifty houses lining the highroad,
clothes-shops and taverns for the carters, most
of them, from which exuded a keen and acrid smell
of must, a rich warm smell of dung, and the shops
of blacksmiths, locksmiths, wheelwrights, with a
tumble-down house in the centre, converted into a
chapel for the Sunday services.

To avoid the gaze of these village yokels, all of
whom knew him by sight, Sciaralla turned along
a bridle path that crossed the fields and had soon
gained the sanctuary of Valsanìa.

Apart from the vineyard, the object of Mauro
Mortara's passionate devotion and the pride of
his life, and the ancient Saracen olive grove, the
almond grove and some acres of ploughland, and,
in the wide ravine farther down, the orchard, all
of which formed the portion reserved for Don

Cosmo, all the rest was made over in small lots
to poor peasant portioners, not by the Prince himself, Don Ippolito, to whom this estate belonged
as well, but by subtenants of tenants, who, not
content with living a life of leisure in town on the
toil of these poor creatures, crushed and bled them
with the most pitiless usury, and with a complicated system of customary exactions. The usury
arose from the purchase of seed and various
loans advanced during the year; the exactions
were even more unfair, and were levied at harvest
time. After toiling for a year, the so-called por-
tioner saw carried away, heap after heap, from
his steading practically the whole of his crop; the
heaps for sowing, the heaps for feeding, and for
the *lamp,* and another for the *campiere,* and
another for Our Lady of Sorrows, and San Francesco di Paola, and San Calògero, in fact for
almost every Saint in the Church calendar; so that
as often as not he was left with only the *solame,*
that is to say the few sweepings of grain mixed
with chaff and dust which were left on the floors
after threshing.

The sun had by this time risen, and Captain
Sciaralla could see here and there, over the expanse of the fields, the glittering reflexion from
some pool of rain-water or perhaps a piece of
broken crockery. The whole countryside was
steaming as though a veil of mist hung and quivered over it. Here and there, a group of those

tumble-down, smoke-begrimed hovels which the
peasants called *roba,* house, stable, byre all in
one; and the wife of one of these portioners
emerging from her door to tether the grunting
little pig in the open, followed by three or four
fowls; outside the worm-eaten red door of the
house opposite, another woman was combing the
head of a whimpering little girl; while the men,
with old and primitive ploughs drawn each by an
emaciated mule and a slow-moving donkey that
strained every muscle in the effort, barely
scratched the surface of the soil, after the preliminary watering it had received in the night.

All these poor folk, seeing Sciaralla approach
on his white mare, paused from their labours to
salute him with reverence, as though it were the
Prince in person who was passing. Captain Sciaralla responded with great dignity, raising his
hand to his cap in a military salute, and received
these demonstrations of respect as a compensation in advance for the humiliation that lay in
store for him at the hands of that savage old beast
Mortara. A secret misgiving, however, spoiled
all the pleasure to be derived from these salutes:
in a few minutes, when he entered the other's do-
main, he would be assailed by the dogs, those three
mastiffs more savage than their master who had
obviously taught them to give him this greeting
whenever he came. And Sciaralla might shout
himself hoarse while the creatures were bounding

about him, leaping as high as Titina's head while she, in her turn, skipped like a sheep with terror: Mauro or the *curàtolo,* Ninfa's Vanni, would appear in his own good time to call the dogs off, after the poor wretch had more than once seen death staring him in the face.

With these three mastiffs Mauro Mortara used to converse just as though they had been reasonable beings. He used to say that men did not understand dogs, but that dogs did understand men. "The trouble," he would say, "is that they, poor creatures, cannot express their meaning to us; and so we imagine that they do not understand us and do not listen."

Sciaralla however explained the phenomenon differently. These dogs understood their master so perfectly because he was more canine than themselves. And his theory seemed to receive fresh confirmation this morning.

Mauro was stationed outside the villa; his three cronies on guard round him, their noses pointing in the air. Well, on Sciaralla's arrival, this time, they remained where they were (one of them even yawned), as though they quite understood that their master would fill their part to perfection.

"What do you want here, prowling about at this hour in the morning?" was indeed all the greeting he had from Mauro, who pushed back the hood of the rough greatcoat he was wearing and revealed his head, burdened with its huge shaggy cap.

When vintage drew near, Mauro Mortara ceased to sleep at nights: he kept watch over the vines, patrolling up and down the long alleys with his three mastiffs. Perhaps he had been out there in the open all through the night of storm that had just passed: he was quite capable of it.

Sciaralla saluted him humbly, then, pointing to the dogs, asked:

"Can I dismount?"

"Dismount," growled Mauro. "What have you brought?"

"A letter for Don Cosmo," replied Sciaralla as he slid from the mare's back.

Sciaralla knew that it was forbidden for him to cross the threshold of the villa, as though, with his uniform, he might desecrate that tumble-down, rambling pile of a single storey: he who came from the splendours of Colimbètra, where you could see your face reflected in the very walls! The prohibition did not come, certainly, from Don Cosmo, but from Mortara himself, who actually forbade him to tie the mare to the rings fastened to the balustrade of the rustic stair. He must hold her himself and remain standing there, outside, waiting, as though he had come for alms.

No sooner did Mauro turn to go than the three dogs stole softly up to Captain Sciaralla and began to sniff at him. The poor fellow, standing there with a sinking heart, raised his eyes in supplication to Mortara, who was climbing the stair.

"Don't you dirty your muzzles on those breeches!" said Mauro, after calling the dogs to heel: then added, turning to Sciaralla: "I'm going to send you out a mouthful of coffee, to keep your pecker up."

On reaching the landing, he prepared to give the recognized signal, namely to bring the latch down three times on the pin inside; but, as soon as he raised the latch, the door opened, and Mauro entered the house exclaiming:

"Open? Open again? Was it you opened it?" he asked through the shut door of the kitchen, which had opened for a moment to reveal the nightcapped head of Donna Sara Alàimo, the housekeeper (not the servant, oh dear no!) of Valsanìa.

"I?" shouted Donna Sara from inside the room. "I'm just getting up!"

And, hearing Mauro's step recede, she "made the horns," thrust out the index and little fingers of her right hand, and brandished them after him in a gesture of contempt.

Servant, nothing of the sort—not she: the idea of such a thing! neither his servant, nor anyone's else, in that house. She had the ember-fan in her hand, it was true, she was just going to light the kitchen fire, but she was a real lady, a lady born and bred, she was; who could count cousinship

with Stefano Auriti, the brother-in-law of the
Laurentano, and so, why, you might say, one of
the family herself.

She had been at Valsanìa for many years looking after Don Cosmo, who would perhaps never
have felt any need of her services had not his sister, Donna Caterina, sent her to him from Girgenti, where, like a perfect lady, poor thing, she
was starving decorously to death.

At Valsanìa her days were spent in stroking the
backs of two cats (emasculated, as was proper),
which followed her everywhere about the house
with tails erect; in saying rosaries of fifteen dec-
ades, and endless mumbling of other prayers; but,
to hear her talk, everything was going well solely
because she was there—but for her all would
have been at sixes and sevens! If the crops
ripened, if the fruit-trees bore, if the rain came
when it was wanted. . . . In fact, she behaved as
though she ruled the universe.

Mauro could not abide her. And Donna Sara
reciprocated his feeling cordially; indeed, nothing
gave her greater annoyance than to lay a place
for him too at table, since Don Cosmo had sunk
so low as that, as to bestow so high an honour
upon a son of peasants who was little better than
a clodhopping peasant himself; yes indeed . . .
while she, Donna Sara, a real lady born and bred,
remained in the kitchen and was obliged to wait
upon him.

She went to the window and, seeing Captain Sciaralla below, heaved a deep sigh and wailed inwardly:

"Ah, Placidino, Placidino! Let us offer it to the Lord as a penance for our sins. . . ."

Meanwhile Mauro had gone into Don Cosmo's bathroom.

Everything was old-fashioned and rustic in this old and neglected villa: cracked and uneven the rough terracotta tiles of the floor; the walls and ceilings black with smoke; the window-shutters and furniture paintless and worm-eaten; and everything seemed to reek with an odour of dry grain, parched straw, hay withered in the scorching heat of those sun-baked fields.

In the bathroom Don Cosmo, in woollen drawers, his hairy chest bare, his feet unstockinged in their old slippers, was preparing for his regular ablutions, with a dozen sponges, great and small, laid out on the washing stand. He sponged himself all over, every morning, even in winter, with cold water; and this was his one pleasure in life: the height of insanity, though, it seemed to Mauro who every morning, if he washed at all, would wash "just the mug," as he himself put it, meaning his face alone.

"Have you been sleeping with the front door open again?"

"Why not?" said Don Cosmo, as though sur-

prised at such a question; and went on, scratching
his short, curling grey beard: "Come, now!"

"Will you never open your eyes?" Mauro pursued the point. "What have I always said?
Great baby! We'll have to find a tutor, a nurse
for you. . . . Holy God, what sort of man are
you? Didn't you read the newspaper yesterday?
About those gallows birds who say they've nothing
to eat and are going to overthrow everything that
we've shed our blood to set up? The scoundrels!"

What with Mauro's frenzied gesticulations, Don
Cosmo had not observed that he had a letter in
his hand, and had quietly begun to lather his bald
and highly polished scalp. Irritated by his calm,
Mauro went on:

"And if they were all like you. . . . Gad, it's
a lucky thing I'm here! Old as I am, they would
have me to reckon with! Me, do you understand?
Me!"

"In that case," Don Cosmo said quietly, turning to face him, "I can still sleep with the door
open."

The newspapers, at Valsanìa, arrived only at
long intervals, when already converted to their
humble and possibly more useful function of wrap-
ping parcels. Mauro used to straighten out the
sheets with loving care, passing his hands over
them again and again to smooth out the folds and
creases; and, surmounting with monkish patience

the enormous difficulty of reading them (since it was only late in life that he had taught himself to spell), would browse upon them for weeks at a time, committing their contents to memory from beginning to end. Any news was fresh to him, a distant echo of the life of the great world beyond.

In the last newspaper that had come into his hands thus by chance, he had read, the day before, of a strike of sulphur workers in a village of the province and of their forming themselves into a *Fascio di Lavoratori*.

"The vindication of the proletariat!"

Humph! He had made Don Cosmo explain these two long words, a Sibylline utterance to him, and all night long, sheltering in his hut from the pelting rain, had pondered and pondered, groaning with a holy horror at these enemies of their country.

He did not deign to reply to this last speech of Don Cosmo, who, to his mind, must have a screw loose also, but handed him Don Ippolito's letter.

"One of his mountebanks brought it here: Scia-ralla the Captain."

"For me?" asked Don Cosmo in surprise, scooping up the water in the hollow of his hands. "Ippolito has written to me? Wonders will never cease. . . . Open it, read it to me: my hands are wet. . . ."

"Dry them, then!" Mauro told him curtly. "You know that I don't choose to be mixed up in

your brother's affairs. But it doesn't look like
his writing."

"Ah, Préola," observed Don Cosmo, studying
the envelope.

The letter had been written by the secretary at
Don Ippolito's dictation, and was merely signed
by him. As he read it, Don Cosmo knitted his
brows at the opening lines, then gradually re-
laxed the tension of his forehead and eyes in a
pained stupefaction; let his eyelids droop; let the
hand droop that held the letter.

"Ah, poor fellow. . . . So it is true. . . ."

"What is?" growled Mauro, stung by curiosity.

"He's done for himself, done for himself," exclaimed Don Cosmo. "If he yields that point,
there's no way out of it . . . he's ruined. . . ."

"Tell me what is the matter, holy devil!" repeated Mauro, growing more and more curious.

But Don Cosmo only gazed at him for a while
in silence, nodding his head, as though he saw his
brother standing before him and were commiser-
ating him bitterly.

"He asks me for the villa——" he answered at
length, letting the words fall from his lips one by
one, "the villa, for Flaminio Salvo."

"Here?" asked Mauro, with a start, as though
Don Cosmo had struck him a blow in the face.
"Here," he repeated, drawing back. "Flaminio
Salvo, in General Laurentano's villa?"

But Don Cosmo was not furious like Mauro at

the imagined profanation of the villa: what he did feel was a pained stupefaction at what was implied by his brother's offer of hospitality to Salvo. A few days earlier a friend of his, Leonardo Costa, who came now and then to see him from the neighbouring seaport, had told him of the rumour that was going round Girgenti of a forthcoming marriage between Don Ippolito and Salvo's sister, a maiden lady of a certain age. Don Cosmo had refused to believe it: his brother Ippolito was two years his senior, a man of sixty-five; for the last ten years he had been a widower, and had always seemed inconsolable, though he maintained his composure, for the death of his wife, that dear, good woman. . . . Impossible! And yet. . . .

"You will answer no?" said Mauro menacingly, after a moment's silence. Don Cosmo threw up his arms and sighed, his eyes shut:

"It would be no use! Besides . . ."

"What?" Mauro interrupted him. "Salvo, that canting money-lender, here? I shall walk out of the house, if he comes! Good God, have you forgotten that his father went to the *Te Deum* when yours was banished? And didn't he, he himself as a young man, guide the Bourbon police to the house where Don Stefano Auriti was hiding with your sister, when the nobles of Palermo sent the keys of the city to Satriano in Caltanisetta? Have you forgotten all that? I remember every

word of it, as if it was in a printed book! Let
him come to Valsanìa, now, if you dare! But the
General's room, no! Not that! The key of the
camerone is in my keeping! There he shall not
set foot, or I kill him, take the word of Mauro
Mortara!"

Don Cosmo did not stir, nor did he seem to
awake from his pained astonishment, at this long
outburst. More than once he had been on the
point of giving Mauro to understand that the idea
of a United Italy had never entered the head of
Gerlando Laurentano, his father, and that the
Sicilian Parliament of 1848, in which his father
had served for some months as Minister for War,
had never suggested either an Italian Confedera-
tion or annexation to Italy, but a self-contained
Kingdom of Sicily with a King of Sicily, that was
all. This had been the aspiration of all the good
old Sicilians; an aspiration which, if finally it had
in certain respects been pushed farther, had never
gone beyond a form of Federation, in which each
separate state was to conserve its own liberty and
autonomy. But he had never said anything to him
about it; nor did he think of saying anything now;
but rather allowed Mauro, snorting and quivering
with rage, to turn his back on him and go off to
shut himself in the old Prince's room, a room as
sacred to him as the Country itself, the cradle of
Freedom and now almost its temple.

Down below, in the meantime, outside the villa,

poor Sciaralla was still waiting for the promised
coffee: a sip of hot coffee, by Jove, and a good
blaze to warm himself at. . . . Waiting, waiting:
until he too forgot about them and began to worry
over the delay in answering the letter. He ought
to have had the answer in his pocket overnight,
had he carried out Préola's instructions. He was
thinking that by this time the Prince, over at Colimbètra, had perhaps risen from his bed and was
asking his secretary for the answer. And here
was he still waiting for it! Did it take all this
time to read the letter and jot down a couple of
lines in reply? Or could it be that Mortara had
deliberately refrained from giving it to Don
Cosmo?

And Captain Sciaralla groaned; he lost his temper, next, with Titina, who would not remain still
for an instant, tormented by the flies.

"Be quiet! Be quiet! Be quiet!"

Three tugs at the bridle. Titina closed her tear-
ful eyes with so sorrowful a resignation that Sciaralla at once repented of his ill temper.

"You're right, poor girl! They haven't given
you so much as a wisp of hay either."

And he heaved a long sigh.

Finally Don Cosmo appeared at one of the windows of the villa. At the sound of opening shutters, Sciaralla turned hurriedly to look up. But
Don Cosmo appeared surprised to see him still
there.

"Hallo, Placido! What are you waiting for?"

"Why, Excellency, the answer!" groaned the Captain, clasping his hands.

Don Cosmo knitted his brows.

"Does it need an answer?"

"What!" Sciaralla replied in exasperation. "When I've been waiting here for the last hour!"

There, he might have known it! That old ruffian had never said a word about it!

"You're right, my boy, just wait a moment," said Don Cosmo, and withdrew from the window.

He reflected that his brother attached great importance to even the most trifling formalities (stuff and nonsense, *he* called them), and would regard it as a deliberate insult, or, to say the least, a grave discourtesy if he did not receive an answer; he therefore took up a sheet of coarse paper yellow with age; dipped his clotted pen in a bottle of rusty ink and, without sitting down, on the marble top of the chest of drawers, set to work to frame an answer, which finally, after immense pains, found expression in these terms:

Valsanìa, 22nd September, 1892.

My dear Ippolito,

You are perhaps not aware of the deplorable state into which this tumble-down old shanty has fallen; I myself am the only person who could possibly live in it, since I regard myself as already detached from this wicked world, nor do I make any complaint! If you consider, notwithstanding this, that there is no alternative to letting the Salvo family come and vegetate here; be so good, please, as to warn them that we have absolutely nothing here, and that they should bring with them all their household gear and such other furniture as they think they may need.

I have more to say and would say it, did I not feel that it would be vain to hope that any argument of mine might prove effective. And so I shall add no more, but remain

Your affectionate brother

Cosmo

He shut the envelope with a sigh and returned to the window. Captain Sciaralla ran towards the house, took off his cap and caught the letter in it.

"I kiss Your Excellency's hands!"

A spring, and he was in the saddle.

"Like the wind, Titina!"

Bow-wow-wow! The three mastiffs, startled from their sleep, ran after him for a long way, to bid him farewell after their own fashion.

Don Cosmo remained at the window: his eyes followed the galloping figure of Captain Sciaralla until it was hidden by a turn in the road; then the growling, panting return of the three mastiffs, after their futile pursuit and futile barking. When the three animals finally lay down on the ground again, at the foot of the stair, stretched out their heads over their forepaws and shut their eyes to return to their interrupted slumbers, he, as he gazed down at them, shook his head gently and smiled to hear, amid the surrounding silence, one of them heave a deep sigh. In the light of this settling down again to sleep and of this sigh, neither their barking nor their pursuit of Scia-ralla seemed to him any longer to be futile. It was like this: the three animals had protested against the coming of the man who had disturbed their slumber; now that they supposed they had driven him away, they shewed their wisdom by going to sleep again.

"For it is the wisdom of the dog," thought Don Cosmo, heaving a deep sigh in his turn, "after he has eaten and satisfied the other needs of the body, to let the rest of his time pass in sleep."

He looked at the trees that stood facing the villa: they too seemed to him to be absorbed in an endless dream, from which the light of day, the air that stirred their foliage, might try in vain to arouse them. For some time now, the long faint rustle of their leaves in the wind had wafted him a message, as though from an infinite dis-tance, of the vanity of all things and the crushing tedium of life.

CHAPTER II

No offence meant.

A T the request of Flaminio Salvo, whose work
at the bank, with all the other business to
which he had to attend, never left him a moment's
leisure, Ignazio Capolino, his former brother-in-
law, and Ninì De Vincentis, a young friend of the
family, came down next morning in a carriage
from Girgenti to Valsanìa to make the necessary
arrangements for the flitting: a duty that was
highly gratifying to both, though for different, indeed diametrically opposite reasons.

The carts, loaded up with furniture, had started
some time in advance from Girgenti and must
already have arrived at Valsanìa. The conversation between the pair in the carriage had turned
to the projected marriage between Donna Adelaide Salvo, Don Flaminio's sister, and the Prince
of Laurentano.

"No, no: it's too bad! It's too bad!" sneered
Capolino. "Poor Adelaide, it is too bad really,
after waiting fifty years! Let us be honest about
it."

Ninì De Vincentis kept on blinking, as though
to confine within his fine, almond-shaped, velvety

black eyes his distaste for such mockery. At the same time, the expression on his long sallow face was intended to shew at least an attempt to smile, to shew that he saw the joke, that he was making some response to Capolino's hilarity, immoderate and unseemly as it was.

"Yes, a marriage in name!" the latter went on, implacably, since there was no one to hear him (Ninì, the good Ninì, bread of angels, was less than no one). "In name only, for, whatever we may say, be it good or bad, the law is the law, my dear fellow. Religious and political views, if they count at all, what figure do they cut compared with the law? Now the Prince, as you know, makes it a *sine qua non* that there shall be a religious ceremony only; with his views, he cannot allow anything more. And so, a marriage that will not be legally binding, do you follow me? It will be a fine affair, oh! charming . . . it will require courage too, that I don't deny: but what about poor Adelaide?"

And Capolino gave another sardonic laugh, as though, to his mind, Adelaide Salvo was not the woman best fitted for this latter-day form of heroism, which was being demanded of her, for this bold challenge to society as lawfully constituted.

Ninì De Vincentis remained silent, mumbling his lips, still stiffened in a painful smile, in the hope that his silence might stem the torrent of his companion's derision.

The idea! Capolino only abounded all the more.

"Why is she doing it?" he went on, as though conducting an examination of the mature bride in question. "To get into society, with all the privileges of a lady? I should say it was the way out of society, if anything. She is going to shut herself up at Colimbètra! And, a monastic enclosure in every sense of the word, don't you know? The Prince, to say the very least, must be a man of five or six and sixty."

He broke off at a gesture of protest from De Vincentis.

"Why, my dear fellow! Oh, I know, you profess to be a perfect angel, but this is a question of marriage; and one has to think of such things, when a man has reached that age. . . . *Vis, vis, vis*—why, the priests say as much themselves. And so, society can be ruled out. She becomes a Princess, you say, and Princess of Laurentano: let us say, Queen of Colimbètra! Very good: but to me, to you, to all of us who regard a church marriage not merely as superior to the civil rite, but as the only real and valid rite; the rite which, being sufficient in the eyes of God, ought to be more than sufficient in the eyes of men. The rest of humanity, however, are under no obligation to recognize and respect her, outside the walls of Colimbètra, as Princess of Laurentano; Landino, for instance, the son of the former marriage, is not obliged to respect her as his mother-in-law. What else is there, then? Money . . . she is not doing it for that reason, certainly, seeing all the money there is in her own family. If she were doing it for that, poor Adelaide, I'm greatly afraid she might end up like myself. . . ."

Here Capolino laughed again, but his laughter was like the spluttering of a snail in the fire.

After an endless struggle, he had succeeded in obtaining as his wife a sister of Flaminio Salvo, almost a hunchback, younger by two years than Donna Adelaide; and in creating an enviable position for himself with her dowry. A dream of prosperity, alas! A sorry world, and sorry are they that put their trust in it! Five years later, his wife having died, and, worst of all, died childless, he had been obliged to refund her dowry to Salvo, and had relapsed into his former state, with an endless supply of ideas, each one finer and more daring than the last, in his fertile brain, ideas which, in an instant, had been deprived of the blessed support of cash. He had allowed himself six months of profound grief, followed by six more of invincible melancholy, hoping by one or other of these demonstrations to melt the heart of Salvo's remaining sister, who was none other than Donna Adelaide herself.

But Donna Adelaide's heart was not so easily softened: strongly guarded within the stout and ample fortress of her bosom, it had for two years held out against his siege, a siege of polite attentions, courtesies, devotion; it had finally repulsed and summarily routed a supreme and decisive assault, and Capolino had been obliged to beat an orderly retreat. Six months more of profound grief, of invincible melancholy; and then, finally, armed with a second wife, young, pretty and extremely vivacious, he had returned under better auspices to the assault of Flaminio Salvo's household.

Malicious gossip said that it was thanks to Nicoletta Spoto, that is to say his young, pretty and extremely vivacious wife, who had at once become almost a regular companion to Donna Adelaide and to Don Flaminio's only daughter, Dianella Salvo, that Capolino had dropped into a post at the bank as its secretary and legal adviser. But if we listened to what every little bird has to say. . . . For the last year he had been living in luxury and abundance; both he and his wife made use of Salvo's carriage as though it were their own; an accomplished horseman, every Sunday he might be seen swaggering up and down the Viale della Passeggiata on a magnificent chestnut out of Salvo's stable; finally, with the latter's unqualified support, he had managed to create himself, to have himself accepted as leader of the militant clerical party, who, upon the retirement of the Deputy Fazello, would, in the next few days, offer to adopt him as their candidate in the approaching general election.

To the pure soul of Ninì De Vincentis it never occurred for an instant to suspect that all this bitterness on Capolino's part towards Donna Adelaide might have a secret, unconfessable reason. As he did not suppose that anyone could ever have been aware of his own timid, pure, burning love for Dianella Salvo, Don Flaminio's now invalid daughter, so he had never been conscious in the past of Capolino's vain, persistent siege of Donna Adelaide, nor did he now believe one word of the malicious tittle-tattle at the expense of that dear Signora Nicoletta, Capolino's new wife.

Ninì De Vincentis was incapable of discovering an ulterior motive in anyone; nor would the thought of money ever have flashed across his mind. In this respect, he was like a blind man. For years on end, indeed, after the death of his parents, he had let himself be robbed, himself and his elder brother Vincente, by a dishonest agent, Don Jaco Pacia by name, who had managed to get his affairs into such a tangle that poor Ninì, having some time ago demanded a written statement of his accounts, had felt his brain reel when he examined it. And he had been obliged to go for the first time to Salvo's bank for an advance upon his securities. After this he had been obliged to return again and again to the same bank; and finally, acting upon the advice of his agent, had suggested that Salvo should cancel the debt by taking over the splendid property of Primosole, an offer which Salvo had immediately accepted, acquiring at the same time the eternal gratitude of Nini, who naturally had not the slightest suspicion of a secret agreement between Pacia, his agent, and the banker. He was in love with Dianella Salvo, and could look upon Don Flaminio in no other light than as her father.

Now he would have given anything for the girl, who had just escaped by a miracle from an attack of typhoid, to go and recuperate at Primosole, in what had been his mother's old home, where everything would have spoken to her of him, with the melancholy, tender sweetness of maternal memories. But the doctors had advised Salvo to give his daughter sea air. And Nini thought, with regret, that down by the sea at Valsania he would have only the rarest opportunities of going to see her. He took comfort for the moment in the thought that he would be superintending the preparation of her room, the nest which was to shelter her for the next few months.

As though Capolino had read the thoughts of his young friend, whose ingenuous aspirations he had long since and without difficulty discerned, he concluded his opening speech, after his outburst of laughter, with a "That will do!" and went on, rubbing his hands:

"We shall be there in a moment. You will be looking after Dianuccia's room, eh? I shall see to Donna Vittoriona's."

Ninì, plunged in confusion at finding his thoughts read like this, shewed a keen anxiety on behalf of the latter lady, who was Salvo's wife, and had been for many years insane.

"Yes, yes," he said, "we must take care, Heaven help her, that this change of scene does not upset her too much. . . ."

"There's no fear of that!" Capolino interrupted him. "You'll see that she doesn't even notice it. She will go calmly on with her interminable knitting, which (*on dit*) is a mile long already. She knits stockings for the Almighty, you know. Night and day. . . . And she tries to make the two Vincentian Sisters who look after her work at them with her. . . ."

Ninì shook his head sorrowfully.

The carriage, a little way beyond the Seta, turned into the grounds of Valsanìa from the high road. The gate had collapsed: one half of it only, covered in rust, remained standing, fastened to a pillar; the other pillar had long since crumbled in pieces. The carriage drive running across this other part of the estate, which also was let out to portioners, was neglected like everything else, half-hidden by tufts of grass, among which might be seen the fresh ruts left that morning by the carts with the furniture.

Ninì De Vincentis gazed about him upon this scene of desolation, without saying a word, but Capolino, that devil of a talker, Capolino, the inexhaustible windbag, went on talking for them both.

"The invalid," he said, with a grimace, "won't find life here very cheerful, what do you say?"

"It is pretty gloomy," sighed Ninì.

"I don't mean only the place," Capolino went on, "I am thinking of the people here as well. A pair of specimens, my dear fellow! You'll see them in a minute. Mah . . . This country holiday is being taken more for Donna Adelaide, who is not coming down, than for Dianuccia, who may perhaps suspect as much and will bear it calmly as usual, in her love for her aunt. . . . Ah! He's a great man, Flaminio, whatever you may say!"

"The air here is good, though," the young man observed, seeking to attenuate, to some slight extent, his companion's harsh judgment of Salvo.

"Excellent, excellent," agreed Capolino, and, from that moment, withdrew into a frowning silence in which he remained absorbed until they reached the villa.

Philosophy? Pe-ew, pe-ew, pe-ew . . .

The carts had just arrived, together with the basket chaise which had brought a couple of Salvo's menservants, a maid and two upholsterers. Donna Sara Alàimo, on the landing at the head of the stair, was clapping her hands in jubilation at the sight of those four mountains of finery on the carts below.

"Be quick and unload them!" Capolino told the servants and drivers, as he sprang from the carriage, brandishing his cane in the air. Then, racing up the stairs, he inquired of Donna Sara, "Don Cosmo?"

And without waiting for an answer he made his way into the old barn of a house with Ninì De Vincentis, who followed in his footsteps like a stray dog.

"Unload!" one of the servants echoed, mimicking, to his comrades' merriment, the tone of voice and imperious gesture of this self-appointed master.

Don Cosmo was running frantically from one to another of the rooms freshly scrubbed out by Donna Sara, who for the last twenty-four hours, ever since she had heard that the Salvo family were coming, had been making a great to-do, and had even persuaded Don Cosmo to have the rooms cleared of their decrepit furniture, so that the millionaire guests might not see such tokens of poverty in a princely house.

"Most honourable Don Cosmo!" exclaimed Capolino, running him to earth at last in one of the rooms, after he too had run all over the house in search of him. "All in disorder, eh? Perbacco!"

"No, no," Don Cosmo hastened to reply, so as to cut short any pretence of ceremony, his nostrils wrinkling at the acrid smell of mould which infested the house, still damp after its recent and unaccustomed cleansing. "I was looking for some corner where I can sit without being in anybody's way."

Capolino was about to protest; but Don Cosmo stopped him:

"Let me explain! I seek my own convenience and theirs at the same time: is that right? Keep covered, pray, keep covered!"

He raised his hand, as he spoke, to caress the trim little black tuft on the chin of Ninì De Vincentis.

"You've grown into a fine man, my boy! And I, good Lord, have grown into an old one! And your brother Vincente? Still at his Arabic?"

"Still!" replied Ninì, with a smile.

"Ah! Those fourteen volumes of Arabic manuscripts must be pressing like fourteen millstones, in the world beyond, on the soul of Conte Lucchesi-Palli, who insisted on presenting them to our Library to be the poor boy's ruin!"

"He has deciphered ten of them already," said Ninì. "He has still four left . . . so big!"

"He must hurry up and finish them!" Don Cosmo concluded in a fatherly tone. "And you too, my boy, you should keep an eye on your affairs: I know things aren't going any too well. . . . Use your judgment!"

Capolino, meanwhile, at the window, was making the open pane serve him as a looking-glass, and smoothing the short mutton-chop whiskers, already slightly grizzled, that adorned his cheeks. He was not handsome, but had a pair of keen and fervent eyes, which prevented one from noticing the harsh irregularity of his features, and gave a pleasing animation to the whole of his lean dark face.

Hearing a lull in the conversation between Laurentano and Ninì, he pretended to be engaged in trying to settle the orientation of the villa.

"A southern exposure, this, isn't it? But you have chosen this room for yourself, perhaps, Don Cosmo?"

"Any room will do for me," replied Laurentano. "There are plenty of spare bedrooms, you'll find, but they're all like this, in the most wretched condition. . . . It is all old, avvocato, it is all old. . . . Now, if we go out by this door . . . (no, you are not to stand on ceremony: really, what point is there in saying a thing is not old when it is? You have only to look at it!) I was saying, if we go out by this door, we come to this long corridor, which divides the house in two: all the bedrooms on this side face the south; those on the other side, the north. The entrance hall bisects the corridor, and splits the villa into two identical wings, except that at this end we have a big room, the door of which is behind me, and at the other end we have a terrace. It's quite simple."

"Good, good, good," Capolino expressed his approval. "Then we have a big room as well?"

Don Cosmo smiled and shook his head; then proceeded to explain what this *camerone* was, what state it was in and who was its guardian.

"Good God!" exclaimed Capolino.

"It would be better, therefore," Don Cosmo concluded, "if you were to settle in the other half of the house, where you'll be undisturbed. I had chosen this room for myself on purpose . . ."

Capolino once more agreed; and, as the servants had already brought the first load upstairs, made off with Ninì to the other wing. Don Cosmo remained in the bedroom, to which, with the help of Donna Sara, he transported all his books. The poor housekeeper, feeling the weight of all this learning, could not for the life of her understand how Don Cosmo, who had absorbed it all into his person, could continue to live in the clouds as he did. Don Cosmo, his nostrils still wrinkled, could not for his part understand why there was such a damp smell everywhere that morning. But perhaps he did not distinguish clearly between the smell and the annoyance he derived from the thought that from now onwards, by the coming of his guests, all his old lazy habits would be shattered, and for an indefinite period!

Presently Capolino returned, leaving the other wing of the house to De Vincentis, who had shewn a far greater capacity for the work in hand: so at least he declared. As a matter of fact, he came to put into execution one of the objects for which he had readily undertaken to act for Salvo: namely, that he might discover Don Cosmo's attitude with regard to his brother's marriage, or "feel his pulse" in the matter, to use his own expression.

There seemed no hope now that the marriage might come to nothing; but, knowing the discrepancy, indeed the incompatible opposition between Salvo's and Don Cosmo's thoughts and feelings, he liked to suppose that some friction, some actual conflict might arise from the former's stay at Valsanìa. Don Cosmo's was so abstract and solitary a spirit that the life of the world could not succeed in penetrating his consciousness with all its fictions and artifices and persuasions, which spontaneously transfigure it for most people; and often, for that reason, from the frozen peak of his stoical indifference, he let fall like an avalanche the most naked of truths.

"Oh, what a lot of books!" exclaimed Capolino as he entered the room. "But you still keep on studying . . . Romagnosi, Rosmini, Hegel, Kant . . ."

As he read each name on the backs of the books he opened his eyes wider, as though punctuating the names with marks of exclamation that grew longer and longer.

"Philosophy, eh?"

"Poetry!" sighed Don Cosmo, waving his hand vaguely in the air, and closing his eyes.

"What's that you say, Don Cosmo? I don't understand."

"Why, yes," Laurentano assured him, with a fresh sigh. "For study, my dear sir, there is little or nothing: what there is is enjoyment of the grandeur of the human intellect, which on a hypothesis, that is to say on a cloud (you follow me?) builds up castles, pinnacles and towers: all these various systems of philosophy, my dear avvocato, which seem to me . . . do you know what they seem to me? churches, chapels, shrines, temples, of different styles, poised in the air . . ."

"Ah yes, I see . . ." Capolino tried to interrupt him, fingering the back of his neck.

But Don Cosmo, who never spoke as a rule, his one responsive chord having been struck, could not restrain himself:

"Breathe, and the whole structure collapses; breathe, and all these castles which tower like mountains crumble, because there is nothing inside them: a void, my dear sir, all the more crushing the taller and more solemn the structure is: a void and the silence of the mystery . . ."

Capolino had withdrawn into his shell, to collect his thoughts, stimulated by the passion with which Don Cosmo spoke, to reply, to bring him down to earth; and waited anxiously for an opportunity; when it came, he broke out:

"And yet . . ."

"No, there's nothing to be said! Let us drop the subject!" Don Cosmo at once cut him short, laying a hand on his shoulder. "All nonsense, my dear avvocato!"

Fortunately, at that moment, Mauro Mortara down below, on the lawn that flanked the villa, on the side looking towards the vineyard and the sea, began to summon with his invariable cry of "Pe-ew, pe-ew, pe-ew" the innumerable flock of pigeons which he was in the habit of feeding twice daily.

Don Cosmo and Capolino went out on the balcony. Ninì too leaned out to watch from the railings of the farthest balcony at the end of the house, while the menservants and maids and upholsterers looked down from the terrace.

The white ferment of wings invariably ended in a tremendous scrimmage, since the ration of peas had long remained unaltered, while the pigeons had multiplied beyond reckoning and lived now almost in a wild state, scattered about the estate and the surrounding fields. They knew their dinner-hour, however, and would arrive punctually, in dense whirring clouds, from all directions; cooing impatiently, in a great tumult, they would invade the roofs of the villa itself, of the peasants' houses, the straw rick, the dovecot, the barn, the mill and the wineshed; and if Mauro was at all behind time, forgetting them or absorbed in his own memories, a numerous deputation would flutter down from the roofs and go in quest of him, through the door of his well known room in the basement: the deputation would gradually swell into a crowd, until presently the whole lawn was aswarm with fluttering wings and cooing throats, while ever so many more remained hovering in the air, finding no room to alight.

"Stupendous, a stupendous sight!" Capolino kept on exclaiming.

Yes, and the only sight in which Don Cosmo took any pleasure. On hearing the clamorous whirr of all those wings he would always rise from table and go out to the balcony to watch. Besides, it was the signal for his own dinner as well. Having scattered the peas round him several times and finally emptied the basket over the pigeons, Mauro would come upstairs, and the two of them would sit down together.

Don Cosmo remembered with annoyance that on this occasion, however, Mauro would not be coming up; he had said to him overnight:

"This is the last time that I feed with you. Because you will do me the courtesy of believing me when I say that I will not sit down to table with Flaminio Salvo."

Now, on the lawn beneath, he was standing among his pigeons with lowered head. Capolino

watched him from the balcony, as though he had
some rare animal before his eyes.

"Do I speak to him?" he whispered to Don
Cosmo.

The latter made a negative sign with his hand.

"A bear, what?" Capolino went on. "But a
fine type!"

"A bear," Don Cosmo repeated, as he withdrew
from the balcony.

Metastasio.

A few minutes later, in the dining-room in the
other part of the house, which had meanwhile been
richly furnished by the upholsterers, Capolino
made a fresh attempt to "feel Don Cosmo's pulse"
in the matter we know of. He certainly would
not repeat the mistake of leading the conversation
to the books of philosophy.

Don Cosmo was lost in admiration of the room,
which had suddenly been made unrecognisable.

"A perfect miracle!" he exclaimed, bringing his
hand down upon the shoulder of Ninì De Vincentis. "One might be at Colimbètra!"

Capolino at once caught the ball in its flight.

"You haven't been there for years and years,
to Colimbètra, eh?"

Don Cosmo thought for a moment.

"About ten . . ." and remained lost in medita-
tion, without saying another word. But Capo-

lino, baiting his question so as to force an answer:

"When your sister-in-law died there, wasn't it?"

"Yes," was Laurentano's dry response.

And Capolino sighed:

"Donna Teresa Montalto . . . what a lady! what a loss! A true lady of the old school!"

And, after a pause, heavy with feigned grief, a fresh sigh, of a different kind:

"Mah! *Cosa bella mortal passa e non dura!*"

Donna Sara Alàimo, the housekeeper, who at the moment was waiting at table, seeking to raise herself in the eyes of the guests from her humble and unbefitting state, was tempted to interpose, and asked timidly, with a wistful smile:

"Metastasio, isn't it?"

Ninì turned round and gazed at her in bewilderment; Don Cosmo shaped his lips to emit a special laugh of his own, consisting of a triple "Oh, oh, oh!" loud, deep and sombre. But Capolino, seeing that there was a risk of his breaking the eggs in his basket just at the propitious moment, retorted crossly:

"Leopardi, Leopardi . . ."

"Petrarch, excuse me, dear avvocato, Petrarch!" Don Cosmo protested with outspread hands. "I appeal to Ninì!"

"Oh, of course, Petrarch, what a fool I am! *Muor giovine colui che al cielo è caro* . . ." Capo-

lino at once continued the quotation. "I was
thinking of something else. . . . And so you . . .
so you have never seen your brother again since?"

Don Cosmo suddenly resumed his somnolent
air; half shut his eyes; nodded his head in assent.

"Always buried alive down here!" Capolino
proceeded to explain to De Vincentis, as though
the latter were not aware of this. "Different
tastes, I can understand . . . indeed, diametrically
opposed, since Don Ippolito is fond of . . . of
company, can't do without it. . . . And perhaps,
if I may say so, after his loss, he would have
greatly preferred not to be left alone, without any
of his family round him. . . . But, with you here;
his son always in Rome . . . and . . ."

Don Cosmo, who had by this time grasped, but
in his own way, Capolino's purpose, to cut him
short came out with:

"And so he does right to marry again, you
mean? We are quite of one mind as to that! But
you know," he went on, turning to Ninì, "my fine
fellow, haven't you made up your mind yet?"

Ninì, finding himself thus suddenly drawn into
the conversation, turned crimson:

"I?"

"Look how he's blushing!" exclaimed Capolino, and burst out laughing, in his rage.

"Then there is some one?" Don Cosmo inquired, tapping his chest with his finger, over the
heart.

"I should just think there was!" exclaimed Capolino, laughing louder than ever.

Ninì, on pins and needles, mortified, shocked by this unseemly laughter, protested with marked emphasis:

"I assure you, there's absolutely nothing of the sort! Please don't say such things!"

"Of course not! San Luigi Gonzaga!" Capolino went on, prolonging his forced laughter. "Or rather . . . why, yes, where's Donna Sara? he is, really, Metastasio, a Metastasio hero, Don Cosmo! Or, shall we say, an angel . . . but not one of the angels they have at Alcamo, remember! Do you know, Don Cosmo, that at Alcamo they call the little pigs angels?"

Ninì became genuinely distressed; turned pale; and said in a firm voice:

"You annoy me, avvocato!"

"I shan't say another word!" Capolino promised, recovering his composure.

Don Cosmo remained uneasy, without understanding at first what had happened; then opened his mouth to emit an "ah!" which stuck in his throat. Could it be a question, perhaps, of Salvo's daughter? Why, of course. . . . It had never occurred to him. He had never yet seen her. But of course! Excellent! A fortune for this dear Ninì! And he could not help saying to him:

"Don't distress yourself, my boy. It's a very

serious matter. You have no time to lose, in your position."

Ninì was writhing in his chair, as though trying to endure without screaming the pricking of a hundred pins all over his body. Capolino held his breath and waited for the avalanche to fall. Don Cosmo was unable to account for the effect that his words had produced, and looked in bewilderment at each of the others in turn.

"Have I said something wrong?" he asked. "Forgive me. I shan't say another word either."

Ninì was truly living in heaven, in a heaven lighted by a special sun of his own which was waiting there ready to rise, which had not yet risen and would perhaps never rise. He let it stay there, behind the rugged mountains of reality, and preferred to remain in the vain, roseate light of a perpetual dawn, since his sun, when it did rise, was not ever to set again, and the shadows, of necessity, remained tenuous and almost diaphanous. He had already been assailed by the doubt that Salvo, at present, might not be disposed to listen to his proposal of marriage, supposing that he were to force himself to make it. But he had always shrunk from considering and weighing that doubt, in order not to disturb the spotless dream of his whole life. And, not because this doubt had proved an obstacle, but because he did really lack the courage to translate into action an ideal which he had maintained at so lofty an altitude, that he

almost feared to see it shattered by the slightest
contact with reality, he had never made up his
mind, not indeed to make a formal proposal, but
even to come to an understanding with Dianella
Salvo. And now, the suspicion that he might be
doing so in view of the girl's dowry, which would
re-establish his own financial position, caused him
acute pain, poisoned for him all joy in this service
which he had rendered for love, but which might
however appear to have had a baser motive; and,
as though all of a sudden his sun had fallen from
the sky, all at once the world grew dark about him,
and when the rooms had been put in order, and he,
his throat choking with anguish, had made a final
tour of inspection, he was unable to bestow, as he
had intended, on the pillow on Dianella's bed his
kiss of welcome, that she, unawares, might find it
there, that night, when she retired to rest.

All for a pair of pumpkins.

Meanwhile Don Cosmo and Capolino, a pair of
tiny black dots beneath the soaring arch of a sky
that smouldered with the fire of the setting sun,
had left the house and were strolling up and down
the long straight avenue, forming a sort of hem
on the left side of the crest from which a wide and
deep ravine, known as the *vallone,* ran abruptly
down.

It seemed as though some convulsion of the

earth's surface had rent the tableland asunder at
that point and poured it down towards the sea.

The estate of Valsanìa lay on one side, its farthest olives running down into the ravine, a gulf
of ashen shadows, out of which arose mulberries,
carubs, oranges, lemons, rejoicing in a rivulet of
water which ran down from a spring that burst
from the ground at the head of the ravine, in the
mysterious cave of San Calògero.

On the other side of the ravine, at a correspond-
ing level, were the wooded lands of Platanìa,
which to the south towered menacingly over the
railway line, where, emerging from its tunnel beneath Valsanìa, it followed the coastline as far as
Porto Empedocle.

The band of flame and gold of the sunset broke
up into a marvellous fantastic patchwork seen
through the intense green of the distant trees,
across the ravine. On the near side, over the almonds and olives of Valsanìa, the first cool shades
of evening, tender, light and melancholy, were
already hovering.

This twilight hour, when the things around him
in the gathering dusk, retaining more intensely
the last light of day, seemed almost to be enam-
elled in their several colours, was more sacred
than any other to Don Cosmo in his solitude. He
kept constantly in mind his sense of his own pre-
carious existence in the place of his habitation,
nor did he let this distress him. This feeling,

which melted lightly and vaguely into the impenetrable mystery of the world around him, made every responsibility, every thought, an intolerable burden. We may imagine, then, how shattering he must have found Capolino's conversation, which kept turning with fervour to the success of Salvo's undertakings, to a great scheme which he was planning at the moment, with the manager of his sulphur pits, the engineer Aurelio Costa, for improving the conditions of the sulphur industry, which for many years past had been deplorable.

"A new kind of conscience, his," said Capolino. "Lucid, precise and complex, Don Cosmo, like a modern machine, of steel. He always knows what he is doing, and never makes a mistake!"

"Lucky fellow! Lucky fellow!" Don Cosmo repeated, with half shut eyes, and an air of resigned endurance.

"And a true believer, you know!" Capolino went on. "A religious man!"

"Lucky fellow!"

"It's a marvel how, with all his responsibilities, he manages to find time to bother about our Party. And how zealously he has embraced our cause!"

Presently, however, Capolino changed the subject, observing that Don Cosmo had ceased to listen to him. He drew closer to him, laid a hand on his arm, and said quietly, with a sorrowful air:

"That poor Ninì! I'm certain he's crying now,
don't you know, just because we teased him a bit
at table. Desperately in love, poor boy! But the
girl, eh? No, alas, she's not for him. . . ."

"Is she engaged to somebody else?" asked Don
Cosmo, coming to a halt.

"No; not officially, no!" Capolino promptly assured him. "But . . . this is between ourselves,
though, please: you mustn't breathe a word of it!
My belief is, dear Don Cosmo, that the girl is
really less sick in body than in mind."

"Touched, eh?"

"Touched. That is perhaps the one thing her
father has done wrong. There Flaminio made a
mistake .. . . yes, there are no two ways about it,
he made a mistake!"

Don Cosmo stopped again, nodded his head
several times and said, in his most serious tone:

"So you see that even he can be mistaken, my
dear avvocato."

"Well, when the devil, you know, had him properly caught that time!" Capolino went on. "You
know, of course, that Flaminio . . . it must be
ten years ago; no, what am I saying, fifteen years
ago at least; anyhow, fifteen years ago, more or
less, he came within an inch of drowning. . . .
Didn't you know that? Why, bathing in the sea,
at Porto Empedocle. An absurd business, believe
me, absurd and terrible at the same time! All for
a pair of pumpkins. . . ."

"Pumpkins? Tell me about it," said Don Cosmo, stirred by unwonted curiosity.

"Why, yes," Capolino went on. "He was bathing, at the Casotti. He can't swim, and, to be on the safe side, was keeping within the enclosure, where the water came more or less up to his chest. Suddenly (the devil take them!) he saw a pair of pumpkins bobbing along towards him, which some boy or other had presumably left in the sea. He took hold of them. As he stood crouching down, so that the water should come up to his neck (what a sorry figure a man cuts in the water, my dear Don Cosmo, a man who can't swim!), he had the unlucky inspiration to put the pair of pumpkins underneath him, as a support, with the string that held them together; he sat down on the string, and, as the pumpkins, naturally, floated on, and he had let go of the fence to see whether they were strong enough to keep him afloat with his feet off the bottom, suddenly, plump! he lost his balance and slipped over head downwards, under the water!"

"Oh, I say!" exclaimed Don Cosmo in alarm.

"You can imagine," Capolino went on, "how he began splashing with his feet to regain his balance. But, as ill luck would have it, his feet became entangled in the string of the pumpkins, and, struggle as he might under the water, he could not succeed in getting them free."

"Don't, please! oh dear, oh dear!" gasped Don

Cosmo, with a convulsive tightening of his fists and all his features.

But Capolino went on:

"You will admit that it was really absurd for a man to be on the point of drowning in an enclosed bathing place, with crowds of people round him, who never noticed him and never came to his rescue, not suspecting for a moment that he was struggling there with death staring him in the face! And he would have been drowned, as sure as God's in heaven, had not a boy of thirteen—this Aurelio Costa, who is now a qualified engineer and manager of Salvo's sulphur pits at Aragona and Comitini—caught sight of a pair of feet kicking desperately on the surface and gone over to him, greatly amused, to set him free."

"Ah, I begin to understand," said Don Cosmo. "And now the daughter . . ."

"The daughter . . . the daughter . . ." Capolino chewed the word. "Flaminio, you will understand, had to discharge his debt to the boy, and discharged it in proportion to the danger he had run and the terror he had felt. They told him that the boy was the son of a poor weighman on the beach where the sulphur is loaded . . ."

"Costa, yes, Leonardo Costa," Don Cosmo broke in. "He's a friend of mine. He comes up here to see me sometimes, on Sundays, from Porto Empedocle."

"You know, then, that he works for Flaminio

now?'' Capolino went on. ''Flaminio took him from the scales and gave him a job in his big sulphur deposit on the east shore. As for his son Aurelio, he determined to make the boy's fortune, without counting the cost; not only that, but he took him away with him, brought him up in his own house, with his own children, Dianuccia and the other one, the little boy that died. That tragedy, too, must certainly have helped to increase his affection for the boy. Affection, though, I should say, up to a certain point only. For the same reason for which he would not give his daughter now to Ninì De Vincentis, he would never give her, I imagine, to Aurelio Costa, his dependent, remember!''

''Mah!'' Don Cosmo exclaimed, shrugging his shoulders. ''With all his money, and with an only daughter . . .''

''Why, no . . . no . . .'' replied Capolino. ''I quite admit that if anything were to happen to him, all his fortune would be bound to pass to somebody, to his son-in-law, whoever his son-in-law might be. But Flaminio will take good care to choose his man first! He's not the sort of person to indulge in rosy dreams of romance. His daughter may. . . . Yes, and romance in the true sense of the word, mind! Because the true nature of her secret malady has come to my knowledge, through certain private channels; Flaminio knows it too, I believe, or at any rate suspects it; but

the other, the engineer Costa (an excellent young
fellow, remember! A solid young fellow, fully
aware of his position and of all that he owes to
his benefactor), knows nothing whatever about it,
has not the remotest conception of it; I can be
quite certain of that, because I have proof posi-
tive, evidence of an intimate nature. The engineer . . ."

At this point Capolino broke off, having caught
sight of a man at the far end of the avenue who
came running towards them, waving his arms.

"Who's that?" he asked, stopping short and
knitting his brows.

It was Marco Préola, bathed in sweat, gasping
for breath and covered in dust, his stockings fes-
tooned about his broken shoes. He was dead beat.

"Here we are! Here we are!" he began to
shout, as he drew near. "He's come!"

"Auriti?" inquired Capolino.

"Yes, sir," Préola went on. "For the election:
there's no doubt about it! I've run all the way
from Girgenti to tell you."

He removed his battered hat, and with a dirty
handkerchief mopped the sweat that trickled from
his matted locks.

"My nephew?" inquired Don Cosmo, rooted to
the ground with astonishment.

At once Capolino, with a mortified air, set to
work to inform him, first of Fazello's resignation,
then of the pressure that had been put upon him-

self to accept the candidature, and of the rumours
that were going about Girgenti as to this unexpected arrival of Roberto Auriti. Rumours . . .
rumours which he, Capolino, refused to accept for
two reasons. First of all, the respect that he felt
for Auriti, a respect which did not permit him to
suppose that, without an invitation, he would
have come down to contest a seat which Fazello
was resigning of his own free will. The Party
Association, which represented the majority of the
electors, as had been shewn by countless indisput-
able proofs, remained solid, even after Giacinto
Fazello's withdrawal. The other reason was of a
more private nature, and was this: that it would
be a grief, a very great grief to him to have as a
by no means redoubtable opponent, in an unequal
contest, a man who, notwithstanding the differences of opinion in his family, was nevertheless
related to the Laurentano brothers, whom he revered and by whose friendship he regarded himself as honoured. No, no: he preferred to believe
that Auriti had come to Girgenti only to pay his
mother and sister a visit.

"What's that you say, avvocato?" Marco Préola burst forth, throwing off with a shrug of his
shoulders the long and tedious speech in which
Capolino had been stealthily endeavouring to give
a specimen of his political views. "When a pack of
rascals went to meet him at the station, students
from the Technical Institute? When the Mafia

and the Masons have come to town, led by Guido Verònica and Giambattista Mattina? There's no doubt about it, I tell you! He's come for the election. . . ."

While Capolino and Préola were discussing the matter, Don Cosmo's eyes, nose and mouth were acting a remarkable pantomime: winking and wrinkling and twisting. . . . Living in exile as he did, his mind always absorbed in thoughts of eternity, his eyes turned to the stars, or to the sea at his feet, or to the deserted country round about, finding himself suddenly assailed by all these topical trivialities, he felt as though he were being stung by a swarm of irritating insects.

"Gesù! Gesù! It's unbelievable. . . . What foolishness . . ."

"And now, a glass of wine, Si-don Co'," exclaimed Marco Préola, to bring the discussion to a happy ending. "Your honour must do me the favour of a glass of wine. I'm finished! I've been all round Girgenti looking for our dear avvocato; they told me I should find him out here at Valsanìa, and off I dashed at once on foot by the Spina Santa. Look at me! My throat's properly burning."

"Go along, go and get something to drink at the house," Don Cosmo told him.

"And isn't Don Mauro there?" asked Préola. "I'm afraid," he added, with a laugh. "He fired a gun at me, last year it was. . . . He says I came here, into the grounds, to shoot his pigeons. Word of honour, Si-don Cosmo, it's not true! It was after the turtle-doves I came. Perhaps, now and then, I don't say, I may have made a bad shot. I fired, and, quick as lightning, I heard a shot come. . . . Lucky I turned round at once. Bang! In the seat of my breeches, a shower of pellets. . . . May I be damned to hell, Si-don Co', I swear to you, if it weren't for the respect I owe to the Laurentano family . . . I got a dose from both barrels and, my word of honour . . ."

From the other end of the avenue came a jingle of bells. The trio, who had drawn near to the villa, talking together, turned round to look. Capolino called out:

"Ninì! Ninì! Here are the carriages! They're arriving!"

Ninì hurried down from the house; the menservants came down also, with Donna Sara Alàimo and the maids, who by this time were firm friends.

The carriages proved to be two victorias. In the first sat Don Flaminio with his daughter; in the second the lunatic with two nurses. Don Cosmo expected to see Donna Adelaide, the bride to be, alight from one of the carriages also: he was disappointed. Ninì De Vincentis had not the courage to step forward and offer Dianella his arm. With a throbbing heart and eyes misty with emotion he caught a glimpse of her drawn white face through her thick green travelling veil, and

followed her with his gaze while, leaning on Capolino's arm, closely wrapped in a heavy cloak, she
climbed slowly up the stair, like an old woman,
amid the obsequious greetings of Donna Sara
Alàimo.

Donna Victoria, whose enormous girth made
her alight with difficulty, stood between the two
nurses, with fixed, vacant eyes in her large, pale
face, framed in the humble black woollen shawl
which she wore over her head; she gazed for a
while like this at Don Cosmo; then parted her
fleshy, almost colourless lips in a mournful smile
and said, with a respectful bow:

"Signor Priore . . ."

One of the nurses took her by the hand, while
Don Cosmo, standing by Salvo, shut his eyes in
distress at the spectacle. Ninì followed the mad
woman.

"Thank you," said Flaminio Salvo, pressing
Don Cosmo's hand. "I need not say more to
you."

"No, no . . ." Laurentano made haste to reply,
still disturbed and moved by the sad spectacle,
feeling a sudden profound pity for this man who,
in his enviable position of power, had in that moment conveyed to him, by that handclasp, the sense
of his utter misery.

CHAPTER III

Not even a pinch of dust!

"THIS way, Sir, this way, follow me," the gentleman who accompanied him was told by the old manservant with the splayed feet, which made him walk in all directions at once, his legs bent under him so that his knees knocked together.

They passed, on thick carpets, through three communicating rooms, in each of which the servant, as he passed, threw open the shutters inside the long windows. The rooms however remained in shadow, whether because of the thickness of the curtains or because of the lowness of the house itself, overtopped by the houses opposite which kept out the light. Having opened the shutters, the servant looked round each room and sighed, as much as to say: "You see how well furnished it is? And yet it is never used!"

At length they came to the drawing-room at the end, with its panelled walls divided by gilt mouldings.

The gentleman drew from an elegant pocket-book an armorial visiting card, turned down one corner and handed the card to the servant, who, pointing to a door which led out of the drawing-room, said:

"One moment, please. Cavalier Préola's in there."

"Préola the father?"

"The son."

"Is he a Cavaliere too?"

"To me," the old man protested, making a deep bow and placing his hand on his heart, "all the gentry are Cavalieri!"

And, as he hobbled away on his splayed feet, he glanced furtively at the card, and read: *Cav. Gian Battista Mattina.*

("So this one really is a Cavaliere, it seems.")

Mattina remained standing, lost in thought, in the middle of the room; then shrugged his shoulders irritably; threw a careless glance round the room; caught sight of a mirror on the opposite wall and went across to it.

In the huge mirror, by the dim light, his own reflexion looked to him like a ghost; and he felt a vague momentary uneasiness as he gazed at it.

All the furniture, the carpet, the curtains exhaled that peculiar smell of old things that have grown stale with disuse; almost the atmosphere of another age.

Mattina looked round the room again with a strange sense of discomfort at the silent immobility of these old things which had stood there, year after year, unused and lifeless. He moved nearer to the mirror to study his reflexion more closely, turning his head slowly, screwing up under his tired, deeply shadowed eyes the ends of his thick moustaches, kept black with the help of some lotion, in contrast to the prematurely grey head which gave such an air of solemnity to his swarthy face. Suddenly a prolonged yawn made him part his lips in a grimace, and, as he let it escape, he contracted his features in an expression of boredom and disgust. He was just turning away from the mirror when, lowering his gaze to the surface of the bracket that supported it, he noticed a quantity of neat little worm-casts, arranged there as though in a pattern, and bent down, curious to examine them. They had done their work well, those worms! And yet nobody seemed to give them any credit for their labour. . . . The fruit of it, however, was there, plainly visible, saying: "This is done now. Take it away!" He put out his hand to one of the little heaps, took up a pinch of it and rubbed his fingers together. Nothing! Not even dust. . . . And, examining the balls of his thumb and forefinger, he went and sat down upon a comfortable armchair by the sofa. Having taken his seat, he shook the chair slightly, as though to test its solidity.

"Not even dust. . . . Nothing!"

With a grimace he picked up from the round table in front of the sofa an album on the first page of which was a photograph of the master of the house, Canon Agrò.

Mattina had always felt that Canon Pompeo

Agrò bore a strange resemblance to some large
bird, the name of which escaped him. Certainly
his nose, broad at the base and ending in a sharp
point, stuck out from his face just like a beak.
It was, however, in the keen little grey eyes, beneath a high and narrow forehead, that one de-
tected all the astute, subtle and persistent malice
for which Agrò was notorious.

Mattina studied the face as though he were trying to discover from its lineaments the reason for
the invitation he had received overnight. What
the deuce could Agrò want with him? Was the
breach between this most gentlemanly of Canons
and the Clerical Party, a breach that had created
such a scandal in the town, an actual fact or was
it not rather a concerted, insidious pose, with the
object of hoodwinking the ingenuous Auriti, of
penetrating into the enemy's camp and discovering his plan of campaign? Ah, if one trusted a
fox. . . . This secret interview with Préola, for
instance. . . . Was the whole thing an elaborate
plot?

He raised his eyes, looked round the room again
and once more felt himself disturbed by the silent
immobility of those old things, so useless and lifeless, as though, now that he had laid bare their
rottenness, they were watching him with greater
hostility than ever.

He heard, through the chain of rooms, the old
servant's voice repeating:

"This way, Sir, this way, follow me."

He laid down the album and looked towards the door.

"Hallo! Veronica . . ."

"My dear Titta," replied Guido Veronica, advancing into the middle of the room.

He removed his spectacles, in order to polish them with the handkerchief which he held in readiness in his other hand, blinked his myopic, almond-shaped eyes, and with the thumb and forefinger of his stumpy hand rubbed the bridge of his nose, where it was scarred by the continual pressure of his glasses; and was making his way towards the sofa facing Mattina; but the latter, rising, took him by the arm and murmured:

"Wait, I want you to look at something."

And led him across to the bracelet to shew him all those little heaps of sawdust.

Veronica, not understanding what he was intended to look at, and being extremely short-sighted, bent down until his nose was almost touching the top of the bracket.

"Worms?" he then remarked, but without any show of interest, looking indeed coldly at Mattina, as though to inquire why he had shewn him them: and went and sat down on the armchair.

Whereupon, *"Tu quoque?"* Mattina queried, feeling uncomfortable and seeking to hide his annoyance. "How are things going?"

"I don't know what it's all about," Veronica

answered, with the air of a person trying to keep
a secret.

"Oh, no more do I," Mattina hastened to add,
in a tone of indifference.

And he let his glance rest casually on Veronica's
brow, furrowed by three long scars running in
different directions: trophies won on the duelling
ground.

"Have you come from Rome?"

"No. From Palermo."

"Shall you be staying here long?"

"I don't know."

Veronica made it evident, by these curt re-
sponses, that he intended to keep his own counsel,
so as not to give himself any importance by what
he could say if he chose.

Indeed his plan for the time being was as follows: to show irritation, or rather boredom and
distrust. Unfortunately for himself he had, as
everyone knew, an ideal: the Country, represented by, nay bodily incarnate in the person of
a famous old statesman defeated some years since
in the course of a tumultuous sitting of Parliament, after a petty and disloyal campaign. For
this Minister's sake he had let himself be provoked into duel after duel, and had invariably
been defeated; he had hurled back, in the columns
of the newspapers, in language unprecedented in
its violence, the insults offered by the opposition.
But now, this Minister having fallen, the country

had fallen as well: the pigmy rabble were triumphant: it was not anger that he felt; it was a disgrace to be alive, in such times. He did not for a moment believe that Roberto Auriti could win, even with the support of the Government; but his revered Elder—who still entertained the most childish illusions as to the future of the country—had ordered him to go down to Girgenti and to fight for Auriti; he knew that Auriti's reason for undertaking the campaign had been not so much the pressure put upon him by the Government as the old statesman's insistent demand; and so here he was at Girgenti. Simply that he might not fail in his duty, he was now here in response to an invitation from Agrò, a Canon, he to whom priests were like a red rag to a bull. Here he was; he must resign himself. Notwithstanding, however, the misgivings with which he had allowed himself to set out upon this electoral mission, he felt a certain irritation, now, on finding himself placed on a level with a mere Mattina, associated with him as a fellow-conspirator in the little plot which Canon Agrò was apparently trying to weave.

Mattina stirred in his seat, with a grunt, and assumed a different posture.

"He's keeping us waiting," he said.

"Whom has he got in there?" asked Guido Verònica, with no trace of impatience.

Mattina leaned forward and said in a whisper:

"Young Préola, Ignazio Capolino's bottle-washer. The servant told me. What do you think? I ask you and I ask myself, what are we two here for?"

"We shall hear presently," sighed Verònica.

"I shouldn't like——"

Mattina stopped short, seeing the door open and the long, lean, stooping form of Canon Pompeo Agrò enter the room.

I supply the ammunition.

Signalling with both hands to his guests to remain seated, Pompeo Agrò began in a shrill, strident little voice:

"I ask your pardon. . . . Do not rise, please, do not rise. My dear Verònica; most eminent Cavaliere. Here, Cavaliere, come and sit here, beside me: I'm not afraid, as you know, of your youthful excesses."

"Youthful, yes!" smiled Mattina, pointing to his grizzled pate.

The Canon drew an old silver watch from his pocket.

"Your hair, eh . . . you shed your hair, you mean, but not your spots. Ten o'clock already, perbacco! I've wasted the whole morning. . . . Mah!"

His face clouded over; he sat for a moment undecided whether or not to speak; then, as though giving articulate form to his suspended ejaculation:

"Gratitude: there's no such thing!"

He shook his head, and went on:

"Would you two gentlemen mind coming with me for a moment?"

"Where?" inquired Mattina.

"To call on Roberto Auriti . . . such a dear friend of mine . . . we have been friends, as you know, from our schooldays. And our fathers, before us. The dearest friends; oh! closer than brothers. Comrades in arms, eh? Roberto's father fell at Milazzo; mine at Volturno. They made history. People ought to bear that in mind in the town, instead of making such a fuss about my . . . what do they call it, again? Desertion, eh? . . . my desertion. My cassock! Yes, my friends. But beneath the cassock beats a heart; and I too have some regard for the sacred ties of friendship, as well as . . . as well as . . ."

The Canon meant to imply "for my country"; he let this be understood by a wave of his hand and stemmed the torrent of his generous sentiments.

He was making an effort to speak in appropriate language, with a subtle smile on his lips, and kept on rubbing his dry, bony hands together under his chin, as though he were washing them at the fountain of his polished phrases, polished indeed, yet not limpid or continuous in their flow,

The Old and the Young 103

but issuing almost in jerks, with frequent hesitations and odd pauses. From time to time, as he raised his drooping eyelids, he afforded a glimpse of a sidelong, fugitive glance, so different from his usual expression that at once the onlooker imagined that this man must, in his private life, when alone with himself, have more than one profoundly secret affliction, which made him astute and crafty, and that there must be obscure workings in his mind.

"Before we start," he went on, with a change of tone, "just a word or two of explanation. I may have thought out . . . put together, shall I say, a little plan of campaign. I don't make it publicly known, of course. You gentlemen will do the fighting; I shall supply the ammunition. That is all. Weighing every consideration carefully, our most formidable adversary is who? Capolino? No; but the man who is behind him: Salvo, who was his brother-in-law, and is a most powerful person. Now I know from a trustworthy source that Salvo, until a few days ago, was absolutely determined not to permit this . . . this appearance of Capolino upon the scene."

"Quite so," Mattina agreed. "Because of the arrangements for a marriage between his sister and the Prince of Laurentano."

"Precisely!" the Canon endorsed his remark. "But Salvo went the length of promising him his support as soon as he learned that the Prince did not intend to consider Auriti as one of his family, and had ordered the Party not to pay any attention to him either. Things being so, our friend Roberto's chances become almost desperate. Let us not make any mistake about that."

"Oh, I know that!" groaned Verònica.

The Canon at once cut him short with a wave of his hand, and went on:

"But if we, now, let us suppose that we, my friends, in spite of the concession made by the Prince, were to succeed in binding the giant Salvo hand and foot . . . what about that? Well, that is my plan."

Pompeo Agrò, having held out this bait to their curiosity, remained for a while with his hands outstretched in the air beneath his chin; then withdrew and clenched them; he shut his eyes as well, to collect his thoughts; emitted a second "Well!" as a hook to keep his hearers' attention fixed, and relapsed again for a while into silence.

"You gentlemen know the conditions in which the marriage is to be celebrated, by Laurentano's express wish. Now these conditions, as I have planned things, should become the . . . what shall we say? the chink in Salvo's armour."

"The heel of Achilles," Mattina suggested, his interest quickening.

"Precisely! Yes, Achilles!" Agrò agreed. "And now let me explain. It must certainly be an important point with Salvo, he having agreed

to these conditions, that the Prince's son, who
lives in Rome (I fancy he's called Gerlando, eh?
after his grandfather: Gerlandino, Landino),
shall not be, or at least shall not shew himself
openly opposed to his father's marriage. Indeed,
I know that Salvo has definitely insisted upon the
young man's being present at the marriage ceremony, as a recognition on his side of the bond and
as a pledge of his honour as a gentleman for the
future. I am not acquainted with this Gerlandino, but I know that he is made of quite a different stuff . . . of quite a different type, let us
say, from his father."

"The very opposite!" exclaimed Verònica. "I
know him well."

"Oh, capital!" Agrò went on. "He, therefore,
even admitting that he does not see eye to eye
with Roberto Auriti either, if he has to choose
between the two, I mean between him and a man
like Capolino, will naturally prefer, I imagine,
that his cousin should win."

Guido Verònica, at this point, sat up and
heaved a long sigh, as though to rid himself of
a momentary illusion, and said:

"Ah, no, I don't think that, you know! I don't
really believe that Lando mixes himself up in that
sort of thing. . . ."

"Allow me to speak," the Canon resumed, in a
harsher tone. . . . "I have no desire that he
should be mixed up in it: I wish only to learn from

you, who have lived so long in Rome and know
the young man, whether the antagonism, if we
may so express it, between Don Ippolito Laurentano and Donna Caterina Auriti exists between
their sons also.''

"No, nothing of that sort!" Verònica at once
rejoined. "In fact, they are great friends.''

"That is enough for me!" the Canon exclaimed,
slapping the back of one hand with the palm of
the other. "It is more than enough for me! If
the father does not intend to take into consideration the fact of Auriti's being related to himself,
the son on the other hand may, or easily might.
And there we have Salvo, the giant, bound hand
and foot!"

Pompeo Agrò wished to exult for a moment in
this initial victory, and cast a sharp glance, with
a slightly disdainful smile, first at Verònica, then
at Mattina, who were both of them now pledged
to the execution of his plan, which at least was
deemed worthy of their consideration. Then, like
a general not content with winning his battle upon
the table only, by the rules of tactics, he came
down to pointing out the material difficulties of the
undertaking.

"The point," he said, "will be to persuade that
dear fellow Roberto to make use of this ex-
pedient. Especially since we shall at least need
a private letter from Gerlandino, which we can

shew, or communicate in some way to Salvo (do you see?), a letter addressed either to Salvo himself, which will be difficult, or to Roberto or to some other of his friends: to yourself, for instance, my dear Verònica: in short, a proof, a document."

Guido Verònica did not wish to state in so many words that he could not expect to receive a letter from Lando, with whom he was not on any real terms of friendship; he did indeed consider Agrò's plan ingenious, but felt it to be impracticable, perhaps, in view of the exaggerated punctiliousness of Roberto, who . . . who . . . yes, patriotic services, quite so. . . . "Spotless integrity!" Agrò put in. "Yes," Verònica conceded, "and brains as well, if you like; but . . . but . . . as things are at present . . . the Prefect irritates him, and it seems that his friends irritate him as well. Anyhow, it will be a serious matter! I, for my own part, would gladly let myself be flayed alive to help him; but . . ."

He broke off; beat his brow with his hand, and exclaimed:

"I have it! Giulio . . . there's Giulio . . . Roberto's brother, who at this very moment is one of D'Atri, the Minister's, private secretaries: eh, perbacco! We can write to him . . . he is on the most intimate terms with Lando. We can easily get anything we want out of Giulio, without letting anything out to Roberto, who would put all sorts of difficulties in the way. There, that's settled!"

"Splendid! Splendid!" the Canon kept on exclaiming, beside himself with joy.

Only Mattina was left like a vessel whose sail has not succeeded in catching the wind. Seeing the other two vessels skim so smoothly ahead, without a thought of himself left lagging in their wake, he felt crushed; he wanted to express his own opinion, and, having nothing else to say, tried the effect of a breath of contrary wind, and the interposition of a few reefs and shallows.

"Very good," he said, "but won't it be too late, my friends? Let us consider! Before the letter can be delivered in Rome, even if we act with the utmost speed, and the answer arrive here—it will take at least a week, at a moderate estimate. Salvo will have plenty of time to commit himself so deeply that he will not be able to draw back afterwards."

"Oh, I should like to see him!" exclaimed the Canon with a titter, and raised his hand as though greeting the absent Salvo. "No, I say, no! Never, ne-ver, ne-ver. . . . Do you mean that he is so greatly attached to Capolino?"

"But his dignity, surely!" the Cavaliere retorted, as though his own were at stake. "A fine figure he would cut! Why, don't you know that this very day, in the office of the *Empedocle*, the selection is to be officially announced, with the support of Salvo and all the committee of the Party? It's no laughing matter.''

"In that case," Verònica hurriedly interposed, "to speed matters up, we can send Giulio an urgent telegram at once, in cipher.''

"Excellent!" the Canon again expressed his approval, leaving Mattina defeated.

"Yes, yes," Verònica went on, "Roberto has a private code with his brother. Don't let us lose any more time. . . . Or rather . . . wait! . . . now that I think of it . . . Selmi . . . perdio!''

"Selmi?" the Canon asked, baffled by the sound of the name, which fell thus suddenly like an insurmountable obstacle upon the path which he had made so smooth. "The Deputy Selmi?''

"Corrado Selmi, yes," answered Verònica. "I saw him at Palermo. . . . He has promised Roberto that he'll come here, and indeed that he will make a speech . . .''

"Well?" came from Agrò. "Surely, a Member of Parliament of such authority, a true patriot . . .''

"That's all very well," Verònica interrupted, screwing up his eyes, and waving his hand in the air. "A patriot, well and good! But he's rotten to the core, my dear Canon. Debts . . . scandals . . . rumours . . . and God forbid poor Roberto should suffer on his account. That is not the point, however. . . . It is Lando Laurentano I am thinking of . . .''

And Guido Verònica pulled his fingers until the
joints cracked, as though to cleanse them of the
annoyance which he felt at the thought of Selmi.

"I don't understand . . ." observed the
Canon. "Do you mean that between Laurentano
and Selmi . . .?"

"I should just say so!" exclaimed Verònica.
"A deadly enmity!"

"There's a lady in the case," put in Mattina,
gravely, screwing up his eyes, overjoyed at this
obstacle.

And the Canon, his curiosity aroused:

"Ah, indeed? A lady?"

"It's an old story," Verònica replied. "It's all
over now, as far as I'm aware; but, not more than
a year ago, Corrado Selmi—I tell you this because the whole of Rome knows it already—was
the lover of Donna Giannetta d'Atri, the wife of
the man who is now Minister."

The Canon held up his hand:

"Ugh, how disgraceful! And this . . . and
this Donna Giannetta, who might she have been?"

"Why, a Montalto!" said Verònica. "Lando's
cousin. . . . You know that the Prince's first wife
was a Montalto."

"Ah, so that's how it is! And, I suppose, the
young man . . ."

"As a boy, yes, in a cousinly way. . . . I don't
really know much about that. The fact remains
that Lando Laurentano challenged Selmi twice.

. . . And so, you can understand, if Selmi comes
here now to support Roberto's candidature . . ."

"Quite so, quite so . . . now I understand!"
exclaimed the Canon. "He must be stopped! Yes,
he must be stopped!"

"It may perhaps not be difficult," Verònica
concluded. "Because Corrado Selmi will have
his own campaign to fight in his constituency.
. . . Anyhow, we shall see. Now let us go at once
to Roberto."

The Canon rose.

"I am ready," he said. "The carriage is at
the door. One moment, if you please. I must
just fetch my hat and cloak."

A minute later, Verònica and Mattina saw the
old splay-footed servant appear, in the garb of a
Jehu, and took their places in the carriage with
Agrò.

As they came up from the Ràbato, by the Piazza
San Domenico, they at once noticed an unusual
commotion along the main street. Four or five
street arabs, running along and stopping at intervals, were bawling the name of the clerical newspaper, *Empedocle,* which they appeared to be sell-
ing like hot cakes.

"L'Impìducli! L'Impìducli!"

And everywhere groups were forming, some
to read, others in an excited discussion of some
article, evidently violent, that appeared in the
paper.

Verònica, seeing one of these vendors pass by the carriage, could not resist the temptation, and while the Canon—who, in the streets of the town, at that time, felt that he was in the midst of an enemy camp—advised: "Better wait till we get home!" he made the boy fling a copy of the paper into the carriage. It was seized by Mattina.

"Shall I read it to you?"

And he began to read in a low tone the leading article, which was evidently what was arousing such a ferment among the populace.

It was headed *A patriot for family reasons,* and dealt (without mentioning names, but the slanderous intention was unmistakable) with the memory of Stefano Auriti, Roberto's father, distorting with the most odious, vilest calumny the romantic story of his love for Caterina Laurentano; the young couple's elopement shortly before the revolution of 1848; the part played by Stefano Auriti in that revolution "not indeed from love of his country, but for family reasons entirely, that is to say in the hope of acquiring a dowry together with the forgiveness of his involuntary father-in-law, a wealthy man and a Liberal, it is true, but a man, alas, of an inflexibility of character proof against any machination."

Gradually, as he went on reading, Mattina's voice changed to a note of contempt, fired by the indignation of Agrò, who broke out from time to time, putting his hands over his ears and flinging himself back in his seat:

"Oh, the cowards! The cowards!"

At a certain stage in his reading Mattina saw the paper torn from his hands. Guido Verònica, white as a sheet, his face distorted with anger, flung open the door of the carriage, quivering with emotion, sprang out and, without heeding the Canon's appeals, first of all hurled himself into a group of people, in the midst of whom was Capolino, whom he then struck in the face with the newspaper, rubbing his nose in it.

The assault came as such a thunderbolt that everyone stood for a moment dazed with astonishment, before falling upon the aggressor: people ran up shouting from all sides: in the middle the fight grew furious: sticks whirled in the air, amid shouts and imprecations. Mattina had neither time nor opportunity to fly to Verònica's rescue; but presently the crowd began to dissolve: the protagonists were separated. The Canon shouted frantically from the carriage to Mattina. He heard him at length, and turned; but at that moment caught sight of Verònica, without hat or spectacles, his clothes torn and muddy, panting for breath amid a crowd of young men who were evidently defending him, and ran to join him. He returned, a moment later, to the Canon's carriage.

"It's nothing," he said; "keep calm; let us

drive on; he is with friends; he has got well out of it."

The Canon was trembling all over.

"Oh Lord, oh Lord, what a scandal! But why? Disgusting creatures. . . . He ought not to have dirtied his hands with them. . . . And what is to happen next?"

"Oh," remarked Mattina with a trace of contempt in his voice, "a duel; it's quite simple . . . or a prosecution, if our holy religion does not allow the scoundrel to accept responsibility for the slanders which it has not prevented him from uttering."

"We will leave out religion, if you don't mind, Cavaliere," Pompeo Agrò said soothingly. "It has nothing to do with this, nor, if you will allow me to say so, has Capolino."

"How is that?"

"Let me explain. I know who wrote the article, that filthy thing. Préola, Préola who came this morning to see me—I don't know who sent him. . . . The ungrateful wretch! Dregs of humanity!"

"But Capolino," Mattina objected, "is the editor of the paper and must have passed the article."

"I would swear, I would thrust my hand in the flames," replied the Canon, "that he had not read it first. He is my adversary, look, yet I know him to be incapable of any such vile conduct.

. . . And now, what are we going to find at Roberto's?''

The bitter tongue.

Donna Caterina Auriti-Laurentano lived with her daughter Anna, also a widow, and her grandson, in an old and sombre house beneath the Badia Grande.

The house had belonged to Michele Del Re, Anna's husband, who had had nothing else to bequeath to his youthful widow and to their only son, Antonio, now about eighteen years old.

You went up to it by narrow, slippery lanes, broken up into steps, unevenly cobbled, often heaped with filth, reeking with the medley of foul smells that issued from the little shops, dark as caves, shops mostly of the spinners of maccheroni, which they hung outside to dry on poles and trestles, and from the hovels of the pauper women who spent whole days sitting on their doorsteps, days that were all alike, seeing the same people at the same hours, hearing the usual disputes bandied about from door to door by two or more shrill-tongued gossips over their brats, one of whom, as they played together, had had his hair torn out or his scalp cut open. The sole variety, now and again, was the passing of the Blessed Sacrament; the priest beneath the canopy, the tinkling bell, the choir of godly women:

Oggi e sempre sia lodato
nostro Dio sacramentato. . . .

Her husband having died after barely three
years of married life, Anna Auriti herself was
virtually dead to the world. Indeed, since the day
of her bereavement, she had never left the house
again, not even to hear mass on Sundays; she had
never shewn her face in public, not even through
the panes of the windows that were never fully
opened. Only the nuns at the Badia Grande, peering through the bars of their own windows, had
caught glimpses of her from above, when she
came out, towards dusk, for a breath of air in the
narrow little terraced garden of the house, which
rested against the dark, towering bulk of their
abbey, originally the baronial stronghold of the
Chiaramonte. Nor indeed could those nuns have
felt any envy of a woman as strictly cloistered as
themselves. Like them, if not with even greater
simplicity, she dressed in black, always; like them,
she concealed beneath a black silk kerchief, fastened under her chin, the hair which, if it was
not cropped close, was no longer tended with any
care, being merely parted in two strands and
twisted in a loose knot at the back of her head;
those beautiful, abundant chestnut tresses which
at one time, carefully arranged, had given such
charm to her pale, gentle, sweet face.

Donna Caterina had scrupulously shared her
daughter's seclusion, and had worn black also,
ever since 1860, the date of her husband's heroic
death at Milazzo.

Of tall stature, rigid, thin, she had not however
her daughter's air of calm and sorrowful resignation. The terrible griefs that had been her constant portion, the gnawing tooth of pride, the firm-
ness of character which, at the cost of incredible
sacrifices, she had unflinchingly maintained when
faced with the most cruel vicissitudes of fortune,
had so altered the lineaments of her face that it
no longer preserved any trace of her former
beauty. Her nose had grown long and pointed and
overhung her withered lips, hollowed here and
there where she had lost a tooth; her cheeks were
sunken; her chin thrust forwards. But it was her
eyes more than anything else, beneath her bushy
black brows, that showed the ruin of her face: the
eyelids had begun to droop, one more than the
other; and the eye that was the more nearly
hidden of the two, with its slow glance misty with
intense suffering, gave to her spent, waxen face
the aspect of some horrible mask of grief. Her
hair, meanwhile, had remained black and glossy,
as though on purpose to bring into prominence
the mutilation of her other features and to con-
tradict the popular belief that the hair turns white
with sorrow.

There was nothing, literally nothing that Donna
Caterina Laurentano had not endured, including
the pangs of hunger, she who had been born in
luxury, brought up amid the splendours of a
princely house: hunger when, after the revolution

of 1848 had been crushed, a girl of eighteen, with her infant son Roberto, she had had to go into exile in Piedmont with her husband, excluded with forty-three others from the amnesty, and sentenced to the forfeiture of his modest fortune. Her father, Don Gerlando Laurentano, who also was among the forty-three proscripts, had invited her at the time to go with him to Malta, his place of banishment, but on the condition that she would definitely abandon Stefano Auriti. And she? She had refused the offer with scorn; and more scornfully still had afterwards refused the charity of her brother Ippolito, who with a few other unworthy representatives of the Sicilian nobility had gone to do homage to Satriano at Palermo, and had obtained from him the restitution of the property confiscated from his father. And she had gone to Turin with her husband, like a pair of blind and helpless waifs, to beg the bread of life for their child.

None of the other exiles, of the Sicilians who had migrated there, would believe at first that she, a woman of such exalted birth, the only daughter of the Prince of Laurentano, had brought nothing away with her, was receiving no support from her family; and Stefano Auriti had accordingly been hindered in every possible way by his own companions in misfortune in his desperate search for some minor employment that would provide him with bread, mere bread alone for his wife and himself. And then she had fallen seriously ill, and for five months had lain in hospital, through charitable intervention, after endless sufferings, and by charitable intervention the little Roberto had been brought up in another institution. At length and with due compunction their fellow-exiles had revised their judgment, and vied with one another in helping Stefano Auriti. On coming out of hospital she had received the news that her father, Don Gerlando Laurentano, had died by his own hand at Burmula, by poison.

Of the twelve years spent at Turin, ending in 1860, Donna Caterina retained now only a vague, confused memory, as of a life that she had not actually lived but had rather imagined in some strange and violent dream, interspersed at the same time with bright glimpses, certain joyous, ardent moments of patriotic enthusiasm.

Ineradicably stamped upon her heart, however, was the hour of her awakening from that dream: when the news came to her that Stefano Auriti, who had set sail with his twelve-year-old son from Quarto, with Garibaldi, for the liberation of Sicily, had fallen in battle at Milazzo.

Even the favour of letting her go mad had God withheld from her at that moment! And she had been obliged to feel, almost to behold her wifely heart (stricken, dealt its deathblow out there in

Sicily) crawl bleeding in the footsteps of her
young son, left now without a father's protection
to carry on the war.

They had collected a fund for her at Turin, and
with the two little orphans, Giulio and Anna, who
had been born there, she had returned to Sicily,
her now liberated fatherland; but as a widow, in
deep mourning, and more wretched than when she
had left home: amid the universal rejoicing, she,
with her two little ones, dressed likewise in black.
Roberto had before this entered Naples with Garibaldi, and was now fighting beneath the walls of
Caserta, side by side with Mauro Mortara.

She had been taken into the house of the Alàimo,
poor relatives of Stefano Auriti. Once again her
brother Ippolito, now in retreat at Colimbètra, had
offered to assist her; and once again, with undi-
minished scorn, she had refused his offer, to
the amazement and consternation of the Alàimo
family, whose guest she was. Poor people, poor
in intellect and in heart as well as in purse, what
bitterness of spirit they had caused her! She had
been obliged to see herself regarded by them as
by the bitterest enemies of her dignity, which they
did not understand; thoroughly capable as they
were of begging and accepting in secret the assistance that she had declined, not content with the
work which she performed in the house and what
she managed to procure from outside to enable

her to earn a fair recompense for the trifling expense that she caused them.

She had raised her head a little from that horrible degradation on the return of Roberto, welcomed by the whole town in a frenzy of joy. Even now, when she recalled that day, that moment, a thrill would run through her poor flesh. Ah, with what exultation, with what a frenzy of love and grief she had clasped to her bosom the son who returned alone, without his father, the youthful hero of the Red Shirt, whom the populace had borne to her shoulder-high in triumph.

The Provisional Government had granted her a monthly allowance, and to Roberto—since at his age nothing else could be done for him—a scholarship at Palermo. He had forfeited this scholarship a few years later, to follow Garibaldi to the conquest of Rome. But against the torrent of young blood which was to have replenished the dried veins of Rome reasons of state had set up, at Aspromonte, a dyke of fraternal bosoms; and Roberto, with the rest, had been taken prisoner and confined first at Spezia, then in the Forte Monteratti at Genoa. Regaining his freedom, he had returned to his books, but not for long. In 1866 he was once more following Garibaldi. Only in 1871 had he succeeded in taking his degree in Law; and at once had gone to Rome to provide, after all these tumultuous changes of fortune, for his own needs and for those of his family. Some

years later, he had been joined by his brother
Giulio. Anna, at Girgenti, had meanwhile found
a husband, and Donna Caterina—until Roberto in
Rome with the flame of his heroic spirit, with his
own exceptional claims to recognition and his exceptional talents, should have forged ahead and
paved the way to a splendid future, worthy of his
past, and consoled her at length for all the bitter
hardships she had suffered and for the degradation which had been the bitterest of all—had gone
to live in the house of her son-in-law Michele
Del Re.

His death, three years later, her daughter's bereavement, the poverty that once again fell upon
them, seemed powerless to arouse her from a
deeper and more intense sorrow into which she
had sunk. Her son, that son of whom such great
things were expected, her Roberto, up yonder,
amid the turmoil and confusion of the new life of
the Third Capital, amid the obscene babel of all
the people who were tumbling over one another,
clamouring for rewards, picking up honours and
favours, her Roberto was lost! Regarding all that
he had done for his country as nothing more than
a sacred duty, he had never sought nor would he
have known how to establish any claim to a reward; he had perhaps hoped, perhaps waited for
his friends and comrades to remember him in his
modest dignity. Perhaps also his finer feelings
had conquered him and had kept him aloof.

And what utter ruin had come in Sicily to all
the illusions, all the fervid faith, by which the
torch of revolt had been kindled! Poor island,
treated as conquered territory! Poor islanders,
treated as savages, who must first be civilized.
And the *Continentals* had descended upon them to
civilize them: down had come the new soldiery,
that infamous column led by a renegade, the
Hungarian Colonel Eberhardt, who had come to
Sicily first with Garibaldi and had then been one
of those who fired upon him at Aspromonte, and
that other, the little Savoyard subaltern Dupuy,
the incendiary; down had come all the offscourings
of the bureaucracy; and disputes and duels and
scenes of savagery; and the Prefecture of Medici,
and the courts martial, and burglaries, murders,
highway robberies, planned and carried out by the
new police in the name of the King's Government;
and falsification and suppression of documents
and scandalous political trials: all through the
first government by the parliamentary Right!
And then the Left had come into power, and they
too had begun with special measures for Sicily;
and usurpations and frauds and extortions and
scandalous favouritism and a scandalous waste of
public money; prefects, delegates, magistrates
pledged to the service of the ministerial Deputies,
and shameless partisanships and electoral in-
trigues; an unfair distribution of taxation, reck-
less expenditure, degrading servilities; oppres-

sion of the conquered and of the workers, assisted
and protected by the law, with impunity guaran-
teed to the oppressors. . . .

For the last day or two—ever since Roberto's
arrival at Girgenti—had been streaming from the
bitter tongue of Donna Caterina Auriti this vehe-
ment flood of cruel memories, harsh reproaches,
fierce accusations. As she looked at her son, from
beneath her drooping eyelids, with that almost
sightless eye, she emptied her heart of all the bitterness accumulated and stored up in all those
long years; of all the grief with which she had
fed and envenomed her heart.

"What do you hope for? What do you want?"
she asked him. "What have you come here to
do?"

And Roberto Auriti, overpowered by this on-
slaught from his mother, remained frowningly
silent, with bent head and shut eyes.

He was now a man of three and forty: already
bald, but vigorous, with a herculean chest, handsome in a manly way, his face sharply defined by
his thick black eyebrows, that almost met above
his nose, and by a short beard, black also, he sat
there steeped in shame and confusion, like a feeble
little boy in the presence of this mother who, albeit
crushed by age and sorrow, retained so much
strength of character and such ardent spirits.

He felt that he really was defeated, did Roberto
Auriti. His strength of character, overstrained

by the heroic efforts of his boyhood, had gradually
declined when brought face to face with the new,
hideous warfare, a fight for gold, a fight for the
base conquest of office. And he had even asked for
preferment himself, not for himself, for his
brother Giulio, and had secured a berth for him
in the Treasury. For himself he had relied upon
the scanty, uncertain profits of the legal profession: profits which, for all that, left him often by
no means at rest in his mind, not because he did
not regard them as a fair reward for his work,
for the zeal he shewed; but because the majority
of his briefs came to him by way of his friends
the Sicilian Deputies, from Corrado Selmi especially, and in more than one instance he had
the suspicion that his case had been won not so
much by his own talents as by their improper and
by no means disinterested intervention. But he,
since the death of his brother-in-law Michele
Del Re, had his mother and widowed sister and
nephew to support at Girgenti; apart from the
fact that in Rome, for some years past, he had no
longer lived alone.

His mother of course was not unaware that he
was living in Rome with a woman, for whom with
her old-fashioned prejudices and the puritanical
strictness of her morals she could not feel any
respect; she had never uttered a word to him about
this; but he could feel the harsh condemnation
in the maternal heart, a fresh bitterness—unjusti-

fied, to his mind—which his mother refrained
from expressing to him in order not to humiliate
him, not to wound him further.

But perhaps Donna Caterina, at such moments
as this, did not give the matter a thought, wholly
absorbed as she was in setting before her son,
with an inexhaustible ardour, the painful memories of their family and the wretched condition of
the place.

And it was during this fervid, black description
that they were surprised by Canon Pompeo Agrò
and Mattina.

Things were better in the old days!

The warm cordiality with which Roberto Auriti
welcomed him made it plain to Agrò that the other
knew nothing as yet of that vile article in the
newspaper. He introduced Mattina, and paid his
respects to his hostess.

Donna Caterina waited for the preliminary exchange of greetings and for the friends to express
their joy at meeting again after so many years;
then resumed, turning to Agrò:

"For goodness' sake, Monsignore, do you, who
are a true friend to him, tell him so too. We are
all friends here. This gentleman too, since you
have brought him to the house, must be a friend.
I am trying to persuade my son not to undertake
this campaign."

"Mamma," Roberto besought her, with a pained smile.

"Yes, yes," his mother insisted. "Do you gentlemen tell him. What has he done, and why, in the name of what cause does he come here to-day to ask for the votes of the people? In the name perhaps of all that he did as a boy, in the name of his dead father, in the name of the sacrifices and of the sacred ideals for which those sacrifices were made and that agony endured? Why, he will make people laugh at him!"

"Oh, no, Donna Caterina, but why?" Canon Agrò tried to interrupt her, laying his hand on his heart, as though wounded. "Don't say that."

"Laugh at him! Laugh at him!" she went on with increasing warmth. "Perhaps you will kindly tell us, then, how those ideals have been converted to reality for the people of Sicily? What have they gained by them? How have they been treated? Oppressed, taxed, neglected, slandered! The ideals of Forty-eight and Sixty? Why, all the old people here cry: *Things were better in the old days!* And I say the same, do you hear? I, Caterina Laurentano, Stefano Auriti's widow!"

"Oh, Mamma, Mamma!" Roberto implored, putting his hands over his ears.

To which his mother at once rejoined:

"Yes, my son: things were better in the old

days, because then at least we had the hope and comfort of a better future, the hope that sustained us and made us overcome all the tribulations you may or may not remember, at Turin. . . . Things were better then! You may be sure that people do not wish to hear anything more about those ideals. They paid too high a price for them, and now they have had enough! Away with you, get back to Rome. Because I will not, I cannot endure your coming here in the name of the Government that is over us. You have not been a thief, my son; you have not lent your hand to all the injustices, to the vilenesses of the unfair, one-sided administration of our communes, bound hand and foot for years past to the local cliques, which abuse them in every way under the protection of the Prefects and Deputies; you have not supported the infamous power of the gangs who are poisoning the air of our towns, as the malaria poisons our countryside! Why, then, are you here? What claim have you to be elected? Who is supporting you? Who wants you?"

At this moment Guido Verònica entered the room, clothed and in his right mind. He had gone up to the hotel, after the scuffle, to change his clothes, and had left word there that if anyone should come in search of him, he would be back by three o'clock. At once Agrò and Mattina signalled to him that Roberto knew nothing of what had happened. Donna Caterina had risen to her

feet to urge her son to decline the support of the
Government, which for that matter would be
valueless in the coming contest, and to accept the
challenge rather in the name of the oppressed
populace. He would not win, of course; but at
least his defeat would not be dishonouring, and
would serve as a warning to the Government.

"For you will see," she concluded. "I make a
safe prophecy: before a year has passed, we shall
witness scenes of bloodshed: the people can endure no more and are making their preparations,
and before long they will rise in revolt."

Guido Verònica thrust out his plump hands before him, and shook his head:

"For heaven's sake, dear lady, for heaven's
sake do not say such things; they sound horrible
on your lips! Leave them to the instigators, to
the demagogues who, without meaning it, are
playing the Clericals' game! Forgive me, Canon; but that is just what is happening! A handful of ambitious rascals, who sow the seeds of dis-
cord to force their way into the municipal and provincial councils and into Parliament itself;
another handful of ignoble enemies of their country who dream of a separate Sicily under British
protection, like Malta! And then there is France,
our beloved Latin sister, blowing on the embers
and sending money to-day in the hope of reaping
her reward to-morrow by some insane, hole-and-
corner rebellion inspired by the Mafia!"

"Indeed?" broke out Donna Caterina, who could no longer restrain herself. "So you re-assure yourself like that, do you? But these are calumnies, the same old calumnies that our Minis-ters repeat, echoing the Prefects and the petty tyrants of the local committees; calumnies meant to cloak thirty years and more of bad govern-ment; calumnies not so much odious, perhaps, as ludicrous! Here we have famine, my dear sir, on the farms and in the sulphur pits; here we have big estates, the feudal tyranny of the so-called *cappelli,* the so-called gentry, municipal taxes that squeeze the last drop of blood from people who have not so much as the price of a crust of bread; here we have all the extortions that can be made with impunity, by taking advantage of the appal-ling ignorance of these poor serfs, bestialized by their poverty. Do you hold your peace! Hold your peace!"

Guido Verònica gave a nervous smile, bowing and extending his arms; then turned to Roberto:

"Oh, by the way—excuse me, Signora!—I want to borrow your cipher-book, to send an urgent telegram to Rome."

"Of course, yes, good, good!" exclaimed Canon Agrò, rousing himself from the pained attitude he had assumed during Donna Caterina's violent harangue.

Roberto left the room to fetch the cipher-book. The conversation between the three friends and the old lady died away; then Agrò, to break an awkward silence, groaned:

"Ah, the conditions of life in our poor country are certainly sad indeed!"

And the conversation revived for a little, but without warmth. The three men had a secret understanding among themselves, and were also angry and appalled by the scandal of the newspaper article: they exchanged significant glances, and would have liked to be left to themselves for a moment to discuss the best way of breaking the news to Roberto. But Donna Caterina did not leave the room.

"Do you know whether Corrado Selmi," Guido Verònica asked her, "has written to Roberto that he's coming?"

"He's coming, he's coming," she replied, shaking her head with bitter scorn.

"I have been thinking," Verònica murmured to Agrò and Mattina. "All the better if he does come. Indeed, I shall send him a telegram asking him to come at once, *for me*, you understand. In that way, Lando. . . . Hush, here's Roberto."

But it was not Roberto: there entered the room instead a tall, thin youth, to whom the glasses perched on the bridge of his nose, uniting his bushy eyebrows, gave an air of grim and rigid tenacity. It was Antonio Del Re, the nephew. Always extremely pale, his face at that moment seemed to be made of wax.

"Have you seen the *Empedocle?*" he asked, with quivering lips and nostrils.

Canon Agrò and Mattina quickly raised their hands to prevent him from saying more.

"Attacking Roberto?" asked Donna Caterina.

"Attacking grandfather!" the boy replied, quivering. "A handful of mud! And attacking you!"

"Filth! Filth!" exclaimed Agrò. "For heaven's sake, don't let poor Roberto hear about it!"

"He's reading it now," said his nephew, scornfully.

"No! No!" cried Agrò, springing to his feet. "Oh, Lord in heaven, we ought to have warned him! The scoundrels have already had the lesson they deserved from our friend Verònica. For heaven's sake, go to him, Donna Caterina. . . . Rashness, rashness, my boy!"

Donna Caterina hurried from the room; but it was too late. Roberto Auriti, unaware of what Verònica had just done, had dashed off—pale as death, his face contorted in a spasmodic smile, groping like a blind man—to the office of the newspaper, by Porta Atenèa. He had there found the committee of the Party assembled, with Flaminio Salvo at their head, to proclaim, immediately after the assault upon him, the candidature of Ignazio Capolino. To the old porter, who stood on guard in the waiting room, outside the glass door of the editor's office, he had said—still with the same strange smile—that Roberto Auriti wished to speak to the editor. Inside the office a sudden silence had fallen; then the following excited words came to his ears:

"No, gentlemen! Let me go, it is my affair; I wrote the article, and I will answer for it!"

He had not even seen who it was that came to meet him: he had flung himself upon the man like a wild beast, had lifted him bodily in the air and hurled him with such force against the door as to burst it open, with a great crash of shattered glass.

When Verònica, Mattina, and his nephew Del Re came dashing upon the scene, amid the crowd of people that had rushed in from all parts of the building at the shouts that rose from the editor's room, Marco Préola, his face streaming with blood and a knife in his hand, was struggling frantically, shouting:

"Leave me alone, curse you, leave me alone! If you let him go now, I shall kill him next time! Leave me alone! Leave me alone!"

CHAPTER IV

Gellias alone stands firm.

INSIDE the entrance hall, among the palms and laurels, with the coloured glass panes of the front door as a background, the precious headless statue of Venus Urania, dug up at Colimbètra from the ground on which the sumptuous villa now stood, seemed as though it were not for shame at her own nakedness that she held her arm upraised to cover the ideal face, which everyone who paused to admire her at once imagined, bent slightly forward, as though it were actually there; but in order that she might not see kneeling before her, outside the door of the chapel which opened on the right, all those men so strangely attired: Captain Sciaralla's Bourbon company.

Mass was just coming to an end. Inside the chapel, that gleamed with marbles and stucco, were only the Prince, Don Ippolito, bowed in prayer on his gilded and damask-covered faldstool before the altar; behind him, Lisi Préola, his secretary; behind him again, the women of the household: the housekeeper and two young maids.

134

The male servants must be content with hearing mass from the hall; only Liborio, the Prince's favoured butler, in kneebreeches and silk stockings, was allowed to take his place on the threshold of the chapel, more inside than out; and this concession seemed to Sciaralla an act of sheer injustice on Préola's part.

In his capacity as Captain, he felt that he deserved a seat at least by the side of Préola himself, if not immediately next to the Prince.

Openly, no; he did not complain openly; prudence forbade; but it caused him acute annoyance. And he had confessed this as a sin of envy to Don Lagàipa, who came to Colimbètra every Sunday to say mass.

"In the sight of God at least we ought all to be equal, surely!"

All, except the Prince; that went without saying.

But was not he, Sciaralla, complaining because he wished to be favoured, brought forward, distinguished from his subordinates, in the sight of God? It wore the horns, then, the horns and hoofs of the devil, this secret desire of his, which at first sight seemed reasonable enough.

So Don Illuminato Lagàipa had stopped Sciaralla's mouth.

And Sciaralla heaved a deep sigh.

A real temptation of the devil, meanwhile, was that naked statue, standing in front of the chapel there, to all the men of the bodyguard who were obliged to remain outside. While their lips repeated the prayers, their eyes strayed towards it, and . . . certain heating passions! His Excellency the Prince, such a religious man as he was, ought never to have left that naked figure exposed to view. Oh dreadful! It seemed to be alive, it seemed. . . . The poor maidservants lowered their eyes whenever they passed by it; even Don Illuminato lowered his, the old hypocrite!

Meanwhile the marvellous form of the headless goddess smiled and bloomed, emerging from a gulf in time, begotten of a Grecian chisel, of a craftsman unconscious that his handiwork was to survive for so long and to speak to a profane race in a diabolical tongue, there at Colimbètra, the ornament now of an entrance hall, amid tubs of laurels and palms.

Mass at an end, the men of the bodyguard stood at attention on either side of the doorway, for the passage of the Prince, who made his way to the Museum.

This was the name given to the ground-floor rooms on the other side of the hall, where, among tall hothouse plants, was displayed the collection of antiquities, of priceless value: statues, sarcophagi, vases, inscriptions, dug up at Colimbètra, which Don Ippolito had described many years before in his *Memorie d'Akragas*, together with the

precious cabinet of medals to be seen upstairs, in
the drawing-room of the villa.

The famous Akragantine Colimbètra of antiquity was actually much farther down, at the
lowest point of the plain, where three valleys meet
and the rocks divide and the line of the rugged
brow, upon which the Temples stand, is broken
by a wide gap. At this spot, now known as the
Abbadia Bassa, the Akragantines, a century after
the foundation of their city, had formed their fish-
pond, a great basin of water extending to the
Hypsas, its bank combining with the river to form
part of the fortifications of the city.

Colimbètra had been the name given by Don
Ippolito to his property because he too, up above
at its western extremity, had formed a basin of
water, fed in winter by the torrent that ran below Bonamorone and in summer by a lade, the
creaking wheel of which was turned from morning
to night by a blind mare. All round this basin
was a delicious grove of oranges and pomegran-
ates.

In the Museum Don Ippolito was in the habit of
spending the whole morning intent upon his impassioned and uninterrupted study of Akragantine antiquities. He was at present engaged in
tracing, in a fresh volume, the historical topo-
graphy of the primitive city, with the help of
long and minute investigations on the spot, since
his modern Colimbètra covered the precise ground

that had once been the heart of the Greek Akragas.

Beside one of the broad windows of the inner room, hung with light pink curtains, stood the massive inlaid writing table; but Don Ippolito composed as a rule mentally, as he wandered through the rooms; he would construct in the old manner two or three periods big with *laonde* and *conciossiachè,* and would then go and commit them to writing on the great sheets that lay ready upon the table, often without bothering to sit down. With one hand on his chin, clasping his lordly beard, which still preserved the last traces, a faint suggestion of its original golden hue, the Prince, tall, vigorous, still extremely handsome, notwithstanding his age and his baldness, would pause before one or other of his relics, and gaze at it as though his clear blue eyes, beneath their contracted brows, were intent on the deciphering of some inscription or of the symbolical figures upon some archaic vase. At times he would wave his hand, or part his perfectly shaped lips, red with a youthful freshness, in a faint smile of satisfaction, if he thought that he had found a decisive, triumphant argument with which to defeat his topographical predecessors.

On his desk that morning a volume of the *Histories* of Polybius, in the Greek text, lay open at Book IX, Chapter 27, at the page where reference is made to the Akragantine Acropolis.

A most serious problem had been distracting

Don Ippolito for some months past, with regard to
the site of this Acropolis.

"Am I disturbing you?" inquired, bowing on
the threshold of this inner room, Don Illuminato
Lagàipa, who had meanwhile removed his sacred
vestments and partaken of his usual breakfast of
chocolate and biscuits.

He was a short, thickset priest, stunted in body
but far from stunted in mind, with a swarthy,
sunburned face in which the blue eyes, too pale
for his complexion, seemed to wander helplessly.
A good man, at bottom, peace-loving and no
bigot; here, in the presence of the Prince, who
made him stay to dinner every Sunday, he assumed, to gratify his host, an air of rigid and bel-
licose intransigence, at which he would afterwards
laugh, discussing things philosophically with his
old and faithful Fifa, the meek ass which carried
him back to his bit of glebe by the graveyard of
Bonamorone, a few acres of land which—even if
they were conscious of the rapid passage of life—
nevertheless, under this King or that, yielded their
harvest year in year out, and registered the effects
of rain and sunshine, ignorant of political and
social changes.

"It is Sunday to-day, and we must abstain
from work," he added, holding up his hand with a
smile.

"It is not real work, that I do," Don Ippolito
told him with a modest, graceful gesture.

"No, of course not! *Otia, otia,* according to Cicero!" Don Lagàipa corrected himself. "You are right. I looked in to tell you that yesterday morning, before I went off to my glebe, Monsignore did me the honour of charging me with a message to Your Excellency."

"Monsignor Montoro?"

"Yes. He told me to warn Your Excellency that to-day, this afternoon, God willing, he is coming here, to talk, I suppose, about the coming election. Eh," he sighed, interlacing his fingers and waving his locked hands. "It seems the old enemy feels his horns smarting. . . . War, war . . . tempest! I hear that a couple of very queer fish have arrived from Palermo, at the invitation, they say, of Canon Agrò . . . yes, two who are well-known as bottle washers to the heads of the mafia . . . yes, of the infamous band of masons . . . one Mattina and one Verònica. . . ."

"Agrò?" came grimly from Don Ippolito Laurentano, whose attention had been caught by the name and ignored the rest of the speech. "Then Agrò does really intend to step down into the arena, with no sense of decency, no respect even for the cloth he wears?"

"Ah!" Don Lagàipa again sighed. "He is my superior . . . superior . . . but I am only repeating what is said . . . *relata refero* . . . he cannot get over, they say, his not having been made Bishop instead of our Most Excellent Monsignor

Montoro. He thinks he is saving his face with
. . . with the plea of the old ties of friendship
that bind him to Auriti. . . ."

"A fine friendship to boast of!" growled Laurentano. "For a priest!"

"But Agrò . . ." Don Illuminato began. He
shut his eyes, shook his head, emitted a third
sigh: "Ah, it is a complicated business . . .
yes, I tell you . . . it is becoming very delicate. . . ."

"For me?" cried Don Ippolito, springing to
his feet (and his polished scalp reddened). "Delicate for me? I would have Monsignor Montoro
know . . . he should know it already; I do not
own and I have never owned this Garibaldesco,
Roberto Auriti, as my nephew. I do not even
know him by sight: he has never been here, nor
would I for that matter have allowed him to cross
my threshold. And so, under orders from his
Government, with no invitation from the people,
he is coming here, is he, with the mad hope of
taking Giacinto Fazello's place? Very good. He
shall have what he deserves. Without paying any
consideration to my unfortunate and in-vo-lun-
ta-ry kinship, let us fight and win!"

"Ah, fight, fight, yes indeed! We shall have to
fight!" said Don Illuminato, knitting his brows
fiercely over his pale, watery eyes. "Even if we
are fated not to win. . . ."

"And why not?" asked Don Ippolito sternly.

"What possible chance can Auriti have of winning? What does Agrò matter?"

"But . . . people say . . . the Prefecture . . ." and Don Illuminato scratched his bristling jowl.

"It has no hold!" the Prince at once retorted. "We saw that at the last municipal election."

"Quite so, quite so . . ." Don Lagàipa agreed. "Still . . . with the mafia taking the field, now . . . the police befriending him . . . all the evil arts . . . they say . . . and now there's a man coming . . . I don't know his name, a bigwig . . . a Deputy . . . Selmi, I think I heard some one say . . ."

Don Ippolito remained silent for a while, an expression of disgust on his face; then, shaking his fist, broke out:

"Filangieri! Filangieri!"

Lagàipa shook his head with a groan at this invocation, which fell frequently from the Prince's lips and was always accompanied by this gesture of furious rage.

"Filangieri!"

He knew with what veneration Don Ippolito Laurentano still cherished the memory of Satriano, the blessed repressor of the Sicilian Revolution of 1848, the far-seeing, energetic restorer of law and order after the sixteen months of the *obscene revolutionary bonfire*. The horror of those sixteen months had remained vividly in the

Prince's mind, especially the brutal assaults of the populace upon hereditary privileges and religious belief. Satriano had been to him as the sun in his splendour, triumphant over that subversive storm; and like a sun, when the clouds had passed, he had blazed in the Sicilian sky from the Norman palace in Palermo, thrown open in a series of brilliant entertainments to surround his authority with a Napoleonic prestige. There, in the palace, Don Ippolito had met Donna Teresa Montalto, then a young girl, whom Satriano had afterwards condescended to give away in person at her marriage, taking great pains to secure from the King, for him, the bridegroom, the Order of San Gennaro, which his father had worn before him. The storm had broken once more in 1860: from his retreat at Colimbètra he could hear the distant rumble: from there he fought with all his might, within the small circuit of his native town: the Bourbon cause was for the moment lost; they must fight next to secure the triumph of the ecclesiastical power; Rome once restored to the Pope, anything might happen! In the meantime, they must at all costs prevent Giacinto Fazello's seat in Parliament from being usurped by Roberto Auriti.

"Besides," he went on, "Auriti has lost any standing he may ever have had in the place. He has not been here for the last twenty years."

"Still, friendship, you know . . ." Lagàipa

gently opposed, "he may have some friends here still . . ."

"Friendship counts for nothing in these days," Don Ippolito replied curtly. "Weighed against material interests, it is nothing!"

So saying, he took from the table the volume of Polybius, which was lying open, and instinctively raised it to his eyes. At once they turned to the passage which he had read and worried over so often, the *crux* about that wretched Acropolis. He lost interest in the conversation; read the passage through once again, his mind again filled with the controversy that was disturbing him; sighed; shut the book, keeping his forefinger between the pages, and, placing it behind his back, said:

"In fact, Don Illuminato, we have got to win! I, myself, look, have at this moment up against me an army of erudite Germans; topographers; historians ancient and modern, of all nations; popular tradition; yet I do not call myself beaten. The field of battle is here. Here I await them!"

He showed him the book, tapping the page with his knuckles, and went on:

"How would you translate the words: κατ' αὐτὰς τὰς θερινὰς ἀνατολάς?"

Under the shock of this fourfold "ass" which fell upon him like four sudden blows, poor Don Illuminato Lagàipa almost reeled. He felt that he had not deserved such treatment. Don Ippolito smiled; then, slipping his arm through the other's, went on:

"Come with me. I shall explain to you in a couple of words what I mean."

They went out upon the vast lawn in front of the villa; walked some way to the right of it; then, turning round, the Prince pointed out to the priest the wide stretch of land that rose behind the villa in a precipitous ascent, crowned at its summit by an isolated mound, iron-red, a hillock completely escarped all round.

"That, now, is the Akrean hill," he began. "The thing on the top, our famous Rupe Atenea. Very good. Polybius says: *The high part* (the citadel, the so-called Acropolis, in fact) *overhangs the city* (observe) *in the direction of the sunrise in summer.* And will you kindly tell me where the sun rises in summer? Perhaps from behind the hill on which Girgenti stands? No! It rises over there, from the Rupe. And so it was up there, if anywhere, that the Acropolis stood, and not upon the site of the modern Girgenti, as these German Doctors try to make out. I shall prove it . . . I shall prove it! Let them put Camicus up there . . . Cocale's palace . . . Omphax . . . anything they like . . . but not the Acropolis."

And with a wave of his hand he swept aside Girgenti, which appeared for a moment, standing up to the left of the Rock, and lower down.

"There," he went on, pointing again to the Rupe Atenea and gathering inspiration, "there, to yonder sublime watch-tower and sanctuary only, not an acropolis, not an acropolis, a shrine of the patron deities, Gellias climbed, quivering with rage and scorn, to the temple of the Goddess Athena, dedicated also to Zeus Atabirius, and set fire to it to save it from profanation. After a siege of eight months, reduced by famine, the Akragantines, in terror of death, abandon the aged, the children and the infirm and flee, protected by the Syracusan Daphneus, by the Gela gate. The eight hundred Campanians have withdrawn from the hill; the vile Desippus has sought a place of safety; any further resistance is useless. Gellias alone stands firm! He hopes by faith to preserve his life, and retires to the sanctuary of Athena. Its walls dismantled, its marvellous buildings in ruins, the whole city is burning here below; and he from above, gazing down at the vast and awful holocaust which raises a funeral pall of flame and smoke between land and sea, elects to perish in the fire of the Goddess."

"A stupendous description, stupendous!" exclaimed Lagàipa, his eyes starting from his head.

Below them, on the second of the three broad flowering terraces that led down to the villa like three steps of a giant staircase, Placido Sciaralla and Lisi Préola, leaning upon the marble balustrade, had broken off their conversation and now stood nodding their heads, marvelling like the priest at the fire of the Prince's utterance, albeit at that distance they had not caught a single word.

Don Ippolito Laurentano, still carried away by excitement, stood gazing with his deep blue eyes at the magnificent panorama. Where he had just been picturing the terrible fire and destruction, there reigned now the unconscious peace of the countryside; where had been the heart of the ancient city rose now a grove of almond trees and olives, the grove which for that reason still bore the name *della Civita*. The almond boughs had begun to shed their leaves, with the approach of autumn, and, among the perennial boughs of the ashen-grey olives, seemed almost ethereal, assumed a tint of roseate gold in the sunlight.

Beyond the grove, on the long brow of the hill, rose the remains of the famous temples, which seemed to have been set there on purpose, on the skyline, to enhance the marvellous view from the princely villa. Beyond the brow, the table-land, on which the ancient city had stood in its splendour and might, fell in a sheer and rocky precipice to the plain of San Gregorio, formed by the alluvial deposits of the Akragas: a calm, luminous plain, stretching out until it ended, far away, in the sea.

"I cannot abide these Teutons," said the Prince, as he returned with Don Illuminato Lagàipa to the Museum, "these Teutons who, being impotent now in the use of arms, invade us with their books and come and talk nonsense in our country, where so much nonsense is being talked and done already."

At this moment they heard the rumble of a carriage upon the sunken road behind the villa, and Don Ippolito knitted his brows. A moment later Liborio, the butler, entered the room, confused, speechless with surprise.

"Pa-pardon me, Your Excellency," he stammered. "The . . . the Signora has arrived from Girgenti."

"What Signora?" inquired the Prince.

"Your sister . . . Donna Caterina."

Don Ippolito stood motionless for a moment as though stunned by a sudden blow on the head. His nostrils twitched, he turned pale. Then, all of a sudden, the blood surged to his head. He shut his eyes, again grew pale, knitted his brows, clenched his fists, and, with his heart hammering against his ribs, asked:

"Here? Where is she?"

"Upstairs, Excellency, in the drawing-room," Liborio replied; and, after a pause, seeing that the Prince was still perplexed, inquired:

"Have I done wrong?"

Don Ippolito gazed at him for some time, as though he had not heard; then said:

"No. . . ."

And he left the room, without so much as a glance at Lagàipa. His mind in a turmoil, he was trying to think of some possible explanation of this extraordinary visit, unwilling, incapable of admitting the explanation that had first flashed across his mind, to wit that his sister, she who in one misfortune after another had invariably refused with obstinate pride, nay with contempt, every offer of assistance, had now come to intercede on behalf of her son Roberto. But what else could she require of him?

The tragic phantom.

When he had climbed the stairs, he was so burdened by anxiety, a prey to so stifling an agitation, that he was obliged to stop for a moment on the threshold. Should he go in? Present himself to her in that state? No. He must regain his composure first. And he stole off on tiptoe to his bedroom. There, instinctively, he made for the case in which were preserved a portrait of her in miniature, taken when she was a girl of sixteen, and the two letters that she had written him, letters without heading or signature, one from Turin, after the violent death of their father, the other from Girgenti, on her return from exile, after the death of her husband.

The first, the more faded sheet of the two, ran as follows:

The property confiscated from Gerlando Laurentano by the Bourbon Government, was restored to his son Ippolito by Carlo Filangieri di Satriano. I have no further interest, therefore, in my patrimony. The wife and son of Stefano Auriti will not eat the bread of an enemy of their country.

The other was more laconic:

Thank you. For the widow and orphans, the poor relatives of Stefano Auriti will provide. From you, nothing. Thank you.

He thrust the two letters aside and fixed his gaze on the miniature, which he had removed from the drawing-room in his father's house after his sister's elopement with Stefano Auriti.

Since then—it was now forty-five years ago— he had not set eyes on her again!

How could he look again now, after all those years, after that endless succession of calamities, upon this lovely young girl whom he saw before him, blooming, in a deeply cut bodice, dressed in the quaint old fashion, with those keen, thoughtful eyes?

He shut the case again, after casting another glance at the two scornful notes; and sombre, frowning, made his way to the drawing-room.

Raising the curtain at the door, he saw, with eyes clouded by emotion, his sister standing to receive him, tall, dressed in black. He stopped just inside the threshold, overpowered by a crushing

stupor at the sight of that ravaged, unrecogniz-
able face.

"Caterina," he murmured, as he stood there,
and instinctively held out his arms to her.

She did not move: she remained there, in the
middle of the room, waxen-pale in her heavy
widow's weeds, with drawn face and shut eyes;
proud, exalted, hardened by the strain of waiting
for him. She let him come to her and barely
touched his hand with her own cold, lifeless hand,
gazing at him now with those weary eyes of hers,
clouded by grief, half-hidden and that unequally,
by her drooping eyelids.

"Sit down," said her brother, lowering his eyes,
as though afraid to look at her, and pointed to
the sofa and armchairs by the wall on the left.

They sat down, and remained for a long time
incapable of speech, in a silence that throbbed with intense, violent emotion. Don Ippolito
shut his eyes. His sister, after making several
attempts to swallow a lump in her throat, said
finally, in a hoarse voice:

"Roberto is here."

Don Ippolito started; opened his eyes again,
and, instinctively, let them range round the room,
as though—bewildered amid the tumultuous flood
of intimate memories—he were afraid of an am-
bush.

"Not here," Donna Caterina went on with a
cold, bitter, barely perceptible smile, "on your

alien ground. At Girgenti, since the day before yesterday."

Don Ippolito, overwhelmed, nodded his head several times to indicate that he was aware of this.

"And I know why he has come," he added in a sombre tone; then raised his head and looked at his sister with a painful effort: "What can I . . ."

"Nothing . . . oh, nothing," Donna Caterina made haste to reply. "I wish you to fight against him with all your force. It would be the last straw if you too were to support him, and he won the election by your party's votes!"

"You know quite well . . ." her brother attempted to interpose.

"I know, I know," Donna Caterina promptly silenced him with a wave of her hand. "But fight him, Ippolito, not knife in hand, not stealing out to dig up graves, like a hyaena, to lay bare sacred tombs from which the dead might rise and make you die of fright."

"Gently, gently," said Don Ippolito, holding out hands that trembled, not so much in protest as to placate this tragic phantom of his sister in her tremendous agitation. "I do not understand what you mean. . . ."

"It is burning my hands," said Donna Caterina, flinging upon the little table by the sofa a much crumpled copy of the *Empedocle.*

Don Ippolito picked up the sheet, opened it and began to read.

"With such dirty weapons. . . . Attacking a dead man . . ." Donna Caterina murmured, as a commentary upon her brother's reading.

Breathless with emotion, she watched him read the article and observed the expression of disgust on his face.

"Roberto," she continued, "went to the office of this paper. He met there the writer of the article, who is the son, they tell me, of one of your . . . serfs here, Préola. He seized him and flung him against a door. They tore the man from him. . . . Now the man, armed with a knife (which he brandishes!) threatens to kill him; and only this morning he was seen lurking outside my house. But I am not afraid of him; I am afraid that Roberto may compromise himself again and soil his hands. . . . Is this how you choose to fight him?"

Don Ippolito who, as he went on reading, had listened in suspense to her story, at this last question recoiled, indignant, as though his sister had struck him in the face, by associating him with the abject creature who had written the article.

He rose stiffly to his feet; but at once controlled himself and went to ring a bell. To Liborio, who promptly appeared in the doorway, he gave the order: "Préola!"

Presently the old secretary entered bowing, ob-

sequious, indeed crawling, as though he had been
driven into the room by blows. He was wearing
a long and heavy frock coat. From his low collar, which was too large for him, his huge, bald,
bony, beardless head emerged like the head of a
flayed calf.

"Yes, Your Excellency?"

"Send over at once to Girgenti for your son,"
the Prince ordered him. "He is to come here
immediately! I wish to speak to him."

"Your Excellency, allow me," Préola ventured to say, bowing and scraping even lower,
with his hand on his heart, while the network of
veins started out on his crimson scalp, "allow me
to present my most humble duty to the most excellent lady, your sister . . ."

"That will do, I tell you!" the Prince shouted
angrily. "I know what I have to say to your
son. Or rather, listen! He disgusts me so, that
I do not wish either to speak to him or to see him.
You shall say to him that if he dares to show his
ugly face again in the streets of Girgenti, you
will be turned out of the house: I shall dismiss you
instantly! Is that clear?"

Préola extracted a handkerchief from the tail
pocket of his coat and assented, reiterated his assent, as he mopped his scalp; then pressed the
handkerchief to his eyes and sobbed until his
whole body shook.

"A gallowsbird . . . a gallowsbird . . ." he

moaned. "He is disgracing me, Your Excellency. . . . I am sending him away, to Tunis. . . . I have made all the arrangements already. . . . Meanwhile, I shall have him fetched here at once. Forgive me, have pity on me, Your Excellency."

And he left the room, bowing and scraping, with the handkerchief to his lips.

Donna Caterina rose.

"By this," Don Ippolito told her, "I do not mean in the least to forfeit any of my rights in the fight for my principles against your son."

Donna Caterina raised her eyes to a large portrait in oils of Francesco II, and to another of King Bomba, which had pride of place in the magnificent drawing-room, on one wall: bowed her head and said:

"That is understood. I told you so myself."

And she prepared to leave the room.

"Caterina!" Don Ippolito called after her, as she was reaching the door. "You are not going away like that? Perhaps we may never see each other again. . . . You came here . . ."

"Like a ghost from the tomb . . ." she said, shaking her head.

"And I should not have known you," her brother went on. "Because . . . wait here a moment: let me show you how I remembered you, Caterina."

He hastened to fetch the miniature from the case in his bedroom, and handed it to her:

"Look. . . . Do you remember?"

Donna Caterina at first felt a violent shock at the sight of her own youthful image, and drew back her head; then took the miniature from his hands, went over to the balcony and began to study it. Those lifeless eyes had long had no tears left to shed, and now tears welled in them. Her brother, too, was silently crying.

"Would you like to keep it?" he asked her in broken accents.

She shook her head, wiping her eyes with her black-bordered handkerchief, and hurriedly returned the miniature to him.

"Dead," she said. "Good-bye."

Don Ippolito escorted her to the door of the villa; helped her into the carriage; pressed a long kiss on her hand; then followed her with his gaze until the carriage turned from the short avenue on the left to pass through the gate of the villa. There one of the bodyguard, in Bourbon uniform, had thought fit to take up his post, to present arms. Don Ippolito noticed him and stamped his foot with rage.

"These tomfooleries!" he growled, glaring at Captain Sciaralla, who was standing in the hall.

He retired upstairs, shut himself up in his bedroom, and from there sent his apologies to Don Illuminato for not asking him to remain to luncheon.

The shades of night.

Monsignor Montoro arrived at four o'clock in his silent carriage, drawn by a pair of active mules in blinkers.

He was accompanied by Vincente De Vincentis, the Arabic scholar, who that day had forsaken the library of Itria for the adjoining Episcopal Palace, and had sought relief in speech, in speaking for all the days and months on end in which, as though he had left his tongue as a marker between the pages of those blessed Arabic manuscripts, he had remained as dumb as a fish.

He had talked in the carriage too, during their drive, in starts and bursts and dashes which convulsed all his meagre, bony, quivering little body with its lean red face always frowning, and eyes fixed and hard behind his powerful glasses.

More than once the Bishop, with his soft womanish hands or his honeyed voice, with its measured inflexions, suffused, one felt, with a pure, protecting authority, had urged him to calm himself; he was now recommending, quietly, prudence, prudence, as they passed through the gate of the villa amid the reverent salutes of the bodyguard; and once again, with a motion of his hand, "prudence," before alighting from the carriage.

The visitors were at once conducted by Liborio to the drawing-room, but passed out on to the marble terrace supported by the columns of the porch, to enjoy the magnificent outlook over land and sea.

Looking down, they could trace the whole line of the distant coast against the crude azure of the boundless sea, from Punta Bianca, to the east, which stood out like a silver spur, on and on, with bays and promontories more or less gently curving, to Monte Rossello on the west, the ruddy glare of whose beacon was visible only at night. For a short space only, almost bisecting the gentle, sweeping curve, the coast line was broken by the mouth of the Hypsas.

Don Ippolito joined them presently, in great excitement, not yet recovered from the serious disturbance which his sister's visit had caused him.

"I've brought our friend De Vincentis with me," Monsignor Montoro at once began, "because there is something he wishes to see in your Museum, my dear Prince. If you will send some one with him, we can remain out here, in this bower of bliss: I cannot tear myself away from it. But first of all De Vincentis has a favour to ask of you."

"Yes," the other broke out, as though he had received an electric shock. "I meant to come out by myself, this morning. But Monsignore said no, he said, 'better come with me.' It is a very serious matter, very serious indeed. . . ."

"Let us hear what it is," said the Prince, in-

viting him with a wave of his hand to resume his
seat on the chair of woven rushes on the terrace.

De Vincentis stooped to see where the chair
was; then sitting down and gripping the arms of
it with his dry, hooked little hands, he burst
out:

"Ruined, Don Ippolito! We are ruined!"

"No, come now . . . no . . ." Monsignore
tried to correct this statement, holding out a hand
burdened with his episcopal ring.

"Ruined, Monsignore, allow me to say!"
De Vincentis repeated; and his hollow red cheeks
turned livid. "And the cause of our ruin is my
brother Ninì! He has been to . . . to . . ."

Once again the Bishop's hands were outstretched; De Vincentis observed the gesture in
time and caught himself up. But the Prince had
already guessed his meaning.

"To Salvo," he said soothingly. "I know that
you have surrendered to him . . ."

"Ninì! Ninì!" screamed De Vincentis. "Primosole . . . Ninì! It was he that surrendered it.
. . . I know nothing, I tell you; nothing at all
about it; I'm in the dark, a blind man. . . . And
he is blinder than I am, stupid, mad, lovesick.
. . . What is the word? A *transfer* of Primosole. . . . Yes! I have signed the receipt . . .
although . . . only the farm, you know, has been
paid for, and that in a way that makes one
laugh . . ."

"No, why?" Monsignore again interrupted him, gravely.

"Cry, then!" retorted De Vincentis, who had now completely lost his head. "Does that satisfy you? Eighty-five thousand lire, and the villa thrown in! My mother's old home, there . . ."

And he pointed with his hand towards the east, over the ridge of the Sperone, to the higher hill beyond known as *Torre che parla,* and shaped like a couchant lion, its coat and mane supplied by a dense growth of olives.

"Forty-two thousand," he went on, "was for bills that had fallen due: the rest, clean vanished, blown to the winds in less than two years! Where? How? Now I hear that he's talking of letting Salvo have the Milione estate as well. And what have we left? Debts to Salvo . . . our other debts . . . I know, I've heard all about it. . . . You are going to marry, I'm told, his sister . . . Donna Adelaide . . ."

"And what has that got to do with it?" asked the Prince, puzzled, vexed, looking at Monsignor Montoro.

"I congratulate you, mind, I congratulate you. . . ." went on De Vincentis promptly, turning as red as a lobster. "We are ruined, though, all the same!"

And he rose so that the others should not see the tears behind his gold-rimmed glasses.

Don Ippolito looked again at the Bishop, in search of enlightenment.

"Let me explain," said the Bishop in a grave tone, a tone of regret at the young man's disobedience, and let droop over his clear pale prominent eyes a pair of eyelids as thin as layers of onion-skin. "Let me explain. I know that Flaminio Salvo has already made over the Primosole estate to his sister, and that he is prepared, when the time comes, to make over Milione as well. But I am distressed at the way in which our friend Vincente has expressed himself, because . . . because that is not the way in which to refer to people who are held in the highest esteem, people from whom perhaps, without knowing it, we may have received some benefit."

De Vincentis, who was standing with his back to them while he wiped his eyes, turned round at the Bishop's closing words.

"Benefit?"

"Yes, my son. You cannot tell, because, unfortunately, you have never taken any interest in your affairs. You now see the disastrous state they are in, and feel the need to inculpate somebody, wrongly; instead of applying a remedy. Was not that why you came here?"

De Vincentis, who was still speechless with emotion, nodded his head.

"It would be better," Monsignore went on, "if

you were to go downstairs; if you will allow him, Prince. I shall explain to the Prince what it is that you want."

Don Ippolito rose and asked De Vincentis to accompany him; then, at the head of the stair, handed him over to Liborio, to whom he gave the key of the Museum, and returned to the Bishop, who greeted him with a sigh, waving his clasped hands.

"A couple of poor wretches, he and his brother! Flaminio Salvo, I assure you, Prince, has treated them like a true friend. Without taking any . . . don't for goodness' sake let us say usury, there was never any thought of that; without asking for interest, he first of all lent them very considerable sums; he next had an offer from themselves of an estate with which he, a banker, wrapped up in business, you can understand, does not know what to do: any other creditor would have put the place up to auction, to recover his outlay. Instead of which he has acted in a friendly spirit, and has continued to open his purse to the brothers, who spend and spend . . . I can't think how, upon what . . . they have no vices, poor fellows, that I must say; the best boys in the world; but not very much brain. The fact of the matter is that they are sailing on troubled waters."

"Do they want help from me?" Don Ippolito asked, in a tone which let it be understood that he would be perfectly willing to afford such help.

"No, no," Monsignore replied anxiously. "To
ask for something which, I am sure, will be refused. De Vincentis believes that Ninì, his younger
brother, is in love with Flaminio Salvo's daughter, and . . ."

"And?" the Prince echoed.

But he had understood already; and the conversation ended, Sicilian fashion, in an exchange
of significant gestures. Don Ippolito laid both
hands on his bosom and asked with his eyes: "Am
I expected to convey the request to Salvo?"
Monsignore nodded a melancholy assent; the other
first of all shook his head in refusal, then raised
his shoulders and one hand in a vague gesture,
as much as to say: "I shan't do it, but supposing
I did?" Monsignore sighed, and that was all.

They sat for a while in silence.

Don Ippolito, for some years past, had been
confusedly aware that this Monsignor Montoro
was a grave burden to him, not so much in the
flesh as in the spirit, as though with the dead
weight of his pink, too well cared for person, he
were encumbering all sorts of things round about
him and dependent upon him, and preventing any
development. What things, he would, to tell the
truth, have found it hard to say; but obviously,
with that figure, with that pink inert cumbersome
flabbiness, he must be allowing any number of
things to slide which another man, perhaps, in his
place, more active and less effeminate, would have

set in motion, would indeed have stirred up and carried to a conclusion.

Monsignore for his part was aware that between him and the Prince there existed a feeling not easy to define, which often on one side or the other shrank instinctively back, leaving a yawning gulf between them which gave rise in each of them to a faintly gnawing bitterness.

Perhaps this gulf was created by a subject upon which Monsignore knew that he must not touch, and which was yet so intimate a part of the Prince's life: to wit, his archaeological studies, his worship of the past. He could not venture upon this subject, for fear of its furnishing Don Ippolito with an excuse for referring again to a matter of which he, a man of the world and absolutely free from superstition, did not wish to hear any more. More than once the Prince had endeavoured to persuade him to devote at least a small portion of the considerable emoluments of his See to the restoration of the old Cathedral, a splendid example of Norman art, ruined in the eighteenth century by horrible incrustations of stucco and the most vulgar gilding. He had refused, telling the Prince that, should he ever succeed in putting aside any savings, he would prefer to establish a fund with which he might bring back to the Convent of Sant'Alfonso, next door to the Cathedral, the Liguorine Fathers who had been expelled after 1860.

Don Ippolito took not the slightest interest in
the improvements that had been effected in his
native town by the new administrations which had
replaced the *decurie* and *intendenti* of his day.
Albeit he allowed himself no rest from the fray
and shewed a spirit resolute to attain the goal, he
no longer believed in his heart of hearts that he
would ever set eyes again on the town from which
he had banished himself. He saw it in imagination as it had been before that fatal year, still
with its *burgi* and *stazzoni,* that is to say its ricks
of straw and its kilns on the marshy space outside
Porta di Ponte; still with the three great crosses
of the Calvary on the brow of the hill, from which
year by year, on Good Friday, sermons were
preached to the whole population assembled beneath, and still with the old garden which one of
his devoted friends, Colonel Flores, commander
of the Bourbon garrison, seeking to ingratiate the
citizens, had laid out there ten years before the
Revolution. He knew that this garden had been
destroyed to enlarge the terrace on the side looking towards the sea; he knew that on the marshy
space there now rose a huge palace, intended to
house the provincial offices and to be the headquarters of the Prefecture. But this too was in
his eyes an unworthy usurpation, since the foundation stone of the palace had been laid in 1858 by
a philanthropic Bishop, who intended to build a
great hospice there for the poor; wherefore the old

people still spoke of it as the Palazzo della Beneficenza.

He would have liked the Cathedral to be restored by Monsignor Montoro, because the churches . . . ah, those were not buildings which the new people could take any pleasure in adorning; and they were the one thing for which he felt a profound regret. There came to him, in his banishment, the sound of the bells of the nearer churches. He knew every one of them, and would say: "There, that's the Badia Grande ringing now . . . that's San Pietro now . . . that's San Francesco . . ."

There came, this evening, too, to break the long silence into which he and the Bishop, out there on the terrace, had drifted, the sound of the Angelus from the chapel of San Pietro. The sky, which a moment earlier had been an intense blue, was all suffused with violet light; and beneath, among the already harvested fields, in the gathering dusk, there stood out among the stripped almond trees a line of tall nocturnal cypresses, like a vigilant picket on guard over the Temple of Concord that soared majestic into the air from the crest of the hill.

Monsignor Montoro removed his zucchetto and bowed his head slightly, shutting his eyes; the Prince crossed himself, and joined him in silent prayer.

After which, "Have you heard of the scandals," the Bishop inquired gravely, "which are bound, I fear, to disturb our peaceful diocese?"

Don Ippolito nodded his head, with half-shut eyes.

"My sister has been here."

"Here?" the Bishop asked in utter amazement.

Don Ippolito thereupon told him briefly of his sister's visit and of the violent shock that it had given him.

"Oh, I understand! I understand!" exclaimed Monsignore, raising his clasped, white hands and letting his own eyelids droop also.

"So altered . . ." Don Ippolito heaved a deep sigh.

To change the conversation, Monsignor Montoro, after drawing a long breath, groaned:

"And now our paladin is determined to take the field at all costs; and that will be a fresh scandal, which I should have liked to avoid if possible. . . ."

"Capolino?" Don Ippolito frowned. "Is he going to fight?"

"Why, yes! He has been assaulted . . ."

"He? It was Préola!"

"He too! You haven't heard the whole story, then? Our friend Capolino was assaulted in the morning by one Verònica, who was then in the company of Agrò, who is giving me so much trouble. . . ."

"She never told me. . . ." Don Ippolito's murmur was barely audible.

"Because it appears," Monsignore explained, "at least this is what people are saying in the town, it appears that Auriti knew nothing about the quarrel in the morning. It may be so. We shall have to turn a blind eye, because the insult, oh, the insult was very serious; they flung the paper in his face, on the public highway. . . . You know that our friend Capolino is a hot-tempered man, a regular knight-errant. . . . It was impossible to make him listen to reason, to make him observe the Christian precept. He has sent the challenge already. . . ."

"I know that he is a good swordsman," said Don Ippolito grimly. "When all is said and done, it will do no harm to teach one of these fellows a lesson, and take them all down a peg. For my own part, Monsignore, I said as much to my own sister, a fight to a finish!"

"But of course! The victory, the victory is ours, beyond question," was the Bishop's conclusion.

Another spell of silence followed; then Monsignore roused himself and inquired: "Landino?" as though it had just occurred to him to put this question, which was as a matter of fact the true reason of his visit.

It was he who had planned this marriage be-

tween Donna Adelaide Salvo and Don Ippolito;
he had given the latter to understand that only
out of regard for him had Flaminio Salvo agreed
to his sister's contracting this invalid marriage,
invalid at least in the eyes of the State; but that
he was anxious—and quite rightly—that the son
of the first marriage should acknowledge his
mother-in-law, and should be present at the religious ceremony: in dealing with a gentleman of
his quality, the mere fact of his presence would
be sufficient to cover all eventualities.

Don Ippolito's face darkened.

After a long inward struggle, he had written to
his son, who had been brought up entirely away
from home; first of all at Palermo, among his
Montalto relatives, then in Rome; so that the two
were not on intimate terms. He knew that his
son had ideas and sentiments diametrically opposed to his own, although they had never had
occasion to discuss anything together. He was
far from satisfied with the manner in which he
had informed his son of his decision to make this
second marriage, and with the terms in which he
had expressed his desire to have his son with him
at Colimbètra for the wedding. Too many excuses: loneliness, old age, the need of loving attention. . . . He felt that he had degraded himself in his son's eyes. His feeling of disgust and
degradation was, however, not due merely to a

badly drafted letter: it sprang from a cause more
intimate and profound, in his own heart.

Without having originally any deliberate intention, he had let himself be persuaded into putting
into effect a plan which at first sight he had
deemed impracticable; the serious obstacle of his
own scruples overcome, the bride found, the marriage arranged, he had suddenly found himself
bound by an engagement which he had not suf-
ficiently weighed, and had been powerless to draw
back upon any pretext. The Salvo family, even
if they had no title of nobility, were nevertheless
of ancient blood; the bride's age was suitable; no
serious objection could be made to her appearance, in the photograph they had shewn him of
Donna Adelaide; and then there was the satisfaction of the deference paid to his political and religious principles. . . . Yes, yes; but the cherished
memory of Donna Teresa Montalto? and his humiliating consciousness of his own weakness? He
had been powerless to hold out against the secret
terror that had been assailing him for some time
past, in his loneliness, at the thought of his old
age, especially at night, when he shut himself up
in his bedroom and, looking at his hands, found
himself thinking that . . . yes, death is always
hovering over all of us, children, young men and
old, invisible, ready at any moment to clutch us;
but, as we see drawing gradually nearer the limit
set to man's life upon earth, and when already,

year after year, for mile after mile of our journey, we have somehow avoided the assault of that
invisible companion, then gradually, on the one
hand, the illusion of a probable escape diminishes,
and there grows, on the other hand, and over-
powers us the cold, dark sense of the tremendous
necessity of meeting him, of finding ourselves of
a sudden facing him as man to man, in the narrow span of time that remains to us. And he felt
his breath fail; he felt his throat tightened by an
inexpressible anguish. His hands filled him with
horror. His hands were the only part of him, so
far, that showed signs of age: their swollen
knuckles, their wrinkled skin. Yes, his hands had
begun to die. Often they became numb. And he
could no longer, at night, as he lay on his back in
bed, bear to see them folded upon his belly. And
yet this was his natural posture: he must stretch
himself out thus to woo sleep. But no: he saw
himself lying dead, with those hands as it were
turned to stone upon his belly; and at once he
would lose patience, assume another posture, tor-
ment himself far into the night. . . .

For this reason he had expressed the desire for
a more intimate companionship; and now his desire was being put into effect; but secretly it filled
him with irritation and shame. He felt that this
desire had acquired the power over him of a will
that was no longer his own. An alien force indeed had assumed control over him and was guid-

ing him and leading him astray, powerless any
longer to resist; like a horse that has given the
first impetus to a carriage upon a downward slope,
now by the carriage itself, or rather by the force
that he had given it, he felt himself thrust and
driven on against his will.

"Has not answered?" Monsignore put in, to
break the dark ring of silence into which the Prince
had withdrawn. "Very well; I only wished to know
He will answer. In the meantime . . . listen: we
have talked to Flaminio about the formal introduction. It can be arranged at Valsanìa, I suppose? Donna Adelaide will go down to see her
niece and her poor sister-in-law; you, from this
house, by the road, without passing through the
town, can go to call upon your brother and his
guests. Is that all right? In the course of the
week. You shall choose the day."

"At once," said the Prince, mastering himself
with a violent effort. "To-morrow."

"Too soon . . ." Monsignore observed with a
smile. "We shall have to warn them . . . to give
them time. . . . The day after to-morrow perhaps,—no: it's a Tuesday. Women, you know,
attach importance to these things. It will have
to be Wednesday."

And he rose, with an effort and with due regard
to his plump, pink, effeminately cared-for person,
sighing:

"Bene eveniat! That poor boy . . ." he went on, alluding to De Vincentis. "If we could find any way of soothing him. . . . I should be so glad. . . . Mah!"

At the foot of the stair Monsignore Montoro stopped the Prince and, pointing to the door of the Museum, in which De Vincentis was, murmured:

"Don't let him see you. You can bid him good-bye from the terrace. Good evening."

The Prince kissed his ring and went upstairs again. A minute later, from the terrace, he bowed to the Bishop and waved his hand to De Vincentis, who took off his hat, evidently without recognising him. He remained there, sitting by the balustrade, watching, over the dead silence of the fields, the shadows gradually deepening, the ruddy streak of sunset, which became livid and seemed to smoke over the distant blue sea, above which in the background, loomed the dark olive-groves of Montelusa, to the right of the gleaming mouth of the Hypsas. High up in the sky a sickle moon was beginning to shine.

Don Ippolito gazed at the temples where they stood grouped austere and solemn in the dusk, and felt a vague sorrow for these survivors from another world and another life. Among all the famous monuments of the vanished city, to them alone had it been granted to witness this remote age: the only living things once, amid the appalling destruction of the city; the only dead things now amid all that life of the trees that throbbed, in the silence, with leaves and wings. From the intervening hill of Tamburello there seemed to be moving up towards the Temple of Hera Lacinia, poised there aloft, almost vertically above the ravine of the Akragas, a long and dense procession of ancient, hoary olives; and one there was, in advance of the rest, bowed over its kneeling trunk, as though overpowered by the imminent majesty of the sacred columns; and perhaps it was praying for peace upon those deserted slopes, for peace from those temples, phantoms of another world and of a far different life. Hot, flaming, clamorous, the civilisation that at one time reigned upon those slopes had melted away, being founded upon sentiment and illusion: raucous with machinery, ice-cold, the civilisation of to-day, founded upon reason, came sweeping down from the north, like a sheet of snow.

Suddenly, through the darkness that had now fallen, there sounded the distant cry of a horned owl, like a sob.

Don Ippolito felt a lump gather suddenly in his throat. He looked at the stars which were now twinkling in the sky, and fancied that their bright tremor was being answered from the deserted fields by the tremulous shrill song of the grasshoppers. Then he saw, beyond the river-bed, to the east, the wavering light of four dark lanterns mount the steep ridge of the Sperone.

It was Sciaralla, who was climbing the hill with his three companions, to mount their ineffectual guard at the barrack-room above.

CHAPTER V

A cloudy dawn.

AS the first glimmer of dawn filtered down
through the thick, leathery leaves of the wild
fig-tree that overshadowed the end of the vineyard, Mauro Mortara, sitting propped against its
trunk, knitted his brows, stretched his arms,
straightened his back and emitted a rumbling
sound from his throat and nose.

With the return of consciousness he blinked two
or three times; he hungered still for the warm
darkness of sleep; but at that moment he heard a
cock crow from a distant farmyard, and a second
cock, farther off still, crow in answer; he heard
a flutter of wings close at hand, and roused himself.

The three mastiffs, crouching beneath the tree
by his side, watched him with moist, anxious eyes,
greeting him affectionately with their tails. But
their master only stared at them, annoyed that
they should have seen him asleep; then stared at
his own legs, stretching out rigid upon the muddy
soil of the vineyard; earth upon earth; shook his
woollen cloak from his shoulders; rubbed his
watery eyes with the back of his hand; last of

all took from the bag that was hanging from a branch three crusts of stale bread and tossed them to the dogs; rose, with an effort, to his feet and, hanging his cloak on the tree, and shouldering his gun, set off still half asleep through the vineyard.

He could no longer manage to keep awake all night: cautiously, at a certain hour, as though someone might be watching him, he would retire to his lair under the fig-tree; for a moment only, he told himself; but the effort to arouse himself became greater every morning. His legs were no longer what they had once been; neither was the strength of his wrist.

Ah, his beautiful vineyard. . . . Yes, this year's vintage he might perhaps live to taste; but the next? He shrugged his shoulders, as much as to say: "Sufficient for the day . . ." and yawned at the first light of morning which seemed to be finding a difficulty in rousing the world to its toil; he looked out over the vast expanse of fields, over which the last shades of night were slow in scattering; then turned to look at the sea, down below, dark blue and vaporous between the bristling agaves and the fat grey stumps of prickly pear, that rose and writhed in the raw, murky air.

The setting moon, which had risen late that night, was still halfway up the sky, surprised there by daybreak, and was already fading in the crude morning light. Here and there in the fields, through that light veil of whitish vapour, smoke

rose from the fires on which the almond husks
were burning.

For the last two days, however, Mauro Mortara had been less worried. He still kept a dog-
like watch round the villa; but then, reflecting that
Flaminio Salvo set off every morning at that hour
for either Girgenti or Porto Empedocle, and did
not return until late in the evening, he heaved a
sigh of relief, as though the aspect of the building became more agreeable to him with the knowledge that the other was not there. There remained, it was true, with their servants, his wife
and daughter; but the wife, a poor lunatic, quiet
and harmless; and the daughter . . . it seemed
impossible! she, for all she was daughter to that
"bad Christian," was not bad herself, no, far
from it. . . .

And Mauro unconsciously threw a glance over
his shoulder, to see whether Donna Dianella had
come out yet to the vineyard.

In the few days that she had spent at Valsanìa,
she had almost completely recovered; she rose
betimes every morning; waited until her father
had driven off in his carriage, and then came and
joined Mauro out here in the vineyard, and asked
him endless questions about the country: about
the olives and how they were tended; the mulberries, which in March gather fresh blood and, when
they are in love, and ready to shoot, become soft
as dough; then she would stop beneath the um-

brella of the solitary pine down yonder, where
the tableland dropped to the sea, to watch the sun
rise over the heights of the Crocca, far away on
the horizon, livid at first, then gradually waxing
blue, aerial, almost fragile. The first thing to be
gilded by the sun, every morning, was that pine,
which stood out in majesty against the harsh,
solid azure of the sea, the tenuous, empty azure
of the sky.

In a few days Dianella had wrought a miracle:
the bear was tamed. The expression on her face,
the gentle and at the same time proud nobility of
her bearing, the melancholy sweetness of her gaze
and smile, the softness of her voice had wrought
the miracle, quietly, naturally, challenging and
conquering the sullen rudeness of the old savage.

While she was speaking, now and again, there
would come into her voice and eyes a sudden
opacity, as though her spirit vanished from time
to time behind some word or expression and
strayed far away, into unknown tracts; she would
lose herself there and take a long time to return,
would ask: "What were we saying?" and smile,
because she herself could not account for what
had happened to her. Often too, at the slightest
contact with any harsh reality, she would feel a
sudden dismay or rather the sense of a chill
shadow closing in upon her, and would knit her
brows. Immediately, however, she would cancel
with another of her sweet smiles the involuntary,

angry impulse, opening wide a pair of sparkling eyes, her spirits quite restored.

"Why should anyone seek to injure me?" she seemed to be saying to herself. "Am I not facing life, trustful and serene?"

Her trustfulness radiated from her every action, her every glance, and was irresistible.

Even Mortara's three savage mastiffs—you ought to have seen the fuss they made of her whenever she appeared. They too kept on turning, one after another, to gaze in the direction of the villa, as though they expected her. And Mauro, not to go too far away, hung about examining first one cane then another, whose clusters, jealously guarded treasures, he had already exhibited, almost grape by grape, to Dianella, with a gruff delight in the praises that she heaped upon them amid her exclamations of wonder:

"Oh, look at all these!"

"A good load, eh? And this cane, look . . ."

"A tree . . . it's like a fruit tree!"

"And here, this one . . ."

"Oh, there are more bunches than leaves! Can the vine bear the weight of all these grapes?"

"Yes, if we don't have bad weather. . . ."

"That would be a pity! And this one," she would ask, noticing a vine on the ground. "Was it the wind? Oh, it has still to be tied. . . ."

Or again, going farther afield:

"And these? Wild vines? New grafts; I see.

Splendid, splendid. . . . Ah, it is worth while to
be alive after all!"

And her voice seemed to thrill with her joy in
the pure air and the sunshine, the same joy that
quivered in the throats of the larks.

For this morning Mauro had promised her a
visit to the General's *camerone,* to the "Shrine
of Liberty." But the dogs, all of a sudden,
pricked up their ears; first one then another stole
across without barking towards the footpath beneath the vineyard, along the edge of the ravine.

"Don Ma'! Don Ma'!" came presently in a
breathless voice from below.

Mauro recognized the voice as that of Leonardo
Costa, his friend from Porto Empedocle; and
called the dogs to heel.

"Here, Scampirro! Here, Nèula! Come here,
Turco!"

But the dogs had recognized Costa also and had
stopped at the boundary of the vineyard, wag-
ging their tails at him from above.

Mauro appeared beside them.

"The chief? Has he gone?" Leonardo Costa
panted.

He was a little man with a crisp, rusty beard
and hair, a face baked by the sun and eyes
scorched by sulphur dust. He wore a pair of gold
earrings and a big white hat covered in dust and
stained with sweat. He had come hurrying from

Porto Empedocle, by the coast, along the railway line.

"I don't know," Mauro answered crossly.

"Will you please call to him, to wait; I have something important to tell him."

Mauro shook his head.

"Run, you will still catch him. . . . What has been happening?"

Leonardo Costa, as he ran, shouted back at him: "Trouble! Bad trouble in the sulphur pits!"

"Curse him and his sulphur pits!" Mauro muttered to himself.

Flaminio Salvo was coming down the steps from the villa to get into the waiting carriage when Leonardo Costa emerged from the path to the west, among the olives, shouting:

"Stop! Stop!"

"Who's that? What's the matter?" Salvo asked with a start of surprise.

"I kiss Your Honour's hands," said Costa, removing his hat as he approached, dripping with sweat and gasping for breath. "I am done . . . I meant to come last night . . . but then . . ."

"Then what? What has happened? What's wrong with you?" Salvo interrupted him sharply.

"At Aragona—Comitini—all the sulphur workers—on strike!" Costa announced.

Flaminio Salvo looked at him with cold anger, stroking the long grey side-whiskers which, with

his gold spectacles, gave him something of the air
of a diplomat, and said, contemptuously:

"I was aware of that."

"Yes, Sir. But late last night," Costa went on,
"some people from Aragona came to Porto Empedocle and told us that the place had been like
hell let loose all day. . . ."

"The sulphur workers?"

"Yes, Sir: hewers, carriers, burners, carters,
weighmen: all of them! They even cut the tele-
graph wire. I'm told they attacked my son's
house, and that Aurelio stood up to them, as best
he could. . . ."

Flaminio Salvo, at this point, turned and looked
narrowly into the eyes of Dianella, who had come
out to the carriage. This strange glance, directed
at the girl in the middle of their conversation, disturbed Costa, who turned likewise to look at the
"Signorinella," as he called her. Her pallor
changed to a crimson flush, then at once returned.

"Well?" shouted Flaminio Salvo angrily

"Yes, Sir," Costa went on, disconcerted. "The
worst of it is, we've no troops handy; the whole
village is in their hands. Only a couple of carabinieri, the serjeant and corporal. . . . What can
they do?"

"And what can I do from here, will you tell me
that?" Salvo cried in a fury of rage. "Your son
Aurelio, what is he? The Managing Engineer,
from the *École des Mines* in Paris, what is he?

A puppet? Does he need me to pull the string from here, to make him act?"

"Oh no, Sir," said Leonardo Costa, drawing back a pace, as though Salvo had lashed him across the face. "Your Honour may rest assured that my son Aurelio knows what to do. A strong head and a stout heart . . . it's not for me to say . . . but face to face with two thousand men, what with sulphur workers and carters, Your Honour will agree. . . . Besides, the real trouble is something else, outside the village. Aurelio sent word to me last night that they had waylaid on the road the eight carts of coal that were going to the pits on Monte Diesi."

"Indeed?" Salvo sneered.

"Your Honour knows," Costa went on, "that up there coal is as necessary to the pumps as bread to a starving man, and more. Your Honour is going to Girgenti? Do go at once to the Prefect and get him to send troops to Aragona station, as many as he can, to provide an escort for the coal to the pits. There are seven truckloads there to replenish the store at the pit; the carters are on strike too; but the coal can be loaded on mules and donkeys, with an armed escort: it will take us longer, but at least we can avoid any danger of the great pit, the Cace (Heaven forbid!), flooding. . . ."

"Let it flood! Let it flood!" Flaminio Salvo broke out, furious, throwing his arms in the air.

"Let the whole show go to blazes! I don't give
a damn for it! I shall close down, d'you hear?
And send you all packing, you, your son, all of
you, from top to bottom, all of you! A clean
sweep! Drive on!" he told the coachman.

The carriage started, and Flaminio drove off
without so much as turning to bid his daughter
good-bye.

This extraordinary outburst had brought Don
Cosmo to one of the windows, while Donna Sara
Alàimo had appeared at the head of the steps.
Both of them, as well as Dianella and Costa below, stood rooted to the ground. Finally Costa
stirred himself, raised his head in the direction
of the window and gave a bitter greeting:

"I kiss your hands, Si-don Cosmo! He's quite
right: he's the master! But, by Our Lord on the
Cross, believe me, Si-don Cosmo dear, believe me,
Signorinella: they're not to blame! They really
are starving; the distress is terrible!"

Donna Sara from the stairhead shook her bonneted head, her eyes raised to heaven.

"The Government takes its share," Costa continued, "and the Province takes its share; the
Comune takes its share, and the chairman and the
vice-chairman and the manager and the engineer
and the foreman. . . . What can there be left over
for the men who work underground and under
everybody, and have to carry all the rest on their
backs and are crushed down? Oh Lord! I am

only a poor wretch, an ignorant clown is all I am, well and good: let him trample me underfoot if he likes! But my son, Lord in heaven, no, he mustn't lay a finger on my son! We owe everything to him, it is true; but even he himself, if he is still where he is, my revered master, who can give me a slap in the face, if he likes, since I get everything from him, indeed I kiss his hands; if he is still where he is, giving orders, and enjoying his wealth and prosperity, he owes it, all the same, to my son, he does: you know that, Signorinella, and you too, perhaps, Si-don Cosmo . . . we're quits!"

"Quite so, quite so," Laurentano sighed from the window. "That business of the pumpkins . . ."

"What pumpkins?" asked Donna Sara Alàimo, her curiosity aroused.

"Mah!" said Costa. "You must get the story another time from the Signorinella here, who knows my son well, since they were brought up together, with the other boy, her little brother, whom the Lord took to Himself, which was the undoing of them all. The poor Signora, there (whom I can remember so well, such a beauty, a ray of sunshine!), went out of her mind over it; and he, poor gentleman . . . anyone with children of his own can feel for him. . . ."

Dianella, her heart wrung by her father's harshness, at this memory could contain herself no longer and, to conceal her emotion, took the path by which Costa had come and disappeared among the olives.

At once Donna Sara, and after her Don Cosmo invited Costa to come upstairs, to rest for a moment after his journey and not to expose his heated body to the morning breeze. Donna Sara would have liked to do more: to offer him a cup of coffee; but, lest she should lose a word of the voluble discourse on which Costa had at once embarked with Don Cosmo on the subject of Salvo, now that the latter's daughter was out of earshot, pretended that such an idea had not occurred to her.

"We know what we're saying, good Lord, we know what we're saying, Si-don Co'! What was he, when all's said and done? I myself, yes, have gone barefoot, and carried loads on my back, I say it and I am proud of it; on my back I've carried sulphur and coal, from the beach to the lighters. What is the Latin proverb? *Necessitas non abita legge.* Yes, Sir; and I've been a dock labourer, and I'm proud of it, a wretched weighman at the landing-stage for the customs, and I'm proud of it. But he, what was he? Of noble family, yes, Sir; but a mere broker, he was, who would come down on foot from Girgenti to Porto Empedocle, all covered in dust by the Spinasanta road, because he hadn't the money even to take a carriage or to hire a donkey, before the railway came. And his first profits, how did he come by them? God knows, and there's many a man that knows, alive and dead. Then he took on the contract for the first railways, he and his brother-in-law who lives in Rome now, the engineering gentleman, the banker, the Commendatore, Don Francesco Vella; we know him too. . . ."

"Ah," put in Donna Sara, "he has another sister then, has he?"

"And why not?" replied Costa, interrupting the series of inclinations with which he had accompanied this string of titles, "Donna Rosa, the eldest of them all, the wife of" (here he bowed again) "Commendatore Francesco Vella, a big pot in the Railway Department now. This line here, from Girgenti to Porto Empedocle, wasn't it he that built it? Nothing like making hay when the sun shines! Hundreds of thousands of lire, sister; money in hatfuls, heaped like sand on the shore. . . . Two bridges and four tunnels. . . . Round a bend there; into a cutting here. . . . Then other contracts for lines. . . . All his fortune came to him from that, am I not right, Si-don Co'? We know what we're talking about!"

"But the pumpkins? The pumpkins?" Donna Sara repeated her question.

Costa was obliged to relate to her in the minutest detail the famous story of the pumpkins; and Donna Sara rewarded him with the most vivacious exclamations of stupefaction, terror, amazement that the local dialect contained, clapping her hands at intervals, to arouse Don Cosmo, who, knowing the story already, had relapsed into his habitual philosophical lethargy. He did rouse himself at length, but without opening his eyes; thrust forward his hand, saying:

"Still . . ."

"Ah, yes!" Costa at once rejoined, with emphasis, beating his breast with both hands. "In all conscience, we have but the one soul, before God, and I must tell the truth. But my son, oh, Si-don Cosmo——" (and Costa held up his hand with the thumb and forefinger joined, as though holding a pair of scales) "every son is a son, but mine! He's perfection! Straight as a die! The top of all his classes! As soon as he had taken his degree, off he went to compete for the scholarship to study abroad. . . . There were, sister, more than four hundred young engineers from all parts of Italy: he left them all behind him, every one of them! And he stayed abroad four years, in Paris, London, Belgium, Austria. As soon as he got back to Rome, without his having to breathe a word even, the Government gave him a post in the Corps of Mining Engineers, and sent him off to Sardinia, to Iglesias, where he did a piece of work all in colours about a mountain. . . . Sarrubbas . . . I don't remember . . . oh, Sarrabus, yes, that's right, Sarrabus (they speak Turkish, in Sardinia), a piece of work, sister, that would leave you gaping open-mouthed. He didn't stay there long, not much more than a year, because a French company, one of those that . . . sacks of money . . . saw his map, and it fairly took their breath away. I'm not saying it because he's my son; but you may take all the engineers in existence, here and elsewhere, he can wipe the floor with them! However. This French company said to him, here's the key of our safe, my boy, help yourself to as much as you want. My son, while he was making up his mind whether to accept or not, came down here on a holiday—it will be six or seven months ago, now—to consult with me and the chief, his benefactor, whom he respects as his second father, and quite rightly! The chief himself advised him not to accept, because he wanted him for himself, do you understand? To look after his sulphur pits at Aragona and Comitini. Enough is as good as a feast, we say. . . . He consented, but at a sacrifice, upon my word! And after all this, now, now he's a puppet, did you hear? . . . Holy Christ!''

Leonardo Costa held up his arm, rose, heaved a nasal sigh, shaking his head, and took up his white hat from the seat. He ought to have left at once, but whenever he began talking about that son of his, the glory, the golden pillar of his house, he could never leave off.

''I kiss your hands, Si-don Cosmo, let me be going. Donna Sara, your most humble servant.''

"Oh, but wait!" that lady exclaimed, pretending to have just thought of it, now that the conversation was at an end. "A drop of coffee . . ."

"No, no thank you," Costa fenced. "I'm in a great hurry!"

"Five minutes!" said Donna Sara, lifting her hands as though to imply: "The world won't come to an end!"

And she turned to go. But Costa, sitting down again, sighed, turning to Don Cosmo:

"There's a wicked woman, Si-don Co', a wicked woman, who has been making mischief for some time past between my son and Don Flaminio; I know it!"

And Donna Sara was powerless to cross the threshold: she turned back, screwed up her eyes, wrinkled her nose and asked with a little twitch of her head: "Who is she?"

"Don't tempt me to speak evil, Donna Sara dear!" groaned Costa. "I've said too much already!"

Donna Sara, however, had already guessed who the wicked woman was to whom he referred, and went indoors, exclaiming with upraised hands:

"What a world! Oh, what a world!"

Like a rivulet.

Dianella was in no hurry that morning to join Mauro in the vineyard. That sharp, hard glance with which her father, in his anger, had suddenly turned upon her, while Costa was speaking of the danger that threatened his son at Aragona, had disturbed her profoundly; it had recalled to her memory in a flash a similar look which he had given her many years before, when her little brother had died and her mother had gone mad.

She had been eleven years old at the time.

And, more than her brother's death, more than her mother's terrible affliction, there had remained indelibly fixed in her mind the impression of that glare of hatred cast at her—a little girl still almost unconscious, uncertain, bewildered between play and mourning—by her father in the frenzy of his grief.

"Couldn't you have died instead?" had been its unmistakable message.

Quite so. Precisely so. And Dianella understood perfectly now why her father would not have hesitated for a moment to sacrifice her life in exchange for her brother's.

All the care and affection and caresses and presents which he had since then lavished upon her had been powerless to thaw the lump of ice into which that glance had frozen in her innermost consciousness. Often she felt ashamed of herself, conscious that the warmth of his paternal affection could no longer succeed in penetrating her heart, but was instinctively repulsed by that hard, frozen core.

On what principle did he still go on working
with such desperate energy? Piling up that vast
fortune? Not for her benefit, certainly; was it
from a spontaneous, overpowering necessity of his
own nature; to acquire mastery over everyone
else; to be feared and respected; or perhaps also
to blunt the sharp edge of his sufferings in business or to take his revenge in his own way upon
the fate that had struck him such a blow? But
in certain moments of anger (as just now), or of
weariness and loss of confidence, he let it be seen
quite plainly that all his undertakings and his
efforts and life itself had no longer any purpose
for him, now that he had lost the heir to his name,
him who was to have carried on the tradition of
his power and fortune.

For some time past, convinced of this, Dianella,
albeit incapable of even imagining her own life
stripped of all the luxury by which she was surrounded, had begun to feel a secret contempt for
her father's riches, to which one day (might that
day be far distant!) she would be left the sole
heir, of necessity and without any satisfaction to
herself. How often, seeing him tired or angry,
had she not felt inclined to say to him: "Stop!
Give it up! Why do you go on increasing it, if
this is to be the end of it all?" And something
more than this, something very different would
she have liked to say to him, had she been able
to converse with her father heart to heart, with-

out words, that is to say without moving her lips
or hearing with her ears.

From what she had been able to gather by her
superfine intuition and to penetrate with those
silently watchful eyes, and from certain utterances
which she could not help overhearing, she was
already aware that her father's riches, if not
altogether evilly acquired, had nevertheless made
many victims in the neighbourhood. Cruel had
fate been to him, cruel was the revenge that he
took upon fate. He wanted everything for himself; to feel everything in his own grasp: sulphur
pits and land and factories, the commerce and industry of the entire Province. Why? Why, if he
went on working without any love left, almost
without any object left to work for? Why heap
upon her frail shoulders—his daughter's . . . a
loved, yes, but not a cherished daughter, for all
that she was now his only child—a crushing burden, all those riches, which many people were perhaps cursing secretly and which certainly would
not bring her any happiness?

Dismay and anger too, at times, Dianella felt at
the thought, foreseeing all too plainly that her
heart might well remain crushed beneath that
mountain of gold.

And yet she had nourished the illusion, until
quite recently, that her father would leave her
free to choose; that indeed he had himself helped

her in her choice, by his benefaction to the man
who as a boy had saved his life.

Nimble and bold, dark-skinned, like a figure
cast in bronze, with black curling hair and eyes
that darted fire, Aurelio Costa had seemed to her
when she first saw him, as a boy of thirteen; and
for years after that he had been her playmate,
hers and her brother's. They were not conscious
then of the gulf that lay between them. But afterwards, by degrees, Aurelio had become steadily
more timid and circumspect. She had been barely
twelve when he, at eighteen, had gone away to
matriculate at the University of Palermo in the
Faculty of Engineering; and she had wept floods
of tears—still like an unconscious little girl—at
their parting. What a joyful occasion had been
his return, at the end of his first year! So
hilarious, so full of jubilation had those holidays
been that her father, as soon as Aurelio had left,
had taken her aside and quietly, in the politest
language, stroking her hair, had given her to
understand that she would have done better to
restrain herself, seeing that Costa was now a young
man, and it was not proper therefore to address
him any longer as *tu*. She—without at the time
understanding why—had felt her cheeks flame.
Good heavens, what next, then? Call him *Lei?*
Was he not still the same Aurelio? No, he was
no longer the same, not even to her; and she had

been made well aware of this the year after, when he returned again; and increasingly so after his third, and fourth, and fifth years at the University, when finally he returned with a splendid degree and with the intention of winning that scholarship for study abroad. He, yes, it was he who was no longer the same; for she, on the other hand . . . with her lips, yes, "Signor Aurelio," but with her eyes she still continued to address him as *tu*. Before leaving the Island, he had come to thank his benefactor, to swear him undying gratitude; and to her he had scarcely known what to say, had scarcely ventured to look at her, and certainly, certainly had not noticed how pale her cheeks were nor how her hand trembled.

After his departure, she had many times heard her father speak of the really exceptional worth of this young man and of the splendid future that was in store for him, and extol himself for all that he had done for him, for having treated him as a son. Naturally these speeches had given ever fresh fuel to the hidden fire in her heart and had strengthened the ever growing hope that her father, having lost his only son, and having virtually created this other, to whom moreover he owed his own life, would prefer that to him, rather than to some comparative stranger, his wealth and his daughter should one day pass.

She had been greatly confirmed in this hope a few months since, when Aurelio, on his return

from Sardinia, had been appointed manager of
the sulphur pits by her father.

She had not set eyes on him since his departure
for Paris. Oppressed, amid her useless luxury,
by the pettiness of life in Girgenti, an old town,
not indeed boorish but weary, listless in the uni-
formity of its long silent days; each day occupied
by the same round of visits from the three or
four families of her acquaintance, who vied with
one another in shewing their affection for and
trust in herself, who was like a little queen of the
place, amid the invariable witticisms of the invariable young bloods, enervated, turned silly
by their narrow and impoverished provincial
life; she had felt herself quicken at the sight of
him, so manly a creature, his own master henceforward, free to tread the path he had conquered
by his strength, tenacity and hard work.

Her joy at seeing him again was however suddenly clouded. There happened to be calling upon
her that day Nicoletta Spoto, who for the last
year or so had been married to Capolino. She
had noticed a curious embarrassment, a keen
emotion, both in her guest and in Aurelio when
the latter, on being shewn into the drawing-room,
had bowed in greeting. Then, as soon as her
father had carried Aurelio off to his study,
Signora Capolino, breathing again, had related
with fiery vivacity to her and to her aunt Adelaide
how that poor fellow, without a penny to his name,

had nevertheless dared to ask for her hand in
marriage, immediately upon obtaining his post as
a government engineer in Sardinia, remembering
perhaps a few innocent glances that had been exchanged between them years and years earlier,
when he was still a young student at the Institute.
They could imagine the horror that she, Lellè
Spoto, had felt at such a request, and how she had
hastened to decline it, especially as the preliminary arrangements were already under way for
her marriage to Ignazio Capolino.

Dianella had felt her heart sink in her bosom
at these sudden, unexpected tidings; she had certainly turned all the colours of the rainbow and
certainly she had betrayed herself to the other
woman, of whose secret and illicit relations with
her father she was already aware. She had not
said anything to her, but when Aurelio, after his
long interview with her father, had returned to
the drawing-room, she, quivering with excitement,
had greeted him with an exaggerated welcome, re-
minding him of the times they had spent together,
their games, their mutual confidences. And more
than once she had rejoiced to see the other bite
her lip and turn pale.

Dianella hoped that Aurelio, on that occasion at
least, had understood. She had at once forgiven
him in her heart for a betrayal of which he could
not have been conscious at the time: yes, he could
have had no thought of her, must have supposed

that he could not dare to raise his eyes to her
level; but . . . at the same time, ah! was it really
to that other woman, a woman in every respect
unworthy of him, that his thoughts had turned?
And the other woman's refusal of him had seemed
to her almost an insult directed at herself. Still,
after all, he had been in Paris; the vivacity, the
capricious frivolity of Nicoletta Spoto might
therefore prove a great attraction in his eyes, re-
minding him probably of some other woman that
he had known there. Being himself of the humblest origin, he had imagined perhaps that he
would be making a great stride, were he to ally
himself with a family like the Spoto, extremely
wealthy at one time, now impoverished, but still
one of the leading families in the place.

And now, it was obvious, the lady in question,
taking advantage of the power she had acquired
over the father, was avenging herself for the
affront she had received on that occasion. Dianella herself had noticed that for some time past
her father no longer seemed satisfied with Aurelio
Costa; and that for the last few evenings there,
in the villa, in conversation with Don Cosmo
Laurentano, he had laid stress upon certain de-
mands which gave her food for thought.

She disapproved privately of this strange marriage between her aunt and the Prince Don Ippolito, she was almost ashamed of it, suspecting
her father of a hidden motive; namely, that he

wished to make use of this marriage, which was
certainly not honourable, to force his way into the
Laurentano family and gradually absorb their
fortune also. For the last few evenings, at supper, his conversation with Don Cosmo had dwelt,
insistently, upon the Prince's son, Lando Laurentano, who was living in Rome. Why?

Absorbed in these reflections, Dianella had sat
down under an olive on the brink of the deep ravine, and was gazing at the steep bank on the other
side, on which a herd of goats were grazing that
had come down from the estate of Platanìa.

The day after her arrival in the country, she
had felt a new life suddenly spring up within her.
The air of wild rusticity which the old villa had
asumed in its neglected state; the profound melancholy which that neglect seemed to have diffused
all around, over the avenues and the solitary
paths, almost hidden in moss and rockrose, where
the air—cool in the shade of the olives and almond
trees or of the tall hedges of prickly pear—was
steeped in fragrance, the bitter fragrance of sloes,
the strong and pungent fragrance of mint and
sage; and that wide precipitous ravine; and the
bright and blithe proximity of the sea; and those
old trees, untended, shaggy with random shoots,
dreaming in the stillness of the vast solitude, were
in pleasant harmony with the state of mind in
which she found herself.

Now, however, those remarks by her father

. . . his anger with Aurelio . . . and this strike
of sulphur workers at Aragona . . . the threats.
. . . And she, alone there, with literally no one to
whom she might pour out her heart! To have a
mother and not to be able to turn to her, and to
see her mother before her eyes, worse than dead
—alive and lifeless. . . .

There wandered for some way, among the occasional clumps of reeds in the bottom of the ravine,
a rivulet which at a certain point in its course
had been dammed in the construction of the railway. She fixed her gaze on it, and immediately it
occurred to her that she herself had been left precisely in the condition of that rivulet, like a rivulet
whose course some unknown hand by a mischiev-
ous caprice had blocked, near its source, with huge
and heavy stones; on one side the water had
spread out in a stagnant pool, and on the other
the stream had filtered underground among sand
and pebbles. Oh, what an unquenchable thirst remained in her for a mother's love! But she flew
to her mother, and that mother did not recognize
her as her own daughter. A daughter's grief so
close and urgent aroused no response whatever in
that spent consciousness.

"Vittoria Vivona of Alessandria della Rocca,"
her mother would say of herself in a voice that
seemed to come from far away. "A beautiful
girl! A beautiful girl! She had hair that reached
to the ground; it took three women to brush

it. . . . She sang and played. She played the organ, too, in church, at Santa Maria dell' Udienza, and the little angels gathered round to hear her, on their knees with their hands clasped, so. . . . She was to have married a rich man in Girgenti; but she took a headache, and died. . . ."

Dianella could no longer restrain her tears, and began to weep silently, with a bitter delight in her solitude. But the silence round about her was so complete, so intense and immemorial the day-dream of the earth and of everything upon it, that suddenly she felt herself somehow absorbed in it, fascinated by it. Burdened with an infinite, resigned sadness seemed to her now those trees, absorbed in their perennial dream, from which the wind sought in vain to arouse them. She perceived, in that mysterious, disturbing intimacy with unpeopled nature, the slightest movements, the faintest sounds, the vague rustle of the leaves, the hum of insects; and ceased to feel that she was living only for herself; she lived for an instant, unconscious and yet alertly wondering, with the earth, as though her soul had been diffused among and confused with all these country things. Ah, what a freshness of childhood in the grass that grew round about her! And how rose-pink her hand looked against the tender green of those leaves! Oh, look, a ladybird, a stray venturer, out of its season, running over her hand. . . . How pretty it was! It glistened like a little

jewel! Could the earth then, among all the sad
and ugly things it bore, produce things so pretty
and charming also?

It ran, as though in answer to her question,
across the leaves, across her hand, light and cool
as the breath of joy. Dianella sighed and waited
with her hand on the grass for the insect to find
its way back among the leaves, then drew back
with a start at the joyous, unexpected arrival of
the three mastiffs, which gathered round her, or
rather sprang upon her, impatient, thrusting one
another aside, eager to feel her hand caressing
their heads. And they would not allow her to
rise. Finally Mauro Mortara overtook them.

"Have you been feeling unwell?" he inquired,
grimly, without looking at her.

"No . . . it's nothing . . ." she replied, shield-
ing herself with her arms from the paws and
tongues of the dogs, and smiling sadly. "A little
tired. . . ."

"Here!" Mauro shouted to the three mastiffs
to leave her in peace.

And immediately they became still, as though
turned to stone by his shout. Dianella rose to her
feet and stooped to stroke their heads once more,
as an apology for the disturbance.

"Poor things . . . poor things . . ."

"If you wish to come . . ." Mauro suggested.

"I'm ready. To see the General's room. I'm
so curious. . . ."

She was embarrassed when speaking to him by the uncertainty whether to address him as *voi* or *tu*.

"Has your father gone?"

"Yes, yes," she made haste to assure him; and at once repented of her haste, which might betray the same sense of relief in herself that everyone else felt in her father's absence. "At Aragona," she said, "the sulphur workers have mutinied. We shall have to get soldiers and carabinieri sent there."

"Powder and shot!" Mauro at once expressed his approval, nodding his head vigorously. "I swear to you, old as I am, I'd enroll as a constable!"

"Perhaps . . ." Dianella attempted to put in.

But Mortara cut her short with one of his favourite ejaculations: *"Oh Marasantissima, lasciatevi servire!"*

He would not allow any argument, this Mauro Mortara. In his perpetual meditative wanderings through his rustic solitude, he had systematized his world for himself after his own fashion, and walked in that world, confident, like a god, stroking his long white beard, his eyes beaming at the satisfactory explanations which he had managed to find for everything. Everything that occurred to him must comply with the rules of this world of his. If anything refused to comply, he would cut it out, ruthlessly, or pretend not to notice it. Woe to any who contradicted him!

"*Oh Marasantissima, lasciatevi servire!* What do they want? I should like to know what they want! Do they reason or do they not? The Government, what is it? The Government is the Government. And we ought all to obey, from the highest to the lowest, all of us, each in his own station, and think of the community! Why should these gaolbirds, wretched ungrateful dogs that they are, come and spoil for us old men the satisfaction of seeing that community, Italy, changed by our efforts to a Power of the first rank? They find the table spread, the soup ladled out for them, and they spit in it, do you hear? But if everyone was to think only of himself, how could the ship keep afloat? Can't a man rise or fall, in these days, by his own deserts? What have you deserved? Bread and onions? Live on bread and onions! I can tell you that a man can be quite happy, living on bread and onions, I have lived on them myself. But if you honestly deserve something more, go ahead, prove your merit, you will advance! No, my friends, no. . . . The ass says to-day to his master: 'Down on all fours; I'm going to ride now. . . .' And all the time, look: Tunis is over there!"

He turned towards the sea and with outstretched arm pointed, frowning, to a spot on the far horizon. Dianella turned to look, without understanding what Tunis had to do with it. She let him talk and did not once interrupt, except to shew her approval of all these patriotic utterances.

"Over there!" Mauro repeated angrily. "And the French are there, who stole it from us by fraud! And to-morrow we may have them here on our own soil, do you understand? I swear to you, there are times when I lie awake all night, biting my hands with rage! And instead of keeping that in mind, those scoundrels there take it into their heads to strike, to squabble among themselves! It's all the priests' doing, you know. Double-dyed rascals! Scum of all the vices! Sinks of iniquity! Quietly fanning the flames, so as to dismember Italy once again. . . . The Sanfedisti! The Sanfedisti! I have to keep eyes at the back of my head, because they have sworn to destroy me, and watch every step I take. But they've found their match in me. . . . Look here!"

And he shewed Dianella the brace of Neapolitan pistols that hung from his belt.

In the shrine.

This visit to the famous "General's room," known simply as the *Camerone,* was indeed a special favour conferred upon Dianella Salvo. Mauro Mortara, who kept the key of this room, never allowed anyone to enter it. And not the door only, but the shutters of the two balconies and of the other window were kept permanently closed, as though the light and air, given free access, might put to flight the memories gathered and hoarded there with such jealous veneration.

Certainly, after the old Prince's departure into exile, door and windows had been flung open time and again; but Mortara, since his return to Valsanìa, had kept the shutters at least permanently closed, and was under the illusion that they had been like that always, and that those walls therefore still enclosed the very breath of the General, the atmosphere of those bygone days.

This illusion was strengthened by the sight of the furniture, which had been left untouched, except for the canopied brass bed which had been stripped of its mattress, boards and heavy curtains.

This half-light was admirably suited for the awakening of distant memories!

Mauro invariably began by making a short tour of the room; stopped in front of some decrepit piece of furniture, on which the veneering had warped and split in places; then went and sat down on the sofa covered with a green stuff, now yellow with age, with a cylindrical bolster in the angle of each end, and there, with half-shut eyes, stroking his long white beard with his stunted, muscular little hand, he would give rein to his thoughts, or more often his memories, dis-

tracted, absorbed, like a praying worshipper in
church.

He was not disturbed even by the rats which at
times created an infernal din on the terrace above,
the floor of which, to prevent the ceiling of the
camerone from collapsing, had had to be covered
with sheets of metal. This remedy had availed
but little and not for long; the strips of metal had
gaped and shrunk in the sun, to the great delight
of the rats who had come scampering back, and
concealed themselves underneath; and the ceiling
had already begun to bulge, and dripped in winter
from two or three cracks, while the walls even in
summer retained two large patches of damp en-
crusted with mould.

Don Cosmo did not trouble about it: he scarcely
ever set foot in the camerone; Mauro did not wish
it to be restored: he had but a short time to live
and was determined that everything should remain as it was; he knew that, after his death, no
one would take the trouble to look after this
"Shrine of Liberty"; and the ceiling might then
come down altogether or be repaired. Every year,
in the meantime, as autumn drew round, he would
go up to the terrace and would join together and
fasten down the strips of metal with big stones,
and on the floor of the camerone place buckets
and basins to catch the drip. The drops fell clang-
ing into them, one by one; and by their rhythmical
cadence seemed to assent to being thus collected.

Dianella, as she entered the room, received a sudden shock at the unexpected sight of a stuffed animal which, in the dim light, seemed to be alive there against the opposite wall, in the corner, with lowered tail and head turned to one side, cat-like.

"What a fright it gave me!" she exclaimed with a nervous laugh, covering her face with her hands. "I never expected such a thing. . . . What is it?"

"A leopard," said Mauro.

"What a beauty!"

And Dianella put out her hand to stroke the dappled skin; but at once drew it back covered in dust, and noticed that the animal had lost one of its glass eyes, the left.

"I presented another one, the companion to this," Mauro went on, "to the Institute Museum, at Girgenti. Haven't you ever seen it? There's a case of my stuff in the Museum. Next to the leopard, there's a hyaena, a great big one, and above them an imperial eagle. On the case is a label: *Shot, stuffed and presented by Mauro Mortara.* Yes, indeed. But come over here, first. I want you to look at something else."

He led her across to the broken-down old sofa.

Hanging upon the wall behind it were four medals, two of silver, the others of bronze, pinned to a frayed and faded velvet shield. Over the shield was a framed letter, written in a minute hand upon a sheet of paper that had once been blue.

"Ah, the medals!" Dianella exclaimed.

"No," said Mauro, with emotion, shutting his eyes. "The letter. Read the letter."

Dianella went nearer to the sofa and read the signature first: "Gerlando Laurentano."

"The General?"

Mauro, his eyes still shut, nodded gravely in assent.

And Dianella read:

> Burmula, December 22, 1852.
>
> My friends,
>
> The news from France of Louis Napoleon's *Coup d'État* must certainly present a long and serious hindrance to the movement in support of our sacred cause, and postpone for an indefinite period our return to Sicily.
>
> At my age, I cannot any longer endure the burden of this life of exile.
>
> I feel that I shall no longer be fit to lend my right arm to the Country when she, in the fulness of time, shall have need of it. All the less reason, therefore, to drag out any longer an existence that is painful to myself and harmful to my children.
>
> You, who are younger than I, have still such a reason; go on living, therefore, for the country and think sometimes with affection of
>
> > Yours,
> >
> > GERLANDO LAURENTANO.

Dianella turned to look at Mortaro who, withdrawn into himself, his eyes now wide open and staring, his features contracted and his hand covering his mouth, was endeavouring to stifle the sobs that broke from him in the tangle of his beard.

"It's years since I last read it," he murmured when he was able to speak.

He stood for a long time nodding his head, then went on:

"He played me false that time. He wrote the letter and dressed himself up in his best, as if he was going to a ball. I was in the kitchen; he called me. 'Take this letter to Mariano Gioeni, at La Valletta.' The other Sicilian exiles were at La Valletta, who had all been together here, in this room, before Forty-Eight, at the time of the conspiracy. I can see them now: Don Giovanni Ricci-Gramitto, the poet, Don Mariano Gioeni and his brother Don Francesco, Don Francesco De Luca, Don Gerlando Bianchini, Don Vincenzo Barresi: all here; and myself down below, keeping guard. However! I took the letter. . . . How should I know what was in it? When I got back to Burmula, I found him dead."

"Had he killed himself?" Dianella asked in alarm.

"With poison," Mauro answered. "He hadn't had time even to draw his other leg up on the bed. What a handsome man he was! You've seen Don Ippolito? He was handsomer. Yes, taller, straight upright, with a pair of eyes that flashed fire: a Saint George! Even when he was an old man, the women would all fall in love with him."

He shut his eyes again and in a low tone repeated the closing words of the letter, which he knew by heart:

"You, who are younger than I, have still such a reason; go on living, therefore, for the country and think sometimes with affection of yours, Gerlando Laurentano. You see? And I did go on living; as he wished. And here, under the letter, which I made Don Mariano Gioeni give me back, I decided to hang up my medals, by way of an answer. But I had to win them first! Sit down, sit down here; you mustn't tire yourself. . . ."

Dianella sat down on the old sofa. At that moment, Donna Sara Alàimo, hearing the sound of voices in the camerone and seeing the unusual spectacle of the door standing ajar, thrust in her bonneted head to inspect.

"What do you want here?" Mauro Mortara sprang upon her as the leopard, had it been alive, might have sprung. "This is no place for you!"

"Pooh!" said Donna Sara, quickly withdrawing her head. "Who spoke to you, pray?"

Mauro hastily barred the door.

"I could throttle that woman! I can't abide her, I can't endure the sight of her, that old spy of the priests! So she dares to poke her nose in here now, does she? She never did that before.

It's the priests that are keeping her here, you know? Taking advantage of Don Cosmo's silliness. The Sanfedisti, the Sanfedisti . . ."

"But do they really exist still, these Sanfedisti?" Dianella inquired with a kindly smile.

"*Oh Marasantissima, lasciatevi servire!*" Mortara once more exclaimed. "Do they exist? They may perhaps call themselves by some other name now; but they are still the same. An infernal sect, scattered all over the world! They have spies everywhere: I came upon one in Turkey, even, just fancy! At Constantinople."

"Have you travelled as far as that?" asked Dianella.

"As far as that? A great deal farther!" Mauro replied with a smile of satisfaction. "Where have I not been and what have I not done? Let us count up; but ten fingers aren't enough: herd boy, farm labourer, servant, ship's boy, dock labourer, able seaman, stoker, cook, bathing attendant, big game hunter, then one of Garibaldi's volunteers, orderly to Bixio; then, after the Revolution, head jailer: three hundred prisoners I had on my hands at Santo Vito, when they tried to escape; and here I am ending up as a peasant again. The story of my life? It wouldn't be believed, if anybody tried to tell it."

He stroked his beard for a while in silence, while his green eyes glowed again, at the thrill of his memories.

"Cut down the trunk of a tree," he said, "and cast it into the sea, far out from the shore. Where will it drift to? I was like a tree-trunk, born and bred up here, at Valsanìa. The storm came and uprooted me. First the General went with his comrades; I went off two days later, by night, in a sailing ship, as the way was then; a big boat of the kind they call tartans. I can laugh at it now. If you knew how frightened I was, though, that night, on the sea!"

"The first time?"

"Who had ever done such a thing before? Black, pitch black, sky and sea. Only the spread sail showed a glimmer of white. The stars, thousands of stars, high up above, looked like dust. The sea was dashing and breaking against the tartan's sides, and the mast rocked. Then the moon came out, and the brute grew calm. The crew were smoking their pipes and chatting together in the bows; I, down in the hold, among the bales and coils of tarred rope, could see the light of their pipes; I was crying, with my eyes wide open, and never noticed it. The tears fell on my hands. I was like a child of five; and I was three and thirty! Good-bye, Sicily; good-bye, Valsanìa; Girgenti, that you see from far out, standing up on the hill; good-bye, bells of San Gerlando, whose hum used to reach me in the silence of the fields; good-bye, trees that I knew every one apart. . . . You can't imagine how, when you are far out at

sea, all the precious things that you are leaving
behind come back to you, and take hold of you
and tear your heart! I could see certain spots
here, at Valsanìa, just as if I had been there;
better, in fact; I noticed certain things that I had
never noticed before; how the blades of grass
quivered in the north-easterly breeze, a stone that
had dropped from the wall, a tree that had begun
to lean over a bit, and could be put straight, I
could count every leaf upon it. . . . However! At
daybreak, I reached Malta. First of all you touch
the island of Gozzo. . . . Malta, you must understand, takes in the sea, like a big bay. Every
here and there is an inlet. On one of these is
Burmula, where the General had taken a room.
Great big harbours, forests of masts; and people
of every race and nation: Arabs, Turks, Bedouins,
Moroccans; besides English, French, Spaniards.
A hundred tongues spoken. In Sixty there was
an outbreak of cholera, brought by the Jews from
Susa, who had fine women with them, oh, beauties!
but, do you know, young girls of sixteen or
eighteen like yourself. . . ."

"Oh, I am older than that," said Dianella.

"Older? You don't look it. They painted their
faces. With no need," Mauro went on, "just like
old women. A pity! Fine girls! They brought
the cholera, I was saying: a terrible epidemic!
Just imagine that at Burmula, a small village, in
one day, there were eight hundred deaths. They

were dying like flies. But when a man is down, death has no terror for him. I used to eat egg-fruit and tomatoes, like anything: I did it on purpose. I had learned a Maltese song and used to sing it night and day, sitting astride a window-sill. For I was in love. . . ."

"Indeed? Out there?" Dianella asked, in surprise.

"Not there," replied Mauro. "I had left a peasant girl here, at Valsanìa, whom I used to court: Serafina. . . . She married another man, barely a year after. And I used to sing. . . . Would you like to hear the song? I remember it still."

He shut his eyes, threw back his head and began to hum in falsetto, pronouncing the words of the popular ditty after his own fashion:

Ahi me kalbi, kentu giœni . . .

Dianella gazed at him in wonder, with a feeling of emotion, of bitter sweetness, which was diffused also by the plaintive rhythm of that air drawn from a far off time and place, which awakened on the old man's lips a faint echo of his adventurous youth. She had never for an instant suspected beneath the rough and hairy rind of Mortara any such store of tender memories.

"How pretty it is!" she said. "Sing it again!"

Mauro, deeply moved, shook his finger in refusal.

"I can't; I have no voice. . . . Do you know
what the first words mean? *Ah me, my heart, how
it aches.* I don't remember what the rest means.
The General was so fond of that song. He was
always making me sing it. Eh, I had a good voice,
then. . . . Are you looking at the leopard? Now
I'll tell you about that."

And he went on to tell her how, after the General's death, left alone at Burmula, and not wishing to return to Sicily, where he had already come
under suspicion, he had gone to La Valletta.
There, the Sicilian exiles had wished to help him;
but he, knowing in what a wretched plight they
themselves were, had refused all offers of help
and had taken up work in the harbour, as a ship's
boy, a dock labourer, an able seaman. They were
short of hands, the population having been deci-
mated by the cholera. Then he had embarked on
a British vessel as a stoker. For more than six
months he had been buried alive there, in the
massive, roaring belly of the ship, roasting himself at the fire that had to be fed day and night,
without ever knowing whither she was bound.
The English engineers would look at him and
laugh—why, he could not imagine—and one day
they had taken him by force and presented him,
all grimy and tattered as he was, to the captain—
a little red-faced man with a big brown beard
almost down to his knees—and the captain had
slapped him on the back several times, praising

him perhaps for his zeal. And indeed, throughout all those months, he had never given himself a moment's rest, not even to snatch a mouthful of food; he had lost his appetite: all he could do was to drink, to cool the burning heat of his body which, down below there, was tortured for want of air! His only amusement, when the ship lay in some harbour, was an old cookery book, all dog's-eared, from which he had learned to spell out the alphabet with the help of the ship's cook, also an Italian, who had long ago emigrated to Malta.

An amusement and a godsend to him, that book! Because, one day, the cook, having fallen seriously ill, had to be put ashore at Smyrna, and, failing anyone else, he, the inheritor of the book and of its culinary lore, had been put to the test of that other fire. He had flung himself with all his energy into this new calling and in a short time had managed to give the captain such satisfaction that he, seeing his new cook about to fall ill like the other, had of his own accord found him a place in the kitchen of an English family, of great wealth, who lived in Constantinople.

But the illness he had contracted on board ship had not allowed him to remain for long in this post, owing to an unfortunate accident that befell him one day. A chemist from Alcamo, established for many years there, in Constantinople, to whom he would repair now and again to hear the

sound of his native dialect, had tried to poison
him. Yes! Instead of a dose of the oil of sweet
almonds, he had given him apparently oil of bitter
almonds. Was he a spy of the priests, of the Sanfedisti, too? An unintentional error? The idea!
He could well remember how one day the man had
dared to rebuke him sharply over the affair of the
hanged Franciscan, which he had told him, simply
as a joke. Ah, but having recovered by a miracle,
after about three months, from his poisoning, he
had made the fellow pay dearly for his crime.
With his fist (here Mauro showed his fist with a
smile) he had laid him out on the floor of his shop.
He had a huge iron ring on his finger, like a
twisted nail, which he had bought at Smyrna, and
with this—without meaning to, of course!—he had
fractured the man's skull.

After the first alarming shock of seeing the man
fall to the ground in a heap, before his eyes,
streaming with blood, he had taken to his heels
and a few hours later had set sail on board a vessel bound for a small port in Asia Minor. He
could not remember the name of the little seaside
town in which he had landed: it was summer and
he had at once found employment as a bathing attendant.

"Have you ever heard of Orazio Antinori?"
Mortara inquired at this stage.

"The explorer? Yes," said Dianella.

"He came there, one day, to bathe," Mauro

went on, "with another Italian. I heard them
talking, and went up to them. Antinori was engaging people to go out shooting big game in the
Libyan desert. He liked the look of me, and took
me on. We went out there; we sent him the beasts
we shot; he stuffed them and then sent them off
to the museums, London, Vienna. . . . When I
came back from the expedition, as he had taken a
fancy to me, knowing I could be trusted, I helped
him to prepare his materials, and while I was
doing so, quietly picked up his secrets. So I
learned how to stuff animals; and when he left,
I went on shooting game and sending home specimens on my own account. Let me tell you about
one adventure we had. One day, we had lost our
way, he and I, and were half dead with hunger and
thirst. Suddenly we caught sight of some fig-trees
and made a dash for them, as you can imagine.
But the best figs were high up and we couldn't
reach them. Then I, the peasant, what did I do?
I went off and came back in a minute with a reed,
a fine long one; I split it a little way at one end
and set to work to gather the ripest figs from the
top, oozing tears of milk: they were like honey, I
can tell you! Antinori stood watching me and
gnashing his teeth with rage. At length he could
stand it no longer and shouted: 'What are you
doing? Stop, will you? Are you going to leave
me to be killed by the Turks?' I knew the answer
to that. Without saying a word, I put out my arm

and handed him the reed. I went off and got
another, and we went on calmly stealing figs. Ah,
Antinori . . . he liked me, and helped me a lot,
even after he had gone away. I stayed there
more than six years. Then I heard that Garibaldi
had landed at Marsala; I flew back at once to
Sicily. I landed at Messina; I joined the volunteers at Milazzo. Don Stefano Auriti died in my
arms. He couldn't speak, he gave me a look begging me to take care of his son, Don Roberto, his
twelve year old lion cub. . . . How we fought! At
Reggio it was I that opened fire, do you know?
The first shot fired was mine! Then Bixio took
me as his orderly. . . . What a day that was, at
Volturno! But now, after all the things I have
seen and been through, I have had enough, why
not! Italy is great! Italy stands at the head of
the nations! She lays down the law to the world!
And I can say that I too, poor ignorant wretch
that I am, have done something, without making
any talk about it. I can go to the King and say
to him: 'Your Majesty, in the throne you're sitting on, if it's not a leg or a crossbar, there's a
little peg somewhere that was stuck there by me.
I've done my share for you, my lad!' And I am
content. I go about Valsanìa here, I see the tele-
graph wires, I hear the pole hum, as if there was
a nest of hornets inside it, and my chest swells;
I say: 'The fruits of the Revolution!' I go over
there, I see the railway, the train burrowing un-

derground, in the tunnel below Valsanìa, which is like a dream to me; and I say 'The fruits of the Revolution!' I go and stand under the pine, there, I look towards the sea, I see Porto Empedocle, which at the time when I left for Malta had nothing but the tower, the Rastiglio, the Old Harbour and a few hovels, and has now grown to be almost a town; I see the two long breakwaters of the new harbour, which make me think of a pair of arms stretched out to all the ships of all the civilized nations of the earth, as much as to say: 'Come! Come! Italy has risen again, Italy embraces you all, offers you all the riches of her sulphur, the riches of her gardens!' Fruit of the Revolution, this too, I think, and—would you believe it?—I burst out crying like a child, for joy. . . ."

So saying, he took from the open bosom of his coarse flannel shirt a big handkerchief of blue cotton, and wiped his eyes, which really were filled with tears.

Dianella felt her own eyes too grow moist. This old man who inspired such terror, who had killed one man, as though it were nothing, and had caused the death of another, simply out of an insane suspicion, who went about armed to the teeth, always within an inch of shedding fresh blood, quick to anger as he was and savage and proud; there he was crying like a child in front of her; he was crying from tenderness, from satisfaction at the work that had been accomplished, which he saw to be without fault and glorious; he cried, exalting himself in his deeds and in the greatness of his country, for which he had suffered so much and fought so well, without ever asking for any reward, generous and fierce, faithful as a dog and bold as a lion. Not his pigeons, nor the peace of the fields, nor the custody of his vineyard, nor the song of the larks could succeed in calming his spirit after all those years; this camerone was, so to speak, his church; and he came out of it reeling like a drunken man, and wandered up and down the solitary paths, under the almond trees and olives, talking to himself of battles and conspiracies, looking askance at the sea in the direction of Tunis, from whence he imagined a surprise attack by the French. . . .

A jingle of bells and the sound of carriage wheels came suddenly to distract Dianella from these reflexions and Mauro from his tears.

"Your father?" he asked, his face at once darkening, as he replaced his handkerchief in the bosom of his shirt.

Dianella rose in alarm, and ran to the window to look out between the slats of the shutters. She remained there. From the carriage, which had drawn up in front of the villa, there alighted her father, home again, and Aurelio Costa—he!—in his working clothes.

"Off with you, off with you," Mauro said to

her, almost thrusting her from the room. "I'll shut up and get away!"

Dianella went out into the corridor and saw at the far end of it Costa and her father, on their way to the latter's room, the door of which they shut behind them. Whereupon Mauro Mortara, like a wild animal surprised in its lair, crept stealthily away, without another word to her.

She stood there in perplexity, profoundly moved, not knowing what to make of her father's unexpected and unprecedented return. Evidently, both his return and Aurelio Costa's visit had some connection with the reports of the disturbances at Aragona. Something very serious indeed must have happened. Had Aurelio run away? No: Dianella refused even to imagine such a thing. Perhaps it was her father himself that had sent for him. With what object?

She was tempted to retire to her own room, next door to her father's, in the hope of hearing some of their conversation through the wall; but she remembered the look her father had given her, that morning, and held back; she remained, however, as though drawn in opposite directions, in the entrance hall.

"Your Papa," Donna Sara Alàimo informed her, thrusting her head out from behind the kitchen door.

Dianella nodded.

"With the engineer," Donna Sara went on, in a whisper.

Dianella again nodded to shew that she knew this already, and went out to the head of the outside stair. The carriage was still there, waiting, at the foot of the steps. So her father was starting off again immediately? Perhaps he had come back to fetch some of his papers.

"Are you going to Porto Empedocle at once?" she asked the coachman.

"Yes, Your Excellency," was his answer.

And out came her father and Costa, in evident haste. Flaminio Salvo did not expect to find his daughter at the head of the steps, and, on catching sight of her, drew back a little, without stopping, smiled at her and waved his hand in farewell. Aurelio Costa, who followed him, stopped for a moment in confusion, and was about to take off his travelling cap; but Salvo called out to him: "Come along, come along. . . ."

Dianella, pale, hardly able to breathe, saw them get into the carriage and drive off, without turning their heads, and followed them with her eyes until they disappeared among the trees of the avenue.

How Aurelio had altered! So agitated. . . . He looked ill, aged, with his unshaven chin. . . . Dianella remembered the opinion that Nicoletta Capolino had expressed of him. She would have liked to see him more independent of her father; would have liked him, notwithstanding her father's imperious summons, to stop at the head of the steps, if only to bid her good day. Instead of at once obeying the call. . . .

Perhaps the moment. . . . What could have been happening at the pit?

An ambush.

Flaminio Salvo came home late that evening, in high spirits, as he always was when he had taken an important decision.

At supper he apologized to Don Cosmo for his outburst that morning; explaining that his gorge rose at the endless worries that kept pouring upon him from those sulphur pits at Aragona, and that he had decided to close them.

"And so," he exclaimed, "those fine gentlemen can do a little striking for my amusement, and will have more time to listen to the sermons of their humanitarian priests. Let them live upon sermons! A fine thing, the humanitarian gospel, Don Cosmo, if you keep to one page! If they were to turn the page. . . . But you won't find them doing that! They are quite right; but their reason is here!"

And he tapped his stomach.

"Go and explain to them that the fiscal policy pursued by the Italian Government has been a regular gold mine to the industry and capitalists of Northern Italy, and an utter disaster to the South and to our poor Island; that for years past taxation and our other burdens have been steadily increasing and our output steadily falling; that with the price to which sulphur has now fallen not only is it absolutely impossible to treat them more generously, but it is sheer madness to carry on the industry at all. . . . I have kept the sulphur pits open for their sake, to let them have at least a crust of bread. They strike, do they? Most considerate of them! That means to say that they can get along without work. A public holiday! Cakes and ale!''

''Life!'' sighed Don Cosmo, his lips drooping. ''When you come to think it over. . . . The sulphur, of course . . . our industries . . . this tablecloth here, damask . . . this cut glass . . . the bronze lamp . . . all this nonsense on the table . . . and in the house . . . and all over the place . . . steamers on the sea, railways, balloons in the air. . . . We are mad, upon my word of honour it's mad we are. . . . Yes: they serve, they serve to fill up to a certain extent that supreme nonsense which we call life, to give it a certain form, a certain consistency. . . . Mah! I swear to you, there are moments when I don't know whether it is I that am mad, I who understand nothing about it, or the people who seriously believe that they do understand something about it, and talk and move as if they really had some definite goal in front of them, which, when they reached it, would not appear futile in their own eyes. I should begin, my dear sir, by breaking this glass. Then I should pull down the house. . . . To begin all over again, possibly! . . . You say that those poor fellows have their reason here? They are fortunate, my friend! And woe to them if they reach satiety. . . . Where do you keep your reason? Where is mine?"

And he rose from the table.

A little later, Flaminio Salvo and Dianella were standing by the window. The night was dark as pitch. The profound stars, that studded and enlarged the firmament, failed to shed any light on the earth. The grasshoppers were chiming uninterruptedly in the distance, and, now and then, from the depths of the valley rose the agonising note of an owl, like a sob. The darkness, the silence round the villa was at intervals pierced here and there and set throbbing by the swift shriek of unseen bats. Then the moon rose, fiery red, where the cloister of Monserrato loomed large against the sky, and the leaves stirred faintly over the whole countryside. A dog, far away, howled.

"Have you nothing, Dianella, nothing at all to say to your father?" Salvo asked, without looking at her, in a sorrowful tone, as though in the spirit he were straying far afield beyond the window.

"I?" said Dianella, puzzled and almost tongue-tied. "Nothing. . . . What could I have to say to you?"

"Nothing, then," her father went on. "No tiny, tiny secret . . . nothing, eh? I am glad of that. Because you, my poor child, have only me, alas, and I have so many worries. . . . And to-day . . . what a day it has been! . . . Do you know what most people lack? The sense of what is opportune. I don't mean to imply that I should have said yes, if the request had been put to me on some other day, in some other way; but I should have said no, a little more politely at least, after I had spoken to you."

Dianella was afraid, as she listened to her father's calm, slow utterance, that he might hear the violent beating of her heart, held in an agony of suspense, amid the impetuous boiling of all the blood in her veins.

"They came to me . . . you understand what I mean," Salvo went on, turning and gazing into her eyes. "And I, being certain that my good daughter, who is such a sensible girl, could never, even for a moment, have fixed her attention upon a young man—oh, a good young man, yes; but still, for all sorts of reasons, neither suitable nor worthy—I, caught at a really inopportune moment, refused, point blank. Let us think now, can't you guess?"

"No. . . ." Dianella breathed rather than uttered the word, while her bosom heaved in a welter of mingled emotions.

"You can't guess, really?" her father insisted, with a smile, as though conscious of the torture he was inflicting upon her. "Come, have a try. . . ."

"I . . . I couldn't . . ." she stammered.

"Then I shall have to tell you," her father concluded, "so that you may know where you are. De Vincentis. . . ."

"Ah!" exclaimed Dianella, with an irrepressible peal of laughter. "That poor Ninì!"

"That poor Ninì," her father echoed, shaking his head and smiling himself also. "Then you expected it?"

"No, I swear to you," Dianella hastily and emphatically replied. "I had noticed, yes. . . ."

"But you were thinking of some one else?" her father was prompt with the question, looking more sharply at her.

Dianella remained silent for a moment, meeting her father's gaze with a firm coldness.

"I have already said no."

The suspicion that her father had intended by this speech to set a trap for her had turned to certainty. Perhaps it was not even true that Ninì De Vincentis had made him this proposal. And that her father should have made use of him, a penniless youth of noble birth, only too much of a gentleman, as though to bring him into derision,

seemed hateful to her, knowing as she did that
De Vincentis was another of her father's victims.

He said nothing more; he remained for a while
at the window, looking out, then turned away with
a sigh and bade his daughter good night before
going off to bed.

"Good night," Dianella answered him, coldly.

As soon as her father had left the room, she
buried her face in her hands and cried, cried im-
petuously, silently, stifling her sobs. She felt
that her father had been amusing himself by
lacerating her heart, like a cat playing with a
mouse. Why, oh why was he so cruel, even with
his own daughter, when it would have been so easy
for him to be kind to everyone? If he really
wished her to tell him her secret, when he re-
minded her that she had no one else in whom to
confide but himself, why, at the very moment in
which he set before her the cruel fate that had
robbed her of a mother's counsel and love, did he
lay a trap for her? And so, no; it was now obvious: he did not wish her to be in love with
Aurelio. He had shut down the sulphur pits; perhaps he had put into effect his threat of that morning: "I'll send you all packing!" Aurelio too?
Oh, Aurelio could get on without him now! If
he lost that post, there were plenty more, and
better, that he would at once be able to find. And
this perhaps (why, surely), annoyed her father all
the more, namely that he should have put the

young man in a position to get on without him, and have done so because of an obligation which bound him to the young man. He wanted people to be pliable tools in his hands; instead of which, Aurelio might rise against him, where he most dreaded rebellion, in the heart of his daughter. Yes, yes, because he knew very well that she was in love with him. If Aurelio had only known it too! But what was to happen meanwhile, if her father had really shut down the pits and dismissed him? Aurelio would go away again, might return perhaps to Sardinia, without the slightest suspicion of her love for him, and there, perhaps . . .

Dianella again buried her face in her hands. In the agonizing void, fastening her attention, unconsciously, on the dense, continuous chime of the grasshoppers, it seemed to her that it, in the silence, became at every moment louder and more intense; she thought of the disturbances at Aragona and Comitini; and that fervid chorus became then to her, of a sudden, the distant, vague clamour of a populace in revolt, to whom Aurelio, turned rebel, was going, to make himself their leader and avenger. And she? and she?

She took her hands from her face: like a dream now appeared to her the desolate peace of the countryside, spread out before her in the moist pale light of the moon. And a cool, unlooked-for spring of tenderness burst from her heart; and fresh tears dimmed her eyes.

Ah, it was beautiful all the same, how beautiful, the spectacle of that profound moonlit night over the country, with those ancient trees, motionless in their sad perennial dream, raising their trunks from the earth's bosom, with those hills behind which enclosed, dark against the sky, the mystery of the most distant ages, with that tremulous limpid persistent song of the grasshoppers which, scattered among the grass of the plain, seemed to be urging forgetfulness of everything.

Between grasshoppers and trees, moon and hills, was there not perhaps a mysterious concert, from which man remained excluded?   So much beauty was not created for men, who at that hour, weary, closed their eyes in sleep; it would last all night long, unseen by any eye, in the silence of the countryside, after she too had closed her window. Perhaps this was what the invisible bat wanted, that shrieked as it flitted past outside, hurt and attracted by the light: did it want her to cease from disturbing by her vigil the nocturnal mysterious concert of solitary nature?

Dianella shut the window: she left open just a chink of one of the inside shutters, and, through this breathing space, her hands clasped before her lips, prayed in silence for all that beauty which remained outside, animated of a sudden in her

eyes by the spirit of God, Whom men offended
with their turbulent and sordid passions. Casting
a farewell glance at the avenue leading from the
villa, she observed a shadow passing along it, a
bald scalp that gleamed in the moonlight. Don
Cosmo? It was he.

Ah, immersed, out there, in the spirit of God,
he perhaps was not conscious of it! He was pac-
ing up and down the avenue, at that hour of the
night, his hands clasped behind his back, absorbed
still, she might be certain, in his own dark and
vain meditations.

CHAPTER VI

On guard

NEITHER appeals to the electors printed in letters a foot high on paper of every hue, nor any unusual animation along the tortuous streets of the old city. And yet the day fixed for the parliamentary election was close at hand.

But boredom had long since yawned in the face of charlatanry, which had lost its voice. The ladder for the assault of the walls, of the bastions, had rotted in its hands, the gluepot was broken.

Charlatanry had assumed the respectable disguise of a priest, and, collected, cautious, hypocritical, went on its way, concealing amid the folds of the priestly cloak the stick of the big drum, converted into an aspergill.

The townsfolk had no difficulty in recognizing it beneath this disguise: they let it go about as it chose; they even respected it; provided, of course, that it did not weary them with too many sermons; it lent them money, besides, on the quiet— at a high rate of interest, but still it lent it; while publicly, with a large subsidy from Salvo and others from minor investors, it had opened a Catholic People's Bank—in the approved interest of Holy Mother Church.

The public offices, the Prefecture, the Customs and Excise, the national schools, the law courts, still gave a little movement, though barely more than mechanical, to the town: the tide of life was now flowing elsewhere. The industry, the trade, all the true activity in short, had transferred itself, some time since, to Porto Empedocle, yellow with sulphur, white with lime, dusty and noisy, grown in a short time into one of the busiest and most crowded marts on the island.

But even there, the superabundance of the sulphur in the primitive conditions in which the industry was carried on, people's ignorance of the uses to which the substance was applied and of the profits that could be derived from it, the absence of capital on a large scale, the need of or greed for a quick return, all brought it about that this natural wealth of the soil, which should have meant the wealth of the inhabitants, was swallowed up day by day in the holds of the British, American, French and German trading steamers, leaving all those who lived by the industry or the trade with their backs broken by hard toil, their pockets empty and their minds poisoned by the savage and insidious warfare with which they fought for the wretched sums paid as purchase money or freight for goods which their own activity had cheapened.

At Girgenti, only the summary courts and the assize courts were really busy, open as they were all the year round. Up at the Culmo delle Forche the gaol of Santo Vito was always overflowing with prisoners, who sometimes had to wait three or four years before being tried. And it was a good thing that, in the majority of cases, there was no danger of innocence being injured by this enforced delay.

The town was quiet on the whole; but in the country districts and villages of the Province crimes of bloodshed, spontaneous or hired, due to sudden quarrels or to schemes of vengeance, and highway robberies and cattle stealing and kidnappings and extortion of ransom were incessant and numberless, the fruit of misery, of savage ignorance, of hard and brutalizing toil, of vast, burnt, barren tracts of land insufficiently policed.

There, to the Piazza Sant'Anna, where the law courts were, in the centre of the town, the litigants came flocking from all parts of the Province, rough, stunted folk, baked by the sun, gesticulating in a thousand vivaciously expressive ways: owners of land or sulphur at law with their tenants or with the warehousemen of Porto Empedocle, and brokers and agents and lawyers and messengers; there came crowding in the dazed, loutish peasants from Grotte or Favara, Racalmato or Raffadali or Montaperto, sulphur workers or farm labourers, most of them, with grimed

and sunburned faces and foxy eyes, dressed in
their thick holiday clothes of dark blue broadcloth
with headgear of strange fashion: conical caps, of
velvet; cowls, of knitted cotton; or Paduan caps;
with rings or chains of gold in their ears, come to
give evidence or to visit their relatives in prison.
They spoke, all of them, in deep guttural tones
or with full-throated and voluble interjections.
Sparks flew from the cobbled roadways at the
heavy tread of their iron-shod boots, made of raw-
hide, high, solid and clumsy. And they brought
with them their womenfolk, mothers and wives
and daughters and sisters, with eyes that shrank
in terror or flashed with a puzzled shy anxiety, in
gowns of barracan; with short broadcloth capes,
white or black, and brightly coloured kerchiefs on
their heads, tied below the chin; some of them
with the lobes of their ears torn by the weight
of their ornaments, rings, pendants, teardrops;
others garbed in black, their eyes and cheeks
scalded by tears, the relatives of some murdered
man.

Among these, when they were unescorted, would
circulate, sharp-eyed and slinking, an old bawd or
two to tempt the younger and better looking of
them, who flushed crimson with shame but yielded
nevertheless at times and were led away, overcome by confusion and trembling, to make a sur-
render of their bodies, without any pleasure to
themselves, so as not to return to the village

empty-handed, to buy for the fatherless little ones at home a pair of shoes or a little frock. (Such bargains! A poor girl ought not to miss the opportunity. No one would ever know. . . . Quick, quick. . . . A sin, yes, but God read what was in the heart. . . .)

The many idlers of the town strolled meanwhile up and down, up and down, always at the same pace, dropping with boredom, with the automatic gait of lunatics, up and down the principal street, the only level road in the place, bearing a fine Greek name, Via Atenea, but as narrow and tortuous as all the rest.

Via Atenea, Rupe Atenea, Empedocle . . . names: illuminating names, which made all the more dreary the poverty and squalor of things and places. The Akragas of the Greeks, the Agrigentum of the Romans had ended in the Kerkent of the Musulmans, and the brand of the Arabs had remained indelibly stamped on the minds and manners of the people. A taciturn slothfulness, a sensitive and jealous distrust.

From the Bosco della Civita, the heart of the vanished ancient city, there ran up at one time to the hill on which the new town sits in squalor a long avenue of tall, austere cypresses, as though to point the way for death. Few of these now remained; one, the tallest and darkest, still rose beneath the town's one public avenue, called Viale della Passeggiata, the only beautiful thing that

the town possessed, lying open as it did to the
magnificent view of the whole vast expanse of
country, undulating in hills and valleys and
plains, and of the sea beyond, contained in the
boundless curve of the horizon. This cypress,
standing out blue and majestic, after the flames
of the marvellous sunsets had died down, against
the lowland darkening with the blue of night,
seemed to embody in itself the infinite sadness of
the silence exhaled from places once so clamorous
with life. Here, to-day, death sat enthroned.
Commanded, from the top of the hill, by the old
Norman cathedral dedicated to San Gerlando, the
Bishop's palace and the Seminary, Girgenti was
the city of priests and passing bells. From morning to night, the thirty churches exchanged, in
long, slow peals, the note of mourning and the call
to prayer, diffusing over all a horrid gloom. Not
a day went by that you did not see passing in
funeral procession the grey-clad orphan girls of
the Boccone del Povero: pale and bent, their
wasted little faces all eyes, with veils on their
heads, medals on their bosoms and tapers in their
hands. Anyone, for a modest fee, might secure
their escort; and nothing was sadder than the
sight of all that girlhood oppressed by the spectre
of death, which they must follow thus, day after
day, at a crawling pace, taper in hand, its flame
flickering invisible in the sunlight.

Who, in such a state of mind, could take any

interest in a parliamentary election? No one had
any faith in institutions, nor had ever had any
such faith. Corruption was borne as a chronic,
irremediable evil; and he was deemed a simpleton
or a madman, impostor or self-seeker, who ventured to raise his voice against it.

At that moment, the idlers were talking less of
the approaching election than of the duel between
the candidate Ignazio Capolino and Guido Verònica.

The violent intrusion of Roberto Auriti had
complicated the question at issue. Guido Verònica had at once accepted Capolino's challenge;
he had asked however for a few days' grace in
order to provide himself with seconds. And there
had come from Palermo the Deputy Corrado
Selmi, with another gentleman, who professed to
be a famous swordsman. Roberto Auriti, meanwhile, being debarred from fighting Préola and
not wishing that anyone else should avenge his
father's memory for the vile insult offered to it,
had claimed the right to fight Capolino first. The
latter's seconds, as also Verònica himself, had opposed this claim. In Capolino's name, his seconds
had honourably declared their regret for Préola's
article, which had found its way surreptitiously
into the newspaper. The person actually responsible for the insult being thus disowned by his own
party, being moreover admittedly unqualified to
take the field and having in the meantime been

expelled from Girgenti, Auriti was no longer in a position to demand satisfaction; and a single duel was to be fought, in order that the affair might terminate honourably: the duel between Verònica and Capolino, for the assault made upon the latter in the open street. Quite right!

This greatly debated quarrel had aroused keen excitement among the townsfolk, quite a number of whom had suddenly revealed a passionate interest in duelling; and this excitement had been raised to the highest pitch by the intervention of so notorious a person as Selmi and by the provoking, Spaniard-like airs of Verònica's other second, the swashbuckler.

But on the other side, the local champion, Ignazio Capolino, had placed himself in good hands also: in those of a certain D'Ambrosio, a distant relative of his wife, who knew how to handle a sword and was not the sort of man to let himself be imposed upon either by the reputation of Corrado Selmi or by the other gentleman's swagger. He stood alone, though, for Capolino's other second was a joke: Ninì De Vincentis, just imagine!

Poor Ninì, he had positively been dragged in by the hair of his head! Sabres, blood—he that was a regular young lady, a lily-bearing San Luigi Gonzaga. He would be sure to faint, when it came to the fight! What on earth was that fellow Capolino thinking about, to go and choose Ninì of all people, as though the town were not full of far

more suitable men! But perhaps D'Ambrosio
had chosen him deliberately, as a piece of bravado.

Ninì was still unaware of the definite refusal
given by Salvo to the offer of marriage which—
under pressure from his brother Vincente—he had
made Monsignor Montoro convey. Capolino had
forced him to accept this position (a terrible one
to him) of second supporter at the duel, giving him
to understand that Salvo would be extremely
grateful to him. Perbacco, was he or was he not
going to give the lie, once and for all, to the reputation for modest, girlish timidity which he had
won in the town? A man! A man! He must
prove that he was a man! Anyhow, paunch and
presence: that was all that was required of him.
Paunch, indeed? Was Ninì required to shew a
paunch? Thin and straight as a lath. . . . Go on,
it was only an expression: "Paunch and presence." Calm and neat as any dandy from Paris,
he was certain to cut a splendid figure.

All four seconds had assembled in the course
of the morning at the Prince of Laurentano's
villa, Colimbètra, where the duel was to be
fought, to make the necessary arrangements and
to choose the ground. No one out there would
dare to interrupt the proceedings. The Prince
was going, on the following morning, to Valsanìa,
to be introduced to his bride, as had been arranged; immediately after his departure, the duel
was to begin.

The peripatetic idlers, from the Viale della Passeggiata, watched the four seconds drive back from Colimbètra.

Ignazio Capolino, meanwhile, was waiting for his seconds to return, strolling with the officials of the Party upon the wide marble terrace, outside the Club which, like so many other things there, was called Empedocle.

This duel, on the very eve of the election, had increased his importance and had won him friends. He made a show of not being in the least concerned, and this display of entire indifference aroused an admiring approbation in the friends who strolled by his side. He had already begun his tour of the constituency, and was now describing the enthusiastic welcome he had received the day before in the suburban district of Favara. He would have liked to go that day to the other suburb, Siculiana, where the electors were impatiently awaiting him; but D'Ambrosio, his master, his tyrant for the time being, had absolutely forbidden this, for fear of his tiring himself unduly.

He was sorry, for the sake of his friends at Siculiana, that was all. They too had prepared a great welcome for him. His victory was assured, notwithstanding the threats and high-handedness of the Government, and the Prefect's orders, and police persecution. Roberto Auriti would or might have a majority of a handful of votes only in the

village of Comitini, where Pompeo Agrò num-
bered many friends.

Capolino gave this information with genuine
regret for his opponent, and this regret was genuinely shared by all that heard him. Because it
was well known that Auriti had never reaped any
reward from the Liberal principles for which he
had fought in his boyhood, nor from his persistent
loyalty to them in later life; and that it was certainly not in the hope of reaping any reward from
them that he had come to ask for the votes of his
fellow citizens, but almost as a duty that was imposed upon him or perhaps under the ingenuous
illusion that he had a sufficient claim to those votes
in the respect due to his honesty. No one denied
him that respect, indeed everybody was quite prepared to do him some honour proportionate to his
deserts. But the honour of electing him to Parliament, no, what an idea! That honour was not,
could not be for him; and the clearest proof of
this lay in the ingenuousness of such an illusion.

When his seconds arrived, Capolino withdrew
with them to a corner of the big morning room of
the Club.

Ninì De Vincentis appeared dazed, his face
mottled as though it had been pinched all over,
and his eyes glistening, absent and sullen. D'Ambrosio, tall and fair, short-sighted, restless, with
a horse face, arched shoulders, an enormous chest
and long, bony legs, was speaking volubly, run-

ning all his words together. He was the most
plain-spoken of men, and people put up with his
plain speech not only because they knew him to
be quarrelsome, but because he often made them
laugh. His insults became blunted and lost their
sting in the laughter with which they were received, and so he was able to insult everyone, and
to shout the vilest abuse in people's faces without
anyone's feeling offended or hurt.

"Do me a blessed favour," he began, "and tell
my cousin Nicoletta to leave you alone to-night, as
you have to fight for your holy devils. For your
holy ideals, I should say. You're getting an old
man, Gnazio, do you know that? Hold out your
arm: let me see whether it shakes."

Capolino with a smile held out his arm.

"Good," D'Ambrosio went on. "We'll pump
the lead into them, my boy. I mean it! First of
all, pistols. Three rounds each at five-and-twenty
paces. (Nini must remember not to stop his ears
when he hears the bang.) Then the sabres. As
far as the sabres are concerned, we're in clover;
but the pistols—Gnazio, my boy, you're getting
old, and I fear. . . . Oh, well; come along home
with me. There's the courtyard. I want to see
how well you can shoot."

Capolino tried to resist; but there was no way
out of it; he was obliged to go, as also was Nini,
to accustom his ears to the sound.

They went up the steep Via di Lena, where a

brawl seemed to be in progress, a mob of people
gathered round some one who was singing. It was
nothing! Only the fish-hawkers who, having just
arrived from the harbour, and dismounted from
their loaded mules, were crying fresh fish amid
the crowd, with a long and cheerful lilt. The trio
proceeded by the increasingly steep ascent of Bac
Bac, and came out by the highest of the city gates,
that to the north, the old name of which, likewise
of Arabic origin, Bâb-er-rjiah (Gate of the
Winds) had been corrupted to Biberia.

D'Ambrosio lived up there in an old house with
its *baglio* (an immense cobbled yard) and a water
tank in the middle, keeping house with his aged
mother, to whom he paid a more than religious
devotion. The poor old lady was deaf, and
lived in constant anxiety, in a continual tremor
for that hotheaded son of hers. A half-knitted
stocking in her hands, she was always looking out
from one of the windows. She saw the hill, on
which Girgenti stands, drop precipitously to the
Val Sollano, intersected by a network of dusty
roads. The view to the front was vast and moun-
tainous. To the right, rose dark and looming
Monte Caltafaraci; beyond, in the background,
San Benedetto; from there extended the plain of
Consòlida and, still looking westward, the plain
of Clerici, beyond the mountain of Carapezza and
the nearer Montaperto. Below, and just opposite, the chalky face of the Serra Ferlucchia

shewed the cavernous mouths of the sulphur pits and the bleak white mounds of burnt refuse. Far away, at the boundary of the Province, rose cloud-capped and majestic Monte Gemini, one of the highest peaks in Sicily. The grey, arid, hard asperity of the landscape was relieved only here and there by an occasional dark carub.

D'Ambrosio left his friends to wait in the court-yard; he went upstairs and came down again a moment later with a big duelling revolver and a box of cartridges; with a stick of charcoal he sketched a few lines on the wall, by the empty stable, the form of a man, Guido Verònica; then stepped out twenty-five paces from the wall.

"Here, Gnazio! I shall clap my hands three times; at the third, you fire! Are you ready?"

Capolino had submitted to this test as to a joke, without enthusiasm. Only when he saw facing him, on the wall, the human target which now seemed with an affectation of lifelessness to be awaiting his shots, but to-morrow would be step-ping out to meet him, detaching itself from the wall, with live arms and legs, pointing the muzzle of a similar pistol at himself, Capolino, his lips frozen in a smile, knitted his brows and resolutely fired.

D'Ambrosio declared himself highly satisfied with the test; then, just for fun, tried to force Ninì to fire at the mark as well.

Ninì proved as obstinate as a mule. But D'Ambrosio would not rest until he had compelled him to fire; whereupon he burst out in a wild peal of laughter:

"Upon my word, he shut his eyes, both of them! A glass of water! A glass of water!"

And he ran to support him, as though Ninì were about to faint. But he did not prolong the joke farther. He began to speak with great fervour of Corrado Selmi:

"A charming fellow! He looks quite a young man, you know? And he was out on the 4th of April, in the affair at La Gancia. . . . He must be at least fifty. . . . He looks thirty-five, thirty-eight at the very most. . . . Clever as they make 'em, broad-minded, an all round man. They say he has more debts than there are hairs on his head. I can well believe it! And . . . oh, a game-cock! Mad on the hens. His Excellency the Minister D'Atri ought to know something about that. . . ."

Having arranged that they should meet again on the following morning, Capolino went away with Ninì De Vincentis.

"Don't forget about Nicoletta! Keep a prudent vigil!" D'Ambrosio called after him from the door of the courtyard, making a trumpet of his hands; then, as though he had caught sight of a mad dog: "Look out, Gnazio, look out, man! He's after you! He's after you!"

Capolino and Ninì De Vincentis turned round

to look, laughing, and saw close behind them Nocio Pigna, *Propaganda,* who was coming down by the same way, with his long arm dangling and the other balanced on his knee. *Propaganda* also turned, angrily, to face D'Ambrosio, opened his lustrous madman's eyes and, raising his arm, hurled at him the word which to him was the deepest brand of infamy:

"Ignorante!"

Propaganda and Company.

And he had a better right, now, than ever to stamp with this brand all his enemies, bourgeois and priests and nobles, had Propaganda: the *Fascio,* in spite of the Prefect and Town Council, the Police and the military authorities, had at length succeeded in establishing itself.

Yes, my friends, even at Girgenti, in the town of crows and passing bells, the Fascio.

He looked up, swelling with pride, and with an air of patronage, at those old hovels of the San Michele quarter, dens of misery; at those old lanes, crooked, filthy, deep-rutted; and his eyes blazed.

More than with his fellow men, he felt himself in harmony now with the worn, blackened stones of those hovels, the gaping cobbles of those breakneck lanes; he talked to them in his heart; said to them "Bye and bye!" It was for the honour of the town, first and foremost, that he had fought and was fighting, that it might not be said that Girgenti alone, when the whole Island was in a ferment, remained silent and dead. Soon those houses, soon those streets would be jubilant with a new life.

It was a serious matter, however, that it must cost him so much labour to persuade other people to advance their own interests; that everyone must compel him to wear himself out, to grow so heated in that task of persuasion that he might almost be suspected of having some secret motive or hope of profit!

Who was making him do it? Really, now! He had been thrust on one side, almost expelled from society, had become superfluous in his own home. Peaceably and forcibly people had said and proved to him that they could get on without him; that they no longer had any need of him. After squeezing him like a lemon, seducing one of his daughters, befouling his grey hair with mud, after slandering and defaming him, they proposed now to fling him away, did they? Oh, no! Things of that sort were not done to Pigna. Not only was he not superfluous, he intended, by Jove, to be positively indispensable; indispensable, in spite of them all! And very soon they would realize this, the *ignoranti* who refused to acknowledge him. If other people worked to support him, all that he gained was the leisure to work in his turn for other people; with this further consideration, that the help given to him was meagre, after all, and provided only the humblest essentials of life; whereas the help that he gave to others, the work that he performed was great, and provided for the higher needs. Easy, comfortable, his work? Oh yes, a regular bed of roses, to be sure! Dashing about from morning to night, racing up and down upon that fine pair of shanks that God had given him, shouting himself hoarse, wasting his breath, anybody could imagine what a pleasant life his must be!

Like a beleagured fortress, everything in which had been used as a missile to repel the assaults from without, so that the inside was left empty, Nocio Pigna had posted, in front and in rear and all about him, reasons and sentiments, all his own misfortunes, as weapons of defence against the people who were toiling remorselessly to destroy his reputation. The more he spoke, the more the sound of his own words increased his conviction and his passion. But by dint of always repeating the same things, in the same order, he had let them become stereotyped in a form in which they lost all their efficacy; his lips, one might say, were stopped up, like guns that emitted nothing but noise, smoke and wads. Inside there was nothing left. He was a man who spoke, and nothing more.

Meanwhile, he had brought the Fascio into being. That it was really composed entirely of

working men, people were inclined to doubt. Not
even Propaganda himself would have made bold,
perhaps, to assert that the non-working element
in his membership was as yet very numerous. But
the great thing was to begin; and this is how
things gradually are begun.

Certainly a fine haul, a solemn enrolment with
several thousand members collected in a single
day would have been possible only at Porto Empedocle, among the *men of the sea,* the carters,
the crews of the lighters, the lads in the warehouses, the weighmen and porters. But at Porto
Empedocle. . . . Hush, for the love of God!
Nocio Pigna could not bear to hear the place men-
tioned: the memory of the hot reception he had
had there was like an ever open wound in his
heart, and the merest touch would set it endlessly
throbbing. Breed of dogs, offscourings of civilization! To have the sea, my friends, constantly
before their eyes; what are you laughing at? the
divine sea, the immensity of it! to have planted
their own homes upon the beach, in readiness for
the ships of distant lands, to have placed their life,
in other words, at the mercy of foreigners; and,
my friends, no spirit of human brotherhood! Of
all that sea they could behold nothing more than
the beach, or rather the filth only upon the beach,
their own sewage running down the open drains.
That sea, oh, that sea ought to have boiled with
rage, with contempt, to have reared up a mighty

wave and submerged it, engulfed it, that town of carrion!

Here, at Girgenti, one had to work like the ants, with patience! He had begun to negotiate with the presidents of sundry local guilds: but those linked hands, the symbol of the mutual benefit societies, hands amputated at the wrist, bloodless, that is to say with no political colour, or hands clasping the blessed rosary and olive branch of some Catholic club, found it hard to unlink themselves, found it hard to extend themselves in brotherly greeting to the workers in other trades and callings, as they had done at Catania, at Palermo, to form a wider circle, a union of all the forces of the proletariat, in short, the Fascio of Fasci.

Luca Lizio had already written to Rome to Don Lando Laurentano (who was one of themselves, God be praised, a Prince and a Socialist!), so that he might give the necessary impetus to all the doubtful and wavering: a single word from him, a sign would be ample. They were waiting from day to day for his reply, which was perhaps being delayed by the displeasure which his father's absurd marriage must be causing the young Prince.

Meanwhile he, Nocio Pigna, was losing no time and was not letting himself be cast down by the obstacles in his way. He realized that it would be foolish to attach too much importance to those guilds: in a dead town like Girgenti, devoid of any

industry, where for years past they had ceased
to build any fresh houses and everything was per-
ishing in slow and silent decay; where not only
did the inhabitants never seek any expensive
amusement, but everyone was trying to restrict
his most modest requirements; masons and smiths,
tailors and cobblers depended too much on the few
so-called gentry; and the secret discontent would
certainly not find in them the courage to declare
itself openly, when the occasion arose. In a day
or two they would all be voting for that rascal
Capolino, at a nod from Don Flaminio Salvo. And
yet, by joining, by enrolling in the Party, the
workmen might serve as an example to the peasants; might draw them in, indeed. Like sheep,
those peasants were, poor creatures! Sheep,
though, that knew the cruelty of the rapacious
hands that shore and milked them; sheep that, if
they succeeded in acquiring a consciousness of
their rights, in forming the least conception of
that famous "virtue of their force," would turn
in an instant into wolves.

A section of them, meanwhile, lived scattered
about the country, and did not come up to the
town, perched high on its hill, save on Sundays
and holidays. Those of them who were called *gar-
zoni,* the least sunken in poverty, since they drew
a meagre wage throughout the year, were too
much afraid of the bailiffs, or *curàtoli* or *sopra-
stanti,* savage taskmasters in the service of the

landlords. There remained the day labourers,
those who, after sixteen hours of toil (when they
were fortunate enough to find any work) came
back to the town at night shouldering their
tools, with aching backs and each with fifteen
soldi or so in his pocket. At these Nocio Pigna
marvelled; they were the majority; but clay, clay,
clay, into which God had not breathed; or else
poverty had long since quenched that breath;
dried clay which gave you a painful surprise if,
in looking at you, it moved its eyes, or in speaking, its lips.

He had taken a lease of the huge building of a
derelict cereal factory on the Piano di Gamez, next
door to his own house, capable of holding five
hundred members and more: a trifle damp, perhaps, a trifle dark; but what of that; by lighting
two or three candles one could see fairly well in
the daytime. He had fitted it up as best he could,
chiefly with his own hands. Ten tablets on the
walls, five a side, with the sacramental mottoes of
the Party, blazoned upon some old hangings of
imitation damask, which, had they been able to
speak, might have been heard muttering endless
Paters and Aves to themselves: once upon a time,
indeed, they had served to decorate, upon festal
occasions, the church of San Pietro, where Nocio
Pigna had been employed as sacristan. The old
incumbent had made him a present of them at
the time. He had exhumed them from the chest

in which for years they had been folded away with
camphor and pepper, a discredited treasure, and
now there they were, and—Luca Lizio might say
what he pleased—did make a splendid show. Besides, to attract the peasants, it did not seem a
bad idea to Nocio Pigna that the Fascio should
have a somewhat churchlike air; and on the president's table he had set a crucifix as well. Behind
the table was displayed the red flag embroidered
by his daughter Rita, Luca's "companion". And
Luca sat there, from morning to night, studying
Marx (Markis, Pigna called him), writing, cor-
responding with the presidents of the other Fasci
of the Province and with those of the whole
Island and with Milan and Rome. A stranger,
passing by the open door of the Fascio, might at
times have supposed that he was engaged in extracting a piece of dirt from his nose and then
flicking it away with his fingers; but what an idea!
dirt, indeed! at such moments, Luca was thinking:
with that finger in his nose, he was thinking: when
he was thinking, Luca became so absent-minded
that he did not even notice the trumpet blasts of
the five "brethren" constituting the band, who, to
tell the truth, were a perfect plague. But it did
not do to blow cold upon juvenile ardour. Five
of the students from the Technical Institute who
had been among the first to join the Party: Rocco
Ventura, who had taken his accountant's certificate that year, Mondino Miccichè, Bernardo Rad-

dusa, Totò Licalsi and Emanuele Garofalo,
helped Luca with his correspondence. They had
found a messenger who had assumed the office of
secret police, a certain "Pìspisa," who hung about
all day long gossiping with his official brethren.
The forty members, who would soon swell to four
hundred, four thousand, had already elected their
decurions, each with his brave red *fascia* on his
collar-band. To provide against the arrest of
the President, that is to say of Luca Lizio, the
Council had elected a Secret President in Rocco
Ventura.

For already both Pigna himself and Lizio had
been summoned together *ad audiendum verbum*
by Cavalier Franco, the Commissary of Police.

Oh, most polite, with his fair hair and rosy
cheeks and his smile, blinking his fine languid blue
eyes or stroking with a white, ladylike hand the
little golden beard that forked from his chin,
Cavalier Franco had made them a little speech,
which Pigna never wearied of repeating to all and
sundry, mimicking his voice and gestures.

The red, the red of flag and *fasce* was what had
most offended the Signor Commissario. Why,
yes, like bulls, the police lost their heads at the
sight of anything red. . . .

Not that Cavalier Franco had been in the least
infuriated: a polite policemanship, his, outwardly
at least. All he wished to know was, why *red*,
when after all there were so many other pretty

colours to choose among: orange yellow, pea green. . . . And one other thing he wished to know: why these two gentlemen in particular, Lizio and Pigna, had undertaken this task. What did they expect from it? What did they hope to gain? A seat on the Town Council, or higher still even, in Parliament? Nothing of that sort? Then why? From a disinterested love of their neighbour? From a sense of social justice? Fine words. Yes, he was gracious enough to admit, himself, that the condition of the farm labourer was really unjust. But were they so certain that they would be doing him a service in raising him above that condition? People who live in darkness need spend nothing on light; and light is expensive, and makes people see things that they never saw before; and the more they see the more they require, my friends! Now, in what does true wealth, true happiness consist? In having few requirements. And so . . . and so . . ." in short, a little applied philosophy, and the following conclusion:

"My dear Sirs, I am not going to have you arrested, even though you wish it yourselves. You say that the conflict is bound to come, if the conditions in which your clients are living do not improve? Very good. I beg you to remember the story of the pitcher that went too often to the well. . . . And that is my last word!"

Cavalier Franco had been half annoyed, half irritated by Luca's silence; during his speech it was to Luca that he had turned, and he could scarcely conceal his irritation at hearing himself answered by Pigna. But how was Luca to tell him the reason of his silence?

Poor Luca, what an affliction! He would have been less to be pitied, had he been blind. A born orator, born to harangue crowds, a type of the true public character, all for other people, no thought for himself—and to have his lips sealed by a freak of destiny! He wrote, he found an outlet in writing, and struck sparks from his pen, flakes of hell fire; then raged, poor fellow, gnawed his fingers, moaned aloud, when he heard his stuff read aloud without the right tone, the proper emphasis, the fire that he had put into it. No one was satisfactory, not even Celsina, the only one of Pigna's daughters who, aflame with the new ideas, had made a religion, a regular religion of them. Rita too, yes, a little, before her baby came. . . . But what was Rita compared with Celsina?

Another thorn, another thorn this which made Nocio Pigna's heart bleed: that he could not send to the University this daughter who had passed out at the head of the honours list from the Technical Institute, to the amazement of everybody there, principal, professors and fellow students. To any imbecile whose father was a rich man, the way lay open and smooth; to Celsina, every way was barred; Celsina was condemned to moulder

here, in this rotten town of *ignoranti*. So much
for social justice!

Meanwhile, this evening, on the eve of the election, she was to make her first public appearance;
to deliver an address at the headquarters of the
Fascio. Nocio Pigna had been running round all
morning preparing for this solemn occasion.

They were short of chairs.

If each member had brought his own chair with
him, and had left it there. . . . For the present,
he did not even expect them to pay the wretched
weekly subscription with strict punctuality. But
they might at least have presented a chair each,
great heavens, for their own use! Nothing. . . .

In one way and another he had managed to
scrape together a score or so. He thought of all the
chairs that were in the churches; of those that had
been in his own custody at one time, at San Pietro;
he thought of the cartloads of them that were
taken down every Sunday to the semi-circle at the
end of the Viale della Passeggiata, where the military band played. Chairs in abundance, for the
godly in one place, for the worldly in the other!
And in the Fascio, nothing! The fault of the members, though, when all was said; so much the
worse, then, for them! They would have to stand.

He was making for home, when from an alley
that debouched on the Piazza he heard himself
softly called by somebody who was lying in wait
for him there, muffled in a hood.

"Pst, pst. . . ."

A peasant! His heart gave a bound. He went towards the man eagerly.

"Your Exc'ency's servant. May I say a word to you?"

"What's that you say?" Nocio Pigna asked him, going nearer to him, dismayed by the air of suspicion and mystery with which the man approached him, speaking through his hood which left his eyes alone barely visible. "Do you wish to speak to me?"

"Yes, Sir; the other indicated the reply more by his gesture than in words.

"Here I am, my son," Pigna hastened to assure him. "Come this way. . . . Let us go inside. . . ."

And he pointed to the door of the Fascio.

But the man shook his head and at once drew back farther into the alley. Pigna followed him.

"Don't be frightened. There's nobody there. What do you want to say to me?"

The man in the hood hesitated still for a little before replying; glanced round him with sharp, suspicious eyes, then murmured, still through his hood: "I was told a secret. . . . Some one who knows. . . . He says. . . ."

And he broke off again.

"Speak, my son," Pigna encouraged him. "We are alone here. . . . What did they tell you?"

The sharp suspicious eyes beneath the hood

revealed the painful effort that the stranger was making to overcome his reluctance to speak. Finally, cowering against the wall and laying his hand, still under cover of his cloak, upon Pigna's arm, he asked in the lowest of tones:

"Is it here that they're dividing up the land?"

Nocio Pigna, half bewildered by all this mystification, stood looking doubtfully at him for a while, his mouth gaping.

"The land?" he said. "The land, no, my son."

The other thereupon tilted his chin and shut his eyes, as a sign that he understood. He sighed:

"I see. It seemed too good to be true! They were fooling me."

And he turned on his heel. Nocio Pigna caught hold of him.

"Why fooling you? No, my son. . . . Listen . . ."

"Your Exc'ency must excuse me," said the other, stopping for Pigna to make way. "It is no use. I understand. Let me go. . . ."

"Wait, my dear fellow, you don't give me time to explain. . . ." Pigna made haste to add. "The land, yes, that will come too. . . . It is only a matter of will! If we wish it. . . . It all lies in that!"

The other continued to shake his head with a dark and bitter incredulity; then said:

"But what are we to wish for, we poor folk? What can we wish for?"

Pigna shook with anger:

"Then I'm to give you the land, is that it? First of all there must be the will for it, in you and in everyone, without fear, you understand? There's no question of fighting, keep that well in mind! Indeed we want to sing hymns of peace, my dear man. The Fascio is like a church! And anyone who enters the Fascio . . ."

"Your Exc'ency, please let me go. . . ."

"Wait, I wish to say one thing more to you: anyone who enters the Fascio enters it to form part of a corporation which embraces, as you can calculate for yourself, four-fifths of the human race, do you understand? Four-fifths, that is all I have to say."

He waved the four fingers of one hand in front of that pair of eyes: then went on:

"Give us union, good God, and we are everything, we can do everything! The law will be laid down by us: they will be compelled to come to terms with us. Who labours? Who turns the soil? Who sows? Who reaps? Give us either everything or nothing! So much for the moment. Our programme. . . . Come in, I can explain it all to you. . . . "

"Your Ex'cency, please let me go. . . . It is not for me. . . . "

"How is it not for you, you great donkey? When it is concerned entirely with you, your life, your rights? Keep that in mind, son! Look: the Fascio is here. You will always find me."

"Yes, Sir, I kiss your hands. . . . Please, will you forget I ever said a word. . . ."

And turning on his heel he crept furtively away, peering about him as he went. Nocio Pigna followed him for a while with his gaze, shaking his head.

The moustachioed doll.

In the house, the confusion was greater than ever. A distinct advance was discernible, from day to day, towards the social revolution. There were—and their presence could at once be guessed from the street—the five students, former classmates of Celsina. There was also, but sulking and huddled in a corner, Antonio Del Re, the grandson and nephew of Donna Caterina Laurentano and Roberto Auriti. They were all talking at once in loud tones. The giant, to wit Emanuele Garofalo, and little Miccichè who trembled in every limb and sprang about the room like a jack-in-the-box, and the thickset, violent Racalmutese, Bernardo Raddusa, were shouting (but what, it was hard to make out) round his daughter Mita, the eldest of the six who were still at home, the one who worked all day long and often at night as well with Annicchia, who was the third. Round the latter were screaming her sisters Tina and Lilla with Totò Licalsi and Rocco Ventura; Rita was trying to soothe the baby, which was wailing in terror; Celsina, in a towering passion, was quarrelling with Antonio Del Re; and, as though all this babel were nothing, 'Nzulu, the old black poodle, whiskered and half blind, crouching upon a chair with his head in the air, was giving vent to long and modulated howls of protest.

Luca Lizio, in a corner by himself, was holding his head in both hands, as though afraid that their screams might carry it off altogether.

"My dear people, what is the matter? Where are we?" Nocio Pigna shouted, as he entered the room.

They all turned, ran towards him and, in their excitement, began to answer him in chorus. Nocio Pigna stopped his ears.

"Gently! You're deafening me! One at a time!"

"Mita and Annicchia, as usual!" shrilled Tina.

"Putting on airs!" Lilla added.

And Emanuele Garofalo, the giant, waving his arms above his head, in a voice of thunder:

"Downstairs, everybody! Downstairs!"

"Exercise your paternal authority!" put in Mondino Miccichè, twirling his stick in the air.

"I haven't the faintest idea what you're talking about! Hold your tongues!" shouted Nocio Pigna.

They all stopped speaking; but immediately, in the silence that followed, rang out a "Silly idiot!"

hurled by Celsina at Antonio Del Re in such a tone
of concentrated fury that the rest broke into peals
of laughter.

Celsina stepped forward, balanced nimbly on
her pert hips, her bosom swelling, her swarthy
face aflame and her eyes flashing. Amid all that
laughter, her expression of the haughtiest irritation threatened for an instant to break down, her
burning lips curved in an involuntary smile, but
at once she recovered herself and shouted im-
periously and with scorn:

"Come along! Come along! Anyone who
wants to listen, can! If he does not want to
listen . . . I don't care two straws!"

"And now," groaned Nocio Pigna, bending his
fingers and bringing the tips together, "may I be
allowed to know what the devil has been happening?" And at once added, opening his eyes wide:
"But let one of you speak!"

Rocco Ventura spoke, short and plump, with a
bullet nose above a pair of straggling moustaches
which began at the corners of his mouth and at
once ended there, like a pair of commas:

"Nothing," he said, "we were simply proposing to go downstairs, to the room on the ground
floor, to attend the dress rehearsal of Celsina's
speech; that was all."

"And Mita and Annicchia, as usual . . ." added
Tina, who was all dishevelled.

"Putting on airs!" repeated Lilla.

"They don't want to come down; then let them stay here!" said Celsina, from the threshold. "We all know, they are the ants and I am the grasshopper. Come along, let us go down and leave them!"

Pigna looked at his daughters Mita and Annicchia, who remained seated, dressed both of them in black, with pale cheeks and sorrowful eyes; then at Antonio Del Re, who also remained seated, a worried expression on his face, his elbows resting on his knees, biting his nails.

"Get along, get along," he said to the others, who were preparing to follow Celsina down to the room below. "I am just coming. . . . I have a word to say to Don Nino Del Re."

"You'll do nothing of the sort," shouted Celsina, coming back up the wooden stair and appearing in the doorway quivering with emotion. "I forbid you, Papa! I have spoken to Nino, and that is enough! Come downstairs!"

"All right! All right!" said Pigna. "What a fuss! I have another little speech to make to him. . . . Gently now, gently. . . ."

Antonio Del Re straightened himself, sprang to his feet in a sudden access of fury; but, at once repenting of his determination to leave the house, remained where he was, searching only with his eyes, which went straying round the room, for his hat.

"Oh, Holy God, how quick to take offence you

are too! Don't rush away!" exclaimed Nocio Pigna.

"No, let him go, if he wants to go," put in Celsina excitedly. "I shall be only too pleased, as I've already told him! Or rather, wait . . ."

She ran to the next room, which was her bedroom; took from one of the drawers an old doll, the last survivor of her dolls in days gone by, which had turned up again by chance a few days earlier, and to which that beast Emanuele Garofalo, never realizing the distress it would cause her, had taken pen and ink and secretly added a pair of serjeant-major's moustaches; came back and laid it on Antonio Del Re's bosom; and lifted up his arm, so as to clasp it tightly, saying:

"There; that is for you! Something you can love!"

And she ran out of the room and downstairs.

Antonio Del Re flung the doll into the big workbasket, which stood between Mita and Annicchia. Nocio Pigna stood for a while staring at it with knitted brows; bent down to examine it more closely; asked:

"What are they, moustaches?"

Nino's only answer was to pick up the doll again and stick it into his pocket head downwards. Its little legs, one in shoe and stocking, the other bare, remained protruding.

"You're sending the blood to her head!" was Nocio Pigna's comment. "Calm yourself, Don

Ninì, calm yourself! Let us discuss matters. Really, it would be better if you went away. Your position, at the present time, with your uncle in Girgenti, standing. . . . We people here have work to do. It is beginning now; there is little that we can do; but we ought at least to raise one voice in protest. Now I can enter into your feelings as a nephew, and I understand them. You are still a boy, brought up in your family: I know what your thoughts are; certain things cannot be agreeable to you. You ought however to enter a little into my feelings as a father also, to understand my responsibility, do you follow me? And also . . . Don Ninì, I am a man who is exposed to criticism, as you know; a poor man stoned with calumnies from all sides: I laugh at them; but as for you and your family, and also out of respect for your . . . what would Don Landino Laurentano be to you again? Uncle? Cousin? Uncle, isn't he? Of course, yes . . . your mother's first cousin—also out of respect for him, as I was saying, I would not have anyone suspect. . . . Am I not right, Mitina?"

Mita barely raised her eyes from her work and, lowering them again at once, went on sewing. Antonio Del Re had gone across to the balcony window and was gazing out over the deserted Piano di Gamez, still biting his nails.

"Listen," Pigna went on. "This is gospel truth: has not your grandmother done a great injury to herself, to all her family and to you personally . . ."

At this Del Re sprang round and came towards him, brandishing his clenched fists, and shouting:

"That will do! Stop!"

Nocio Pigna gazed at him for a minute, speechless, then said:

"But do you know that the whole lot of you seem to be mad here to-day? I was going to add that the greatest injury of all, she did to the town, by letting all the property that was hers by rights pass into the hands of that brother of hers who . . . But oh, Don Ninì, let us cool our passions and speak plainly! On which side are you? We get no farther, going on like this! I am not trying to force you. But it is time to make up your mind, my dear fellow: either you stand here with us, I mean with the Party, openly; or you remain with your own people. If you don't know, yourself even . . ."

"But she, of all people? She?" Antonio Del Re broke out, almost crying with rage, coming towards him again and clawing the air (he alluded to Celsina). "Why she? Wasn't there yourself? Weren't there all those idiots, Raddusa or Garofalo?"

"What about her?" Pigna was puzzled.

"The address," Antonio explained in an undertone.

"Ah, the address? And what has that got to do

with it? Oh, I see. . . . But forgive me, Don Nino, dear! You're in a different boat! You're going off now to Rome with your uncle, to continue your studies, in the great city; you are going to sit down to a spread table; fees, books, everything provided for you. . . . But think, great God in heaven, think that my daughter here too. . . . Can't you imagine how it must make her blood boil, my poor child, when she thinks that all her work, all her efforts have been in vain? That all her love of study, all her passionate ambition to succeed is to end like this? Let her blow off steam! She ought to be setting the whole town on fire! Would you have her muzzled as well? And by what right, may I ask? What are you doing, what can you do for her? If I don't leave the room, I shall scream. . . ."

And off he went, in a fury, down the wooden stair.

Antonio Del Re had returned to the window and was gazing out. Mita and Annicchia went on working in silence, with bent heads. In that silence all three were conscious of the sound of their own troubled breath, evidence of their inward grief, exasperated by the thought that they could do nothing to prevent or remedy a state of things which was contrary to their nature, to their affections, to their aspirations.

The most troubled of the three was Antonio Del Re. All his grandmother's sombre bitterness

had transfused itself, from his infancy, into his
blood, which it had poisoned; the almost morbid
tenderness of his mother, all shocks and terrors,
caused him distress and annoyance, a humiliating
sense of constraint; the submissive resignation of
his uncle, crushed by the sad vicissitudes of life,
left behind, after running the race in his boyhood
with such dauntless ardour, who yet was determined not to appear beaten, and smiled to shew
that he still had faith in an ideal which no amount
of wrongdoing, no amount of error could, according to him, either damage or dim, made Antonio
angry. He felt, he knew that his uncle's smile
was intended to conceal an ever open sore, in a
mistaken idea of what was proper. But why, instead of concealing it, did not uncle Roberto expose his sore, like his grandmother, like his
friends, all the young men here at Pigna's? In
one respect, however, their exposure of their sores
irritated and disgusted him. The people who had
worked and fought and suffered, it was they who
ought to cry aloud against all their afflictions and
hardships and demand justice and vengeance in
the name of their work and blood and sufferings;
not these boys who had done nothing, who showed
no capacity for doing anything, except chatter to
pass the time, and bind everyone together in a
fascio, the honest with the dishonest, his uncle
with the plotters and intriguers, with all those
patriots for amusement or for reward!

It was not this sense of injustice alone, however, that gave Antonio Del Re an aversion to his comrades. Bred up in the school of a proud and sombre grief, which scorned to seek an outlet in speech, of an abnegation prouder still, which scorned any base envy, if he had thrown himself into the fray, severing every ideal link with his own people, he would neither have uttered a single word, nor have sought companions: with lowered head, set teeth and armed fist, he would have sprung at once into action. The others were there merely to chatter, to amuse themselves with Pigna's daughters.

Antonio Del Re would have refused to admit that his aversion and scorn were largely due to a fierce jealousy.

With the same bottled ardour, with which he would have hurled himself into violent action, he had fallen desperately in love with Celsina, from the very first day on which she, still a little girl with her frocks ending at the knee, had made her entry into the technical school for boys. And Celsina, albeit courted by all his schoolfellows, had responded to his love, at first in secret, then letting the others see what was happening, finally making an open avowal of her feelings and defying the jeers of the disappointed. She had not however shut herself up in his love, she had not come and clung to him as he would have liked; she had remained where she was, in the thick of them all, her heart on her sleeve, her mind divided, prodigal of words, glances, smiles, intoxicated with her triumphs, and with her halo of glory as a rebel against every prejudice, conscious of her own value and athirst to have it noticed, admired, applauded.

The clearer this aspect of her became, the more Antonio realized that he ought not to be in love with her, not only because she did not appeal to him when she was like this, but because, when he thought of his mother and grandmother, he realized that one would regard her with horror, while the other would dismiss her as a silly little flirt. But no: Celsina was neither bad nor silly, as he knew very well; indeed, had he listened to the secret, innermost voice of his own conscience, a voice stifled by respect, shyness, love, instead of condemning Celsina's open rebellion, he would have condemned the too exclusive pride of his grandmother, the too submissive resignation of his mother.

"Don Ninì," Mita called to him in a gentle voice. "Will you come over here a minute?"

Antonio roused himself and went to her; but when he saw her hold up the article of clothing upon which she was at work, as though to take a measurement, he at once drew back shocked, writhing with discomfort.

"No! . . . not just at present. . . ."

"Dear Don Ninì," sighed Mita. "You must

have patience! It has to be finished quickly. . . .
You are going away. . . . Lucky you!''

Mita was engaged in getting ready, with her sister, the linen that he was to take with him to
Rome.

All the best families in the town, including Antonio's grandmother and mother, gave out work
to these two poor sisters, who would often go and
work in their houses also by the day. This was
done out of consideration, or pity rather, for
themselves alone; and they were fully aware of
this, and became every day more humble, the better to deserve it, to shew their gratitude and not to
forfeit their employment. They realized that so
many things had to be overlooked by the people
who were anxious to help them, things which their
father and sisters, instead of attenuating them,
did everything in their power to bring into prominence, as though they deliberately set out to rouse
the whole town against them and to wear out
people's patience and neighbourly charity! But
would not the harm recoil on these two also?
What must people be saying? We, who are out-
siders, are to shew consideration for you, are to
help you, are we, while your own flesh and blood,
those whom you maintain with our assistance, are
to make war upon us? Disorders, scandals,
feuds!

To find some sort of excuse for their father,
Mita and Annicchia forced themselves to believe

that he had really gone out of his mind after Rosa,
the eldest sister's disgrace. Certainly, from that
time onwards their house had been hell let loose.
It was not so much of their father that Mita and
Annicchia complained, with bleeding hearts, as of
their sisters. How on earth could their sisters
fail to understand that only by keeping silence,
only by the humblest, most retiring modesty could
they succeed, if not in obliterating altogether, in
making less apparent the brand of infamy, with
which their house was now marked? Rita, when
the baby left her a moment to herself, and also
Tina and Lilla did indeed help them with their
sewing, basting or machining, on the all too rare
days when work was plentiful; but they worked
without zest, absent-mindedly, the two last especially, since they were not resigned, after the
tragedy, to the abandonment of all hope and all
desire. When they saw these two sisters dress up
and adorn themselves every morning, they felt
their hearts wrung, realizing that they were not
dressing up, were not adorning themselves with
any hope or desire that was honourable: they
themselves must know, alas, that no man whose in-
tentions were honourable would care to be seen
with them now. And from day to day they waited
for Tina and Lilla, with all those young fellows
always dangling round them, to end like Rita.
But if they could only find a good young man, like
Luca! Rita might have fared worse. . . . Be-

cause, when all was said, they were obliged to admit that Luca was good. Only they could not forgive his obstinacy in not legalizing his union with Rita before the law and the altar. He was so good to everyone, and was so fond of the baby and was no trouble at all in the house. Certainly, if he had not made so many enemies with those ideas of his, and had not been so unfortunate, he might have been of great assistance to the family, since, as far as work went, he worked all day long, and must indeed be learned to judge by the number of books he had read and still went on reading.

A little of this respect claimed by his intellect and erudition Mita and Annicchia extended also to Celsina, whose accomplishments dazzled everyone. They dared not criticize Celsina, because really she appeared to them by so many standards to be above the ordinary run, and they agreed with their father that in another place, in other conditions, she would have been sure of a triumphant success! They saw her full of contempt for men —and this was in one respect reassuring. As for men, she had gone and challenged them in their own schools and had beaten every one of them! As a matter of fact, they had not seen their way to approve of that challenge: with greater profit, albeit with less satisfaction to herself, she might have attended the girls' classes and become a teacher. As it was, she was left without a profession. But they were not afraid for the future: some outlet Celsina was certain to find for her talents, in the town or elsewhere. That poor Don Ninì, meanwhile, who was in love with her, and was jealous. . . . So good, poor fellow! But she was not for him, Celsina. If his family should come to hear of it! They were counting the minutes until he should leave for Rome.

Annicchia laid her hand gently upon Mita's arm to draw her attention to the two legs of the doll, which were protruding from his pocket as he still stood at the balcony window. Mita responded with a wistful smile to her sister's smile; then, remembering a request which she had made up her mind the night before to put to the young man, she rose to her feet, laying down her work in the basket, and went timidly over to him.

"Don Ninì," she murmured, "before you go to Rome, you must for the last time do me that great favour, and . . ."

"No, for heaven's sake, no, Mita, don't speak to me of it!" Antonio Del Re violently interrupted her, pressing his hands to his forehead and screwing up his eyes.

"You are ashamed, isn't that it?" said Mita sorrowfully, lowering her gaze.

"No, it's not that! It's not that!" Antonio hastened to assure her. "But now, just at the moment . . . I can't bear to listen to anything, Mita!"

It was a terrible thing that the poor girl wanted of him, a terrible memory recurred to him as he spoke. He looked at her, afraid lest the horror that evidently underlay his refusal might have aroused some suspicion in her. But he saw her fine eyes more sorrowful and humble than ever, eyes which all the tears that they had shed had veiled and dimmed for ever.

Almost every night, indeed, she wept with her whole heart for Rosa, her ruined sister, her fallen sister, who had sunk into the lowest depths of infamy. More than once, not being able herself to go and visit her in the house of shame in which she was at present confined, she had asked Antonio to go there instead of her. And Antonio, the last time that he had gone there, finding her half tipsy . . . horrible! horrible!

A din of shouting, applause, mingled with the wailing of the baby and the barking of the dog, came up at this stage from the room below; and presently 'Nzulu, the old poodle, kicked out of the other room, trembling all over, crouching on his hind legs as though he were trying to sweep the floor with the tuft of his agitated tail, came in and laid his whiskered muzzle on the knees of Mita, who had returned to her seat.

The two sisters, when they saw the poor creature come to them imploring their protection and shelter, began to cry. Whereupon Antonio Del Re, unable to contain himself any longer, crushed his hat down on his head, opened the balcony window and, bestriding the iron railing, while Mita and Annicchia cried in terror: "Oh, gracious, Don Ninì . . . what are you doing? What are you doing?" lowered himself, holding on at first to two of the upright bars of the railing, then let himself drop on to the piazza beneath.

They could hear the thud, and then the sound of something breaking. Mita ran to the window and saw him down below, stooping, groping with outstretched hands, like a blind man, for his hat which had fallen at his feet.

"Don Ninì, you haven't hurt yourself, I hope?"

"It's all right . . ." he answered from below. "My glasses . . . I've lost my glasses."

And, snatching up his hat, he made off.

"He's gone mad!" said Mita. "Can it be possible?"

And she pointed with her hand to the room below, in which Celsina was holding forth.

As he dashed along the Via di Gamez, Antonio Del Re, who without his glasses could not see an inch before his nose, ran into somebody at the corner of the Via Atenea.

"Hallo, Nino!"

He recognized the voice as Corrado Selmi's.

"Let me pass!" he shouted at him, freeing himself with an angry gesture.

A light traveller.

Corrado Selmi had left Veronica at the hotel in the company of his other second, and was now on his way back to Roberto Auriti's house, where he was staying.

For the last four days, whenever he shewed his face in the street, he had seen every eye turned upon him, had noticed that a number of curious spectators would even stop to gaze at him open-mouthed; that others emerged from the shops and planted themselves on the doorsteps, looking over one another's shoulder.

All this curiosity obliged him to assume—what was most unusual with him—a certain air of stiffness. At the same time, he could not help laughing. And he did not know where to look, so that his naturally merry eyes, the frank and open expression of a face that was always smiling might not earn him an unmerited reputation for petulance.

He was indeed and felt himself to be still quite young, in body and in spirit, notwithstanding his age, the changes of fortune and fierce struggles he had borne. He still had not a single white hair, nor had the golden brightness of his moustaches and hair began to fade. He dressed with a gentlemanly and entirely natural elegance, and exhibited in his whole person, in every gesture, every glance, a freshness and youth that were irresistible.

For this persistent youthfulness Corrado Selmi
of Rosàbia was indebted to his keen, constant and
intense love of life, and, at the same time, to his
having always refused to attach the slightest value
to it. He had never consented to burden himself
with any excess of memories or of studies or of
scruples or of clinging aspirations, unlike so many
men who find that inevitably—under such a burden—their knees begin to bend and their shoulders to arch.

A light traveller, such was his usual definition
of himself. And he had always embarked like
this—light and free—upon long, adventurous and
difficult journeys. Nothing to lose, and so, forward march!

On the failure of the insurrection of the 4th of
April, having escaped by a miracle from the Convent of La Gancia, he had at first carried on a
guerrilla warfare with the squadrons round Palermo; he had then served in the 1860 campaign
with Garibaldi until Volturno—but in what fashion? Without ammunition and with an old blun-
derbuss that would not fire, procured from Malta
for six ducats.

In the Chamber, among all his fellow-members
whose brows were pregnant with great thoughts
and their portfolios bulging with reports and
notes and memoranda, he had served upon the
most difficult Committees. Yes, but without either
a pencil or a notebook.

Life, to him, spelt action. And he had always managed to find something to do, of some sort or other; though without making the slightest effort in any direction. And in everything he had secured an easy and spontaneous success, never drawing back, seeking out rather and braving the gravest perils, the most difficult undertakings, the most intricate adventures.

He did not believe, he would not admit that difficulties could exist for a man like himself, always ready for anything. He did not go out to meet life; he faced it, and passed on. Passed on, disarming everyone with his convinced, gay, tranquil confidence: stripping every abstract principle, every rhetorical display from the rigid morality of the Catos, every scruple of modesty from the women's virtue.

Was he to halt, for a moment even, in his race through life, to criticize his own conduct and decide whether he had done well or ill? Of course not! He must not waste time upon criticism, any more than he must attach importance to his own actions. Wrong to-day, right to-morrow. Useless to recall his attention to consider the wrong he had done; he would shrug his shoulders, smile, and go on his way. He was bound to go ahead, at all costs, in any way, without hesitating, letting himself be purified by his incessant activity and by his love of life, and remaining always cheerful

and open, lavish with his favours to everyone,
holding everyone in the hollow of his hand.

Life was for him, in short, a succession of baited
hooks, which drew him this way and that. To
arrest him at one of these, to suspend him from it
in order to criticize him would have been a cruel
injustice.

Now Corrado Selmi was afraid that such an injustice threatened him at this moment: in other
words, that people hoped to hook him by the many
debts which he had been forced to contract, by the
many bills with his signature that were held by
one of the leading banks, the shaky condition of
which was already being exposed. Perhaps at the
opening of the new Session of Parliament the
scandal would come out. He could imagine the
spectacle that would be offered by all the jealous,
bristling guardians of respectability, whom the
fear of committing an action that was not quite
correct had always prevented from doing anything at all, apart from their insipid rhetorical
chatter; feeble, peering egoists, diligent culti-
vators of the arid garden-plot of their own moral
sense, ringed round by a dense hedge of scruples,
though there was nothing for it to guard, since
the garden in question had never yielded anything
but blighted fruit or useless formal flowers!

Debts! Bills! Why, certainly! But he had
always been signing bills, all his life! When he

was eighteen, at Palermo, in the early part of
1860, the Revolutionary Committee were at their
wits' end: they had hopes of Garibaldi, they had
hopes of Vittorio Emanuele and Piedmont, they
had hopes of Mazzini; but funds were lacking and
arms and munitions. Well, he had suggested that
they should take six thousand ducats from the
safe of the Bank of Sicily on the signature of the
wealthiest gentlemen among them. And he had
been the first to sign, though he had not a carlino
in his pocket, for two hundred ducats. The Provisional Government would pay in due course.
How was the Fourth of April made possible? In
this way alone!

And how had he contrived, single-handed, the
reclamation of the marsh lands which formed a
great part of his constituency? Why, by signing
one bill after another! After which the constituency had been rid of malaria, and the debts—as
everyone knew—had remained on his hands, because the cultivation of the reclaimed land, which
he had entrusted to certain inexperienced relatives of his own, had proved a failure, and at present the fruits of his labour were being enjoyed
for the most part by other people who gave him
only the rinds, as and when they chose, but continued to do him the honour of returning him to
Parliament.

It was quite true: apart from the sums bor-
rowed from the Banks for this undertaking and

for others equally advantageous to many, disastrous only to himself; other sums and no small ones he had taken for his own support. Live he must; he neither could nor would live a life of poverty. As a boy he had gone straight from school to take part in the Revolution. For eleven years, until Rome was taken, he had not allowed himself a moment's rest. When the armistice came, left without a profession and with no return for the expenditure of his best years in the service of others, what was he to do? Hang himself? Fortune had not chosen to smile upon him in business; it had granted him other favours, but these had cost him dear, and one—the greatest and worst of them—not in pocket alone.

Corrado Selmi forbade himself any regret for what was past. And yet, now and again, regret for his love affair with Donna Giannetta D'Atri Montalto would assail him with a sudden tightening of the heart. But stronger than any sorrow for the love he had lost was his rage at the blind abandonment of himself in the hands of that woman who for two years had made him the talk of Rome, leading him on to do things that were really mad. It seemed that she had taken a vow to compromise herself and him in every possible way, gripped by a passion for scandal. More for her sake than for his own he had tried at first to restrain her, but had soon lost all restraint himself in the fear that his scruples might give

offence, his prudence appear to her as cow-
ardice.

His heaviest debts had been contracted at this
period, albeit they did not figure under his own
name, out of consideration for the woman who
made him contract them.   Roberto Auriti had
stepped in, with brotherly abnegation, to raise the
money for him from the Bank, after a private ar-
rangement however with the Governor of that institution.

The threatened exposure of the irregularities in
this Bank was therefore less alarming to Corrado
Selmi on his own account than on Roberto Auriti's.
But his alarm was to some extent modified by his
certainty that the Government had many excellent
reasons for preventing any public scandal.   He
well knew that such a scandal would result in the
failure not of one Bank only but of the national
confidence.   The Government's support of his own
re-election, in spite of Francesco D'Atri's being
in office, and their support of Roberto Auriti's
candidature, confirmed him in this certainty.   Before leaving Rome, he had promised Roberto that
he would come down to Girgenti to help him in his
campaign; summoned there in haste by Veronica's
telegram, he had come at once, and had at once
realized the extremely difficult position in which
Roberto found himself placed by his opponents,
a position aggravated now, still further, by this
duel.

He would have done anything in the world to liberate Roberto from all the trials by which he saw him oppressed, to draw him up where he might breathe a different air, to raise him to the position which he knew him to deserve by the qualities of his mind and heart, by all that he had done in his youth; but as soon as he had set foot in his friend's house, at Girgenti, and had met his mother and sister, he had felt his strength fail; in a flash he had seen the reason why Auriti's life had been a failure.

It had seemed like a prison to him, that house! Was it possible that two human beings could have adapted themselves to drag out their existence in that melancholy gloom of bitter and contemptuous boredom? Could have formed so grim, so horrid a conception of life?

He had been unable to resist the temptation to broach this topic with Roberto's mother, in the hope of rousing her from her lethargy.

"But if life is a mere feather, Donna Caterina! A breath, and away it goes. . . . Would you attach any weight to a feather?"

"Would I, dear Selmi?" had been Donna Caterina's answer. "It is not my doing. . . . To you, life is a feather, and flies away; for me, it has turned to lead, my dear Sir. . . ."

"But that is just where you make a mistake!" he had promptly retorted, "turning a feather into lead! Surely, since we have to live, does it not

seem to you essential to keep our spirit in a state
of . . . shall I say, continual fusion? Why arrest this fusion and make the spirit coagulate, fix
it, stiffen it in this gloomy mould of lead?''

Donna Caterina had nodded her head, her lips
curved in a bitter smile.

"Fusion . . . yes! But to keep the spirit, as
you say, in this state of fusion, we must have fire,
my friend! And when, inside you, the furnace is
dead?''

"We must not allow it to die, perbacco!''

"My dear Sir, when the wind is too strong,
when death comes, and breathes upon us . . .
when you look round you and cannot find so much
as a handful of twigs to feed the flame . . .''

"But where do you look for them? Here?
Always mewed up inside these four walls as in a
prison? . . . But Signora Anna, surely . . . is it
possible that Signora Anna . . . I mean to say.
. . .''

He had stopped short, in a sudden embarrassment, observing that Roberto's sister, finding herself drawn into the conversation when she least
expected it, had turned crimson.

Ever since he first set eyes on her, Corrado
Selmi had remained lost in admiration of her pure
and delicate beauty and had suffered instinctively
at the sight of that beauty so mortified by her persistent widow's weeds, and not so much neglected
as despised.

This sudden blush made him afraid lest he had gone a little too far; but at once, overcoming his momentary embarrassment, he had gone on:

"Haven't you a son? And you are obliged, therefore, to live for him, to cherish life for his sake . . . aren't you? I mean to say . . . perhaps I am a little too emphatic in shewing you what is in my mind, when I see all this atmosphere of gloom here, which does not appear to me reasonable. What do you say about it, Signora Anna?"

She had flushed again, had made a painful effort not to lower her eyes, and with a dazed expression and a nervous smile on her lips, shrugging her shoulders slightly, had replied, alluding to her son:

"He is young, still. . . . He can plan his life for himself. . . ."

"But you, then . . . are you old?"

This almost spontaneous question had brought their first conversation to an end.

Now Corrado Selmi was returning to Roberto's house, exhilarated by all that he had seen at the villa of Colimbètra. All those great dolls in Bourbon uniform who had presented arms to him! Sheer lunacy! But what a splendid place, that villa! The Prince—no, he had not shewn his face. Such a pity! He would so much have liked to meet him. . . . There was a man, now, who had taken root, in his affections, in a past epoch . . . and yet he went on living, outside time, outside life

. . . in a most curious fashion (how charming!), projecting from his own period certain images of life, which inevitably, in the reality of to-day, must appear unsubstantial, masks, toys, all those dressed-up dolls there . . . how charming!

"And yet those dolls out there, dear Selmi, which made you laugh," Donna Caterina told him, "to-morrow, at the election here, will defeat you, your friend Roberto, the Prefect, your Government and everybody. . . . Go on laughing, if you can. Shadows? Why, it is we that are the shadows!"

"I am not, if you don't mind, Donna Caterina," said Selmi, laughing and patting his chest. "Spare me this one illusion at least. Why, the Prince, when I went to find him, melted away before me like a shadow. . . . I would have given anything to see him come out to meet me, if only to be quits. . . . Roberto knows all about that . . . to be quits for a certain meeting with his son in Rome, when it fell to my lot to play the shadow. Bah! Patience. . . . Why yes, you are quite right, Donna Caterina; we all persist in being mere shadows, here in Sicily. . . . Inept or discouraged or servile. . . . But when the sun puts the very words to sleep on our lips! I'm not just saying this for the sake of talking, you know: I have studied the question carefully, I assure you. Sicily entered the great Italian family with a public debt of barely eighty-five millions of capital and a small

balance of about twenty-two millions. She brought
in as well all the wealth of her church and crown
property, the accumulation of centuries. On the
other hand, badly off for public works, with no
roads, no harbours, no irrigation, of any sort.
. . . How was the sale of crown property and the
letting of church property carried out? It ought
to have been done with an eye to social advantage,
to the relief of the agricultural classes. To be
sure! It was done with an eye to financial profit.
And we have been obliged to buy back our church
and crown lands and free the rest of our real estate with the colossal sum of something like seven
hundred millions, at the expense, naturally, of the
improvement of our other lands. And that famous
fourth share of all church property allotted to us
by the Law of July 7, 1866? What a mockery!
Why, to begin with, the value of that property was
calculated upon the deliberate understatements
made by the Sicilian clergy when assessed for the
mortmain tax; and from this nominal value, remember, were deducted all the percentages due to
the State and the various charges and cost of administration. And then, if you please, all these
deductions were based upon actual values, with the
further subtraction of the pensions due to the
members of suppressed communities. So that, up
to the present, nothing, practically nothing has
filtered through to our Communes. Now, after all
the sacrifices we have made and accepted out of

patriotism, has not our Island the right to share equally with the other regions of Italy in all the benefits, the improvements of every sort, which those other regions have already secured? But if it has never proved possible, in spite of all my efforts, to collect all the Sicilian Deputies together in an effective group? . . . Oh, don't let us speak of it, Donna Caterina! I should only lose my temper. . . . I do all I can. Then I shrug my shoulders and say: 'It means that we are getting what we deserve. . . .' "

He turned to Roberto, to change the conversation, and went on:

"I say, I saw your opponent's wife yesterday, in the street. My dear fellow, you're simply bound to lose. . . . Oh, what a lovely little lady! Forgive me, ladies, for speaking like this; but I really should not have the heart to win, not even in the sacred name of the Country and of Freedom, if it brought tears to those charming eyes!"

CHAPTER VII

The mask.

NICOLETTA CAPOLINO entered her husband's study dressed to go out, with a curious, broad-brimmed, plumed felt hat on her beautiful raven hair. Full-blooded, lively and eminently alluring, with burning eyes and lips, she exhaled from all her secretly, artfully tended person a voluptuous, intoxicating perfume.

It was a dramatic moment, an interlude in the comedy which husband and wife had been playing day after day for the last two years, even within the privacy of their own four walls, each for the other's benefit, mutually enjoying their own subtlety and daring.

They knew very well, however, both of them knew that they would never succeed in deceiving one another; nor did they attempt to do so. That they were acting from pure love of the art could not be said, seeing that they both secretly loathed the necessity for their make-believes. But if they wished to live together, without causing scandal to other people, without too much disgust at themselves, they realized that they could not do otherwise. And so there they were, eager to dress up, or rather to mask with a polite and pretty falsehood their mutual loathing; to treat the falsehood as a painful and costly work of charity. It took the form, in fact, of a duty, a competition in exquisite courtesies, by means of which husband and wife had in course of time acquired not only an affectionate regard for each other's merits, but actually a sincere mutual gratitude. And they were very nearly in love with one another.

"Gnazio, I can't bear to leave you like this!" she said as she entered the room, as though vexed at a supposed deception, which pained and alarmed her. "Swear to me that you're not going to fight this morning."

"Oh Lord, Lellè, haven't I told you that I'm going to Siculiana!" Capolino replied, raising his hands and letting them rest gently on her arms. "I was to have gone there yesterday, as you know. Don't be alarmed, dear. The duel has been put off until after the election."

"Am I to believe that, really?" she insisted, as she attempted to button her other glove with her already gloved hand.

Capolino would have liked to answer her importunity with a snort of anger; as it was, he smiled; sprang towards her; took her hand, to button her glove for her, and lingered over the task like a lover.

"I can't tell you what a bore it is having to go

to Valsanìa!'' was her next remark, almost murmured in his ear, in faint accents.

"But you must go!'' he exclaimed, looking her in the face, as though to warn her that this note of tenderness—charming and delightful as it was—was, to say the least, out of place at the moment.

"I swear to you!'' she replied, obstinate, but smiling back at him.

Capolino laughed aloud:

"Go! Go! Go! You will enjoy yourself no end! Think of seeing that old walrus Adelaide meet her bridegroom. . . . It will be a sight for the gods! You aren't serious, Lellè?''

"If my mind were at rest . . .'' Nicoletta repeated. "Last night you stayed in here for ever so long. . . . I never heard you come to bed. . . .''

"But all this correspondence about the election, don't you see?'' he said, pointing to the writing table. "Uncle Salesio, surely to goodness, might come and help me with this at least. . . .

"Oh, yes, Uncle Salesio!'' she exclaimed. "If they were jam tarts . . .''

"That will do,'' said Capolino. "Don't waste any more time, off with you. . . . Or are you waiting for the carriage?''

Nicoletta raised her eyes with the air of one resigning herself to accept a statement though not convinced of its truth, and sighed:

"If you really are going to Siculiana, couldn't

you, on your way home this afternoon, look in at
Valsanìa?"

"Why of course, if I can!" he replied. "But
when I'm with friends . . . I shan't be coming
back alone. . . . If I can . . . I mean to say, if I
can manage to leave them . . ."

He put out his lips to kiss her. She drew
back her head, instinctively, afraid of his dis-
arranging her hair.

"Why?" she said.

"Because I like you like that. . . . Aren't you
going to give me a kiss?"

"Gently, though. . . ."

They were interrupted by the old maidservant,
who came in to announce that Salvo's carriage
was at the door. Nicoletta turned at once from her
husband.

"All right, I'm coming," she said to the servant; then giving her hand to her husband: "So
long, then."

"Have a good time," Capolino told her.

This carriage, in a dead-alive town like Girgenti, was really too much of a good thing; a
senseless display of wealth and luxury for which
only a man like Salvo could be forgiven. From
the suburb of Ràbato, in which Capolino lived, to
the Viale della Passeggiata, where Salvo, a few
years earlier, had built himself a charming villa,
one could go on foot in half an hour.

Nicoletta had not the least doubt that her husband was going to fight that morning. But she must not be supposed to know it, if she was to be free to enjoy herself. How many other things there were that she must not be supposed to know, in order that she might be what she was, gay and in love with life! She succeeded, often, by force of will, not indeed in not knowing them, which would have been impossible, but in behaving just as though she did not know them. Surreptitiously, when her gorge rose at them, a deep sigh, and there!—she would raise her spirit above all the miseries that had always oppressed her, almost from the cradle.

She must not know, for instance, that her mother had caused the death—if not by poison, as some slanderous tongue in the town had suggested, certainly of a broken heart—of her father, in order to unite herself in a second marriage with the man whom her daughter called Uncle Salesio, a former clerk in the Spoto Bank.

She had been scarcely five years old when her father died, and yet she remembered him quite well; so much so that her mother had never been able to persuade her to address as "daddy" this second husband much younger than this wife.

He was not a bad man, Uncle Salesio, no; but fatuous, fatuity and vanity incarnate. As soon as he became the husband of Baldassare Spoto's widow, he had seriously believed that this marriage conferred upon him a sort of title of nobility; and the strangest fumes had mounted to his brain; indeed, you might say that his whole soul turned to smoke. Soon however the fuel for that smoke had begun to fail. Wild extravagance. . . . And if only it had brought him any pleasure! What a Chinese torture must they have been to him, all the time, those patent leather shoes, which obliged him to hop along on tiptoe, like a bird! Evil tongues averred that beneath his waistcoat he wore stays, like a woman. Stays, no; a woollen band he did wear, wound tightly and several times about his waist, as a protection to his back, which required support. He was not so old as all that: just a year or two older than Capolino; but senile decay, despite all his precautions and his most loving and assiduous attentions to his person, had begun early in him. He now looked like an automatic figure: everything adjusted, everything pieced together, everything a sham: his teeth, the pink of his cheeks, the black of his waxed moustaches and his little tuft of a beard and his exiguous eyebrows and few remaining hairs; and he walked and moved as though upon springs, with a youthful gait. His eyes, however, among all these chemical applications, almost hidden behind their swollen, lymphatic lids, were eloquent of an infinite distress. For trouble had come upon him after his wife's death. Nicoletta, who might have washed her hands of him, had shewn compassion; she had, however,

taken over the management of what little remained to them; she had insisted, moreover, upon
keeping up appearances, and Uncle Salesio (now
almost mummified) had continued to parade the
streets like a little lord, a prodigy of smartness,
always in silk stockings and patent leather shoes,
walking on tiptoe; but at home, ah, at home the
most rigid economy. So much so that, one day,
Nicoletta had been seen to arrive with a parcel
containing a couple of sham roast fowls, of pasteboard, under her arm. Yes, indeed: two roast
fowls of pasteboard to be displayed on the meagre
table beneath the flyguards of netted wire. Every
day the poor old man set them before him on the
table, to deceive himself: he could not do without
them! And those two pasteboard fowls and a
crust of stale bread (genuine enough, but hard
upon his teeth which were not) now formed the
whole of his daily meal for weeks on end! Because Capolino had not chosen to take him into
his own home, and Uncle Salesio Marullo, left
alone in the gloomy old house which Nicoletta had
made over to him with what little she had managed to save from the wreck, as often as not, being
incapable of limiting his expenditure, when it was
a case of buying a fine necktie or a fine cane, had
to fast—unless, that is to say, he were to call at
Flaminio Salvo's, towards the luncheon hour,
knowing that his step-daughter would be there.
And Nicoletta, who in her shame and rage would

gladly have torn his beard off or his eyes out, had to welcome him with a smile.

She felt that she might have been a good woman, at heart, and that she really had shewn herself to be good at certain moments in her life; but that a perfidious fate had refused to allow her to be good. Wicked she was compelled to be! Everything, every atom of her was false, inside and outside and round about her. And a secret, continual struggle to overcome the stifling sense of disgust, not to feel the chafing of her mask, albeit by now it had grown to her face like a second skin. But she had over her brow a lock of upturned, unruly hair, and she feared at certain moments that her soul might similarly rise up one day in her bosom, in a sudden dash for freedom after all these years of suffocation.

And now, her husband was going to fight a duel? And she herself at a party!

So as not to see, not to be seen by too many people, she told the coachman not to go by the Via Atenea but to take the Santa Lucia road, which ran outside and below the town. She had long ceased to care what people might think when they saw her in Salvo's carriage. It was common knowledge now. Besides, even in this, appearances were to a certain extent saved by Capolino's former connexion with the Salvo family and by her own position with Don Flaminio's daughter.

Audacity had defied malice and, if it had not

entirely conquered it, had obliged it to hold its tongue and to bow down in public places; leaving it to gossip only in private, and even then with a certain philosophical indulgence. For philosophy has this to be said for it: that in the end it always finds a justification for any form of success.

Cards on the table.

Villa Salvo was situated high up, on an airy perch, and commanded the road carved in the hillside from the south. You went up to it by flights of broad steps, which conquered the steep ascent by a series of easy zigzags. At each turn, on the pillars, were four statues of a barbaric ugliness, which certainly did not offer a friendly greeting to visitors, nor appear to be congratulating them on having surmounted another stage in their climb. They were rewarded, however, on reaching the top by an enchanting view over the whole countryside undulating beneath them, with the sea in the distance.

Before mounting to the upper floor of the villa, Nicoletta made straight for Salvo's study on the ground floor; but stopped short on the threshold when she saw that he was not alone.

"Come in, come in," said Flaminio Salvo, bowing, from where he stood in front of the writing table at which a young man was seated, writing busily: Aurelio Costa.

"Forgive me, if . . ." Nicoletta began, looking at Costa, who rose from his chair.

"Nothing of the sort!" Salvo cut her short, stroking his moustaches with a cold smile, to which the slow gaze of his eyes from behind their heavy lids gave a faint suggestion of irony. "Come in . . . I was just having a chat with my engineer."

Then, observing the young man's embarrassment in the lady's presence, he added:

"What! Don't you know one another?"

"By name, of course," Nicoletta replied in a tone of indifference. "I don't think we have ever been properly introduced. . . ."

"Oh, in that case," Salvo went on, "let us observe the formalities: Ingegnere Aurelio Costa, Signora Lellè Capolino-Spoto."

Aurelio Costa, without raising his eyes, or moving from the writing table, made a slight bow. He was well dressed, with no trace of affectation, composed and dignified in his manly beauty, which the unfamiliar setting of a new suit of town clothes made a trifle rough, perhaps, by contrast.

"Is Adelaide ready?" Nicoletta asked Salvo, after examining the young man and acknowledging his protracted bow with a faint smile.

"Just one moment," Salvo replied. "Sit down, Donna Lellè, sit down. I shall run up and see. I think Adelaide must be ready."

And he went to the door.

"But it will be better if I go up too!" Nicoletta called after him.

"No, why?" said Salvo, turning round on the threshold. "Adelaide will be down directly."

He left the room.

Nicoletta refused to sit down; she wandered restlessly about the large room, furnished with a sober luxury.

Aurelio, who was still on his feet, did not know whether he ought to sit down again or not; he was afraid of committing a breach of good manners; but at the same time he was annoyed by the thought that, through a caprice on her part, he was obliged to stand there like a servant in attendance. And really she did seem to be mistress of the house: but on what terms? And he had dreamed for years of making her his, this woman! He himself, in that house, was in Salvo's service too, like her, like Capolino, like everyone; but if she had been his wife, Salvo would certainly not have dared to imagine that he could make use of her for his senile pleasures. As it was, she found herself now placed between two old men, with her blooming, voluptuous beauty contaminated. Did she relish her position? Was she making a display for his benefit of that brazen supremacy? Did she enjoy all this luxury, all the honours that were paid to her for the loss of her own honour? To be sure! In a few days her husband would be in Parliament too. . . . And she, the wife of a

Deputy! With him, on the other hand, what would she have been, supposing her to have succeeded in overcoming her horror—yes, horror!—at the thought of uniting herself with a man of such humble birth? Honour, youth, a pure and sacred love? But the waving plumes and the veil of her broad-brimmed hat meant more to her!

Weary and ashamed, he sat down.

"Oh, of course, do, please," Nicoletta exclaimed, turning round to look at him. "Do forgive me for not telling you. . . . My thoughts were wandering. . . ."

She came towards him; took her stand in front of the writing table, with a sudden, decided, provoking movement of her person.

"You will be staying here now, Ingegnere?"

"Perhaps. . . . I don't know. . . ." he answered, gazing firmly at her in his turn. "At present we are busy planning a scheme. . . . If it comes to anything . . ."

"You will remain here?"

"A manager will be required. . . ."

Nicoletta stood looking at him for a little, without any definite thought in her mind; then, gently lifting her hair from her brow with one hand:

"You studied in Paris, didn't you?"

"Yes," he replied, curtly, breathing in the intoxicating perfume which she exhaled from her irresistible person.

"Paris!" exclaimed Nicoletta Capolino, raising

her chin and half shutting her eyes. "I was there once, on my honeymoon. . . . What a whirl it is! A whirl of splendour. . . . Tell me though, couldn't you go back to government service now, if you wished?"

Aurelio looked at her, puzzled by this sudden digression. He knitted his brows; and replied:

"I don't know. I don't think so. But I should not dream of trying. I should go back on my own account to Sardinia. I am here only to oblige Signor Salvo. I should lose nothing by leaving."

"Oh, I know," she said quickly. "With your talents. . . . That is exactly what I meant! And Signor Salvo certainly won't allow you to escape, if, as you say, he has a scheme in his mind. . . ."

She screwed up her eyes and laid her finger on her lips, remained for a while in thought and continued, with a change of tone:

"But I remember you quite well, d'you know, when you were here before, as a student . . . quite a boy . . . yes, I remember you perfectly now. . . ."

Aurelio made a violent effort to resist the disturbance, the shock that her speech, uttered with so calm an impudence, had given him. What did this woman want of him? Why was she speaking to him like this?

Truly, it was difficult to guess; for Aurelio, indeed, impossible.

This sudden, unlooked-for meeting with him; the impression she had received of him; the thoughts that with her furtive, feminine glance she had read on his brow when she had taken the liberty of invading the study and afterwards during this interval of waiting; the secret humiliation of her own position, which she herself in her heart could not help feeling, in the presence of this young man who once upon a time had asked her to marry him, honourably, because he loved her; the thought that he would now be staying on here in Salvo's house, and that Dianella was secretly in love with him, and that before long he, by force of contact, might become aware of this; and that very soon, therefore—if Dianella persisted until she had overcome her father's opposition—she might have to suffer the indignity of witnessing his betrothal to her employer's daughter, had thrown Nicoletta Capolino into confusion. It would be her duty, then, to watch over the engaged couple; and that young man there, who still showed such mortification at her scornful refusal of his offer; that young man there would be amply revenged upon her: he would presently become her master, he too, as the husband of that Dianella who, she could feel, despised and loathed her. And he was good-looking too, and strong and proud! And still (as she had not failed to observe) still fascinated by herself, offended and indignant as he might be . . . Why, too, had Flaminio Salvo,

who knew the whole story, at once hurried from
the room and left her there alone with him?

She blinked her eyes again, as though to ex-
tinguish the flame of her secret thoughts, and went
on with a curious smile:

"You may remember too, perhaps . . ."

Aurelio, at a loss what to say, raised his eyes
and stared at her with a hard, grim expression.

"Don't think badly of me," she next said, with
a melancholy sweetness, tilting her head sideways.
"Since you are going to stay here and we shall
be seeing one another constantly, let us take this
opportunity of a frank discussion and clear away
a misunderstanding which would weigh upon us
both. . . . People say that I am a thoughtless
creature; so I am, I don't deny it; but I cannot
bear pretences or concealments of any sort or for
any reason, covert thoughts. . . . Are we going to
be friends?"

So saying, she held out to him her pretty, fragile, vigorous, ring-studded hand; and, after he had
taken it, left it lying in his hand for a moment
while she added:

"I'm not saying this, believe me, from coquetry,
nor am I fishing for compliments: you are still a
free man; nothing lost, nothing to regret. Are we
friends?"

And, hearing the breathless approach of Donna
Adelaide Salvo, amid a rustle of silken garments,
she clasped his hand again, hurriedly, with a

definite purpose, as though to give the form and
appearance of a secret treaty to their conversation.

"Off to the fair! Off to the fair!" exclaimed
Donna Adelaide, running into the room waving
her arms, heated and breathless. "Look, Lellè,
look, Ingegnere, my boy, how they have rigged me
up. . . . Oh, Maria Santissima, I feel like a fine
filly in season, all bells and ribbons, waiting to be
taken to the fair. . . . But it's no good arguing
with Flaminio, children; you've got to play: '*Su,
bubbolino, salutami il re*'; and keep on saying
yes, all the time. . . . You're laughing at me?
Laugh if you like. . . ."

They were indeed laughing, Nicoletta Capolino
and Aurelio Costa, while Donna Adelaide with her
arms outstretched spun about the room like a top;
they were laughing also, helplessly, with the pleasure of hearing her express so carelessly and comic-
ally their own secret impression, which they
would never have dreamed not merely of expressing but even of retaining, in such crude terms, in
their own consciousness. This was just what
Donna Adelaide wished. She felt the absurdity
of this strange and tardy marriage, and was placing her cards on the table to disarm the malice
of others.

Endowed with common sense and with a certain
spirit, she had decided that she might as well make
the most of her own privileged position and of

that of her bridegroom, which masked with an arrogant pomp all that was illegal in their marriage.
But she lent herself to the task without enthusiasm, to please her brother almost rather than herself. She knew however that the Prince was an
extremely handsome and well-mannered man.
She herself, already past her prime, since the coming of this charming Nicoletta, who had acquired
such a hold over Flaminio (and quite rightly, oh
yes, a dear girl, a dear girl, sacrificed, poor thing,
by that trickster of a husband!) had grown tired
of her own "terrible maiden-ladyship" as she
called it, and had said yes:

"Su bubbolino, salutami il re!"

Without any civil ceremony; in church only.
What did that matter to her? At her age she
would certainly not be having any children. The
priest's absolution was enough for her, it was
enough for her family and friends, and so away
we go, off to the fair! With a light heart!

Sulkiness was a thing that Donna Adelaide
could not endure. She was troubled by one thing
only: they had told her that the Prince had a long
beard. A man with a long beard must of course
be intensely serious, or at least look as though he
were. She hoped to be able to make him trim it.
Bella Madre Santissima, she would never have
the patience to stroke a great long waterfall of
hair! Shorter, the beard, shorter. . . .

Short and stout, almost neckless, Donna Adelaide was not altogether ugly; indeed she had quite a good face, but her eyes were too bright, with a crude polish like discs of enamel, and dazzlingly bright the teeth all of which she exposed in her frequent peals of laughter. She was always in a state of excitement, burdened as she was and stifled by those two enormous breasts beneath her chin, "monstrous excrescences," as she called them. And hot, hot, hot; she was always hot, and must have air, air, air!

Cassock and frock coat.

The old barrack of Valsanìa could never have anticipated, in the desolate abandonment in which it had existed for so many years, all these frills and feathers, all these gorgeous trimmings, in which the decorators had been dressing it up all the morning. And it seemed to be looking round at them, sorrowful and slightly bewildered, from the innumerable cracks in its walls, in the decrepit plaster that bulged and gapęd everywhere. Oh, look! They had hung up beneath the windows a long festoon of laurel, like a necklace; another necklace higher up, of myrtle, beneath the gutter, with paper rosettes which had terrified the sparrows on the roof. Poor dear little creatures, whom it, their good old hostel, loved so well! There they were, all of them, flown away, away, hiding among the leaves of the trees round about.

. . . And from there they sent back to it shrill cries of dismay, as much as to say:

"Good gracious, what are they doing to you, old friend, what are they doing?"

Bah! It had long been slumbering, their old friend, in the peace of the fields. Remote from the life of men which had almost abandoned it, it had gradually begun to feel itself, in its dream, a part of nature: its stones, in the dream, had begun to feel again their native mountain, from which they had been quarried and shaped; and the moisture of the deep earth had risen and diffused itself through the walls, as the sap rises to the branches of trees through their roots; and here and there in the cracks tufts of grass had sprouted, and the tiles on the roof were coated with moss. The old barrack, as it slept, rejoiced to feel itself thus reabsorbed by the earth, to feel in itself the life of mountain and plants, almost their consciousness, whereby it was now better able to understand the voice of the winds, the voice of its neighbour the sea, the twinkling of the distant stars and the gentle caress of the moon.

But now, look, men were disturbing it again, were dooming it to witness and to receive more of their strange and futile innovations. And who could say what happenings it might yet have to witness in this late autumn of its life!

What a grand new carpet blazing on the old rustic stair, with two green poles for a balustrade! What an escort of potted laurels and bamboos up the steps and along the landing above! And those damask hangings on the window sills and on the eastern terrace to hide the rusty railing! The fine carpet there too, on the terrace, with rush seats and little tables and bowls of flowers. . . . Now they were fixing an awning overhead. The reception and mutual introduction of bride and bridegroom would take place there, since they had failed to wrest from Mauro Mortara the key of the *camerone*.

Since daybreak he had been in hiding, no one knew where.

Don Cosmo, in his shirtsleeves, was tearing about amid the disorder of his bedroom, while Donna Sara Alàimo, her hair still unkempt, bowed over, buried in an old beechwood chest, long and narrow as a coffin, was trying to find him a decent coat in which to make a fitting appearance at the solemn ceremony. There rose from this chest, filled with old garments, a strong and pungent smell of camphor.

"You might at least hold the lid up for me, good Lord!" the poor "housekeeper" moaned in a suffocated voice, as though from the nether regions.

Twice already the lid had fallen upon her back.

And Don Cosmo:

"Nothing of the sort! What's the use, I say,

what's the use? We're in the country here. . . .
Don't bother me. . . ."

"But you must let me dress you . . ." Donna
Sara went on wailing from inside the chest.
"The Lord Bishop is coming . . . the bride is
coming. . . . Do you propose to appear in a
jacket? Let me find it. . . . I know it's here!"

"And I tell you that it's not there!"

"But I've seen it with my own eyes! It is
here! It is here!"

She was looking for an old frock coat which
Don Cosmo in days gone by had worn once or
twice, and which accordingly had remained brand
new, buried there under the camphor, of old-
fashioned cut, it was true, but a "fashionable garment," all the same. . . .

"Here it is!" Donna Sara cried at last in
triumph, raising her aching back from the chest.
. . . and pulled and pulled and pulled—oh,
gracious, was it as long as all that? . . . and
pulled. . . .

Donna Sara's arms slackened. It was a cassock. The cassock Don Cosmo Laurentano had
worn as a seminarist.

She drew it all out at length, gently, to fold it
properly and bury it again with due reverence.
She shook her head; sighed:

"A real pity! A real pity! Who knows but
you might be Bishop of Girgenti at this moment
instead of Monsignor Montoro. . . ."

"It would be a lively diocese!" muttered Don Cosmo. "Put it away, bury it!"

He had been disturbed by the sudden appearance of this cassock, a spectre of his fervent, boyish faith. Empty and black as the cassock itself had his soul been ever since! What anguish, what tortures it revived in him. . . .

With drooping lips and shut eyes, Don Cosmo let himself be immersed in the remote but still painful memories of his youth, a youth tormented for years on end by the bitter struggle between faith and reason. And reason had conquered faith, but only to be engulfed, in its turn, in that dark, profound, despairing scepticism.

"Was it there or wasn't it?" Donna Sara broke in upon his musings, standing before him with the frock coat spread out on her arms.

Don Cosmo had barely time to put it on. One of the bodyguard (eight of them had come over, by twos and threes, from Colimbètra, in full review order) came clattering in to announce the Bishop's arrival.

Don Cosmo groaned again; tried to raise his arms to express the annoyance that he felt at these tidings; but was unable: the frock coat . . .

"Perfect! It fits you exactly! You look a picture!" Donna Sara assured him.

"A picture indeed!" shouted Don Cosmo. "It's stifling me! I can't breathe!"

And off he went.

He had hoped that the Bishop would be the last
to arrive, and that it would not fall to himself to
receive him and to keep him company until the
other guests came. The thought of them bored
him too, the whole of this pompous tomfoolery
bored him intensely, but more than all or than any
of them the sight of the Lord Bishop, of that
exalted representative of a world from which he
had severed himself after so much suffering,
shocked most of all by the hypocrisy of so many
of his companions, who, albeit secretly assailed by
the very doubts that tormented him, had remained
in that world. And Monsignor Montoro had been
one of them. Now he held out his ring to be
kissed, and had the supreme charge of the souls
of an entire diocese. The unconscious illusions,
the spontaneous and necessary fictions of the soul,
Don Cosmo could and did excuse and commiserate
and felt sympathy for them; but the deliberate fictions, no, especially in that supreme office, in that
ministry of life and death.

"Oh, beautiful! Lovely!" Monsignore was saying meanwhile, as he alighted from the carriage
and stood gazing at the scenery, between Dianella
Salvo and his secretary, a young priest, tall and
thin and pallid, with deep intelligent eyes. "With
the sea so near . . . oh, beautiful! Lovely! . . .
and the valley . . . and the valley . . . and . . ."

He broke off, seeing Don Cosmo coming down
the steps from the decorated old mansion.

"Ah, here he comes! My dear Don Cosmo . . ."

"Monsignore, your most humble servant," said the other, bowing awkwardly.

"My dear fellow, my dear fellow . . ." Monsignore repeated, almost embracing him, and laying a hand on his shoulder. "How many years can it be since we last met. . . . Old men now, eh! old men. . . . You (we can call one another *tu*, I hope, as we did in the old days) you must, if I am not mistaken, be a year or two my senior. . . ."

"Possibly . . . yes," sighed Don Cosmo. "But who counts the years now, my dear Montoro? I know that I have many behind me, and few left to come: and the past years are a burden, and the future years seem to me enormously long. . . . That is all that I know. . . ."

Dianella Salvo, as she looked at Don Cosmo, could not help smiling at the sight of the old frock coat which gripped him under the arms. The pale young priest was smiling furtively also; and the eight men of the bodyguard, posted stiffly at the foot of the steps, stared with distress and mortification at the figure cut by the brother of the Prince their master at this solemn reception. Donna Sara Alàimo had tucked away her hair as best she might under her cap, and had come down to kiss the Bishop's hand, genuflecting to the ground; the two maids had come down with her, also the cook and the manservant, and the wife of the *curàtolo*, Ninfa's Vanni, had come up as well with her three half-naked bandy-legged urchins. Monsignore held out his hand to be kissed and smiled at them all, bowing his head. Then he introduced his secretary to Don Cosmo and, as he climbed the steps to the villa, spoke of the visit he had just paid, in passing, to the chapel of La Seta, and of the welcome he had received from all the folk of that hamlet.

"Such good people . . . such good people . . ."

And he asked Dianella and Donna Sara if they went there on Sundays, to hear mass in the chapel.

"I know that a priest comes out specially from Porto Empedocle, and that those good villagers collect a toll from the passers-by all the week, by the roadside. . . ."

As he entered the villa, he turned to Dianella and inquired:

"Your mother?"

Dianella replied with a disconsolate movement of her arms, turning pale and looking him sorrowfully in the face.

"How very sad!" sighed Monsignore, going and sitting down on the now decorated terrace. "But at least she is calm, eh?"

"She takes in nothing!" exclaimed Donna Sara.

"And she still prays, doesn't she?" the Bishop went on.

"All the time," Dianella answered.

"A consolation for you," observed Monsignore, nodding his head and half shutting his protuberant eyes, "that, in the darkness of her mind, only the light of faith should remain burning. . . . Divine mercy. . . ."

"To lose one's reason!" Don Cosmo muttered.

Monsignore shot an angry glance at him. But Don Cosmo did not observe it: he was lost in his own thoughts.

"I mean to keep her faith, even after she has lost her reason," Monsignore explained.

"Quite so!" Don Cosmo sighed, rousing himself. "It is the other thing that is difficult, my dear Monsignore!"

"I think it would not be advisable, would it, for her to see me?" the Bishop asked, turning again to Dianella as though he had not caught Don Cosmo's words. "Let us leave her, let us leave her in peace. . . . With you, though," he added, softly and with a kindly smile at Don Cosmo, "I should like to resume those heated discussions we used to have long ago, but not now and not here. . . . If you would care to come and see me. . . ."

"Discussions? I'm a perfect fool!" exclaimed Don Cosmo. "I have become a perfect fool, my dear Montoro. . . . I can no longer put two and two together! If one person tells me that two and two make six and another tells me that they make three. . . ."

"Here's the Prince!" broke in Donna Sara,

who was keeping a watch on the avenue from the balustrade of the terrace.

Monsignore rose with Dianella and Don Cosmo to see him arrive. The last ran down to embrace his brother as soon as he should alight from the carriage. There rode upon either side of it Captain Sciaralla and another officer, in review order likewise. The blazing red of their breeches shone out gaily against the green background of the trees and beneath the blue canopy of the sky. It was a closed carriage. The secretary, Lisi Préola, sat facing the Prince.

Donna Sara withdrew from the terrace, leaving only Monsignore, Dianella Salvo and the secretary to watch from the balustrade the exchange of greetings between the brothers.

"I do hope it's not going to rain!"

Don Ippolito Laurentano sprang from the carriage with boyish agility. He was in morning dress with a loose brimmed Panama hat on his head. He kissed his brother and at once drew back to examine him.

"Cosmo, what on earth have you been putting on yourself?" he asked with a smile. "No, my dear fellow, no! Go in at once and take off that relic of antiquity . . ."

Don Cosmo looked at the frock coat; he had forgotten its existence, although he felt it gripping him under the arms.

"Why yes," he said, "I do notice an odour...."

"An odour? why, you stink, my dear fellow!" exclaimed Don Ippolito. "You reek of camphor a mile away!"

He smiled at Monsignore and raised his hat in greeting to Dianella Salvo on the terrace; then began to mount the steps.

"I give you the comforting intelligence that you are a great deal more stupid than I am! Far, far more!" Don Cosmo was saying presently to the "housekeeper" who, ashamed and angry, was by no means convinced that this "fashionable garment" could be out of place on an occasion like this, with a Monsignore present. "And you've given me a headache," Don Cosmo railed, "and you've made me drunk with all your camphor. . . . Off with it, I tell you, take it off at once. . . . I can't skin myself! Give me my own coat, quickly."

When he reappeared on the terrace, Don Ippolito threw up his arms:

"Ah, heaven be praised! Now you look splendid!"

Monsignore and Dianella laughed.

"Donna Sara's ideas! What is one to do?" Don Cosmo sighed, shrugging his shoulders. "I assure you, she's even stupider than I am."

"That I can well believe!" said the Prince with a laugh. "But tell me—Mauro? Where is he? Isn't he to be seen?"

"Humph!" said Don Cosmo. "He's vanished! I've heard nothing of him now for days past, ever since we had the honour . . ."

"I know where he is," said Dianella, acknowledging Don Cosmo's compliment with a graceful bow, while he tried to cut her short. "Under one of the carubs down in the valley. . . . But, please, nobody is supposed to know! We have made friends. . . ."

"Indeed?" Don Ippolito inquired, as his radiant eyes took in the grace and beauty of the girl. "With that bear?"

"He is mad as a hatter!" Don Cosmo announced gravely.

"No, why?" put in Dianella.

"And look who it is that says so, Monsignore!" the Prince exclaimed. "I'd give anything in the world to be able to hide behind a curtain and watch the scenes that must go on between them when they are alone together. . . ."

Don Cosmo nodded his assent and uttered his habitual laugh, the threefold "Oh! oh! oh!"

"They must be rare fun!" Don Ippolito added.

Dianella was gazing with pleasure, with an indefinable satisfaction at this old man, to whom his manly beauty, his firm vigour, his sure mastery of himself, imparted a nobility at once so proud and so serene; she could imagine how exquisite must be his manners without the slightest effort and yet without a trace of affectation, and it pained her to think of him in conjunction with her Aunt Adelaide, a nature so different, so diametrically opposed to his: giggling, impulsive, noisy. What impression was he going to form of her?

They all left the terrace and all, except Monsignore and his secretary, who remained at the front door, went down to the foot of the steps, when the tinkle of silver bells announced the arrival of Flaminio Salvo's carriage from the avenue.

Don Ippolito stepped forward to help the ladies to alight, and caught his bride in the act of exclaiming: "Here we are!" with her arms upstretched towards the roof of the carriage, as though she were casting them from her. He pretended not to notice this awkward gesture, by prolonging his bow, then kissed her hand; he next kissed Donna Nicoletta Capolino's, and vigorously clasped that of Flaminio Salvo, while the two ladies rapturously embraced Dianella, and Don Cosmo stood self-consciously in the background, not knowing whether or how to introduce himself.

Captain Sciaralla on his white mare was like an equestrian statue, at the foot of the steps, facing his rigid platoon.

"Ah! The soldiers! Let me look at the soldiers!" exclaimed Donna Adelaide, waddling off like a goose, without noticing that, at the head of the steps between the potted laurels and bamboos, Monsignore Montoro, his features composed in a

kindly, condescending smile, was bowing to her
for the third time in vain.

Dianella, observing at length Don Cosmo's embarrassment, cut short Nicoletta Capolino's ex-
pansive greetings and stopped her aunt to point
out and present to her her future brother-in-law.

"Oh, of course," said Donna Adelaide, laughing and squeezing his hand in a tight grip. "Such
a pleasure! The hermit of Valsanìa, isn't it? So
delighted! And how nicely they have done the
villa up! Oh, look! Look! Why, there's Monsignore all the time. . . . And nobody told
me!"

She ran towards the steps; the Prince at once
hastened to offer her his arm; Don Cosmo gave
his to Donna Nicoletta, and Dianella went last
with her father.

"Beautifully dressed, those soldiers!" Donna
Adelaide remarked to the Prince, lifting up her
skirt in front with her disengaged hand, so as not
to trip upon the steps. "Truly charming! They
look like a lot of sugar dolls! Charming!"

Then, as she reached the head of the steps:

"Most Excellent Monsignore! I thought that
Your Excellency would be coming at your own
convenience, instead of which here you are, punc-
tual to the minute!"

The Bishop smiled, held out his hand for Donna
Adelaide to kiss his ring, and said to her:

"To have the joy of seeing you like this, on

the Prince's arm, and to bid you welcome, Donna Adelaide, to the house of Laurentano."

"But how very kind, thank you, thank you, truly gracious, Your Excellency!" replied Donna Adelaide, going first into the villa at the Prince's bidding.

Monsignore went in, and then Donna Nicoletta, then Dianella and Salvo and the Bishop's secretary and also Don Cosmo: the Prince choosing to enter last of all. When he emerged on the terrace, he intercepted the gentle gaze of Dianella, anxiously awaiting his coming. Instinctively he responded with a faint smile.

"Fine looking man, isn't he?" Nicoletta Capolino whispered to Dianella. "There certainly won't be any need to clip his beard, as Adelaide says."

"Clip his beard?" asked Dianella.

"Yes," the other replied. "She kept us in fits of laughter in the carriage, with her terror of the Prince's long beard."

"What are you two talking about over there?" Donna Adelaide broke into the conversation at this point. "Are you laughing at us? They are laughing at you and me, my dear Prince. Silly girls! But we must grin and bear it: that's what we are here for; this is our day. . . . Like going to the fair! Flaminio, my boy, don't devour me with your eyes. Give me courage, if anything! I do everything you tell me, always. . . . But let me enjoy myself! I say foolish things, because I'm excited. . . . Come along, Nicoletta! With your permission, Prince, I am going to pay my poor sister-in-law a visit."

And off she went, followed by her niece and by Nicoletta.

At once Salvo, to remove the unfavourable impression left on the Prince's mind by his sister's outburst, explained with an air of mystery that Signora Capolino was unaware that her husband, possibly at that very moment, was fighting a duel, and that she supposed him to be at Siculiana on a tour of his constituency.

"Let us pray to God that all may be well!" sighed Monsignore, in a tone of deep distress, raising his globular eyes to heaven.

"Oh, there's no doubt about that!" smiled Salvo. "A ridiculous adversary, who has been beaten by everybody, always: short, stout and blind as a bat. Whereas our friend Capolino . . ."

"Just after I left the house," said Don Ippolito, "I could see the two carriages in the distance coming along the road towards Colimbètra."

"Why, yes," added Salvo, "by this time, they're certain to be . . ."

He stopped short. They were all silent for a moment, helpless in the grip of terror, and their thoughts flew far away to the other villa where at that moment the duel was being fought. There, was a very different spectacle: two men face to face, two drawn sabres, flashing in the air; here, amid the silence of the fields, the pompous decorations, improvised for a festal occasion which now, strangely enough, appeared to them all to be almost out of place, artificial, forced.

There was indeed, from the moment of their arrival, a certain awkward chill in the spirits of both the Prince and Salvo, which they were each doing his best to conceal. This chill was caused by Landino's reply, which had at last arrived, to his father's letter: the usual congratulations, the usual wishes for the future, delicately worded expressions of his pleasure at the kind and loving companionship that his father would now have; but not a word as to his own coming down to attend the wedding.

Don Ippolito, as he started from Colimbètra, had made up his mind to send Mauro Mortara to Rome, to let Landino know how displeased, how pained his father was with his behaviour, and to try to bring him back to Sicily. He knew that Landino from his earliest boyhood had entertained a deep and tender affection for old Mauro and a keen admiration for his character, for his fanatical loyalty to the memory and ideas of Landino's grandfather, for the almost contemptuous attitude which he had adopted from the beginning and still maintained towards the father, that is to say towards Don Ippolito himself, who for all that was his master. No other envoy was likely to prove so effective. For this savage old rustic was, so to speak, rooted in the heart of the family, the voice of the ancient Valsanìa, their native soil.

He thought he would seize the opportunity of the ladies' absence to go out to the head of the steps and tell Sciaralla to send Ninfa's Vanni down to the gorge to look for Mauro, as he wished to speak to him.

When he returned to the terrace, he found there Donna Adelaide, Donna Nicoletta and Dianella. The two former had taken off their hats. Donna Adelaide's eyes were red with tears and Dianella was paler and Salvo darker than before.

"I did not ask you, Don Flaminio," said the Prince, in a sympathetic tone, "to present me to your wife, because I know, alas . . ."

"Oh, thank you, thank you," Salvo cut him short, shrinking into himself and nodding his head gently, with half shut eyes, as much as to say: "Thank you . . . it is just as though she were not in the house!"

Donna Adelaide had gone across to the balustrade of the terrace and, with her back turned to the party, was wiping her eyes and loudly blowing her nose, saying to Nicoletta Capolino, who was begging her to calm herself:

"I am a great donkey, I know! But how am I to help it? Whenever I see her, whenever I see those eyes of hers, they make me feel so wretched!"

Suddenly, making an effort, she threw up her arms, tossed her head as though she were stifling, panted: "Ufff, that will do for the present!" and turned round smiling.

Two footmen in livery appeared on the terrace with big trays loaded with cups and cakes. After these refreshments, Monsignor Montoro took the floor to announce in a polished little discourse (which was intended, nevertheless, to give the impression of its having been improvised on the spot) the formal promise of marriage that had been exchanged, and proceeded naturally to extol the good old days in which a contract made before God was sufficient by itself, in civilized society, to fasten the bond of matrimony, which religion alone can render sacred and noble, whereas the law of man, the so-called civil law degrades it and almost makes it infamous. . . .

All the rest listened with lowered eyes, religiously, to the Bishop's glowing words. Only Don Cosmo sat with knitted brows and fixed gaze, as though he hoped in one of those words to find the peg for a philosophical discussion. Don Ippolito, seeing him adopt this attitude, became seriously worried about him. Flaminio Salvo, for his part, with that letter from Rome upon his mind, was thinking that it was all very well, what the Bishop was saying, but that meanwhile the Prince's noble son was turning a deaf ear, that the other side were not abiding by their agreement and that his sister, without the slightest guarantee, was allowing herself to be compromised from the start. To Donna Adelaide, this little sermon was like any sacred function, almost like hearing mass: a formality, nothing more. A piece of play-acting, on the other hand, and one that was not very amusing at the moment, it seemed to Nicoletta Capolino, and disgusting to Dianella who was watching the other and could read on her brow all that was passing through her mind.

A light breeze had risen from the sea, and the awning overhead kept on swelling and rising like a balloon, while a corner of the damask hanging slapped insolently against the railing it concealed.

This slapping noise at length distracted the never very close attention that Donna Adelaide had been paying to the little sermon, which had already lasted too long, and, as a cloud borne on the breeze hid the sun for a moment, she bent down to peep out at the sky from under the awning, and could not repress a murmur of:

"I do hope it's not going to rain. . . ."

These few words, although barely audible, had a disastrous effect, as though the entire party (Monsignore, of course, excepted) were irresistibly led to discover an immediate connexion between the threat of rain and this ponderous and interminable sermon.

Don Cosmo opened his eyes and stared; Donna Nicoletta could not repress a titter of laughter;

Don Flaminio frowned; Monsignore stopped short, lost his thread, said:

"Let us hope not," and at once added: "And now to conclude."

He concluded, naturally, with good wishes and congratulations, and the rest of the party rose with great relief.

Donna Adelaide, feeling that she would stifle beneath that awning, suggested going down for a stroll along the avenue. The Prince gave her his arm, Nicoletta went next with Dianella, and Monsignore, Salvo, Don Cosmo and the secretary followed in their wake.

Don Ippolito Laurentano felt his tongue parched and tied by the desperate struggle that was raging within him between his chivalrous instincts, which impelled him to be courteous and attentive to the lady, and the enormous, freezing disappointment and invincible repulsion which her manners, her behaviour, her gestures, her voice, her laugh had at once aroused in him; between the instinctive, overpowering, irresistible need to free himself from her at the earliest possible moment, dismissing without more ado a project which now, when it came to the point, seemed to him to fall so lamentably short of the idea that he had formed of it, and the thought of the serious difficulty of so doing, now that he had definitely pledged himself—with his resentment to boot, secret and bitter, against his absent son, to whom he would ap-

pear to be owning himself beaten, after he had so
far humbled himself as almost to crave his son's
consent to this marriage. He was boiling, lastly,
with the bitterest rage at Monsignore, who had
depicted his bride to him in such deceiving colours: "Lively, a warm heart, an open nature, sincere, vivacious, submissive. . . ." What on earth
was he to say to her now? How bring himself to
address her?

Fortunately, Captain Sciaralla appeared at this
moment, and, standing to attention, announced
that Mortara had come up from the *vallone*.

"Where is he?" said the Prince curtly. "Tell
him to come here."

"Mauro?" Don Cosmo asked. "Oh no, let him
alone, poor fellow. . . . You know what he's
like. . . ."

"Oh, the person they call the Monk?" exclaimed
Donna Adelaide. "Let us go and see him, let us
go at once, Prince, please!"

"No, aunt!" implored Dianella, who was sorry
that she had revealed his hiding place. "It would
hurt his feelings."

"Is he really such a bear, then?" said Donna
Adelaide, puzzled.

"A grizzly bear!" Don Cosmo assured her.

"Just fancy," put in Flaminio Salvo; "after
all this time I have never yet succeeded in setting
eyes on him. . . ."

And Nicoletta inquired:

"Is it true that he wears a goatskin on his head and goes about armed to the teeth?"

"Let you and me go by ourselves, Prince!" was Donna Adelaide's next suggestion. "I do so want to see him . . . I can't wait, come along!"

Mauro was standing outside the door of his room in the basement, staring moodily over the vineyard to the sea. Seeing the Prince with a lady, his face darkened, but, as Don Ippolito gave him a friendly greeting, he advanced towards him and stooped down to kiss him on the breast. His kiss was followed by a sort of sob.

"My old friend," said Don Ippolito, touched by this kiss over his heart, "do you know who this lady is?"

"I can guess; may God give you happiness!" replied Mauro, gazing solemnly at Donna Adelaide, who was staring at him with wide and glistening eyes and a smile on her lips.

"I wish to give you happiness as well," the Prince went on. "Would you like to go to Rome?"

"To Rome? I?" exclaimed Mauro in amazement. "To Rome? You can ask me that? Who knows how many times I would have gone there on foot, as a pilgrim, if my legs . . ."

"Good," the Prince interrupted him, "you shall go there on the steamer and the train. I have a message for you to give to Landino. Come tomorrow to Colimbètra . . . that is to say, not tomorrow . . . let me think! I shall send over for you in the course of the week. I have a lot to say to you."

"And then . . . straight to Rome?" Mauro faltered.

"Immediately!"

"Because I am an old man," Mauro went on. "On my two crooked sevens.[1] And the thought of dying without seeing Rome has always worried me!"

"But will you go dressed like that, to Rome?" Donna Adelaide asked him.

"No, Signora," Mauro replied. "I have a good coat here, of broadcloth, and a black hat, like your bridegroom's."

"And that hairy cap," Donna Adelaide asked again, "how can you wear it? Oh Lord, the very sight of it makes me sick!"

"This cap . . ." Mauro was beginning to explain; but a sudden shout, from the other end of the house, cut him short.

"Don Ippolito, come, quickly! Capolino. . . ."

"What has happened?" screamed Donna Adelaide.

"Wounded?" asked the Prince.

"Yes; badly, it seems. . . ." Salvo answered. "Come!"

"But who says so?"

"One of your men has ridden over from Colim-

[1] The number 77, in Italy, is symbolical of the bent legs of an old man. So the British soldier speaks of "legs-eleven," and the Frenchman says "prendre le train onze." C. K. S. M.

bètra. . . . They have carried him up to your house, wounded in the chest. . . . I don't know yet if it was a sabre or a pistol. . . . And poor Signora Nicoletta, here with us!"

When they reached the villa, Donna Nicoletta was struggling in the arms of the Bishop and Dianella, moaning incessantly:

"My heart told me so! My heart spoke to me! My hat . . . my hat. . . . The carriage, quick. . . . Scoundrels, murderers. . . . Oh, my Gnazio!"

"The carriage is at the door!" Captain Sciaralla came in to announce.

Nicoletta dashed out without saying good-bye to anyone.

"What about you, Prince?" said Salvo.

"Ought I to go too?" asked Don Ippolito.

To which Salvo:

"It would be as well. You, Adelaide, will remain here to-night. Come along. Come along."

The carriage, with Nicoletta, the Prince and Salvo in it, set off at full speed.

"Oh Holy Mother of God, what bad luck!" Donna Adelaide was left exclaiming at the head of the steps, beating her hands together. "But what were they doing with a duel to-day, of all days? Is that fair? Leave God out of it, Monsignore! If you don't mind! What is the good of praying? . . . Your Excellency must excuse me, but is this the sort of trick to play on a poor woman like me?"

CHAPTER VIII

A phantom conclave.

IN the house of Donna Caterina Auriti Laurentano, on the day of the election, were assembled
round Roberto the few friends who had remained
faithful to him, notwithstanding his having ceased
to correspond with them for many years. He had
found them, in the last few days, altered like himself by time and the vicissitudes of life.

For a moment, in the eyes of each of them, as
they embraced their friend, there had kindled and
flashed the old youthful expression of those far
off days, unconscious still of what fate held in
store for them; then immediately, with a slight
shake of their heads, those eyes had grown misty
with emotion, with agonizing regret, while their
lips parted in a sad and bitter smile.

"Who would have said," that misty gaze and
that smile seemed to ask, "who would have told
us then that one day we should have come to
this? That we should have lost so many things,
which were everything in life to us then, and
which we should have thought it impossible to
lose? And yet we have lost them; and life has
remained to us; but what a life: this!"

More painful still was the spectacle of one who
had not noticed, or who pretended not to have
noticed his losses, and showed his unconsciousness
in the care he devoted to his middle-aged person,
which exhibited, in a compassionately enfeebled
form, the airs and graces of another generation.

Each of them had adapted himself as best he
might to his own fate, had made a niche, a position for himself. Sebastiano Ceràulo, a lawyer
who had scraped through his examinations, a fervent improviser of patriotic poetry in the years of
the Revolution, at that time a spirited, impetuous
youth, with a forest of unkempt locks, had been
appointed, by personal influence, secretary in the
Provincial office, and now trained over his scalp
with pitiable industry the wisp of long, carefully
waxed hair that remained on it; he had grown
enormously stout; had taken a wife; had had by
her five children, all girls hot in pursuit of hus-
bands. Marco Sala, sentenced to death by the
Bourbon Government, who notwithstanding had
returned again and again to Sicily from his place
of exile, disguised as a friar, to distribute Mazzini's proclamations by stealth; had gone first of
all into the sulphur business; had done very well
for several years; then had come to grief; and
for some time supported his family by gambling;
finally he had been made keeper of a tobacco
warehouse. Rosario Trigona, who on the 15th of
May, 1860, at Girgenti, while Garibaldi was fight-

ing at Calatafimi, had sallied forth alone, an act
of madness, with a handful of comrades, the tri-
colour in one hand and a long sabre in the other,
to face the three thousand men of the Bourbon
garrison, and who, pursued, under a rain of bullets, had escaped by a miracle, and made his way
on foot to the victorious Garibaldi, running day
and night and dodging the royal army which was
scouring Sicily in search of the Filibuster, who
was by that time at Gibilrossa above Palermo;
Rosario Trigona, crippled now by nephritis,
flabby, bald, toothless and half blind, likewise burdened with a family, was dragging out a wretched
existence on the meagre salary of assistant secretary in the Chamber of Commerce. And Mattia
Gangi, who had flung his cassock to the winds to
take part in the Revolution, now, asthmatic, ir-
ritable, his beard, hair and bushy eyebrows dyed
the colour of egg-fruit, was teaching in the elementary school *alauda est laeta: the lark is blithe.*
"Blithe? Not a bit of it!" he would add, to the
boys who stared, open-eyed. "How is she blithe?
Why is she blithe? She seems blithe to us! She
sings because she is hungry, she sings to call her
mate! Blithe, indeed! Don't you believe it!"
In contrast to him was Filippo Noto, tall, thin and
wasted, but still golden-haired and neat. Before
1860 he had fought a duel with a young officer in
the Bourbon army over a woman and had been
prosecuted; this amorous adventure had served

him as a patriotic precedent; but he cared little
for politics; by dint of hard reading he had succeeded in keeping himself afloat, in moving with
the times, while remaining a lukewarm Conserva-
tive; he was regarded as one of the most experi-
enced members of the Sicilian bar, and was often
briefed to defend the most important civil cases
even at Palermo, Messina, Catania.

These five friends and Canon Agrò were endeavouring to keep the conversation going, talking of impersonal matters, of remote events, re-
calling anecdotes which provoked an occasional
forced laugh; in order simply that the weight of
defeat, however clearly foreseen, might not, with
the additional burden of silence, press too heavily
upon their troubled minds. But as a matter of
fact, gradually, after the first shock of seeing
their friend again and now with their increasing
emotion at renewing the old memories of their
youth, the four walls of their present consciousness were beginning to melt, and they, with a sort
of secret disturbance, which weakened their resistance, became aware that not only were the persons that they now were inhabiting their bodies;
but that those other persons, also, which they
had been years and years before, were living
still and feeling and reasoning with the same
thoughts, the same sentiments that they had supposed to be obscured, cancelled, extinguished
by a long oblivion. There came to life at that

moment in each one of them another unsus-
pected self, that self which each of them had
been thirty years or so earlier; but so living, so
present that, as they looked at themselves, they
received a strange impression, sad and at the same
time absurd, of their present appearance, which
even to themselves seemed scarcely to be real.
There was present, actually present, alive and active in each of them, the past; and the present
had practically ceased to exist.

From time to time, however, there came into
the room Antonio Del Re, who saw them as the
elderly men that they were, and, after listening
for a while to their conversation, felt an ineffable
sadness, the sadness that we feel when we see in
old men who have forgotten for a moment that
they are old, certain passions still vigorous for
things, for people that to us are dead or obsolete:
passions that have their roots in a soil of which
we know nothing, which is no longer ours, which
was the old men's, and which we have passed beyond in our advance, dragging after us their
feeble bodies, not their souls: their souls have
been left behind.

"We had been sitting up playing cards at San
Gerlando," Marco Sala was recounting, "until
nearly midnight, at Giacinto Lumìa's, poor fellow."

"Poor Giacinto!" Trigona sighed, shaking his
head.

"Vincenzo Guarnotta was with us, from Siculi-ana," Sala went on.

"Ah, Vincenzo!" said Roberto Auriti. "What has become of him?"

"Dead," replied Sala. "It must be nine or ten years ago. He had come to Girgenti on business, and was staying at the Convent of Sant' Anna, as he used always to do. Even the Convent is gone now! It was a terrible night: wind, thunder, lightning, rain, rain that seemed to be bringing the roof down. So much so that in the end Giacinto Lumìa invited us all to spend the night there. We should find some sort of shakedown. The others, being bachelors, and Guarnotta, the stranger, ac-cepted the invitation; I, in spite of his entreaties, insisted upon going home so as not to keep my mother (now with God) and my wife in suspense. Before I left the house, Guarnotta, knowing that on my way home I must pass along the Stretto di Sant' Anna, asked me to knock at the gate of the Convent and tell the Brother Porter that he would be sleeping out that night. I promised to do so, and left. I assure you that, as soon as I had started, I regretted that I had not accepted Lumìa's hospitality. What a wind! It carried you off your feet! The rain came lashing down like bullets; and the cold and darkness, a darkness torn to ribbons by the ghastly streaks of light-ning! All the same, as I passed along the Stretto di Sant' Anna, I remembered what Guarnotta had

said, and stopped to knock at the Convent door.
I knocked, and knocked again: nothing happened!
Nobody heard me! It was a wonder I didn't
break down the door. I was just going away, in
a towering rage, when I heard a barred window
open above my head and a voice shout: 'Who's
there?' 'Sala,' say I, 'Marco Sala!' 'All
right!' shouts the voice from above; and with
that I hear the window being shut and bolted. I
stood there gaping. They hadn't given me time
to open my mouth, and yet it was all right? I
shook with rage at the thought that simply to
oblige Guarnotta, who had remained under cover,
I, at the risk of catching my death of cold, had
perhaps made them think me mad or drunk. Who
would ever wander about at that time of night,
in such weather? Well, I had gone a few yards,
when I heard, echoing down the Stretto, the slow
boom of a bell, which made me jump: *'Dong!'*
And the wind made the sound spread, mournfully,
through the night. Then, again, *dong—dong—*
more slow booms; there must have been fifteen
of them; I didn't stop to count. I reached my
house, tore off my clothes which were clinging to
me; dried myself thoroughly; jumped into bed,
and went off to sleep. Next morning, I get up
early, as my habit is, go to answer the door, and
guess what I find there. The bearers with the
bier. As soon as they catch sight of me, they
throw up their arms, start back; stand there

speechless: 'Don Marco! What's this? Your Exc'ency's not dead?' 'You dogs!' I shout, raising my stick. 'Yes, sir,' they go on. . . . 'They sent up to Sant' Anna, last night, to say that Your Exc'ency was dead!' That bell, d'you understand, had been tolling for me. And I had called there myself to report my own death.''

Albeit this little tale was not a merry one, Sala's closing words were drowned in his friends' laughter.

"You laugh, do you?" he said. "And yet, who knows whether I didn't really die that night, my friends! Yes, indeed! I can honestly say that it was the last merry evening of my youth! Perhaps, with constantly thinking about it, the impression of that tolling bell has become fixed in my memory, an evil omen; but it does seem to me that just at that very time my life began to be pent in a torrent of misfortunes, became for me what the Stretto di Sant' Anna was on that night of storm, and that the *dong—dong* of that passing bell has followed me all the way.''

At this point Antonio Del Re reappeared with a fresh telegram. A number of these had already come in from the various polling stations in the constituency. Canon Agrò opened it, cast his eyes over the contents and flung it into a corner, on the chair by the sofa. Neither Roberto nor any of the rest took the trouble to inquire from what district it came, what result it announced. Agrò's gesture and silence had been more than eloquent.

The defeat of the moment, which affected Auriti, made more evident the other, far more serious, irreparable defeat which had been inflicted upon each of them by time and life. And this defeat seemed to be symbolized, in statuesque form, in the person of Donna Caterina Auriti Laurentano, taciturn and brooding.

From time to time Roberto and his friends cast a furtive glance at her, as at a phantom of the days of which they were the futile survivors. Other voices were there in these days, which found no echo in their hearts; other thoughts which did not enter their minds; other energies, other ideals, against which their spirits were sealed in hostile aloofness.

And the proof of this was crudely obvious in that heap of telegrams, lying there on the chair.

There had come forward unexpectedly, in the last few days, but certainly after a long and secret preparation, a third candidate in the shape of one Zappalà of Grotte, a mining expert: whose nomination was openly declared to be an act of protest and assertion by the sulphur workers and farm labourers of the Province, now united in Fasci.

Roberto Auriti had dropped to the third place. In almost all the districts this Zappalà had received more votes than he, putting him thus out of the running, by a quick, contemptuous thrust, as one might kick out of one's path a useless piece of rubbish, a nuisance rather than an obstacle.

At one point, when the telegram arrived from Grotte, which was one of the principal centres of the sulphur industry in the Province, with the report that the voters there had been almost unanimous for Zappalà, it seemed that he might even prove a serious rival to Capolino, and qualify for a second ballot, notwithstanding the enthusiastic support which the clerical champion had received in Girgenti, to console him for his serious injury in the duel.

Trigona, wishing to cloak the truth in a pious fraud, sought to ascribe their defeat principally to the result of this ill-advised duel, to the undue violence shown by Verònica, a stranger, and to the arrogant behaviour of one of his seconds, that Signor what's-his-name, the swashbuckler, which had genuinely shocked and outraged the citizens of Girgenti, in spite of the fact that Selmi, who in the mean time had returned to his own constituency, had done everything in his power to temper their indignation.

Canon Agrò nodded his head in silence. He could not forgive Verònica for having ruined, by that disgraceful scene in public, the strategic plan which he had pondered and constructed with such subtle guile. And that other Cavaliere, Giovan Battista Mattina! Sent to Grotte to support Auriti's candidature, he had played the part of

Judas, going over at the last moment to the Popular Party.

"But who is the fellow?" Mattia Gangi demanded with his habitual savage glare. "What does he represent? What does he live on? What does he do? What sewer has he escaped from? Sleek and overdressed, with the airs of a sovereign prince. . . ."

Canon Agrò shook his head gently, curling his lips in a sneer, then said:

"Kites, my dear friends, kites! He, Verònica, and ever so many more! They are all kites. . . . You see them up overhead, in the seven heavens, you stand open-mouthed gaping at them; and all the time who knows what hand it is that is paying out the string? It may be the hand of some bad woman; or the string may start from the police headquarters, or from some midnight gambling den. . . . No one can tell! The kite meanwhile is there, it takes the wind, flies with it and seems to rule it. Every now and then, a blunder, a swoop, all the signs of a headlong crash. But the unknown hand, down below, sends it up at once with a gentle, cunning twitch or a strong energetic tug, and gets it into the wind again and goes on paying out more and more string. Kites, my dear friends. . . . How many we see! And they all have tails, *et in cauda venenum.* . . ."

Six heads nodded to express their approval, silently and with intense bitterness, of this imaginative flight by Canon Agrò, who himself seemed to remain slightly dazed by it for some moments, and heaved a sigh of relief, as though he had thus eased his spirit of the burden of defeat.

Roberto Auriti was more distressed by his mother's obstinate, brooding silence. She had spoken volubly at first (which was unlike her), seeking to dissuade him from the venture; and weighty had her words been then; weightier still, now, was her silence. She intended that only the facts should speak now, in plain terms, confirming all that she had said.

With a feeling of irritation, he put in:

"Whatever they may be, my friends, kites or serpents . . . we need not consider them! To hear you speak, one would think that I, in coming here, was under some illusion. . . . Nothing of the sort, as you know. I was sent here by One to Whom I could not say no: I should have felt that I was a deserter."

"Poor Christ!" exclaimed Mattia Gangi. "You have come here to be crucified!"

"Not crucified, surely," Roberto smiled. "It was that my offer, with whatever value it might have in the present campaign, might be rejected by my fellow-citizens; and that their answer, given in my name to the Government, might make the Government think that something else is wanted here now for a change!"

"Zappalà, Zappalà is what is wanted!" Mattia Gangi sneered. "How I should love to see Zappalà elected!"

"Mamma," Roberto added softly, laying his hand on his mother's arm, with a smile of bitter resignation, "you can't teach an old donkey . . ."

His mother thrust out her lip and knitted her brows, while the others shouted in chorus, echoing Mattia Gangi's wish that Zappalà might be elected. One Zappalà only? No! Five hundred and eight Zappalàs, one for every constituency in the Peninsula! What scenes there would be in the Chamber! The first thing would be to abolish all the schools! Abolish all taxation! Abolish the army and the police! Law and order, soap and water! The frontiers levelled, and universal brotherhood! Yes, yes, cut the heads off the mountains, reduce them all to hillocks of uniform height! And Mattia Gangi, springing to his feet, began to declaim:

> Al ronzìo di quella lira
> Ci uniremo, gira gira,
>   Tutti in un gomitolo.
> Varietà d'usi e di clima
> Le son 'fisime di prima;
>   E' mutata l'aria.
> I deserti, i monti, i mari,
> Son confini da lunari,
>   Sogni di geografi. . . .

> . . . E tu pur chètati, o Musa,
> Che mi secchi con la scusa
> Dell'amor di patria.
> Son figliuol dell'universo
> E mi sembra tempo perso
> Scriver per l'Italia.[1]

They had all risen to their feet, all except Pompeo Agrò, and were applauding enthusiastically.

"Gentlemen, gentlemen," said Filippo Noto, clawing his cuffs down from under his sleeves, "let us be fair, gentlemen; do not let us find fault with them, when the wrong is all on our side! Yes, on ours! With us Christian people! When we hear them say: 'We intend that to everyone shall be given according to his work! We intend that the spirit of man shall be able to raise itself above material cares! We intend that everyone shall have bread to eat and work to do!' we ignorant bourgeois, we tender-hearted Christians, are the first to applaud. . . ."

"Why, of course! Of course! Of course!" cried Ceràulo. "In the desire for universal happiness, of course! All honest minds are agreed as to that."

"Very good, so they are, and the Socialists

---

[1] To the thrumming of that lyre, we join our hands and round we go, all in a ring. Differences of custom and clime are fancies of the past; we have changed the tune. Deserts, mountains, seas, are frontiers only in the almanacs, dreams of geographers. . . . And do you keep silence now, O Muse, who weary me with the plea of love of country. I am a child of the universe, and it seems to me a waste of time to write for Italy.

(ahem!) open their mouths, and you drop in,"
Filippo Noto promptly retorted. "They give us
a glimpse of an ideal humanity and justice, with
which nobody can find fault, for which everybody
must feel enthusiastic; and so they make prose-
lytes to their cause among those who cannot distinguish between the poetry of the ideal and the
reality of social life, my dear Ceràulo! Simpletons, simpletons who are incapable of asking
themselves even whether the new methods are not
calculated to increase a thousandfold the hardships and the sadness of our vale of tears; am I
not right, Monsignore?"

Pompeo Agrò nodded his head in approval.

"The real danger, gentlemen, lies in this," Noto
went on with increasing warmth: "in the conviction at which we Christians have arrived, that the
movement of the so-called Fourth Estate is inev-
itable, irresistible. . . ."

"It is, it is, it is, alas!" Ceràulo again interrupted him.

"Nothing of the sort! Absolute nonsense!"
shouted Filippo Noto. "The Socialist theory lacks
the support of science, my dear Sir, of science, of
logic, of morals, even of civilization; it cannot
maintain itself, and is bound to collapse like a
crazy dream, like a drunkard's nightmare! I
should like to prove it to you, I should like to
prove it to every one, and first of all to the men
in power who make us look on at the pitiable spec-

tacle of a State that yields, a State that goes astray and burdens itself with things with which it ought not to burden itself!"

He grew somewhat calmer, held up his hands and continued in a different tone:

"Let me explain myself, briefly. The whole procedure is a mistake, from a to z. Just consider! Making provision for the aged, for women, for foundlings, for the sick, may be a matter that really is in the public interest."

"In the interest of humanity," said Trigona.

"Precisely! I quite agree!" Noto assured him. "But from assisting actual misfortune by means of orphanages, night shelters, soup kitchens, it has been an easy, an unconscious step, my friends, to the safeguarding of the proletariat . . ."

"The so-called proletariat," Gangi muttered through his teeth.

" . . . from potential misfortunes as well," Noto went on, "thanks to compulsory insurance against the accidents arising out of employment and against the worker's future incapacitation by old age or sickness. Now does it not seem to you self-evident, my friends, given these first steps, that others will follow which will lead us ever farther in the direction of that Providential State so strongly condemned by the most eminent practical writers? Because, when the public mind has once entertained the idea that the community

ought to look after those who from bodily incapac-
ity are unable to work, it is an easy jump across
the ditch that separates us from the true realm
of socialism, by extending the principle to those
men who are able-bodied and unemployed. And
the fact must be admitted! If these men, notwithstanding their willingness to work, cannot
find work, or if their labour is not adequately rewarded, are they, do you think, less to be pitied
than those who by some physical defect are unable
to work? The effect is the same, gentlemen, unde-
served starvation! And with the proclamation
of the right to work, anyone can see where we
shall end; we have seen it already, for that matter, in France, in 1848 . . ."

At this point a sudden cry of rage from Canon
Agrò interrupted Filippo Noto's speech, which
was beginning to assume the proportions and tone
of a platform oration.

There had come in from Comitini, Agrò's native
village, a letter reporting a fresh betrayal. Rosario Trigona's son had sold himself there to Capolino's party, and was spreading the report that
Roberto Auriti had laid down his arms, was retiring from the fray, and begged his supporters to
vote for the Clerical candidate against the Socialist Zappalà.

Agrò could not contain himself: without pity for
the poor, half-blind father, who was in the room

with him, he heaped coals of fire upon the wretch
who had brought upon him so serious an affront,
there in his own stronghold.

Roberto Auriti made several attempts to stop
him, then hastened to console his friend, who at
first had risen to his feet, horrified, ready to fling
himself upon the letter and upon Agrò, then had
let himself sink heavily down on his chair,
and burst out sobbing, burying his face in his
hands.

"But it's sure to be a slander, Rosario . . . a
slander, you'll find that it is! Your son must have
acted in good faith, believing that he was inter-
preting my wishes. . . . In fact, between the two,
between Capolino and this man Zappalà, why, it
is better that the votes should go to Capolino.
. . . He has decided that I cannot keep up the
struggle . . . and . . ."

"No . . . no . . ." Rosario Trigona moaned
between his sobs, inconsolable. "The wretch!
The wretch!"

Fortunately, they were joined by Mauro Mortara, who had gone from Valsanìa to Colimbètra
to arrange with the Prince for his expedition to
Rome. He knew nothing about the election. Welcomed with joy by Marco Sala, Ceràulo, Gangi,
who had not set eyes on him for years, he thrust
them all aside with his arms and almost fell on
his knees before Donna Caterina, seizing her hand
and kissing it again and again; he then embraced

Roberto and bent down to kiss him on the breast, over his heart.

"To Rome!" he said. "Have you heard? I'm coming to Rome!"

But his jubilation aroused no echo: they were all still disconcerted and upset by Trigona's tears.

"Oh, Don Rosario!" exclaimed Mauro. "Why, what is the matter? Why?"

He looked round the circle and fastened his eyes on Canon Agrò, who appeared the most sombre and disturbed of them all.

"Nothing," Roberto interposed quickly. "A report which is sure to be unfounded. Gentlemen, please! I am pained . . . pained by your distress . . . far more than for myself. Do you wish to make me happy? Let us say nothing more about it. Let bygones be bygones! That will do! You know how fond I am of you all, and why. I do not thank you for what you have done for me, on this occasion, because I know that, if the times have changed, our hearts have not changed, and that you therefore could not help doing for me what you have done. The mistake is ours, really, my friends! And we all know it, and have known it for some time, one in one way, another in another. And so . . . and so that will do: why complain of things now? It has been an additional test, of which I, for my part, did not feel any need. . . . That is all!"

Roberto Auriti was at the end of his patience.

The sight of these friends gathered round him and his mother's silence, Trigona's tears, Agrò's bitter resentment, Noto's frigid pedantry had become unendurable. He was in a hurry to write to Rome, to report the loss of the election without delay to his mistress, to her who for so long had lulled to sleep his aspirations and his dislikes, and with whom he, submerged now in indifference to everything that was not related directly and minutely to her person, lazy and forgetful, satisfied only the brutal appetite of his senses.

In the presence of his mother's nobility, his sister's purity, he felt himself almost instinctively obliged to conceal even from himself his passionate thraldom to this woman who knew all his sorrows. And he wrote to her at night, misrepresenting his own feelings, since to remain at peace with her and to have her docile and prompt to his wishes, he had not ventured to confess to her, before leaving Rome, the true reason for which he was engaging in this contest, but had given her to understand that it was to strengthen his position, by bringing himself—as a Deputy—more into prominence. And in his first letters he had allowed her to hope that victory was not improbable; then gradually had left her in doubt; he had written to her finally that the only thing which mattered to him now was that he should return at once to her side. He went himself to the post with these letters, whereas for all the rest of his correspondence he employed his nephew. And yet he knew that this nephew, next day, would be going with him to take up his university career in Rome and would be living in his house, and would see, therefore, and know everything. But he preferred, so long as he was there, to keep his secret. That unkempt, angular youth was not formed, certainly, to attract anybody's confidence. And Roberto resented the thought of having to take the boy with him, of letting him know, and, through him, his mother and sister, the nature of the life that he was leading in Rome. But how was he to get out of it?

Donna Caterina, meanwhile, was asking Mauro for news of her brother Cosmo, "that lunatic," and of Donna Sara Alàimo.

"Don't speak of them, for pity's sake!" exclaimed Mauro. "I am going to Rome, I tell you, and I know nothing more, I don't wish to know anything more at present!"

"My dear Mauro," Donna Caterina answered him, with a bitter smile, "if that is how it is, shut your eyes, stop your ears tight and go back this very instant to the country: take my advice!"

The bats on the avenue.

When, from the Badia Grande, the party came down to the Via Atenea, they found themselves caught in a stream of people who were cheering the announcement of Ignazio Capolino's election.

Canon Agrò's carriage was obliged to halt. The old butler-coachman with the crooked legs kept cracking his whip: "Hey, by your leave! Hey, by your leave!" How could he ever have imagined that people would be wanting in respect for his master, or that his master could shew fear? And, amid the clamour and confusion, he did not hear the voice of the Canon who was shouting to him:

"Turn back, Cola! Back! Go by the Via del Purgatorio!"

"A hoot of derision, another, a third. . . . Sons of dogs! But Capolino was still in bed, convalescent in the Prince of Laurentano's villa, at Colimbètra, and the demonstration of rejoicing, for want of a direct outlet, was sorely tempted to change there and then into a demonstration of protest against Canon Agrò. Fortunately, the section leaders managed to quell the storm which threatened to burst upon the rashly venturing carriage, showing respect not for Pompeo Agrò, who deserved none; but for the cloth, that was it, the cloth which he disgraced. An occasional hoot, perhaps, as he drove past, would not come amiss; then away, everyone, to the Passeggiata, to assemble beneath Flaminio Salvo's villa!

"Viva Ignazio Capolinòòò!"

"Vivàààà!"

"Three cheers for our new Deput-eee!"

"Vivàààà!"

In the darkness of the night, beneath the faint
glimmer of the street lamps, there passed in a
tumult along the narrow street that torrent of
people, who let themselves be swept on without
the slightest enthusiasm, like a bellowing herd, by
the will of two or three interested persons.

Flaminio Salvo's villa was illuminated from top
to bottom, splendidly, so that it might be visible,
as a sign of triumph, from distant Colimbètra.
Inside were assembled the committee of the Party,
who went out in a body upon the great balcony
with the balustrade of marble, as soon as the roar
of the demonstration reached them from the avenue beneath.

"Viva Flaminio Salvòòò!"

"Vivààà!"

"Viva Ignazio Capolinòòò!"

"Vivààà!"

There came up to the villa a deputation from
the crowd, who were received by Salvo with his
habitual frigid smile, to which the slow stare of
his eyes beneath their heavy lids gave a faintly
ironical expression. And indeed those fifteen or
sixteen excited townsfolk, newly emerging from
the nameless multitude which down below in the
darkness of the avenue sounded so imposing, assuming in an instant each his own name, his own
appearance, standing there, timid, embarrassed,
hesitating, bewildered, obsequious, their hands apparently sewn up in their sleeves, cut a sorry

enough figure amid the splendours of the magnificent drawing-room.

Flaminio Salvo expressed his gratitude to the townsfolk for this solemn affirmation of the popular feeling; gave them the latest report of the Hon. Capolino's condition and, in the presence of the deputation, asked the engineer Aurelio Costa to go off at once to the Prince's villa, to report there the result of the election and this manifestation of joy by the entire population of Girgenti.

Whereupon one of the fifteen, swelling and reddening like a turkey cock, went to the balcony and, between the lamps held up by a pair of footmen, delivered an impassioned harangue to the crowd.

No one gave any thought to the discomfiture of the poor bats on the avenue, which, dazzled by the glare, dropped from above to crawl over the heads of the demonstrators, then, at the shouts, at the clapping of hands, rose again in a panic, uttering shrill cries, as though appealing for help and vengeance to the stars that twinkled merrily in the sky. The extempore orator was saying that Capolino's election was one of the most memorable events in the history of modern Italy; but no one, certainly, could have got it out of the heads of those bats that the whole town was banded together, that evening, to declare a most unprovoked war upon themselves.

The speaker was still declaiming, when Aurelio Costa, mounted upon one of Salvo's chestnuts, which had been hastily saddled, set off at a gallop for Colimbètra.

Lost in the crowd, down there, was Pigna, who had drifted down to the tail of the procession, expurgated, voided (so to speak) from its body by a succession of violent efforts along the whole of the route. Insolence! Oppression! He had been going about his own business, was preparing to cross the Via Atenea, when the crowd surged round him. He had not had time to escape, and then the people in front had thrust him back so that they themselves might pass, and so the flood had engulfed him.   To escape, with those legs and that hunched back, had been impossible; furious, shouting at the top of his voice, he had begun to push in all directions with fists and feet and elbows, to clear a space round him and make his way out; but the crowd, for the fun of taking him along with them as a hostage, had fallen upon him, with shouts of: "Here's Pigna! It's Pigna! Viva Pigna! Abbasso Propaganda! No, Viva! Down with us!" and sticks had begun to fly, and blows were exchanged.   More infuriated than ever, like a boar at bay among a pack of hounds, he had gone so far as to bite those nearest to him; more than once, thrusting out feet and shoulders to disengage an arm, and expecting the crowd to close up behind him, and finding instead a space left by some one who was trying to avoid him, he had been on the point of falling; but immediately some one else had propelled him forward against the back of the man in front, and there, packed tight, gasping like a fish out of water, more sticks and buffets and jeers. And, pushing and pulling, they had tossed him from side to side like a shuttle, ill-treating him in every possible way, until, overpowered, he had let himself go with the crowd, but not on his own feet, no, no! like that, carried away. . . . Oh, the savages! Oh, the scoundrels! Bartered consciences! What a spectacle! Oh Girgenti, disgrace to Sicily and to humanity! A name for scorn and derision! All of them in the sacristy to-morrow, yes, yes, sticking together with the sacred wafers the torn halves of five-lire notes. . . . Yes, up with Capolino and up with Salvo! Up with Bacchus and up with Mammon!

And, exclaiming thus, and looking round with an air of menacing contempt at the crowd assembled beneath Salvo's villa, he now straightened out his battered hat, now rubbed a bruised shoulder, now sighed or groaned, now gave a sniff of disgust; pooh, dregs of humanity! Pooh, vile *ignoranti!*

"All right, Propaga', wait till to-morrow!" some of them shouted. "To-morrow we shall all come and join the Fascio! To-night, we're here: 'Viva Capolinòòò!' (You mustn't believe us, you know? We're only pretending.) 'Viva! Vivààà!'"

Was this the end of a day of battle, this his
reward for all his running to and fro since daybreak between one polling station and another,
alloting their duties to the comrades, giving instructions, ordering the people in one place, per-
suading, inciting, imploring them in another, according to circumstances, that all the votes of the
workers must be given to a worker, their comrade,
perdio! Angelo Zappalà, who would defend their
interests, who would plead their cause in Parliament!

Yes, granted that this popular candidature was
to be of value only as a protest, he might after all
have professed himself satisfied with the result:
yes; but only of the voting in the surrounding
villages! His heart bled, however, for the disgrace of Girgenti, the capital, his native city! A
name for scorn, for derision. . . .

Farewell, love!

When, at length, Pigna, pounded and pum-
melled, with no voice left, ready to drop with
exhaustion, returned home, to the Piano di Gamez,
to swallow a mouthful of supper poisoned by bile,
as he mounted the first steps of the wooden staircase which led from the big room on the ground
floor to the room above, he found standing there
in the darkness, eagerly conversing, Celsina and
Antonio Del Re.

"Hallo, you here?"

"Go upstairs, Papa!" said Celsina. "I'm just saying good-bye to him. He leaves to-morrow."

"Oh, good-night, then," said Pigna. "I mean to say, a good journey to you. . . . You're going off at once, then? I envy you, my dear fellow. Oh, you are certain to see in Rome . . . what relation to you is Don Landino Laurentano? Of course, yes, your uncle, you told me: give him my most humble regards, tell him that Girgenti needs him; Girgenti is a disgrace to the Island. . . ."

"We know all that, Papa," Celsina cut him short, tartly. "Let him talk to me now! Go away!"

"A town of carrion!" muttered Pigna, dragging his crooked shanks painfully upstairs. "Rascals . . . *ohi ohi* . . . *ignoranti*. . . ."

He turned the corner. Immediately the two young people were in each other's arms again. Antonio had lost all self-control; drunken, desperate, he could not tear himself away from her; he sought her lips, as though his were parched with thirst, for another kiss, which penetrated to the inmost depths of his being; another kiss, passionate, burning, endless, in which to give her the whole of himself and to take the whole of her, in the spasm of the most intense longing.

"Stop," she groaned, exhausted, letting her head sink on his bosom.

But he clasped her again, more ardent; quivering more than ever; he wanted her lips again.

"No, stop, Nino," said Celsina, recovering herself. "Stop . . . stop . . ."

She took his hands, pressed them tight; laid them upon her heaving bosom, still holding them; went on:

"So! . . . Now, listen . . . you will see, won't you? you will try. . . . You must do all you can. . . ."

"Yes. . . ."

"Are you listening?"

"Yes. . . ."

"You're not listening! That will do, now, Nino! I've told you, that will do. You're not listening to me. . . ."

"Yes, I am. . . . I will try. . . ."

"What will you try? Let me alone, for heaven's sake!"

"I don't know. . . . I will do all I can. . . . You know I will! Give me another kiss. . . ."

"No! Where will you try?"

"Why, everywhere, everywhere. . . ."

"Yes, a post of any sort . . . even a humble one . . . to begin with, you understand? You know that I can. . . . I will make myself do anything! I must, I must be in Rome, as soon as possible, are you listening?"

"Yes, love . . . love . . . my love!" he gasped;

then gripping her arms, and raving: "What am I to do? Oh, my Celsina. . . . I shall die. . . ."

"Hush!" Celsina warned him. "I don't want them to hear you upstairs."

"Then I'm off. . . . I can't . . ."

"Yes, go, go . . . it's late! They're calling me. You'll write at once, remember?"

"Yes. . . ."

"Good-bye, good-bye."

But he still could not bring himself to let go her hand; he thrust his face close to hers, asked her:

"What will you give me?"

"What do you want?" said she.

"You, all of you! Come with me, come with me!"

"If I could! This instant!"

"Oh, my love. . . . What will you give me?" he repeated. "Something of your own. . . ."

"I haven't anything, my Nino. . . ."

"But I have something of yours, you know, that you gave me."

"I?"

"Haven't you given me anything? Not even your heart, a little?"

"Ah, that. . . ."

"And something else as well. . . . Don't you remember?"

"No. . . ."

"The doll. . . ."

"Ah," smiled Celsina, "that one with the moustaches?"

"Don't laugh, don't laugh. I've rubbed them out, you know. I am taking it with me."

"Baby. . . ."

"D'you know? I had it in bed with me all last night, in my arms. And I shall always . . ."

"Go on! I'm not the doll, you know!"

"I know; but it is yours, it has been yours. . . . Haven't your lips kissed it?"

"Often, when I was little. . . ."

"Very well, then. . . ."

"Go, Nino, go. They're calling me. Good-bye. Don't forget, now. Write to me! Good-bye!"

Another long, long kiss at the front door, and Antonio went away. He stopped in the Piano di Gamez, where not a soul was stirring; and gazed about him, in bewilderment; he gazed up at the motionless vault of heaven, and felt a sense of stupefaction, as though he had passed into a waking dream. How brightly the stars shone! He heard the balcony window open. Celsina leaned out.

"Good-bye. Remember."

"Yes. Good-bye!"

Already she was remote; remote was her voice, remote her form; and that little house, the front of which, clear and bright against the misty blackness of the Piano, reflected the moon's rays, and the Piano itself, the chattering voice of the fountain, and those narrow alleys, crooked and dark, the whole town silent in the night, high on its hill, beneath the stars—everything seemed to him to be henceforward remote; he felt as though he from a distance, with infinite sadness, with infinite pain, were contemplating his own life which remained there, severed from himself.

Light and darkness.

When Aurelio Costa arrived at Colimbètra, Don Ippolito knew already of Capolino's election; and was discussing it in the drawing-room with Don Salesio Marullo and Ninì De Vincentis.

The former had come hurrying from Girgenti on hearing of the result of the duel, a most fortunate result for him; the latter, after the encounter, at which he had been present as a second, had remained at Colimbètra by the victim's bedside.

Uncle Salesio was listening to the Prince with an air of proud condescension, as though he himself were responsible for Capolino's election. And of course he was! Had he not given him his stepdaughter's hand in marriage?

During the last five days uncle Salesio had taken a new lease of life there, amid the splendours of Colimbètra, in which he took as much pride as though they had been his own property. He trod the thick carpets more on tiptoe than ever; pursed his lips at all the pretty and valuable

things he saw; at table he almost fainted with
pleasure at the sight of all that gleaming silver,
or when Liborio, in a swallow-tail coat and white
gloves, handed him the choice dishes which—it
seemed to him almost impossible!—were not made
of pasteboard. And at sunset, notwithstanding
his aching feet, he would go down to the lawn and
walk as far as the gate to enjoy the delight of receiving a military salute from the sentry in his
red breeches and blue greatcoat. The sentry took
an equal delight in saluting him; and each of
them, after the salute, would look at the other and
smile.

Ninì De Vincentis seemed not to have recovered yet from the terror that had overpowered
him when he saw Capolino sink to the ground,
wounded in the chest by Verònica's pistol, at the
second round. It had indeed been a terrible surprise to everybody, that shot. The pistols, by a
tacit understanding between the seconds, had been
loaded in such a way as not to inflict any injury,
their intention being that the actual duel should
begin with the sabres. And it was a lucky thing
that the bullet, striking him without much force,
had barely grazed one of his ribs and swerved
aside from his heart!

But it was not only this terrifying memory that
kept poor Ninì still so crushed and helpless; Nicoletta Capolino had given him plainly to understand that Dianella Salvo was not and never

would be his, even if her father had not met his
suit with so curt a refusal.

After spending the first night by her husband's
bedside, notwithstanding the doctors' assurances
that all danger had fortunately been averted,
Nicoletta had persuaded herself that it no longer
behoved her to play the despairing wife, as she
had done at Valsanìa when the news came that
"her Gnazio" was wounded. And she had begun
to alternate her loving and diligent attention to
her poor wounded "paladin" with a skilful en-
deavour to remain there at Colimbètra, in Don
Ippolito Laurentano's memory, as a most charming guest.

Ah, if only, instead of that walrus Adelaide
Salvo, it had been herself that was presently to
become the queen of this little realm! She felt
that all the good qualities with which nature had
intended to endow her and which her destiny had
chosen to suppress and stifle in her would have revived spontaneously and in time have gained the
upper hand in her; that she would have managed
to bring happiness to the last years of that proud,
magnificently handsome old man, still so fresh
and vigorous!

She guessed how bitter had been his disappointment at the sight of his future bride; but knew
also that no seductive art would prevail over such
a man, who had made a sort of religion of loyalty
to his plighted word. Not a vestige of coquetry,

therefore, must she shew, but must vie with him
in compliments and courtesies, during those days,
without the least affectation. And what words in
season to Uncle Salesio, who would not understand
that there was no longer any reason at all for his
remaining at Colimbètra. He knew his place, and
kept it, quite—rather too much so, indeed—did
Uncle Salesio; and yet . . . and yet! . . .

And for her unrealizable dream; for her longing for a virtuous life; for the incubus which was
the sight of her step-father, so polite and so pre-
posterous, for the disgust she now felt at her long
and hateful pretence of affection for that husband, that worthy companion of her own baser
self, Nicoletta took her revenge in tormenting
Ninì De Vincentis, especially in the evenings, on
the marble terrace, built out upon the columns of
the porch, by speaking to him of Dianella Salvo.

She took a delight in wounding him, knowing
that no affliction, no injustice, could—let alone
making that uncorrupt and incorruptible young
man do anything wrong—provoke a bitter word
from his lips, so much was he the slave of his own
goodness and resigned to it!

She spoke to him mysteriously, in broken sen-
tences, as though not to saturate him, at any one
time, with his own grief.

Ninì was anxious to know on what grounds she
had told him that Dianella Salvo would never be
his, even if her father had given his consent.

"Why? Ah, dear Ninì. . . . There is a reason, a reason that is painful to others besides yourself!"

"What reason?"

"I cannot tell you."

"But to whom else is it painful?"

"To me too, Ninì!"

"To you?" asked Ninì in amazement.

And she, smiling:

"Certainly . . . certainly. . . . You don't see it; and yet there is, there really is a connexion between myself and you and . . . her. What connexion? What can I have in common with you? And yet there is something, dear Ninì . . . there is, there is. . . . You and I are joined by something. It seems impossible, doesn't it? And yet, believe me, we are joined. . . ."

Ninì was left to ponder over this mysterious reason, and felt his heart sink within him.

When Aurelio Costa, ushered by Liborio, entered the drawing-room, Nicoletta was with her husband; but she came in presently and felt an exquisite pleasure in letting herself be seen by him there, in that princely mansion, amid the deference and respect of all the household. Don Ippolito hastened to inform her of the popular demonstration.

"He's resting just now," she said. "I'm afraid of exciting him. . . . But, if they want . . ."

"No, no," the Prince at once assured her. "We

shall find an opportunity of letting him know
to-morrow. . . ."

"On the contrary, I am sure Don Flaminio,"
put in Aurelio Costa, "sent me galloping out here,
at this time of night, so that he might let the electors know then and there that the Honourable
Capolino and the Prince would at once be informed of the demonstration."

"I am sorry for your sake, Ingegnere," said
Nicoletta, "that you have had such a journey.
. . ."

"Not at all!" Costa at once cut her short. "Indeed, it's been a pleasure. . . ."

"Especially as, I don't mind betting," put in
Uncle Salesio, "this is the first time you were ever
at Colimbètra, eh? A marvellous abode, my dear
Ingegnere, marvellous! A regular earthly para-
dise!"

The Prince smiled, made a slight bow, and invited Aurelio Costa to stay to supper.

That evening, Ninì De Vincentis was left in
peace by Nicoletta; but he was not in the least
grateful to her. He had grown to enjoy being
tortured.

But Nicoletta had Aurelio Costa to consider.
And she meant to bewitch him properly, that evening; she meant him to interpret, in his own mind,
all her coaxings and glances and smiles as a compensation for the thankless task set him by Flaminio Salvo, to wit, that of coming out there to

tell them of her husband's triumph; and she
meant that in this compensation which she was
giving him, he should detect a note of resentment
against Salvo himself who, though well aware of
his sentiments, had dispatched him there like a
servant. Did he regard everybody as his pur-
chased slave? It might come to pass, nevertheless, that these slaves, in the end, under such
provocation, would accept the challenge and come
to a mutual understanding! Had they not some
such understanding already? Was there not
already an agreement, a secret pact between
them?

And Nicoletta Capolino's eyes, fastened upon
his, now blazed out ardent and excited, now
languished, misty and disturbed, as though promising an intense, profound pleasure in store. A
slave, in common slavery with her! They would
be avenged upon all the old men who sought to
keep their two young selves enslaved! For her
sake, from now onwards, he would cherish his servile state; and would think no more of becoming
his own master, even if Dianella Salvo should
openly reveal her love to him. A slave, in common
slavery with her!

Aurelio Costa was really like a drunken man,
his face radiant with joy and gratitude to the
lady, when, late in the evening, he left Colimbètra.

He did not know what to think. The blood

pulsed in his veins, and sang in his ears. Was
she playful like that with everyone, naturally or
by acquired habit, or was it for him alone that
she had shaped those smiles, perfected those
glances and coaxing attentions? Ought he to wonder or to feel certain of it? And if certain, why
had this woman thus suddenly made up her mind
to tempt him, to provoke him, to love him, after
receiving his honourable offer of marriage, years
before, with a curt and contemptuous refusal?
Had she repented? Weary, sickened by the infamous part that her husband had assigned to
her, had she decided to rebel and to be avenged,
choosing as her weapon of vengeance the man who
honourably, once upon a time, had wished to make
her his own, and whom she had then maltreated
and perhaps laughed to scorn? Did she wish now
to give him this revenge over the man for whom
she had refused him then? Or was she seeking to
lay a snare for him?

This suspicion, crude and unworthy as it might
appear to him at that moment, had nevertheless
worked its way into his mind among the welter of
possible theories. He was incapable of any great
respect for her.

But what sort of snare? To make him fall in
love, lose his head, to the point of arousing Flaminio Salvo's jealousy and so bringing about his
own dismissal? But had he not told her that he
would be sacrificing nothing, now, were he to leave

Salvo? Besides, what interest could she have in banishing him? How was his presence offensive to her? Did he remind her, in her present misery, of the past? But when it had been she herself who, by that strong, intimate pressure of his hand, had chosen to remind him of that past, so as to sweep away its shadow from between them? And she had seemed to him sincere! Yes, frank and sincere! And how beautiful she was! What a fascination radiated from her whole person! Oh, to be loved by her. . . .

Coming to Flaminio Salvo's villa, now silent and dark, Aurelio Costa put his horse in the stable, and went up to the study, where Salvo was waiting for him. Salvo at once perceived the emotion, the unusual animation on the face and in the speech of the young man, as he apologized for his lateness on the ground that he had been kept to supper by the Prince. As he listened to him, Salvo scrutinized him closely; and—when Aurelio lowered his eyes—accentuated slightly his habitual smile, letting it play over every line of his face, which a trace of fatigue, that evening, made flabbier than usual.

"I expected it," he said, caressing his sidewhiskers.

"I thought that . . ." Aurelio attempted to interpose.

"Why, yes, you were quite right," Salvo at once cut him short. "What a fine colour you've brought back with you! It must be good for one, a ride in the country at this time of night. . . . A beautiful evening! In here, it's stifling. . . . When you are an old man you will remember. . . ."

"I?" asked Aurelio, tempted to smile by the affectionate tone in which Salvo addressed him, albeit the words themselves, after his reflexions on his homeward ride, filled him with suspicion. "Why?"

"No . . . I mean to say, perhaps . . ." Salvo went on, with a vague wave of his hand. "Of course, you are accustomed to that sort of thing. . . . Day and night, always on the go. . . . A busy life, yours! But perhaps this has been a special occasion. When we are old, there come back to us, in flashes, memories, distant visions of ourselves as we were at certain moments . . . and we don't even know why one particular moment and not another has remained stamped on our memory, and suddenly detaches itself and strays to the surface. There was perhaps a more comprehensive memory, of a whole period in our life. It has faded. A single incident is all that remains alive, a single moment, an instant. . . . And you will see yourself again on horseback, on a calm, exquisite night, with stars shining . . . and you will try in vain, perhaps, to recollect what thoughts you had in your mind on that occasion, what feelings were in your heart. . . ."

"But that can happen without our being old," observed Aurelio.

"It is not the same thing," replied Salvo. "You will find that out for yourself."

And he sat for a while with his eyes motionless, fixed in an unseeing gaze.

There was certainly something strange about Salvo too, that evening, and even Aurelio noticed it, as though, during his absence, the other, left alone there in his austere study, had been plunged in thoughts which had bred in him an unaccustomed melancholy. What thoughts? He had evidently been sitting with his elbows on the writing table and his head in his hands, since on his head, which was bald at the top, the few remaining grey hairs on his brow, which he wore parted in the middle and trimmed short, had become disarranged.

Aurelio knew that this imperious spirit was at heart profoundly melancholy, and that Salvo's harsh manner, his violent resentments were no more than instantaneous eruptions of that inveterate, hidden, repressed, inconsolable melancholy. But why had he succumbed so to it on this evening of all evenings, when he should have been rejoicing in his victory?

"All well out there?" asked Salvo, shaking off his abstraction. "Did you see him?"

"No," answered Aurelio, dissembling his embarrassment and confusion, which were perhaps

visible on his face, with the fear of having failed
in part of his duty; he added, however, by way
of excuse, blushing as he spoke: "Because the
Signora said he was resting. . . ."

"On his laurels, eh?" Salvo capped it, then,
tilting his chin and smiling openly, asked:
"And . . . tell me, is she . . . the Signora . . .
pleased?"

Aurelio waved his hands, and, as though the
point had not occurred to him, replied: "She
didn't seem to be. Why?"

"She ought to be pleased," Salvo went on.
"She is going to Rome. . . ."

"Yes, now that her husband . . ."

"In Parliament, in Parliament," Salvo took
him up, tossing his head. "It had to be! In Parliament."

With which he rose from his chair.

"You see, my dear fellow, what are our unpar-
donable faults? And then we complain of our lot!
In a moment such as this, with an enterprise such
as we have been considering, which has already
cost us so much in hard work, has already exposed
me to such risks, I have made them elect Capolino to Parliament. The very man I needed here,
on the spot, wouldn't you say? To talk big in
Rome, when the time comes, at the Ministry of
Industry and Commerce. . . . But it had to be.
You will find that Ignazio gets on splendidly in
Rome: it is the right place for him. Here, he

was in my way. . . . A clean sweep, a clean sweep.
. . . Should the need arise, I can go myself to
Rome, to talk to the Minister. First of all, though,
they must all sign an agreement here, all the pro-
ducers of sulphur, great and small, I want them
all in; with the stipulation that they consent to
restrict their output, if necessary, and to store all
their sulphur in common warehouses. Otherwise,
nothing doing. I am risking my capital for the
salvation of Sicilian industry. I am entitled to in-
sist upon the adhesion and co-operation of all the
interested parties, and upon some slight sacrifice,
if necessary. In the meantime, whereas here we
are seriously considering how to improve the present desperate state of affairs, have you heard
about Grotte? They want to enforce the will of
the majority. . . . Idiots! Enforce it upon whom,
and why? . . . The people who have, to-day, are
worse ruined than those who have not! The majority. . . . What force can a majority have?
Brute force; it can deal you a blow; but the avalanche, when it reaches the ground, crumbles into
fragments at the same time. Oh, how sickening
they are, how sickening! Take them singly, they
are afraid, you understand; and so they gather
a thousand strong to take a step which they could
not take each by himself; take them singly, they
have not a thought among them; and a thousand
empty heads, crowded together, imagine that they
have, and fail to observe that it is the thought of

the madman or mischief-maker who is leading
them. So much for them. And here? Here we
have another spectacle, more sickening still. I
am perhaps growing old, Aurelio.''

''You?'' the other asked, with a smile.

''I am growing old, yes,'' went on Salvo. ''I
am losing the desire to command. What has destroyed it is the servility that I discover in everyone. Men are what I want, men! I see round
about me automata, puppets, mannikins, which I
have to pose in one attitude or another, and which
remain paralysed, as though to mock at me, in the
attitudes I have put them in, until I give them a
cuff that sends them flying. Outwardly, though,
you understand; it is only outwardly that they
allow themselves to be posed! Inside . . . ah, inside they remain hard, with their covert, hostile
thoughts, alive only to themselves. What can
you do with them? Docile outwardly, mild, mal-
leable, with smiling faces, obsequious, they approve of everything you do. Oh, how revolting it
all is! I should like to know why I am losing my
temper like this; why and for whose sake I am
doing it. . . . To-morrow I die. I have had command of men! Yes, indeed: I have allotted his
part to this man and to that, to hundreds who can
never have seen anything more in me than the
part that I represent to them. And of all that
other life, the life of affections and ideas, that
stirs within me, nobody has ever had the remotest

suspicion. . . . With whom would you have me discuss it? It is outside the part that I am expected to play. . . . Now and again, when somebody comes here to see me, to make me angry, I amuse myself by giving him a searching glance, a glance that penetrates his mask, and I see him, then, for an instant, caught and exposed before me, awkward and embarrassed; heaven knows the effort I have to make not to burst out laughing in his face. He would think I had gone mad, at the very least. Even you, my dear fellow, if you could see how you are staring at me at this moment . . ."

"I, no!" Aurelio at once protested, starting back.

Flaminio Salvo shook his head and laughed:

"You too, you too. . . . It is so; it is bound to be so. . . . How can I tell you what I should really like you to do? The pleasure that you would give me, were you to act as I perhaps should act in your place?"

"Why not?" Aurelio asked, rising to his feet. "Tell me. . . ."

"Why not?" Salvo was quick to reply, shrugging his shoulders. "Because I cannot. . . . Can you tell me what you are thinking, what you are feeling, what sort of life you have within you at this moment? . . . You cannot. . . . You stand before me in such relations as there may be between yourself and me: you are my engineer, my

dear son, whom I love, to whom this evening, before a score of marionettes, I gave instructions to
ride over to Colimbètra, a messenger of triumph:
and that is all! What else could I have to say to
you? Only this, perhaps, for your good . . ."

Flaminio Salvo laid his hand on Aurelio's
shoulder:

"Never trace out paths to follow, my boy; nor
habits, nor duties; go ahead, always keep moving;
shake off every fresh incrustation of ideas; seek
your own pleasure, and do not fear the judgment
of other people, or your own either, which may
seem right to you to-day and wrong to-morrow.
You've met Don Cosmo Laurentano? If you only
knew how wise that madman is! Go along now,
it is late; time we were in bed. Good night."

As he walked down the Viale della Passeggiata,
under the dripping trees, in the vast stillness of
the night, Aurelio Costa had the impression of
being no longer able to find himself in himself,
and stopped as though in search of what was
missing.

The thoughts that had been agitating him as to
his own future, in connexion with this colossal
scheme of Salvo's; the provoking smiles, the
words, the attentions of Nicoletta Capolino, out
there at Colimbètra; and here, just now, Salvo's
melancholy, tortuous, puzzling speech seemed to
have divided his spirit piecemeal. Part of it had
remained out there at Colimbètra; the rest here in

the villa, bewildered, disturbed, made suspicious, stunned by Salvo's words. So Nicoletta would be going to Rome? What then? But how was this? Had Salvo wished to be rid of Capolino? Yes, he had said so distinctly: "A clean sweep." Had he been alluding perhaps to her? There had been a certain irony in the question that he put to him: "Is the Signora pleased?" Had he wished to banish her too from his house? Or was it perhaps she that had rebelled against him? Was this why he was so melancholy, in so unusual a frame of mind? And what did Salvo want with him? What meaning was he to extract from the strange things that Salvo had said to him? "How can I tell you the pleasure that you would give me, were you to act as I perhaps should act in your place?" What pleasure? What had he meant by that? A secret, unconfessable desire? Or had he been speaking generally? He had complained that he was surrounded by automata, puppets. . . . And those final words of advice. . . .

Try as he might, he could find no solution. And then, as though leaving outside him, to stray where they would, thoughts and doubts and suspicions, he withdrew into the safe shell of his own consciousness, of the opinion, modest, calm and solid, that he held of himself.

By the mere accident of his having, once upon a time, almost without thinking, plucked Salvo from the jaws of death, he had been brought up to an

enviable position, of which, with his exceptional
natural gifts, and his determination to succeed, he
had managed to render himself worthy. The extent of his good fortune, which everyone admitted
to be deserved, the exaggerated reports of the
honours he had won in his classes, in examinations, in his profession, had meanwhile given him
an importance which he himself admitted to be
excessive, and which proved at times embarrass-
ing. The manner in which he found himself received and treated, the things that people were
saying about him, were a continual proof to him
that he was to others something more than to himself, a different Aurelio Costa, whom he himself
barely recognized, of whom he could form no clear
estimate; he always remained, therefore, in the
company of other people, in an agonized state of
mind, in a strange confused apprehension that he
was falling short of their expectations, failing to
live up to his reputation. He knew how to keep in
his place, but would have preferred to remain in
it quiet and secure; whereas he felt that other
people, he having started to rise when a mere boy,
were still pointing to a higher position as though
it were his by right, and were urging him on, and
refusing to leave him alone. It was not timidity
on his part; it was an awkward reserve, which
often irritated him with other people or with himself, a perpetual alarm, lest some shortcoming
might be discovered in him, were he to stray ever

so little beyond the field of his own knowledge, in which he felt himself to be secure; from the corner in which he could stand firm, at which he had arrived by his own practical merit. His irritation with himself arose also from his seeing that so many men, whom he himself regarded as his inferiors in every respect, managed to forge ahead without effort, and were allowed to pass; whereas he, regarded by everyone as superior even to the conception that he had formed of himself, he lagged behind, and, were he thrust forward, often felt himself embarrassed in his movements, in his speech, and blushed at times like a girl.

To-night, Aurelio Costa was more conscious than ever of that feeling of unaccountable annoyance that was always caused him by his own shadow, as it stretched out before him, growing longer and thinner the farther he went from each of the lighted lamps which kept a lugubrious watch over the sleeping town, after the clamour of the popular demonstration.

Half way along the deserted Via Atenea, he caught sight of Roberto Auriti, by himself; he turned to gaze at him with profound sorrow, and followed him with his eyes, until he saw him turn aside into one of the steep alleys on the left, which led up to the Badia Grande.

Good-bye.

There was no going to bed that night at Donna
Caterina Laurentano's, since Roberto and his
nephew had to set off in the dark, at four o'clock
in the morning.

Anna Del Re was busy with a labour of love,
making the final preparations for her son's departure. What an agony, for her, this parting!
Her whole world, her whole life, for years past,
had been concentrated in love and care for this sole
treasure. How was she to go on living, now, without him? She wept silent tears.

She had brought him up, had guarded him with
her heart and soul, never heeding the reproaches
of her mother, who was afraid of her spoiling him.
Spoil him, indeed! No, no! She had been so worried and tormented, when she saw him grow up
cold and sullen, always and entirely self-absorbed,
and had endeavoured by her manner towards him,
by her ever vigilant care, to thaw him (that was
all!) with a mother's love, to make him more ex-
pansive and confiding.

She did not know what it was in his nature that
kept him aloof from the companionship even of
boys of his own age. A hard worker, indeed he
had worked too hard, until his health was affected;
and when he was not working, he would sit closely
wrapped in certain thoughts which made his

brows more bushy, his eyes harder and more repellent behind his powerful glasses.

"Good heavens, Ninuccio, if you could only see what a face you're making. . . ."

He would reply with a shrug of the shoulders.

Perhaps he was distressed, her Ninuccio, by the family's straitened circumstances, perhaps he was thinking that his grandmother, even without any derogation from her dignity, from her sentiments, might have been a rich woman. Too sunless, certainly, had his childhood and boyhood been made by the dark shadow of all those tragedies in that huge old house, always shrouded in silence, into which the sun, when it did penetrate, never seemed to bring either light or heat.

What a house! She noticed it herself that night, imagining the melancholy aspect it would present to her on the morrow! The furniture worm-eaten, the ceilings grimy, the floors crumbling, the window frames warped and paintless, the wall paper in all the rooms faded. . . . And yet it was constantly cared for and cleaned and put to rights; it seemed as though it too were in some dim way conscious of the misery of life. Corrado Selmi was right; he had accurately interpreted her own secret feeling. . . . Resigned long since to her own fate, she would have wished, if not for herself at any rate for this son of hers, that at length some smile of peace, even a sad smile, should lighten a little the burden, the incu-

bus of those painful memories, that dark rancour
against life, the mute, despairing bitterness of her
mother.

Calm, not peace! The soul of Donna Caterina
Laurentano could know no peace.

Perhaps because she no longer believed in anything? She herself, Anna, did believe, she believed fervently in God, albeit without keeping up
any of the practices of religion. The women of
the neighbourhood never saw her go out to mass,
like her mother; and yet they made a distinction
between the two, guessed that the "young lady"
was religious and, when they caught an occasional
glimpse of her, so beautiful and meek, always
dressed in black, would point their fingers at her
as at a Saint.

Anna's thoughts turned principally upon the
new life, the strange customs among which her
son would presently find himself, in her brother's
house in Rome. She had not the least doubt that
her brother would look after his nephew with the
most loving care; but the woman he had with him?
Her family? All the people who came to Roberto's house? That Corrado Selmi, who, with
his strange fascination, had succeeded in disturbing even her equanimity? Who could tell what
effect he would have upon her Ninuccio, who had
spent all his life here, cooped up with his grandmother and herself!

They had, both of them, spoken frequently and

volubly, with bitterness, of their Roberto's wasted
life, of the irregular connexion that he had
formed, going by the reports that had reached
them from Giulio, the younger brother; reports
that were distinctly vague, for Giulio, who had
always lived in Rome, had lost all family feeling
and tradition, had ceased even to resemble a Sicilian; and was inclined, perhaps, to make excuses
for his elder brother; certainly he attached no
weight, no importance to all manner of things, at
which her mother and she could barely repress
their horror.

She was a teacher of singing, the wife of a tenor
who had lost his voice, Roberto's mistress. And
Giulio had said, with a laugh, that this tenor, a
worthy fellow, sat down every day at Roberto's
table and then retired for the night to the house
of his wife's brother, who kept a sort of college,
a private *conservatorio,* in which the lady taught
singing and her husband filled no less a post than
that of censor. Roberto was a sort of boarder in
this house where now and again, in their more pro-
sperous seasons, another lodger or two were taken
in, for whom there was no room in the brother's
college.

So it was with people like these that her son
would shortly be coming in contact.

More than once Anna had sought to persuade
her mother to suggest to Roberto the removal of
the family to Rome. They would sell this house,

which had harboured so many tragedies, and
would make shift to live as best they might in
Rome, by themselves of course to begin with, by
themselves or with Giulio only. Then possibly, by
slow degrees, in time, their mother might succeed
in detaching Roberto from his companions. . . .
Would it not also be an economy, to combine three
households in one? And to have the whole family
under one roof. . . .

"Dreams!" her mother had said. And she had
refused even to discuss the suggestion.

She knew that neither would Giulio wish to forfeit his personal freedom, nor would Roberto be
able to free himself from his thraldom to that
woman. She herself, moreover, at her age, would
not be able to stand so radical a change of life
and habits.

"Dreams! Dreams! When I die, and Nino is
grown up, you can go with him. . . . He will be
responsible for giving you a new life."

"But in the meantime!" sighed Anna, looking
at her son where he sat in the other room, listening to the conversation of his grandmother and
uncle, his hand buried in his hair, his elbow resting on the table, beneath the lamp that hung from
the ceiling.

He showed no sign either of regret at the pros-
pect of leaving her for about a year, or of joy at
that of going to Rome.

Always the same!

Once only, at the beginning of the previous year, infatuated by a discovery which he thought he had made, a special device of his own for extracting (he said) the electrical energy from the waves of the sea (there had come, that year, to the Technical Institute an excellent professor of physics, who had succeeded in arousing an enthusiasm for that science in all his pupils), he had talked to her with genuine warmth, trying to induce her to prevail upon her mother to ask for a loan of a few thousand lire—not from the "Bourbon uncle," no, indeed!—but from uncle Cosmo: one thousand lire on loan, to construct as best he might the apparatus required for the experiments which he would make out there, at Valsanìa, upon the beach.

Poor boy! She had quickly damped his ardour. His grandmother? Ask her brothers for money? Didn't he know her?

He had at once shut himself up again in his husk of silence, and had refused even to give her a description of his famous discovery. There might have been something in it; who could say? Perhaps it was only a boyish illusion! Anyhow, all that year, he had continued his passionate study of the science, and now, when he went to Rome, proposed to devote himself to it entirely.

Other affections—youthful as he was—other interests, other desires he did not appear to have.

"Ninuccio," she called.

She had finished packing his portmanteau, and required his help in shutting it. He came in at once.

"Too full?" she asked. "You would have all these books in here. . . . Wouldn't it be better to take them out and put them with the others in the case? We can send them after you to-morrow."

"I shall take the case with me," he said. "I don't trust it out of my sight. Heaven knows when it would reach me. . . ."

"But it will be too much weight for you, my boy, don't you think? Impossible. . . . Don't worry about it, you shall have it in a few days. I shall see to that. . . ."

"In that case leave the books here, in the portmanteau. Shall I shut it?"

"Your grandmother hasn't said anything to uncle Roberto in there?" she asked, alluding to her proposal.

"Nothing," her son replied.

"I realize too," sighed Anna, "that it is hardly possible. I should have liked it for your sake. . . . Mah! Ninuccio dear, listen: you must write and tell me everything, always . . . if there is anything you want . . . how you are keeping . . . if you are well. . . . Everything! I shall be glad of a few lines even. . . . But not your first letters, you know. Your first letters must be long ones. . . . I want to know everything! And remember, Ninuccio . . . you must be a little more tidy! You will put away all your linen neatly in the drawers. . . . Don't leave it about as you do here! Uncle Roberto is a very tidy person, you know. . . . You must be tidy too! And that is all I am going to say to you. . . . I know you will do your duty and please your mother and grandmother, who will be left here . . . alone. . . . That is all. . . . It will soon be time. . . ."

They went into the dining-room, where the grandmother and Roberto were seated side by side on the sofa.

"You will live to see it," Donna Caterina was saying. "I should like first to close these tired eyes of mine for ever. But it may perhaps fall to my lot too to behold this sight, if I am to make a good end. There will be some, I don't deny it, who do evil deliberately; but the soil has been prepared for years for an evil sowing. You live in Rome, and neither hear nor see. I wish I were mistaken! But I am not."

She lifted her head to look at her daughter and grandson, saw the tears in Anna's eyes, and exclaimed, raising her arm:

"Let him go, let him leave us! Air! Fresh air! He will be able to breathe. . . . Break through your shell, my boy; and let us stay here, to wait for manna from heaven! In Sixty, dear Roberto, do you know what we were doing here? We were melting our souls in little saucers, like pieces of soap; the Government sent us down a straw each, as a present; and then we, poor fools that we were, set to work to blow into our soapy water, and oh, the bubbles, the bubbles, each one prettier and more iridescent than the last! But then the people began to gape with hunger, and when they gaped, pop went all those wonderful bubbles, one after another, and ended, my son, if you will pardon the expression, in drops of spittle . . . That is the truth!"

The maid came in to say that the carri[age was] at the door, and that the driver, who [was pressed for?] his time, urged them to hurry. It to[ok over?] an hour to drive from Girgenti [to the nearest?] station in Val Sollano.

Anna, candle in hand, on the doorstep, by her mother's side, stood as though overcome, unsatisfied by that last hurried embrace of her son, as he ran with his uncle down the steps of the precipitous alley, in a darkness that was still unbroken.

"My son! My son!" she moaned to herself.

"You will see Ninuccio again," her mother said to her gently. "Shall I see Roberto? Who knows?"

They heard in the profound silence the rumble of the departing wheels. And Anna raised her eyes filled with tears to the sky, in which the stars, for her, were keeping a solemn vigil.

END OF PART I

sign filled with tears to the sky, in which the stars,
for her were keeping a solemn vigil.

END OF PART I.

DATE DUE